House of Demons

"Come along, paleblood," sneered Nurthel. "You have work to do."

Araevin complied, turning to follow the fey'ri sorcerer without any effort of his conscious mind. He fell in behind Nurthel, arms still shackled behind his back, ribs aching from the blow Grimlight had dealt him. Behind him half a dozen fey'ri warriors and a pair of foul vrock-demons marched, watching him carefully for any sign that Sarya's compulsion might be fading. The daemonfey queen was not present, having left to return to her army, but she had ordered Araevin to obey any command given him by Nurthel, instantly and without resistance, and the malignant compulsion she had used to crush his will was sufficiently strong to force Araevin to do exactly as she commanded.

Half-demon, half-elf monsters infest the glades of the High Forest, the mountains around Evereska, and the very halls of Evermeet itself. They claim a birthright that was taken from them so long ago even the elves who imprisoned them forgot they existed. For millennia the daemonfey army planned, grew, and waited.

Until Now.

FORGOTTEN REALMS®

THE LAST MYTHAL

Forsaken House

Farthest Reach

Final Gate

Also by Richard Baker

R.A. Salvatore's War of the Spider Queen, Book III
Condemnation

The City of Ravens
The Shadow Stone
Easy Betrayals

STAR•DRIVE
Zero Point

FORGOTTEN REALMS

FORSAKEN HOUSE

THE LAST MYTHAL
BOOK I

RICHARD BAKER

FORSAKEN HOUSE
The Last Mythal, Book II

©2004 Wizards of the Coast, Inc.

All characters in this book are fictitious. Any resemblance to actual persons, living or dead, is purely coincidental.

This book is protected under the copyright laws of the United States of America. Any reproduction or unauthorized use of the material or artwork contained herein is prohibited without the express written permission of Wizards of the Coast, Inc.

Published by Wizards of the Coast, Inc. FORGOTTEN REALMS, WIZARDS OF THE COAST, and their respective logos are trademarks of Wizards of the Coast, Inc., in the U.S.A. and other countries.

Printed in the U.S.A.

The sale of this book without its cover has not been authorized by the publisher. If you purchased this book without a cover, you should be aware that neither the author nor the publisher has received payment for this "stripped book."

Cover art by Adam Rex
Map by Dennis Kauth
First Printing: August 2004
Library of Congress Catalog Card Number: 2004101418

9 8 7 6 5 4 3 2 1

US ISBN: 978-0-7869-3260-3
620-96562-001-EN

U.S., CANADA,	EUROPEAN HEADQUARTERS
ASIA, PACIFIC, & LATIN AMERICA	Hasbro UK Ltd
Wizards of the Coast, Inc.	Caswell Way
P.O. Box 707	Newport, Gwent NP9 0YH
Renton, WA 98057-0707	GREAT BRITAIN
+1-800-324-6496	Save this address for your records.

Visit our web site at **www.wizards.com**

For Kim

Have I told you lately that I love you?

Acknowledgements

Special thanks to Eric L. Boyd for the excellent Realmslore, Ed Greenwood and Phil Athans for the invaluable advice and guidance, and especially to the Monday night gaming group (Warren Wyman, Ed Stark, James Wyatt, David Noonan, Dale Donovan, and Tim Rhoades). It's been good saving the world with you guys.

THE HIGH ICE
GRIMLIGHT'S LAIR
THE MOONWOOD
REVER REDRUN
SUNDABAR
SILVERYMOON
NETHER MOUNTAINS
MYTH GLAURACH
RIVER RAUVIN
EVERLUND
THE TALONS
HELLGATE KEEP
THE NAMELESS DUNGEON
THE FAR FOREST
THE LOST PEAKS
THE HIGH FOREST
RIVER DELIMBIYR
THE FALLEN LANDS
REITHEILLAETHOR
THE STAR MOUNTAINS
GRAYPEAK MOUNTAINS
THE LONELY MOOR
GRAYCLOAK HILLS
WATERDEEP
HOUSE OF LONG SILENCES
FORGOTTEN FOREST
EVERESKA
THE TRADE WAY
DAGGERFORD
0
40
MILES
N

PROLOGUE

15 Flamerule, The Year of Doom (714 DR)

The end came not at sunset, but an hour after highsun. Nor did mournful rains mark the city's passing, as the bards later sang. It was a sweltering summer afternoon, the forest air thick and hazy. Myth Drannor was burning, and the acrid smoke of many fires hung heavily in the humid air.

Fflar Starbrow Melruth stood wearily on the shattered flagstones of the courtyard before Castle Cormanthor, and took the measure of his enemies. Thousands of savage warriors—orcs, goblins, gnolls, even ogres—stamped and shouted in the square, roaring and shouting in their guttural tongues, clashing axes and spears on their hide-covered shields or shaking jagged swords in the air. Like a great black sea of blood and steel the horde roiled and swarmed, clogging the marble streets and clinging to the feet of the white towers.

Too many, Fflar thought bitterly. And we are too few.

Behind Fflar stood the tattered heart of the Akh Velahr, the Army of Cormanthor. A dozen companies defended the broken castle, none with more than a quarter of its strength left. Tall and stern in their shining hauberks and green cloaks, the soldiers of the city knew they were defeated, but still they held. Each day they fought on, a few more of Myth Drannor's folk escaped to safety in desperate Flights, vanishing through whatever gates could be made to work.

At the head of the enemy host mighty nycaloths crouched eagerly, shadowing their faces with their vast black wings. Each was a great champion of the hells, kindred of the demons and devils whose vile spawn filled the lower planes. To see one such creature free to walk Faerûn was a terrible thing, but there at the head of their army stood gathered more than a dozen of the monsters. Hundreds of lesser yugoloths, creatures like the nycaloths but thankfully less powerful, drove the orcs and ogres into battle before them. Despite the painfully bright sunshine in the court, each nycaloth cast a terrifying shadow over the scene, living storm clouds about to break upon Fflar and his soldiers.

"Do not do this, Fflar," said Elkhazel from beside him. The sun elf swordsman stood a few paces behind him, his golden mail gouged in great furrows across his shoulder and breast. "Withdraw your challenge, I beg you. We may yet hold another few days, long enough for the rest of the Flights to escape."

Fflar kept his eyes on the roaring horde. The orcs and ogres did not advance yet. They held their ground, eager to see the duel to come. Even as he watched, a rift opened in their shouting ranks, and a great shadowed figure, a mighty prince of the nycaloths, made its way deliberately through the ranks. Brazen armor gleamed in the darkness, and a mace as large as a young tree dragged the ground. The bestial roars of the bloodthirsty horde rebounded from the castle walls as their dark captain came forth to battle.

"Nothing but a lord of the infernal realms could hold that horde together," said Fflar. "If I can defeat him, the rest of that rabble may well turn on each other. We could cut our way out of the city while they fight over the spoils."

"Aulmpiter is a mighty foe," Elkhazel replied. "If you should fall...."

"Then you will fight on, as you must," Fflar finished for him as he hefted his sword in his hand. "Do not fear, my friend. Keryvian and I have slain more than one mighty foe this summer. Demron crafted his baneblades well."

"Fflar! Captain of Myth Drannor! Come forth!" bellowed the monstrous figure wading through the enemy ranks. *"I will have you answer for your boasts!"*

"Fflar..." Elkhazel struggled to find words. "Think of Sorenna, and the babe."

Fflar glanced over at his lieutenant and offered a little smile, and said, "She will understand, Elkhazel. I have seen this. It is my hour."

He settled his golden helm on his sweat-soaked brow, and swept Keryvian before his feet several times to remind his hand of the sword's balance, not that he really needed to. The blade seemed to sense the presence of a worthy foe. It shivered in his grasp, giving off a cold, pure whisper of hate.

How many of our heroes have fallen this year? Fflar thought bleakly.

Josidiah Starym could have carved Aulmpiter to pieces with steel and spell in a deadly bladedance. Kerym Tenyajn would have riddled the infernal lord with his blazing arrows of moonfire, slaying Aulmpiter where he stood. But they were dead, and Fflar had to meet the horde's captain. He was exhausted, wounded already in the fighting at sunrise, but he could not let Aulmpiter detect his weakness.

"I am here, Aulmpiter!" he cried. "Your foul minions may have broken our walls and burned our homes, but you will not live to savor your victories! Today Keryvian will send you back to whatever black hells spawned you, monster!"

The nycaloth lord fixed his smoldering gaze on Fflar. Despite his words of bravado, the elf captain could not still a quiver of terror deep in his belly.

"Bold words, elf," Aulmpiter hissed. "I have slain a hundred of your kind this year. They died screaming for mercy. How will you die, I wonder?"

Fflar chose not to answer. He steeled himself, forcing the pain of his wounds and the heavy weight of his fatigue to a place where he would not feel them. Then, with a high, clear cry, he hurled himself at his vast foe, his feet flying over the broken flagstones of the square, the day spinning into timelessness as the chanting orcs fell silent and his heart, his will, his very life narrowed into a brilliant point. Keryvian sang in his hand and Fflar laughed aloud in fey delight.

Aulmpiter roared in rage and threw himself into the air with a powerful sweep of his mighty wings. Fflar leaped up to hew at the nycaloth lord with his brilliant blade. Then Aulmpiter's giant mace came crashing down at him, a thunderbolt of infernal power.

Elf-wrought steel, holy and true, met the brazen maul of the nycaloth lord, and darkness fell in Myth Drannor.

CHAPTER 1

*Midwinter, the Year of Lightning Storms
(1374 DR)*

Angry winter surf boomed and thundered against Tower Reilloch's headland as Araevin Teshurr answered the high mage's summons. He turned his feet to the familiar halls and staircases, stretching out his legs with the long and quick stride he'd learned in countless years of devouring roads and paths in distant Faerûn. Tower Reilloch had been Araevin's home for more than eighty years, but in thoseeight decades he'd been away on far travels more often than not.

Araevin was tall for a sun elf, with all the height of a human but with a slender and more graceful build. He stood half a head higher than most other elves he met. Humans sometimes mistook his manner for cool disdain, but in truth he was simply thoughtful, in the sense that his mind was often engaged on distant things.

He was keenly interested in everything he saw, and he habitually studied his surroundings with an uncanny intensity.

His face set in a small frown, he came to the marble steps leading up to the great hall. Four elf warriors stood watch at the main door, dressed in green cloaks embroidered with a silver starburst insignia over coats of shining mail—Queen's Guards, assigned to Reilloch's garrison.

"Good day," Araevin said to the warriors. "Philaerin has summoned me."

The guard sergeant, a lithe young moon elf, nodded and replied, "Go on in, Mage Araevin. They're expecting you."

He returned her smile awkwardly, then swiftly took the last steps. He was still unused to the simple routine of passing the Tower guards.

Three years ago, he thought, we would have laughed at the notion that Evermeet's Towers required guards.

But in the Year of the Unstrung Harp renegade sun elves had joined forces with human sea-wolves and drow from the deep tunnels of the Underdark to launch a great assault against the island kingdom. A terrible spell launched from a traitorous Tower had obliterated the Tower of the Sun, home to the greatest mage circle of Evermeet. Queen Amlaruil and her supporters had defeated the attack, but a third or more of Evermeet's best mages did not survive the battle against the invaders. Since then soldiers of the queen protected the invaluable remaining Towers against any future attacks . . . and perhaps kept an eye on the circles themselves to make sure that no more scheming mages could gather undetected.

The great doors of blueleaf wood, bound with mithral, opened silently for Araevin. Hesitating only to draw a deep breath and calm his nervousness, he strode into the hall and stood before the Circle of Reilloch Domayr.

Three high mages awaited him near the center of the tall chamber, standing beneath the theurglass and mithral dome that crowned the hall. In Araevin's experience, high mages had no need to resort to trappings such as ceremony or thrones in order to express the power they wielded. Each was a wizard of tremendous accomplishment, the youngest more than five hundred years old, the least among them capable of dueling a dragon and perhaps living to tell the tale. Araevin could sense the Art they wielded as a bright white flame, hidden from sight but powerful nonetheless.

He bowed and said, "You sent for me, Eldest?"

"Welcome, Araevin," said Philaerin. The Eldest of Reilloch Domayr, Philaerin was a moon elf, pale of skin and dark of hair. His expression was grave, but his eyes were kind and thoughtful. He was almost six hundred years old, a very great age for a moon elf, but his face was smooth and unlined. Elves were not truly ageless, of course. The spirit grew stronger, burning brighter and clearer as the years passed, until at last the frail body was no more than a thin envelope through which a brilliant soul shone. "I hope we didn't interrupt anything important."

"Not at all," Araevin replied. "I was inscribing a new wand to sell in Leuthilspar, but it will wait."

"How is Ilsevele?"

"I have not seen her for some time. Her duties lie in Leuthilspar. When I finish the wand I am working on, I think I will visit her."

Araevin smiled as Philaerin's courtesy reminded him of Ilsevele Miritar, his betrothed. It had been several months—or was it a year already?—since Araevin had last seen her. Too long, he decided.

"Your talents as an artificer are well known," said High Mage Kileontheal.

Araevin turned his attention to Philaerin's companions. Kileontheal was a small sun elf seemingly no more than a girl, but she was an illusionist of great power. High Mage Aeramma Durothil was a proud sorcerer from the highborn Durothil family, utterly confident in his powers.

"Crafting wands and such devices supports my studies and travels, High Mage," he answered.

"Your studies and travels," repeated Aeramma.

His manner was brusque and direct. Araevin felt an

unspoken exchange between the three high mages, as if their thoughts darted one to the other in a tangible but unseen form.

They mean to test me, he realized. Not a test of skill, or knowledge, simply . . . personality. What qualities are they looking for? he wondered. What recourse will I have if they do not approve of me?

He calmed his mind with a conscious effort of will as Aeramma continued, "Tell us a little of your journeys in Faerûn, Araevin. You have spent many years away from Evermeet, and we are not familiar with your interests."

Araevin met Aeramma's measuring look with a steady gaze, refusing to show any lack of confidence. "I have spent some years studying elven portals and spell structures throughout northwest Faerûn. Most are relics of Illefarn or Siluvanede."

"Evermeet's libraries were not sufficient for this task?" Kileontheal asked.

"The old elfgates are in Faerûn, not here. Besides, while the Tower's records have often provided me with useful clues, there is no substitute for experience." Araevin glanced at the tiny high mage and added, "As it turns out, our libraries are in need of some updating."

Aeramma Durothil folded his arms across his chest as if the remark had affronted him.

"Is it true you led humans and folk of other barbaric races"—Aeramma used the blunt term *n'tel-quessir,* or "not-People" in the Elvish tongue—"to secrets we hid from them centuries ago? And that you allowed them to despoil our tombs and sacred places?"

Do not give in to anger, Araevin reminded himself.

His eyes smoldered, but he retained his calm.

"It is true that I traveled in the company of *people* other than elves," he said, deliberately referring to them as *Tel'Quessir.* "I formed the Company of the White Star from the best folk I could find regardless of race, because I needed stout and loyal comrades to help me. And it is true that we explored some of the forgotten vaults, towers, and libraries of Illefarn and other long-fallen realms. But it is not true that I despoiled elven tombs, or allowed my companions to do so."

"Did you remove valuables and magical artifacts from places abandoned by the People, or not?" Aeramma demanded.

"What is inherently sacred about a place we have abandoned?" Araevin countered. "Many of our old cities and palaces in Faerûn have become dangerous places. Some are haunted by monsters, some are defended by decaying old spell wards that endanger any who come near, and some were dark and deadly places even before our People left them." He looked away from Aeramma to the other high mages, and said, "We opened no tombs, that I can promise you."

Aeramma seemed unsatisfied by Araevin's answer, but Philaerin chose that moment to step in. The Durothil high mage subsided as the Eldest spoke.

"Ancient ruins and broken mythals are the extent of your interest in Faerûn, then?" asked Philaerin.

"To be honest, no. I have spent a great deal of time traveling the human realms, simply to see them. That was not my intent when I first went to Faerûn to find our lost portals, but you cannot seek out the old places of Illefarn or other elven lands without coming to know the human cities that have grown up along the Sword Coast."

"What do you think of our human friends?"

Araevin considered his answer carefully before replying, "They are a strange folk, so like us in some ways, so different in others . . . a race of young giants who know not their own strength. Once I thought I was jealous of them. Why should humans inherit the lands where our ancestors lived, after all? But in the course of my travels I made the acquaintance of many humans, and I found among them friends whose wisdom would reflect well on any elf five times their age."

"I am sure that there are individuals of outstanding character among humans, Araevin," Kileontheal said. "Yet, as a race, do they not pose a grave danger? Their numbers grow every year. Their realms spring up with the speed of

Forsaken House • 9

a forest fire in Flamerule. They have no reverence for those who have gone before them . . . including us."

"Yet that is an advantage as well as a danger, High Mage." Araevin turned to Philaerin and spread his hands. "We live among the works of our ancestors. We are burdened by their misdeeds, and shackled by their mistakes. What history we write of ourselves in the years to come has already been determined, at least in part, by the wars and grief of ten thousand years. Humans are not bound by the past in the same way we are. Every day is a new beginning for them, an opportunity to discard the mistakes of the day before. We might learn something from that."

Aeramma frowned and asked, "Would you also have us copy their squalid cities, their senseless squabbles, or their fickle gods?"

"It seems to me that you see everyone's faults except our own, High Mage," Araevin said sharply. Despite his determination to remain calm, he was growing angry. The Durothil mage's smug self-assurance was exactly the sort of myopic view that had driven Araevin to seek his answers beyond Evermeet's shores in the first place. "You don't know humans as well as you think."

"Nor do you, if you love them so well," Aeramma retorted.

The noble-born high mage started to frame a more severe reply, but Philaerin raised his hand. He glanced at Kileontheal then at Aeramma. Araevin sensed the lightning-swift flicker of thought from wizard to wizard, and bleakly wondered if Aeramma's thoughts were anything he would care to hear. He settled for clasping his hands before his belt, and waiting. Outside, the surf boomed like distant thunder.

When the high mages appeared to arrive at some consensus, they returned their attention to Araevin.

"We did not call you here to ask you to explain your travels among humans, Araevin," Philaerin said. "We have been considering your request to take up the study of high magic for some time now, and we have arrived at an answer."

Araevin steeled himself against the uncertainty in his stomach. He'd waited two years to hear the response of Tower Reilloch's high mages. He was confident of his lore, and he'd proven himself in his service with the Queen's Spellguard years before, but still . . . no one was made a high mage unless those who already held that exalted rank concurred in the decision.

This is where Aeramma puts me in my place, he thought bitterly.

"You have demonstrated competence and care with your Art in the years that you have studied at Tower Reilloch. Your skill rivals that of any other wizard in our circle who is not a high mage already, and your scholarship is even more noteworthy," Philaerin continued. "All in all, we consider you an excellent candidate for the study of high magic.

"However, you are only two hundred and sixty-six years of age. We would like you to continue your studies here at the Tower for another fifty years or so before we will begin to share with you the power that has been placed in our care."

"Fifty years?" I have been selected! he thought, with no small relief, but at the same time, he almost groaned aloud at the thought of the wait. He inclined his head to Philaerin and said, "Thank you, Eldest, for your confidence in me. But that is a long time, even by our measure. What am I expected to learn in that time that I do not know now?"

"To tell the truth, Araevin, I do not know," Philaerin said with a sigh. "You have shown an excellent grasp of your studies in the Art, and I believe you could embark on the higher studies tomorrow and not fail. But you know as well as I that, questions of skill aside, we do not make high mages of those who are still young, or those whom we do not know well. Your passion does you credit, but you are so young, and you have spent so much time away from Evermeet. We do not think it unreasonable to see what Evermeet and time might teach you."

Araevin did not attempt to conceal his disappointment,

but he accepted the decision with a curt nod. Arguing his case would certainly not convince Philaerin to let him begin sooner. "As you wish, Eldest. I look forward to beginning my studies, when it is time."

"We know you are nearly ready, Araevin," said Kileontheal, not unkindly. "I do not know of a single high mage who began his studies before his three hundredth birthday, and many of us do not take it up until we are a full five centuries in age."

"You are, of course, welcome to continue your studies in another Tower," Philaerin added. "But I hope you will remain here. You have much you could teach our younger mages. Your time will come, sooner than you think. We will wait."

Araevin could think of nothing else to add. He touched his hand to his lips and his brow, and bowed again.

"Of course, Eldest. Sweet water and light laughter, until next we meet."

With his heart a turmoil of frustration and hope, he withdrew from the great hall.

❖ ❖ ❖ ❖ ❖

Araevin left Tower Reilloch the next day, following the old track that led east along the steep headlands and forested hillsides of the rugged northeast coast. In the north, Evermeet was covered in dark pine forest, and the trail threaded its way above striking views of the rocky shore and the angry gray sea. Streamers of windblown mist clung to the hilltops and hid the higher slopes above him as he walked, a sturdy staff in one hand and a light rucksack over his shoulders. The seaborne wind was strong in his face, and the forest sighed and rustled with the gusts.

From time to time he found himself glancing up into the treetops, as if to surprise his old companion Whyllwyst. Every time he caught himself at it, he frowned and pulled his eyes back down to the path before him, trying to ignore the stab of sudden grief. It had been more than ten years since his familiar had died, and yet the small gray gyrfalcon still seemed a part of him. Araevin had thought once or twice about summoning another, but he was still not done grieving. For the time being, he preferred to be alone.

Late in his second day of walking, he came to a particularly rugged headland and turned off the track, following an overgrown trail above a precipitous drop to the rocky strand below. At the end of the path stood a battered lodge, a rustic place of fieldstone and carved cedar beams. Many of its rooms were cleverly sculpted balconies and open colonnades that rambled over the southeast side of the headland, open to the weather. Higher up on the hillside a living spring gave rise to a swift rill that rushed through the center of the house in a moss-grown waterfall. Humans might have built the place of similar materials, but they never would have managed to conceal it so well among the rock and the forest of the headland.

"Glad homeagain," Araevin said softly, but the wind and the surf made no answer.

Araevin had not set foot in the House of Cedars for the better part of thirty years. When he was in Evermeet, he usually stayed in the apartments set aside for him at Tower Reilloch. The elements had been hard on the house. Water stains marked the woodwork, the cedar beams were gray and split, and some of the fieldstone walls had buckled and crumbled with thirty winters of freezing and thawing. He dropped his rucksack to the flagstone floor, and leaned his staff against the lintel with a sigh.

The house seems half a ruin already, he thought. *Has it been so long? We are so changeless, but the world is so impermanent.*

"Well, I can't say I expected to find anyone here," he said aloud.

Few of the Teshurrs remained, after all. His mother and father had passed to Arvandor a hundred years past, and his sister Sana lived in the open, sunny meadows of Dregala at the other end of the island with her husband, children, and grandchildren. Still, he would have hoped that *someone*—at least his cousins Eredhor or Erevyella, or their children—might have made the House of Cedars into a summer home, a hunting lodge, or simply a place to go to escape their daily cares.

Araevin spent the next few days repairing the place as best he could. He had no skill to replace the great timbers—ancestors wiser than he in the ways of living wood had crafted much of the house—but he was able to coax the ancient spells sleeping in the beams back to life, and he had some hope that they would slowly heal themselves in time. Cleaning out the house and redressing the fieldstone was a matter of simple physical labor, which he did not shy from. He opened several of the storage rooms and brought out a few of the old furnishings in order to make the place more comfortable, though he had to resort to magic to dry out and restore many of them. He also spent hours each day clambering all over the headland, wandering the paths he'd haunted as a child while he considered what he wanted to do next.

On returning to the house from one such walk, a tenday after he'd left the Tower, he found a fine gray destrier grazing on the thin grass just outside the house's front door. A light saddle, blanket, and pair of saddlebags worked with a swan design lay nearby, alongside a large leather bow case.

"Well," said a clear voice from behind him, "I was wondering if you were going to turn up."

"Ilsevele!" Araevin exclaimed.

He turned and found her watching him from the doorway. She was lissome and pale, a sun elf with copper-colored hair and a graceful figure, and she wore a simple green and white riding outfit. Even among elves she was thought to be strikingly beautiful, and it had never ceased to amaze Araevin that her heart had turned to him. He had no gift for songs of love or dances beneath the stars, not compared to a dozen other noble-born lords and princes who had wooed her, and yet she had promised herself to him. The sun falling on her shoulders brushed away his melancholy, and he laughed out loud in pure, unintended delight.

"Ilsevele! What are you doing here?"

"Looking for you, of course. You might have taken the trouble to tell your betrothed where you were going before vanishing from the Tower without a word to anyone. Fortunately, my father divined your whereabouts for me. I really should be angry with you, I suppose."

"I didn't mean to be away for long," he said. "Without even thinking about it I found myself here. The house needed caring for, so I tarried to do what I could."

"And to escape some weighty matter of the Tower, I am sure."

"Well ... yes. I suppose I wanted to slip away for a while and think of something besides the affairs of Tower Reilloch."

Ilsevele set her hands on her hips and said, "You needed to escape the Tower for a time, but you didn't think to come visit me? Now I think I am growing angry."

"I thought you would be busy with your duties in Leuthilspar. I did not want to trouble you."

"We are to be married, in case you've forgotten. You are not a trouble to me ... unless I find myself riding all over Evermeet looking for you, because you were not at your lonely little Tower when I chose to slip away from my post to surprise you." Ilsevele poked a finger in his chest. "Next time, send word to me! For some strange reason, I sometimes wonder where you are when we are apart."

Araevin bowed, spread his arms wide, and said, "Lady Miritar, I offer my sincerest apologies."

"Hmph. Well, that must do for now, I suppose." Ilsevele swirled away, gazing at the old house around her. "So this is the place where you were born, all those many ages ago?"

Araevin smiled. The difference in their ages was a standing jest between them. He was almost a hundred years older than she. Of course, among elves there was really no such thing as a winter-and-spring match, as his human friends might have called it. Once an elf was older than a century or so, age really did not matter much—except to high mages, he reminded himself. He stepped ahead of her and led her inside.

"You are gazing on the House of Cedars, ancestral seat of the Teshurr clan, my lady," he said. "I suppose it is not much to look at right now."

"You suppose wrong," Ilsevele said. She ran her hand along a rich cedar balustrade centuries old, admiring the work. Sunlight and shadow dappled the waters of the broad cove below. "This place is beautiful. The sea, the cliffs, the forest . . . to sit in Reverie every night with the sound of the sea in your ears. It's perfect, Araevin."

"My family was content here for a long time."

"Maybe they will be again," Ilsevele said.

"Oh, we've all gone our different ways now. My sister lives in—"

"I wasn't speaking of your sister, you dunderhead." Ilsevele glared at him. "I thought mages of your rank were supposed to be brilliant, Araevin. Honestly, you're as thick as a post sometimes. No, I was thinking of *our* family."

Araevin glanced around the house, as if seeing it for the first time, and said, "I hadn't ever thought of it that way."

"We are to be married in only three years, Araevin, if you haven't forgotten our promises. We will need a place to dwell, won't we?" Ilsevele smiled at him. "I have no intention of taking up residence in an unused corner of your workroom in Reilloch. We will need a place that is ours, dear one, and with a little work, I think this might do quite well."

Araevin stared at her in bemusement. They'd been promised to each other for almost twenty years, and of course their wedding was almost upon them. Yet when he was immersed in his work in the Tower, or traveling across Faerûn, the fact that he was betrothed to a beautiful and clever lady of high family had a way of escaping him. Ilsevele was right. He was thick as a post sometimes.

Ilsevele watched him as if she could follow the course of his thoughts. In truth, Araevin would not put it past her.

"Now—what dire challenge drove you away from the Tower, anyway?"

He started to wave off the question, but then thought better of it. Instead, he sat down beside her.

"The high mages met with me," he said. "I will be permitted to study the high lore."

"Araevin, that's wonderful! I know you have hoped for this."

"In fifty years."

"Oh." Ilsevele frowned. "Well, everyone knows that high mages must have a lifetime of experience before they can safely study the high magic spells." She thought a moment, then her expression brightened. "Perhaps it isn't so bad. That will give us plenty of time to get started on our family."

"There is that," he admitted.

"But?"

"But I find myself wondering what I am to do with myself between now and then." Araevin stared at his hands. "For so long I have always felt that I needed to master one more spell, find one more old book and read it, learn one more secret of the Art, prove myself in one more way. I am afraid that I may find the waiting hard to abide."

"I think you have spent too much time among your human friends," she replied. "There is no hurry, Araevin. And I think you will find that I can demand your full and undivided attention if I so choose."

She reached for him and drew him close, and Araevin was soon forced to concede that Ilsevele could do exactly as she threatened when she wanted.

Later, as the stars came out in the eastern sky and the last fiery glimmers of sunset burned in the clouds of the west, Araevin held her in his arms. Together they listened to the sea's endless voice and the sighing of the breeze in the forest.

"I am going to Faerûn soon," he said softly.

"I know."

"I may be gone for some time. I don't know what I am looking for."

"I know."

"You are not angry with me?" he said.

"Of course not. I am going with you," she replied. She snuggled deeper into his arms. "Some desire in your heart is set on things you cannot find in Evermeet. I want to walk beside you and see what those things are. You will never be wholly mine until I do."

Araevin thought on that for a long time. He found, somewhat to his surprise, that he wanted more than anything to have her come with him, to share the things he saw, to meet the people he knew and visit the places he loved.

"We'll leave in a month, maybe two. I have a few things to finish at the Tower. By summer at the latest, I think. There is no hurry."

❧ ❧ ❧ ❧ ❧

Araevin was deep in Reverie when the call came. He and Ilsevele had tarried at the House of Cedars for two more days, content with each other's company, considering their plans to journey into the world beyond Evermeet's shores. But an hour after moonset, when the night was black and heavy with the wet sea winds and Araevin lay dreaming of times long past, a brilliant white flame impinged on his trance.

A swift, frightened voice interrupted his dreams: *Mages of Reilloch Domayr, rally to the Tower! Demons assail the circle, and many have been slain already. Arm yourselves for battle!*

"Kileontheal?" he cried out, as he roused himself from Reverie.

He could feel the imprint of the High Mage's personality on the sending, as if her pale face hung before him in the darkened room. Araevin leaped to his feet, his mind stumbling over the message.

Demons in the Tower? Impossible! he thought.

Evermeet was warded by mighty spells that prevented creatures of the lower planes from setting foot on the island of the elves. But Kileontheal would not be mistaken about something like that, would she?

"Araevin? Are you well? You cried out," said Ilsevele, who stood at the door of the chamber, a dressing gown wrapped around her body against the cold breeze.

"Demons are attacking the Tower," he said numbly. "The high mages have summoned the circle to its defense. I must go at once."

"I will saddle Swiftwind," Ilsevele said.

"No, it would be a ride of hours. I will teleport there immediately."

"Can you take me?"

Araevin fumbled with his belt, sparing her a single glance. "Yes, but—something is very wrong, Ilsevele. I do not know what sort of danger is waiting there. Maybe you should—"

Ilsevele's eyes burned as she said, "Don't you dare suggest that it might be too dangerous for me, Araevin. I am one of the best spellarchers on this island and I am an officer in the Queen's Guard. If you can take me, you will."

She ducked out of the chamber, only to reappear with her belongings. Slipping out of her dressing gown, she shrugged a light arming coat over her shoulders and began to lace it up as quickly as she could.

Araevin quickly rummaged through the small chest he'd chosen to serve as his dresser and found a long vest of unusual cut. It was fitted with numerous pockets and a long bandolier filled with the ingredients and reagents he needed to cast many of his spells—carefully formed rods of crystal, spirals of copper, pinches of silver powder and dried blood, all the physical components needed to invoke his magic. Then he dashed out into the front hall for his cloak and staff. He was not as well-armed as he might like, since he had only two wands at his belt, but then he had not expected to be summoned into battle when he left the Tower.

"I am ready to go!" he called to Ilsevele.

"One moment!" she said. "I have to set Swiftwind loose. He can find his way back to my father's house."

She hurried past him out into the night, then returned, still lacing up her mithral shirt as she gathered her things. She slipped her feet into stout calf-high boots, threw the green cloak of the Guard around her shoulders, and uncased her bow. It was a powerful weapon of deep red yew, crafted from a rare and magical tree found only in Evermeet. She strung it with a single efficient movement.

"By the way," Ilsevele said, "I hope you're skilled with your teleporting spell. I don't want to find myself a few miles out in the ocean if you miss."

"Don't be concerned." Araevin paused to consider where he needed to go. Kileontheal's call was no more than ten minutes old, but who knew what might have happened in that time? "I'll take us directly to my workshop. It's somewhat out of the way, so I should hope we wouldn't appear in the middle of a battle. And I've a few things there that might prove useful, if matters are as desperate as the high mage indicated."

He extinguished the soft lanterns all around the house with a gesture, then took Ilsevele by the arm and spoke the complex words of a spell.

Magic surged through him like a jolt of living fire, powerful, intoxicating, and frightening all at once. There was an instant of icy darkness, a sensation like falling but subtly different, and Araevin and Ilsevele stood in a large, cluttered chamber. Parchment notes lay scattered haphazardly across the workbenches, and a row of narrow theurglass windows looked out over the seaward walls of the Tower on one side of the room. Ilsevele winced and set out a hand to steady herself against the wall.

"Well, you missed the ocean, so we must be in your workshop," she whispered. "Nothing seems out of the order here. Where now?"

"The great hall," Araevin said. "But first. . . ."

He crossed the room quickly to a theurglass-faced cabinet built into one wall. He whispered an arcane word, and the glass door of the cabinet vanished. Theurglass was strong as steel at need, but those who knew how

20 • Richard Baker

could dismiss it into nothingness or call it back again with a word. Inside the cabinet lay the laspar-wood wand he'd been working on, as well as four more wands and a shirt of gleaming mithral mail. Araevin quickly donned the mail shirt, which was so light it scarcely interfered with even the most difficult spellcasting. He took a wand made of dark zalantar wood, ignoring the others. That one he had ensorcelled with a powerful spell of disruption, meaning to have it at his hip the next time he traveled in Faerûn.

Feeling somewhat better prepared for whatever he might find, he moved to the workshop door and carefully pulled it open, peeking out into the corridor outside. It was dimly lit by enchanted lamps at wide intervals, and showed no signs of enemies or friends. In the distance, some destructive spell rumbled menacingly, shaking the Tower, and Araevin caught the ring of steel on steel from far away.

Araevin set off at a trot, gliding swiftly and softly along the hallway. His workshop was high in a little-used tower. He quickly checked the rest of the floor, and descended a winding staircase to the level below. On the landing he found the first of the fallen—one of the Tower guards, savagely clawed or bitten around the face and throat. Araevin could do nothing for her, and so he and Ilsevele continued, following a long hallway to one of the Tower's libraries. The door stood ajar, with another guardsman lying unconscious at its foot. From the room beyond, Araevin caught the hiss and croak of sinister voices. He glanced at Ilsevele and gave her a steady nod. She set an arrow to her string, and nodded back.

Araevin kicked open the door and stormed inside. Two hulking hellspawned monsters, demons or devils or some such creature, crouched inside, pawing through the books and scrolls. They had chitinous bodies of deep red, and beaklike maws beneath green, multifaceted eyes. Their long arms ended in horrible talons that dangled below their knees. A third creature, almost human or elf in appearance except for his red, fine-scaled skin and sweeping batlike wings, stood across the chamber, examining tomes laid out on a great table beneath the windows.

A demon-elf? Araevin hesitated, certain his eyes had deceived him. The features were elf enough—narrow skull, subtly pointed ears, eyes gently inclined down at the inner corners—but hellish malice glowed in those green eyes, and the bared teeth were small, sharp fangs. His stomach twisted in horror as the monsters wheeled to face him, jaws clacking, while the winged one started to bark out the words to a spell.

From over Araevin's shoulder, a pair of silver arrows streaked out and took the first of the insect fiends in the jaw, vanishing up to the feathers in its foul mouth. It went to all fours, black blood gushing from the wound. Araevin leveled his wand at the others and snapped out the wand's activating word. A shrill, deafening sound split the air as a coruscating blue bolt sprang out from the wand. It blasted past the second insect creature, who ducked away from the blast and snatched up an iron trident, but it caught the winged demon-elf in the midst of his spell and hammered him into the other wall. Bookshelves splintered and heavy tomes cascaded down on the creature.

"Taksha! Erthog! Slay them!" the winged one cried out.

The insect fiend took two steps and hurled its heavy iron trident at Araevin, who yelped despite himself and twisted to one side. He stumbled out of the doorway as the weapon thudded into the door with enough force to bring all three of its points clear through the thick oak. Araevin scrambled to his feet to cast a spell, sending five streaking missiles into the hellborn monster attacking him. The creature came on undeterred, its great talons raking inch-deep furrows in the wall behind him.

"Araevin! What are these things?" Ilsevele called.

She darted into the room herself, circling behind a table and loosing more arrows at the hellspawn. One arrow shattered on the thick plates of the creature's shoulder, but another sank into the eye of the monster who already had two in its throat, and a third punched a hole through

22 • Richard Baker

the membranous wing of the red-scaled sorcerer, just then picking himself up from the ground after Araevin's disrupting bolt.

"Mezzoloths!" Araevin answered.

He'd never encountered the things himself, but he had read of them in his researches—mercenaries of the lower planes, powerful fiends who served any master who could meet their price. The monster Ilsevele had shot crumpled to the ground and abruptly discorporated into black, stinking mist, returning back to whatever foul plane it had been summoned from.

Araevin danced back from his own adversary to gain himself room to use another spell. Having observed the damage wreaked in the library by his first disrupting bolt, he didn't want to use the wand again unless he had to. He started on a spell of dismissal, but the winged demon-elf beat him to the punch, hurling a brilliant white orb into the fray. The spinning white disk exploded into a blast of unearthly cold and razor-sharp splinters of ice, peppering both Araevin and Ilsevele, as well as the pursuing mezzoloth. Araevin grunted in pain, but he kept his feet.

Enough of this, he thought. No sense saving my spells if I let these creatures claw Ilsevele or me to death.

He allowed himself to slide away from the mezzoloth raking at him while carefully focusing his attention on a deadly spell. The insectile monster surged forward, seeking to overwhelm him before he could finish, but Araevin snapped out the last word just as the fiend's beak descended toward him. From his outstretched finger a brilliant emerald ray sprang, taking the mezzoloth full in the chest. The creature seemed to glow bright green, screeching in agony, and it discorporated into sparkling dust and streaming, foul smoke.

Araevin shifted his attention to the bat-winged sorcerer across the room. The demonspawn, hobbled by arrows in its hip and thigh, snarled out a vicious curse that wove a wall of darkness behind it as it ducked through the opposite door.

"Araevin! I can't see it!" Ilsevele cried.

"It fled," Araevin said.

He quickly dispelled the darkness, and glanced at his betrothed. Ilsevele had an arrow on her string. Patches of frostburn gleamed along one arm and the side of her face, but her eyes were bright and hard.

"Are you hurt?" he asked her.

"It's nothing, just a touch of that ice spell the one with the wings threw," she replied. "You?"

"The same," Araevin said, then nodded at the other end of the library. "Come on, we'd better see if more of these things are still roaming around."

They hurried out of the library, but their adversary was nowhere in sight. This corridor was a grand hall, wide and tall, leading to the great hall itself, where Araevin had met with the high mages a tenday-and-a-half before. A furious battle had been fought in the corridor. The walls were scorched by fiery blasts and broken by lightning bolts, and a dozen more elf guards lay dead alongside three of the sinister winged sorcerers.

Araevin halted and stared at the scene in horror. He had known many of the dead guards for decades.

"By the Seldarine," he whispered. "What happened here?"

Violet light flared at the end of the hall, and an ear-splitting thunderbolt shook the Tower.

"Whatever it is, it is not over yet," Ilsevele said.

She and Araevin picked their way through the shattered corridor to the great doors at the end, splintered and hanging crookedly from their hinges. The great hall of Reilloch Domayr lay on the other side of the doorway. The two elves glided up to the smoking oaken doors and peered inside.

In the center of the room, a fierce band of mezzoloths and other hellborn monsters stood around a large iron hoop or ring lying on the marble floor. Elf mages and warriors sheltered behind the tall columns ringing the room, surrounding the creatures. The Tower's defenders hurled spell and arrow at the invaders, even as the yugoloths and their winged sorcerers blasted back at the elves with their own infernal magic, filling the great hall with scathing rays of fire and glowing magical darts. Dead and wounded elves littered the chamber. The iron ring glowed with a ruddy light, and half a dozen of the attackers who had been standing within its confines—including, Araevin noted, the wounded sorcerer who had escaped him in the library, as well as another mezzoloth bearing a large iron coffer—ghosted into nothingness.

"They're teleporting away!" cried several of the elf defenders.

The last of the infernal attackers stepped back into the hoop. Araevin broke from his cover and hurled a blazing sphere of lightning into their midst, while Ilsevele followed, her bow thrumming like a deadly harp as she sent arrow after arrow into the band. Two skeletal demons with swords of blazing bone crumpled under her deadly rain, but one of the winged sorcerers smothered Araevin's lightning orb with a quick countering spell of its own. The demon had a shirt of fine golden scale mail, and wore its long black hair in thick braids laced with gold wire. A jeweled eye patch covered one eye. The creature fixed its good eye on Araevin and grinned maliciously.

"You'll have to do better than that," it rasped.

"As you wish!" Araevin growled. He gestured and snapped out the words of the deadliest spell he could manage, hurling a scything blast of rainbow-colored doom at the invaders. Each glittering ray carried its own deadly energy, and the great hall crackled with the power of Araevin's attack. But the demons within the iron ring were already fading into nothingness, vanishing away from the great hall. Araevin's prismatic blast scoured the space where they had stood only a moment before.

Araevin swore and started forward to see if he could decipher the workings of the teleporting ring, but at that instant an enormous blast of green fire exploded out from the device. Agonizing heat seared Araevin as he hurled himself to the ground, and all around him he heard the screams and cries of those other elves who were too close.

Forsaken House • 25

The chamber fell silent, save for the low crackle of guttering fires and the pelting of the rain, falling through a gap blasted in the great hall's dome. The emerald blast had seemingly contained a spell that carried away the bodies of the winged sorcerers that had fallen, since none of the creatures remained in the great hall. The iron hoop on the floor was nothing but a twisted band of scorched metal, its magic gone. Araevin slowly picked himself up, wincing with pain.

I should have prepared a spell against fire, he thought. *But then, how could I have known that I would become embroiled in a spell battle such as this?*

He turned and looked for Ilsevele, and found her slowly standing up from behind a heavy column that had shielded her from the worst of the blast.

"Ilsevele—?"

"I'm fine," she said. She stared at the hall, her face grim. "Sehanine, have mercy. So many have fallen here. Nothing to do now but see if we can do anything for the wounded."

Araevin nodded, but first he paced over the remains of the iron circle. He picked up a single twisted piece of metal in his fist.

Where are the high mages? he wondered silently. *Have they fallen as well?*

Then, with a sigh, he let the debris clatter to the floor, and turned to help with the injured.

CHAPTER 2

15 Alturiak, the Year of Lightning Storms

As the dim sunrise glimmered in the tower's window slits, Araevin gathered with the surviving mages of Reilloch Domayr in the conservatory. The great hall was in no condition to host a meeting of the circle. He left Ilsevele to lead the Tower guards in scouring the grounds for any enemies who might have been left behind by their comrades' escape.

The conservatory was a large, high-ceilinged hall that occupied the entire upper floor of the gatehouse. It was floored with gleaming old oak, and its paneled walls were finished with dark cherry carved in sylvan scenes. The place was used as a recital hall by the bards and music students who drifted through Tower Reilloch. Araevin had attended many recitals there, but had little gift for music himself. He found five mages waiting for him there.

"Welcome, Araevin," said the Loremaster Quastarte. He was a sun elf of great age, his eyes dark with wisdom in his young-old face, his hair so thin and white it seemed like a nimbus flowing down his shoulders. "We are all here, then."

"We are all that remains?" Araevin asked, astonished.

He glanced around the room, unable to keep himself from looking to see if he had perhaps missed one of his colleagues. Beside Araevin, there had been eight others who held the rank of mage. But only five of Araevin's colleagues were there: Quastarte, the wood elf sorcerer known as Eaglewind, the diviner Yesvellde Shaerim, the half-elf battle-mage Jorildyn, and the young abjurer Faelindel.

"I know that Earelde fell," Araevin continued, "but where are Olleile and Starsong?"

"Both slain in their Reverie. The invaders broke into their chambers before the alarm was raised," Quastarte said.

Aillesel seldarie," Araevin said softly. "The Seldarine preserve us. There is no end to the sorrow of this day." He bowed his head, hesitating before asking his next question. "The high mages?"

"We have not found Philaerin yet," said Quastarte, "but the fact that he was not seen in the battle and has not appeared since leads me to fear the worst. He was not in his chambers."

The others nodded in agreement. If Philaerin lived, he would have defended the Tower.

"Kileontheal lives, but she is grievously wounded," Yesvelde said. Yesvelde was a moon elf, with long dark hair and a distant, ethereal manner to her. She carried a sleek cat in her arms, her familiar Versei. Araevin felt thea quick gray shadow of Whyllwyst flicker across his heart, but made himself focus on Yesvelde's words. "She was struck senseless by a spell of insanity during the fight outside the great hall, a few minutes after issuing her call to the circle. She fled the battle, hurling spells at imaginary foes in the tower halls until she exhausted her power." The illusionist sighed. "I had no means to undo the enchantment afflicting her, so I directed the guards to confine her in her quarters and keep her under constant care until we can find a healer for her."

"Aeramma Durothil is dead," said Eaglewind. He was a grave and quiet fellow for a wood elf, more at home in the solitude of the forest than in the company of his peers. Araevin sometimes suspected that he was a sylvan creature of some sort who simply wore the shape of a wood elf for the convenience of the others, but he had never pressed the question. "I found him in the astrolabe an hour after the raiders fled. It looked like he destroyed a number of those who came against him. I found shadows shaped like demons blasted into the walls there."

"So one high mage is dead, one missing, and one incapacitated," Araevin sighed. "And three of us are dead, as well. What of the initiates and the other folk of the Tower?"

The initiates were the lesser wizards and sorcerers, those who were still new in their studies and not yet accounted members of the Circle. There had been fourteen of them.

Jorildyn, a seasoned battle-mage, stepped forward. He had human blood—something that was quite unusual on Evermeet, and regarded with great suspicion in some quarters—and was thickly built compared to the others, with a gray-streaked beard and a gruff manner.

"Four initiates are dead," the half-elf reported. "We also lost nine of the Tower Guards and several more of the Tower folk. About twenty are wounded, but all should recover with care." His face was grim. "We must see to our defenses at once, and make sure this cannot happen again."

"We will need a high mage for that, and none are available," Araevin observed. "We must suffice, then. Quastarte, you are the eldest among us. I will be content to follow your orders."

"You are a more skillful wizard than I, Araevin. I would not presume to command you. Or any of you, for that matter. I can only suggest what seems wise to me."

Forsaken House • 29

"Then let us hear what seems wise to you, Loremaster," Jorildyn said, "and we will take your suggestions as commands."

Quastarte fell silent, thinking for a moment, then said, "Very well, then. First, someone must carry word of the attack to the Queen in Leuthilspar, the sooner the better. Does anyone have a spell of teleporting prepared?"

"Not I," said Yesvelde.

"I am afraid I used mine to return to the tower when Kileontheal called," Araevin said. "I cannot ready another for hours."

"I have a scroll I can use," said Faelindel. "I will leave at once."

The abjurer bowed to the other mages and left the chamber, striding quickly.

"Jorildyn and Eaglewind—take charge of the Tower defenses. I do not think our attackers will return, but we must not be caught off guard again if they do."

"It will be done," Jorildyn replied.

"Yesvelde, you are a skilled diviner. See if you can learn who our attackers were, and where they came from. We may be able to organize pursuit, if we can learn these things."

The diviner bowed her head, accepting her task.

"What of me?" Araevin asked.

"I want you to carefully examine the vaults, armories, and libraries," Quastarte said. "The hellspawn and their winged masters did not come here simply for mayhem and murder. They must have been looking for something. You know the vaults as well as I. Determine if anything is missing." The old loremaster looked at the other mages. "In the meantime, I will search for Philaerin. If he is not here, perhaps he was cast into another plane or banished to some far realm by our enemies."

Araevin nodded and replied, "I will report back at once if I find anything amiss."

❂ ❂ ❂ ❂ ❂

Over many centuries, the mages who had dwelled at Tower Reilloch had accumulated many magical devices: mighty staves, deadly battle-wands, rings that stored or deflected spells, crystal orbs, enchanted cloaks, and tomes of perilous lore. Many of them had been crafted, forged, or scribed by the circle's own sorcerers and wizards, while others were prizes of battle, or long-forgotten artifacts that had been brought to Reilloch for safekeeping. Araevin had created a few of the things himself, since he was a skilled artificer of magical devices, and he had brought even more to the Tower from his explorations of old elven ruins in Faerûn. His intermittent research into the magical artifices of lost elven realms had required a careful study of the devices stored in the Tower's vaults.

Some of Reilloch's vaults were buried in the deep foundations, others were hidden high atop isolated towers, and a few were in extradimensional spaces that could be reached only through specific doors or chambers in otherwise innocuous portions of the fortress. Most were protected by spells of sealing and concealment that were virtually impenetrable. The vaults containing the most dangerous items were also guarded by lethal spell traps, terrible sigils that would utterly destroy anyone trying to pass them without knowledge of how to do so safely.

The first two vaults Araevin checked were secure, their spells of closing still intact. Araevin quickly inventoried their contents anyway, and found that nothing had been removed. *That makes sense,* he realized. Raiders after a specific target could not afford to waste time deliberately locating and opening each vault, not unless they were confident of defeating the circle in its entirety and holding the Tower in the face of every counterattack that could be thrown at them. Most likely it would be a single vault that had been attacked. He descended into the mazelike levels below the great hall, and found another vault undisturbed. That was not the case with the fourth vault he checked, however.

At the end of a long, low corridor with a ceiling of groined stone stood a door of iron and adamantine leading to a place known as Nandiyerron's Armory, after the archmage who had built the room a thousand years before. Araevin turned into the corridor leading to the armory, and realized at once that something was amiss. Whispers of spectral magic, the remnants of deadly spell traps even he did not understand, whirled and drifted in the heavy air of the passageway, and the door at the far end stood open. The walls and floor were deeply pitted with black, bubbled stone, as if great gouts of acid or fire had been loosed there, and the stink of hot stone still lingered.

Philaerin lay crumpled before the open door, his staff broken in his burned hands.

"Eldest. . . ." Araevin whispered.

He picked his way down the scored passageway and knelt beside the high mage. A black, even hole had been blasted through the center of Philaerin's chest by some slaying spell, but none of the attackers had managed to so much as scratch him otherwise. Araevin glanced at the passage around him, trying to guess at how many spells had been thrown there while the battle raged in the tower above. Demons, yugoloths, and such monsters summoned from the infernal planes did not leave bodies behind when they were slain—they returned to the foul hells from which they had been called forth. Philaerin might have repelled a few attackers, a small army of them, or none at all, but the battle had gone on long enough for many spells to damage the passageway.

Araevin rose and stepped into the vault of Nandiyerron, quickly examining what was left of its contents. All the Tower's vaults stored a number of relatively minor items, such as rings bearing protective enchantments, or arms and armor that any wizard or priest of middling power might make. He was not concerned about things like that. It was not good that such devices had been stolen, but they were not truly dangerous. On the other hand some of the vaults held uniquely dangerous items, things that could do great harm in the wrong hands. And Araevin saw at once that something important was indeed missing from the vault.

"The Gatekeeper's Crystal," he said aloud. "Damnation."

No one knew who had made the Gatekeeper's Crystal, or even when it had been made, but it was a powerful weapon indeed, an artifact that could easily disjoin and destroy magical wards and protections of any sort. The device consisted of three similar shards, each a dagger-shaped wedge of pale unbreakable crystal. Tower Reilloch held only one of the shards. The other two were lost, as far as Araevin knew. But perhaps those who had attacked the Tower knew differently.

"Araevin? Is that you?" Quastarte's voice echoed from the passages outside.

"I am here, Loremaster," Araevin called. He stepped out of the armory and knelt beside Philaerin again. "I have found Philaerin. And I have found what is missing."

The old sun elf entered the passageway and halted.

"Is he—?"

"Yes," said Araevin. "He was trying to keep them from the shard."

"Ah, no," Quastarte breathed as he hurried to the side of the Eldest, tears brimming in his eyes. "So that is what they were after, then. The Seldarine know what sort of evil they plan with it."

"They will need the other two pieces to use the device, won't they?" Araevin asked.

"Each shard is dangerous in its own right," Quastarte said. "But in conjunction, the three shards together are terribly powerful. Almost one thousand years ago the joined crystal was used to destroy the defenses of Myth Ondath. Only five years past, the Harpers used the crystal to throw down the old defenses of Hellgate Keep and raze that fortress of evil. But each time the crystal is used for such a purpose, its three parts separate and hurl themselves across vast distances and into far planes. It took us two years to find this one piece after the Harpers used it against Ascalhorn."

"And now it is gone."

Quastarte sighed and said, "We thought it would be safe here, if anywhere."

Forsaken House • 33

Araevin looked down at the fallen high mage on the pocked stone floor. Philaerin's face was not peaceful in death. His teeth were bared in a rictus of agony, and his eyes were wide and staring. He reached down to compose the Eldest's features, but as his hand neared Philaerin's face, a thin, cold sensation of magic at work briefly kissed his fingertips.

He drew back quickly and said, "Odd. There's a spell on him."

Quastarte leaned close.

"Hmm. Yes, I feel it too. A defense of his? Or some curse of his enemies?"

"It was not very powerful. Not much of a defense or a curse." Araevin considered for a moment. "I will try to negate it."

Quastarte nodded. Araevin drew a breath, then spoke the words of a spell of negation, canceling out the charm he had sensed. To his surprise, the spell crumpled at once, flaring bright blue as it did so. He saw at once that it was a minor dimensional pocket of some sort, a temporary storing place not much larger than a big goblet. The spell ended, and from the imaginary space a small gemstone suddenly appeared, clattering to the ground. It was a deep green, so dark as to be almost black, and a glimmering white star flickered in its depths.

"What in the world?" Araevin breathed.

"A *telkiira!*" Quastarte said. "I have not seen one like this before."

Araevin leaned back, thinking. *Telkiira* were small gemstones that could hold the thoughts or memories of their makers, even potent arcane lore such as spells or the rites necessary to create enchanted items.

"I wonder what this one holds?" he said.

"Whatever it was, Philaerin considered it important enough to conceal from his attackers." Quastarte frowned and picked it up in his hand, studying it carefully, and continued, "It doesn't advertise its secret, it seems. Sometimes all one has to do is touch a *telkiira* in order to find out what it contains. But this one is guarded against casual contact."

"Would the demons return for that, do you think?"

"I don't know," the loremaster said. "But we should make sure that it does not fall into their hands. Perhaps you should hold onto it, Araevin. If the demons do return, you will defend it better than I."

Araevin took the stone and gazed into its depths. It seemed an ordinary gemstone, if a somewhat valuable one.

"Very well," said Araevin. "Since our enemies have shown that they can enter our vaults and know something of where we keep our more powerful relics, it may make sense to keep it close at hand instead of simply hiding it again."

He exchanged a dark look with Quastarte and understood that the old loremaster shared his true concern. The raiders had known their way around Tower Reilloch quite well. They might have prepared their attack for months, secretly scrying the Tower's defenses . . . or perhaps they had had assistance from someone familiar with the Tower's secrets.

"True," Quastarte said, thinking aloud. "Of course, that suggests to me that perhaps you should remove it from the tower entirely. Do you think you might absent yourself for a short time?"

"If you are certain you will not need me here," Araevin replied. He found a silk handkerchief in his pocket and carefully wrapped the *telkiira* within. "I could go to Lord Miritar's estate and visit with Ilsevele and her father for a time. He is a councilor of the realm, and deserves a firsthand report of what happened here. And it would seem perfectly innocuous for Ilsevele and I to go to Elion for a time. No one would think it out of the ordinary, would they?"

The old loremaster grasped Araevin by the shoulder and said, "We may be jumping at shadows, but at this moment I would rather take too many precautions than too few."

"Do not hesitate to summon me back if I am needed," Araevin replied. He stood and slipped the small, silk-wrapped stone into his belt pouch. "Once I am away from here, I will examine the stone more closely to see if I can determine what is hidden inside. It may shed some light on who our attackers were, and what they intend to do with the shard."

"And I will search through Philaerin's tomes and journals to see if he makes any mention of it." Quastarte rose as well. "Come. Before you leave, we must summon the other mages and tell them what has been taken from the Tower."

◈ ◈ ◈ ◈ ◈

Nurthel Floshin stretched wide his black, leathery wings, and dropped closer to the snow-covered ground. He was in a hurry, and he beat his powerful wings tirelessly against the winter sky. Nurthel cut a striking figure, a demonic elf with scarlet-scaled skin and large batlike wings, clad in armor of enchanted golden scales, one eye covered by a rune-scribed patch.

Miles behind him, the rest of his raiding party proceeded on foot, too heavily burdened with their plunder to fly. It was not a particularly good day for flying, anyway. The clouds were low and thick, and freezing rain was falling all across the rugged hills and thick forests of the Delimbiyr Vale.

Nurthel allowed himself a smile of pleasure. The Gatekeeper's Crystal gave him the perfect excuse to hurry on ahead of the other fey'ri. He carried the artifact inside his golden scale shirt, wrapped tightly in a leather pouch. He started gaining altitude again, as the foothills of the Nether Mountains began to mount skyward from the river vale. His mistress had chosen her stronghold with an eye toward remoteness and isolation. None but the most determined—or foolhardy—of travelers passed that way. There the Delimbiyr turned east, fed by numerous streams known as the Talons—swift, racing rivers that descended from the snow-covered mountains to the north.

Nurthel followed the Starsilver, the second of those

streams, and after a few miles found a round hilltop rising up before him. Its slopes were shaped in graceful terraces inundated by the forest, and old white ramparts green with moss and vines climbed across the hillside. Glaurachyndaar, a great city of fallen Eaerlann, had once been known as Myth Glaurach, City of Scrolls. Crumbling colonnades and empty buildings choked with rubble were all that remained of the elven city, but deep catacombs led to hidden armories and jagged chasms beneath the hill.

He wheeled once and dived down through the snow-clad fir trees, alighting in a ruined old courtyard. He shook his wings vigorously, ignoring the quiver of fatigue from his rapid flight, and folded them behind his back. Nurthel made his way through an old archway into the palace proper. A thin crust of snow lay on the uneven ground within the white walls, and most of the halls and corridors were open to the sky above. It struck Nurthel as supremely ironic that the very palace of Myth Glaurach's grand mage should serve as the hidden citadel of she who had once been the most dangerous enemy of the realm of Eaerlann.

He came to a broken white tower and entered. That place at least still had intact floors above, so the ceiling kept out the rain and the snow, but its broad windows were blank and empty, the old theurglass that once covered them long since gone. The chamber possessed a magnificent view of forest-covered hills and snowy mountain peaks beyond. Comfortable furnishings—elegant divans, credenzas, and bookshelves, with a gorgeous tapestry secured on one wall—stood carefully placed in the room's interior so as not to be exposed to the weather.

"My lady!" he cried. "I have returned!"

"So I see, Nurthel." A sinuously graceful figure turned from the wide, empty window. "You took care to conceal your retreat?"

"Yes, my lady. We used the ring gate to return to the ruins of Ascalhorn."

Ascalhorn, the city later known as Hellgate Keep, and later still nothing but a windswept ruin, was almost thirty miles away. The fey'ri lord went to one knee, bowing in the presence of his mistress.

Like the fey'ri who served her, Sarya Dlardrageth possessed both demon and elf blood. But in her case, she was a true daemonfey, and her demonic bloodline was pronounced indeed. The demonspawned sun elves known as fey'ri were descended through several generations from the mating of elf and demon, but Sarya was a princess of House Dlardrageth. Her father was a balor, a great and terrible demon lord. Sarya's skin was deep red and her hair a blazing orange-gold as bright as a flame. She favored gold-embroidered robes of black that overlapped like plates of dark armor, carefully crafted to incorporate powerful defensive enchantments and leave her adequate room to flex her wings in flight or wield the sinister spells at her command.

"You may rise." Sarya said.

She turned her back on the windows and came closer, moving with the restless grace of a predatory animal kept in a space too small for her. Nurthel knew that she used the tower for her own quarters because of the numerous windows and open spaces beyond, since she strongly disliked confining spaces.

"Well, Lord Floshin, let me see my prize," she said.

Nurthel lifted his eyes to his queen's face and stood. Despite her fiendish heritage, she was seductively beautiful, with classic elf features and the figure of a winsome girl. At a glance one might think her no more than twenty years of age . . . but her eyes were cold and malevolent with an ageless evil. Sarya Dlardrageth had first walked the world more than five thousand years past.

"As you command, my lady," he said. He reached beneath his tunic of scale mail and drew out the broken crystal in its pouch, offering it to her. "The paleblood elves and their rabble were careless, as you said they would be. They were not expecting an attack, and we slew dozens before they remembered how to fight."

"No one remembers how to fight, in this diminished age," Sarya replied. "How many did you lose?"

She did not place any great value on her servants' lives, but she didn't have many fey'ri at her command. Each life was a resource not to be wasted lightly.

"Five fey'ri fell to the Tower defenders, my lady. We were careful to carry off the dead. Most of the yugoloths and demons died too, but of course they were summoned and bound for that purpose, and we expected to spend them in battle."

"You have done well, Nurthel. Very well indeed."

Sarya took the bundle from his hand and quickly unwrapped the crystal, discarding the cover. She caressed the device with her taloned hands. The stone was a pale, milky white, perhaps six inches long and triangular in shape, with a curiously beveled base and a long, tapering point. A glimmer of violet fire seemed to dance in its depths. Swirls of phosphorescence drifted in the wake of Sarya's fingertips as she touched the crystal.

"For over five thousand years I dreamed of holding the key to my prison in my hand," she mused, admiring the stone. "Fifty-eight centuries crawled by while I waited and watched. Sharrven and Siluvanede passed away, and I waited. Eaerlann—hated Eaerlann—grew old and decrepit and forgot the ancient enemies her lords had imprisoned beneath their fortresses, and still I waited and watched. The city of Ascalhorn was raised up over my living tomb, and I watched when demons and devils warred in the streets, driving out the simpering humans and their paleblooded friends. Fifty centuries I dreamed of this, Nurthel, and now only five short years after gaining my freedom, the crystal is mine. The irony of it!"

"You are free now, my lady. The ancient treachery of your foes has been undone."

Sarya's eyes narrowed and she said, "Only through the ignorance of foolish adventurers, who thought to cleanse Ascalhorn with no less a weapon than the Gatekeeper's Crystal."

They succeeded in throwing down Hellgate Keep—dying heroically in the process, of course—but they had also managed to crack the deeply buried magical prison in which

Forsaken House • 39

Sarya and her daemonfey sons had been interred thousands of years before the city of Ascalhorn had been raised.

At once Sarya had set about exploring the new world that had grown over the ruins of the one she had known five millennia earlier. In the five years since the Harpers had unknowingly set her free, she had gathered together the remnants of the fey'ri, demonspawned elves who had served House Dlardrageth in the days of her glory. Some, such as Nurthel himself, she had liberated from lesser prisons similar to her own. Others she had found hiding in distant planes, and a handful had survived unimprisoned, hiding amid the cities of her enemies. And she had also turned her attention to unraveling the mystery of her freedom, employing all of her formidable sorcery to learn how and why she had come to be freed.

"I wonder how the palebloods of Evermeet found the third piece," he said.

The daemonfey princess shrugged.

"Most likely it was found by some human mageling or tomb-plunderer," she said, "who recognized it as elf-work and sold it to someone who understood its true worth. My divinations informed me of the crystal's location, but did not suffice to solve the mystery of its travels."

She turned to a golden coffer that stood on one table, and spoke a charm of opening. Inside gleamed two crystals virtually identical to the one she held in her hand. The first segment Sarya had found in the rubble of Hellgate Keep, soon after gaining her freedom. It took her four years, but she eventually found the second piece in a volcano in Avernus, first of the Nine Hells.

She lifted out the other pieces one at a time and joined them, base-to-base. As each segment's lower facet touched that of the neighboring segment, the crystal glowed blue and melded together, forming a seamless, perfect whole. When the last piece was added, the device seemed to hum with power. It resembled a three-pointed star almost a foot in diameter, stronger than steel and imbued with magic beyond mortal means.

"Ah," Sarya purred. "What a pretty trinket this is!"

"Will it work?" Nurthel asked, peering at the artifact.

"Oh, yes," Sarya said. "Nothing can stand against it, though we must be careful, or else it will fly apart and fling its component crystals to the far ends of the multiverse. I dare not invoke its powers here, not within the spell wards of Myth Glaurach—but it will serve for the task I have in mind. I am confident of it."

Sarya replaced the conjoined crystal in its coffer, then set a lethal spell over the chest. She gestured at a decanter of dark wine and a pair of golden goblets across the room, summoning them to her hand.

"Now, what of the rest of your mission? How did that proceed?"

"We battled at least two, perhaps three high mages. We killed the two we were certain of and destroyed a number of lesser mages, too. Some had skill, others were mere novices. We plundered what we could from the Tower, and left before the mages managed to organize their defenses."

"And what of Kaeledhin's key?"

"We did as you directed, my lady. I attended to the matter personally," Nurthel said. The fey'ri lord accepted a goblet from his lady's hand and sipped the fiery vintage within. He dropped his eyes to his golden cup and swirled the wine thoughtfully. "Still . . . I do not see the point of it. We have the Gatekeeper's Crystal. That seems sufficient."

"Perhaps," Sarya replied. She turned and paced absently away, resuming the endless prowling she fell into when her mind was engaged. "But once I use the crystal, it is almost certain to fly apart again, and it may take years to reassemble. I would like a more permanent weapon at my disposal. In any event, it seems that Evermeet will remember our visit for some time."

CHAPTER 3

16 Alturiak, the Year of Lightning Storms

Araevin spent most of the day lending his spells and lore to the restoration of the Tower's magical defenses, aiding Quastarte and the other mages. An hour before sunset, he and Ilsevele left Tower Reilloch, following the coastal track west.

While they walked, Araevin carefully replayed the battle over and over in his mind, setting its every detail in his memory and thinking long and hard on the nature of the Tower's foes. The demons and yugoloths were clearly little more than footsoldiers, brought to the tower in order to destroy its defenders and guard the winged sorcerers. The latter were the creatures that most concerned Araevin. He'd seen at least three of them among the attackers. Each had possessed the narrow face, elegant features, and graceful build of an elf ... along with the fine scales, sinister wings, and supernatural malice of a demon. It shouldn't have been possible for the winged ones to gate their demonic minions into Evermeet, not with the magical wards surrounding the island, but somehow they had managed the feat.

They have elf blood, he thought grimly. They pierced our defenses because Evermeet did not recognize them as enemies. But what manner of elf is so clearly spawned of the lower planes? Not even the cursed drow are so debased.

A couple of hours before dawn, they finally stopped to rest in a small wayside hostel along the road. So far they had seen no signs of anything untoward, but as an extra precaution, Ilsevele stood watch while Araevin prepared his spells. Araevin had used many spells the night before, and he took some time to ready all his powers again. The act of unleashing a spell was fairly simple, a few arcane words, a quick pass of the hands, a pinch of odd reagents. But a wizard often required hours of tedious preparation to ready spells for the quick casting called for in battle. When he finished, they set out again, and reached the Miritar estate on the outskirts of the northern city of Elion late in the afternoon.

The Miritar clan had held Elion and the surrounding land in the name of Evermeet's monarchs for close to five hundred years. Like many other Cormanthorian families, the Miritars had fled Myth Drannor in the last days of that great city, escaping the terrible army that had destroyed the city. They had never been a numerous family, but they claimed the allegiance of a number of less noble clans, and they had proven to be good stewards over the northern lands granted them by the Crown. Seamist, the Miritar seat, was a large, rambling place of white stone walls wreathed in the ever-present mists of the northern shore. Dimly glimpsed colonnades and alluring bowers hovered beneath the dripping fir trees like an ethereal dream.

Two guards in dappled gray cloaks greeted Araevin and Ilsevele as they approached the palace gates.

"Lady Miritar, glad homeagain!" one of them called.

"We wondered where you were when Swiftwind returned unsaddled."

"I sent him along, Rhyste. He is well?"

"Yes, my lady. You'll find him in the stables."

"Good," said Ilsevele. She glanced at Araevin. "Swiftwind knows his way here, unlike some others I can think of." Araevin winced, but she smiled and looked back to the guard. "Is my father here?"

"Yes, my lady," said Rhyste. "He just returned from Leuthilspar. You'll find him taking his dinner in his study, if I am not mistaken."

"Thank you," Ilsevele replied. "Mage Teshurr will be staying with us for a time. Please send word to have a room readied for him."

Ilsevele and Araevin passed into the palace grounds, following a winding path that climbed through the cool groves and elegant buildings to a broad meadow high on the hillside. There a manor house of white stone crowned the palace grounds, looking out over the forested slopes below to the gray sea beyond. An open archway led to a courtyard of undisturbed natural stone open to the sky, grown over with moss and heather. Ilsevele led Araevin to a door on their left and knocked twice before entering.

The room beyond was a broad study, its walls graced by elegantly carved wooden screens and wide windows of mystic theurglass. A writing desk of cherry stood against one wall, beside two tall bookcases of the same wood. On one wall hung the ancient sword Keryvian, a mighty weapon of fallen Myth Drannor that had come into the possession of House Miritar almost three hundreds years before, recovered from the demon-haunted ruins of the city by Ilsevele's father when he was young.

A trim sun elf dressed in robes of green reclined on a divan beneath one of the windows, a book in his hands, a tray of sliced fruit and thin cakes forgotten on the end table. His hair, once a copper red, was streaked with silver, and thin lines framed his mouth and gathered at the corners of his eyes, but he was still graceful and fit. Lord Seiveril Miritar wore his four hundred winters well. He glanced up as Ilsevele and Araevin entered, and smiled warmly.

"Ilsevele! Glad homeagain, my dear. This is an unexpected surprise. And Araevin, too! Welcome to Seamist."

Ilsevele hurried across the room to take her father's hands and kiss his cheek.

"Hello, Father," she said. "It's good to be home."

"Please, join me in my meal," Seiveril said. He waved at the divan, and took in their mud-splashed boots and mist-dampened cloaks with a glance. "You've traveled a fair distance today, I see. Have you come from the Tower, then? How are things there?"

Araevin did not move. He exchanged glances with Ilsevele. Seiveril spied the worried look in Araevin's eyes at once, and paused.

"Something is wrong," he observed quietly.

"The Tower has been attacked, Lord Seiveril," Araevin said. "The night before last. A large band of demons and yugoloths killed many of the Tower's folk, including the high mages Aeramma Durothil and Philaerin, the Eldest. And they stole a dangerous artifact from the Tower vaults."

"*Aillesel seldarie!* Has Amlaruil been told?" Seiveril asked at once.

A high priest of Corellon Larethian, highest of the elf gods, Seiveril served as one of Queen Amlaruil's high councilors. It would not be completely accurate to say that he was lord of the isle's northern coasts, but on the other hand no elf within fifty miles commanded the authority that Seiveril did as a high-ranking cleric and a lord of Evermeet's council.

"We sent a mage to Leuthilspar immediately, and followed her with messengers on horseback," Araevin said. "We left the Loremaster Quastarte in charge, with the other mages to help him defend Tower Reilloch until help arrives."

"I will send assistance immediately, just in case," said Seiveril. He stood and walked to the door, summoning a guard in the mist-gray and sea-blue colors of House Miritar. "Tell Lord Muirreste to ready a company of knights to ride to Tower Reilloch at once," he instructed the fellow. "Ask Muirreste to join me here as soon as he's passed word to his riders. Then send for the mage Earethel, and ask him to join me here too. And tell Sister Thilesil that I will require her to send along five or six initiates of the grove with Muirreste's riders. There are injured to tend. Be swift. I want Muirreste to leave within the hour."

The guard's eyes widened, but he nodded and said, "As you command, Lord Miritar."

Seiveril watched the fellow go, then turned back to Araevin and Ilsevele. He clasped his hands behind his back and fixed his keen gaze on the two of them.

"Now," he said, "start at the beginning then, and tell me exactly what happened."

Araevin nodded. He drew a breath, and recounted the events of the past two days as best he could. He had a tremendous memory for details—one could not be very successful in the study of magic without a mind for such things—and he carefully and completely described the battle, the aftermath, the discovery of Philaerin, and the empty vault.

When he finished, Seiveril paced anxiously around the room.

"Demons, you said?" the lord asked. "I thought Evermeet's wards barred such creatures from the isle."

"They were led by demons that possessed elf blood," Araevin replied. "Or perhaps elves corrupted into demonic shapes. They had black wings and terrible eyes, and they fought with both sword and spell."

"You think the winged ones might have been elves?" Ilsevele said weakly.

"You saw them, too. They had our eyes, our ears, our features, and they were able to slip within Evermeet's wards."

"Demon-blooded elves. . . . Could it be that some of the Dlardrageths survive?" Seiveril mused.

"Dlardrageths?" asked Ilsevele.

Seiveril's eyes grew hard as he explained, "Thousands of years ago, in the early days of Cormanthor, the sun elves of House Dlardrageth—a proud and powerful family—gave themselves to demons, hoping to strengthen their line and gain power enough to seize the Coronal's throne. They were discovered and driven out of Arcorar long before the mythal was raised over Cormanthor." The nobleman sighed. "What was it you said they were seeking in Tower Reilloch?"

"The Gatekeeper's Crystal," said Araevin. "Well, one-third of it, anyway. It is an artifact composed of three smaller crystals. We had one shard of it in Tower Reilloch. I could not begin to guess where the other two pieces are now. I suppose we should assume that whomever attacked the Tower already has his hands on the remaining shards of the crystal."

"We'll find a way to get it back," Seiveril said. "At moonrise I will pray to Corellon Larethian, and prepare divinations to find out who stole the crystal and where they're hiding. We'll assemble an expedition of our best warriors and mages. Whomever dared attack Evermeet herself will not enjoy their success for long."

He passed a hand over his face, his expression grim.

Araevin glanced at Ilsevele and saw that her jaw was set in a determined frown as well. Three years before, Ilyyela Miritar—Seiveril's wife, and Ilsevele's mother—had died during the war launched by the traitorous sun elf Kymil Nimesin. Ilyyela had perished in the catastrophic attack against the Towers of the Sun and Moon. It did not take a sharp mind to guess that Seiveril was sickened by the thought of another attack against Evermeet, following so quickly on the heels of the recent war.

"There is one more thing, Lord Seiveril," he said. "When I found Philaerin, he was dead, but he had managed to hide something from his attackers—a *telkiira*." Araevin reached into the pouch at his belt and produced the small, dark stone. In the daylight of the study, the faint violet gleam in its heart was almost invisible. "Philaerin concealed the gemstone in an extradimensional space. I noticed the spell and dispelled it when we found his body. I do not know for certain, but it seems likely that the high mage deemed this too important to fall into enemy hands and hid it as quickly as he could."

"A *telkiira*?" Seiveril looked up. Araevin handed him the lorestone, and the noble studied it, peering into its depths. "I have not seen one like this before. Do you have any idea what it holds?"

He passed the loregem to Ilsevele, who held it up between her thumb and forefinger and peered closely at it.

"No," Araevin answered, shaking his head. "Philaerin never mentioned it before. I saw several other *telkiira* that he kept, but never that one."

"Strange. I think there is lettering in the stone," Ilsevele said. She looked closer. "Yes, there is. If you stare closely at the flicker in the depths of the gem, it seems to form itself into sigils or runes."

"Be careful!" Araevin said. "Magic runes can hold terrible spells. I'd better have a look at that."

"I know," Ilsevele said, but she recoiled and quickly handed it back to Araevin. "It seems safe enough to handle, anyway. Are you sure you can spot any dangerous sigils before they're triggered?"

"I know a spell or two that can unravel magical traps of that sort." Araevin thought for a moment, and wove a spell of deciphering with a few adroit passes of his hand and whispered words of arcane power. Then he held the loregem up to his eye and looked closely.

At first he saw little more than a dark purple blur, speckled with glimmers of lighter violet from the inner facets of the stone. Then he caught sight of the strange inner gleam, and fixed his eye on that. Instantly the wavering, inconstant flicker grew sharp and clear, forming itself into the shape of a rune that Araevin knew: *dramach*. It was a rune of sealing, a potent defense against intrusion.

Runes and magical signs used as seals could often be bypassed or neutralized by naming them.

Should I proceed? he wondered. Philaerin may have locked this stone for good reason.

On the other hand he would be able to form a much better guess as to the significance of the *telkiira* if he viewed its contents.

Without looking away from the rune glowing in the stone's depths, he said its name softly: *"Dramach."*

The room whirled madly as he felt himself fall into the gem.

Light exploded in his head as a procession of brilliant, burning symbols flashed before his eyes. He caught glimpses of thoughts and knowledge that were not his own, fragments of arcane formulae, images of people and places he did not know—a hoary, vine-grown tower in a black forest, a proud sun elf whose eyes gleamed green in a darkened room, a pale hand arranging three stones identical to the one he held in a wooden case, the sudden appearance of an even larger loregem, the sound of a dozen voices chanting together in some sort of rite. Then the burning symbols returned, pressing themselves indelibly into his mind one at a time, each searing a word of power into his brain.

"Araevin!" Ilsevele cried out in concern. Araevin blinked his eyes clear of the hurtful vision, and found himself sitting awkwardly on the floor, the *telkiira* gripped in his fist. "Araevin! Can you hear me? Are you hurt?"

He stirred slowly, gestured for patience, then said, "No, I am not hurt. The *telkiira* transferred its knowledge to me. The experience is a little unsettling."

"You are fortunate that it was not trapped as you had feared," Seiveril observed. He reached down and helped Araevin to his feet. "You frightened us, Araevin. You simply crumpled without a word. We thought you'd been enspelled."

Araevin said, "Give me a moment. I will be fine."

He gingerly felt his way over to the divan and sat down.

"What did you see in the stone?" Ilsevele asked.

"I am not exactly sure . . . a tower, a pale hand . . . three stones like this one, and a larger stone with a purple star in its heart. I do not understand it."

Forsaken House • 49

Araevin took a deep breath, and carefully called to mind the bright symbols he'd seen.

Spells, he realized. The *telkiira* holds the formulae for a number of spells.

Like a great book, the gemstone recorded page after page of arcane words, lists of reagents, and the directions for casting each of the spells it contained. The spells themselves had not been impressed into his mind. Araevin would have to study the words and gather the reagents in order to make use of any of them, just as he did any time he studied his own spellbook and prepared his spells. But he had unlocked the description of the *telkiira*'s contents, and he could access anything within the lorestone.

He turned his attention to the spells first. The stone held seven of them, he saw. Several he knew already—or, to be more precise, were recorded in the spellbooks he carried in his well-protected rucksack. The spells of teleportation, lightning, the terrible prismatic blast . . . all were quite common among reasonably skillful wizards, so Araevin was not at all surprised to find that the *telkiira* held their formulae. Whomever had created the lorestone long ago had naturally recorded useful spells.

He called to mind the remaining symbols he'd seen in his flash of insight, and recognized two more spells that he knew of but had not yet mastered: a spell that could be used to conjure up powerful, and often dangerous creatures from other planes of existence, and another that could cripple one's enemies with nothing more than a single deadly word of power. But the last two spells in the stone he had never even heard of before. One seemed to be a spell that would turn an enemy's own spell shields and protective mantles against him—a very useful spell for a wizards' duel, to say the least. The last spell was incomplete. Araevin frowned and directed his attention at it again, confirming his initial impression. The *telkiira* recorded only a portion of the spell. The rest of the spell was not there.

"What is it, Araevin?" Seiveril asked. "What have you learned?"

"The *telkiira* records six spells, and part of a seventh," Araevin answered. "That is not unusual. I've heard of elf wizards using *telkiira* as spellbooks." He glanced down at the lorestone in his hand. The lambent light in its heart seemed to flicker a little brighter. "But there is something else here, too. This stone is part of a set. There are two more just like it, and there is a fourth stone as well, larger and more perilous than the others. I think it might be a *selukiira*."

"A high loregem?" Seiveril said. The older elf tapped a finger on his chin. "That would be a prize, would it not? Now I think I see why Philaerin might have chosen to hide this *telkiira*."

"What is a *selukiira*?" Ilsevele asked.

"It is like a *telkiira,* but more powerful," Araevin explained. "A *telkiira* is really not much more than a book. It stores whatever information its creators care to place in it—spells, memories, secrets, anything. When someone accesses the *telkiira,* they can 'read' that information quite quickly and accurately, but their comprehension is limited by their own skill and knowledge.

"But a *selukiira,* a high loregem, is something different. It is a living thing, and it can *teach* those who view it. It is said that a *selukiira* can make an apprentice into a high mage in the blink of an eye, if it so chooses. Or it might destroy the one foolish enough to use it, in order to protect the secrets it holds."

"Do you think Philaerin owned the *selukiira* you saw in the *telkiira*?" Ilsevele asked.

Araevin shook his head and replied, "If he did, he would not have told me. He wouldn't have shared that secret with many people at all. But . . . I don't think the *selukiira* was in Tower Reilloch. This *telkiira* here—" he held up the dark stone in his hand—"seems to indicate the direction and distance to the next stone. I can feel it in my mind, far to the east . . . almost certainly somewhere in Faerûn. And I suspect that if we were to examine the second stone, we would find directions to the third of the set, which would in turn reveal the location of the *selukiira* I saw."

He set the *telkiira* on the low table by the divan, and stood up, frowning as he paced around the room. The study seemed darker, more threatening than it had a right to. Ancient mysteries and hidden peril whispered to Araevin in chill, dead voices.

Seiveril ran a hand through his hair and said, "Well, this is quite a day you have brought to my doorstep, Araevin. One stone missing, one stone found. Deadly battle and foul sorcery on Evermeet's shores. I fear that great and terrible events are afoot."

"I am sorry, Lord Seiveril. It seemed prudent to bring the Tower attack to your attention."

"No, you did well, Araevin. I did not mean to suggest otherwise." Seiveril sighed and continued, "I must go to Leuthilspar and confer with the queen at once. We will see if we can divine the location of those who stole the Gatekeeper's Crystal from Reilloch. Amlaruil will want to send our foremost champions in pursuit of the thieves. In the meantime, Lord Muirreste and his knights should suffice to reinforce Tower Reilloch against any additional raids."

"What about Philaerin's *telkiira*?" Araevin asked.

"Finding the other stones may offer some insight into why the daemonfey wanted them," Ilsevele observed. "And if you know why the daemonfey want the lorestones, we might understand what exactly they are trying to do with the Gatekeeper's Crystal."

"Or perhaps they wanted the *telkiira* because they don't want that high loregem found," Seiveril mused. "Could it be a weapon they fear? Some secret weakness they're afraid we might exploit?" He looked up at Araevin and said, "I will seek Corellon Larethian's guidance in this matter, but for now, take the stone. My heart tells me that we need to answer this riddle that Philaerin has set for us, whether he meant us to or not."

"I think so, too," Araevin said. He picked up the stone and slipped it into the pouch at his belt, murmuring a spell of safekeeping as he did so. "I meant to return to Faerûn soon, anyway. I'll leave tomorrow."

Ilsevele fixed her eyes on him and asked, "*You'll* leave tomorrow?"

"I think," Araevin said, "I meant to say that *we* will leave tomorrow. That is, if your father will allow me to carry you off thousands of miles from home."

"I stopped trying to tell Ilsevele what she could and couldn't do a century ago," Seiveril said with a laugh. "I'm pleased to see that it didn't take you quite so long to learn not to do that. But both of you—be careful."

☙ ☙ ☙ ☙ ☙

In the depths of the High Forest stood a great stone bluff, a rocky tor blanketed by a shaggy cloak of twisted felsul trees and hearty blueleafs. Between the arms of the hill stood a weather-beaten stone door, overgrown with ivy. For years companies of adventurers had gone there to explore its depths and seek out its hidden treasures. They knew it only as the Nameless Dungeon, and had no idea how or why it had come to be built. But the elves of ancient Eaerlann had known the place as Nar Kerymhoarth, the Sleeping Citadel, and refused to name it aloud. They had meant for its secrets to remain hidden for a very long time indeed.

Sarya Dlardrageth studied the door in the stone hill, her arms folded across her chest.

Without taking her eyes away from the door, she asked, "Did any escape?"

"No, my lady," Nurthel replied. "Lord Xhalph slew them all."

The elves of the High Forest and the nearby realms had long maintained a watch over the ancient elven road leading to Nar Kerymhoarth to warn away would-be explorers. Sarya had no particular interest in the sentries, so long as they did not interfere in her business, but she was pleased that her minions had been thorough. There was no point in leaving witnesses, after all.

She gestured to her son Xhalph, who stood nearby. Like her, Xhalph was a true daemonfey, half-elf and half-demon. His father had been a glabrezu, a huge four-armed monstrosity of the Abyss. She did not recall that coupling with any great pleasure, but it had served its purpose. Xhalph was taller and more strongly built than the mightiest human warrior, and he had inherited his demonic father's four arms, which made him quite a dangerous swordsman indeed. Of course, he also had a fierce temper and no gift at all for the study of magic, but all the daemonfey could call upon the infernal power of their heritage to rake their enemies with abyssal spells.

Xhalph carried the Gatekeeper's Crystal in a small casket between his two lower arms. At his mother's command he opened the small chest and offered her the weapon.

"Shall I use it, Mother?" he rumbled.

"No, dear boy. I will do this myself. The magic warding Nar Kerymhoarth is impenetrable, but the Gatekeeper's Crystal can sunder any obstacle. I am curious to see which proves the stronger."

Sarya carefully separated the crystal into its three component parts again. One she kept for herself. The other two pieces she gave to two of her fey'ri, who knelt before her.

"Now, listen closely," she said to the fey'ri. "You two will each take your piece of the crystal and carry it about three hundred yards to each side, so that the three of us form a triangle surrounding Nar Kerymhoarth, with a third at each corner. When you are in position, I will activate the crystal. You are to hold your fragments steady, but do nothing else. I will wield the magic of the device."

"Yes, my lady," the two fey'ri said.

They each took their pieces and set off at once, arrowing through the overcast skies to alight high on the shoulders of the hill, overlooking the cleft in which Sarya and the others stood. The daemonfey queen eyed their positions carefully, then gestured for the fey'ri to separate a little more. Then, content with their placement, she focused her attention on the brilliant crystal in her taloned hands, and summoned forth its power.

Instantly, a blazing line of energy sprang into existence, linking each of the three pieces and forming a triangle of fire above Nar Kerymhoarth's hilltop. Sarya recoiled, but maintained her hold on the gemstone. Despite its brilliance and the ravening power streaming from its depths, it remained cool to the touch and steady in her hand. The actinic light glared back at her from the hoary stone doorway, shadows snapping like banners in a gale.

Her fangs bared in a ferocious grin, Sarya invoked the crystal's most terrible power. In the space of a heartbeat, every spell, every ward, every shred of magic that existed within the bounds of the burning triangle ceased to exist. Ancient enchantments laid thousands of years before, strong enough to bind and hold for uncounted ages, were sundered in the blink of an eye. All the mighty magical power that had been laid into Nar Kerymhoarth's building and its defenses came unshackled in a single calamitous detonation. The force of the blast hurled Sarya and her followers to the ground. Vast portions of the hillside were thrown into the air, and came crashing down in the forest below. Thunder pealed throughout the ancient woods, rumbling like the roar of some massive dragon.

The broken crystal in Sarya's hand shimmered once and vanished. The blazing white lines flickered and guttered out as boulders and splintered trees pelted down from the sky. Sarya growled in frustration, snatching futilely at the vanishing crystal. She rolled over on her hands and knees and looked up the hillside, to where the two assisting fey'ri had stood. Nothing was left there but complete devastation. Their pieces of the crystal were gone as well, along with any trace of the two hapless sorcerers she had pressed into service.

It was not unexpected, she told herself. *The crystal disperses when its full power is invoked—that is the curse—and those who assist in the invocation of its might often pay with their lives.*

It was exactly what had happened when the Harpers destroyed Ascalhorn. The two fey'ri she would not miss,

Forsaken House • 55

but she had hoped that perhaps one portion of the crystal might remain within her grasp after she had finished with it.

"It is done," she hissed at her followers. "You can get up."

Though smaller pieces of rock and splintered wood continued to patter onto the ground around them, Xhalph, Nurthel, and the other fey'ri picked themselves up off the ground. More than a few had suffered injury from the explosion, but Sarya didn't even spare them a glance. Instead she looked on the empty vaults and naked halls of Nar Kerymhoarth, which were bared to the sky.

"I did it," she said, then laughed and sprang to her feet. "I did it!"

She took to the air and flew down into the dungeon, alighting before a great brazen seal set above a huge well in the floor. With a quick invocation, she gestured and hurled the seal aside, laying open the well below.

"Warriors of Reithel!" she called. "Ilviiri! Ursequarra! Come forth!"

From the dark well below her came a flutter of movement. Slowly, laboriously, a single fey'ri climbed into the air, gazing at the ruin around him with malice dripping from his eyes.

"I am free," he hissed.

Other fey'ri followed, struggling to fight their way free of the well, male and female both.

Sarya watched the demonspawned elves emerge, dark delight in her face. She and her two sons had been imprisoned beneath Ascalhorn with dozens more of her followers elsewhere in the old fortresses of fallen Eaerlann. But the great bulk of her army—nearly two thousand of her fey'ri, each a deadly swordsman as well as a skilled sorcerer—had been entombed in Nar Kerymhoarth. That was the army with which she could finally build her empire, after her enemies had cheated her of victory so long ago.

"You!" she called to the first fey'ri. "Do you know who I am?"

The fey'ri turned at the sound of her voice. He was a tall

fellow with long black hair, clad only in a short kilt. Small horns jutted from his forehead. He took one menacing step toward Sarya, then recognition flared in his eyes.

"Lady Sarya!" he said. "You have come to free us! Give me a sword, and for you I will blood it with the warriors of Sharrven!"

"Sharrven is no more," Sarya said. "Nor Eaerlann, nor even Siluvanede. You have been imprisoned a long, long time, my fey'ri."

"How long has it been, my lady?"

"Fifty centuries, warrior. Five thousand years you and your comrades have been imprisoned here."

The fey'ri warrior wailed in anguish, "It was only to be one thousand years! They lied to us!"

"Yes," said Sarya. "The cursed paleblooded elves of Eaerlann and Sharrven lied to you. They bound you and your fellows in Nar Kerymhoarth for a thousand years. And they died, or forgot their promises, or chose not to honor them. You will not have your vengeance upon those who jailed you, warrior. They have gone down into the dust of history, while their watch failed and their cities crumbled. The world has changed beyond recognition, while we dreamed away the centuries in our magical slumber.

"But know this, my fey'ri: All our ancient foes are gone. Now no one remains to oppose us."

❧ ❧ ❧ ❧ ❧

"Araevin, what is it?" Ilsevele set a hand on the mage's arm, a frown on her face.

They stood in a small, wooded glade high on a hillside, a few miles inland from Seamist and the city of Elion. Sunset painted the sky with brilliant rose and pale gold.

"I am not sure," he said. "There was something . . ." He peered toward the east, toward distant Faerûn, thinking. Finally he turned away, shaking his head. "I thought that I felt a tremor in the Weave. Almost as if someone had plucked the string of a great harp a long distance away."

"I thought I felt something too," Ilsevele said. "It came from the east."

"I've felt that before," Araevin said. "The last was two years past when the city of Shade was called back from the Plane of Shadow. Someone has worked mighty magic indeed. I would not be surprised if half the mages in Faerûn just started from their beds."

"The Gatekeeper's Crystal?"

Araevin looked sharply at Ilsevele. She had named his fear before he had himself.

"It could be," he said. "My Circle noticed a similar disturbance about five years ago. That would have been in the Year of the Gauntlet, around the time when the crystal was used to shatter Hellgate Keep. Corellon grant that we're wrong about this."

Ilsevele shrugged and said, "We'll know soon enough."

She picked up her pack and slung it across her back, carefully arranging it so that the rucksack did not interfere with the bow and quiver she wore across her shoulders. Beneath her cloak she wore the arms of a captain of the spellarchers, an embroidered doublet of leather sewn with fine steel rings, strongly enchanted to ward its wearer from harm. A pair of fine elven short swords graced her hips.

"I'm ready," she said.

Araevin nodded and picked up his own pack. He was also dressed for travel in dangerous lands, wearing his shirt of mithral mail beneath a dove-gray tunic, and his scarlet cloak with its magic of warding and protection over all. His bandolier of spell reagents crossed his chest from left hip to right shoulder, and three wands were holstered at his side—the disruption wand he'd used in the fight at Tower Reilloch, plus a pair of additional wands he thought he might find a use for. At his hip he wore the blade of House Teshurr, an enchanted long sword named Moonrill. Spell and wand were his chosen weapons, but he knew how to wield a sword, and long ago an ancestor of his had imbued Moonrill with magic that a mage might find useful at times.

He joined Ilsevele in front of a simple stone marker in the center of the glade. Faded old runes, half-filled with moss, were graven into its surface. Most of Evermeet's old elfgates had been dismantled in the past few decades, as the elves of the isle had come to see the magical portals as weaknesses in their defenses, places from which resourceful enemies could attack the island. But a few had been left standing, secured by powerful defensive spells. Only those who knew the secret of their activation could make use of the elfgates, and with every year the folk of Evermeet grew more careful of that knowledge.

"Where in Faerûn will this gate take us?" Ilsevele asked.

"The Ardeep Forest, not far from the House of Long Silences. Many old portals meet there, and it's close to Waterdeep, where many less magical roads meet."

Araevin hummed an arcane incantation beneath his breath, and passed his hand over the top of the stone marker.

At first nothing happened, but then the stone began to glow with a soft, golden light. Slowly it brightened enough to fill the glade with its pale glow, dancing motes of magic drifting in the air.

"Say farewell to Evermeet," Araevin told Ilsevele. "We'll be in Faerûn in just a moment."

Ilsevele glanced around at the wooded clearing, the sunset sky above, the deep green forest all around. A tear trickled down her cheek. No elf could leave Evermeet easily, especially not for the first time. She whispered a farewell, and they were gone.

CHAPTER 4

19 Alturiak, the Year of Lightning Storms

Gaerradh trotted swiftly through the endless tree-gloom of the High Forest, little more than a shadow herself. She wore her long russet hair tied behind her in a single braid, and carried her longbow easily in one hand. Even though she wore a jerkin of studded leather and carried a pair of axes thrust through her belt, she ran easily. She was a seasoned warrior, well trained in the ways of the forest, and she had long ago learned that the ability to move fast and far was one of an elf scout's best weapons.

Behind her the snow-covered forest floor rustled, and a large, powerful wolf with a silvery coat appeared in the gloom. Long and lean, the predator sprinted after her, bounding over the ground like a white streak, only to fall in alongside the ranger and slow its pace to match hers. Gaerradh glanced down to her side without breaking stride.

"I was wondering where you'd gotten to," she said to the wolf. "Chasing rabbits, I suppose."

Sheeril simply looked up at her with dark eyes and an expression of disdain. Gaerradh was fairly certain that the wolf understood almost everything she said. Gaerradh was comfortable with her own company—one could not serve as a far-ranging scout in the northern marches of the endless woods if one minded being alone for tendays at a time—but Sheeril was as close a friend to her as any elf. Together Gaerradh and Sheeril kept watch over the northern marches of the High Forest, spying out the comings and goings of orc warbands, gangs of trolls, avaricious companies of human freebooters, and the darker and more dangerous creatures of the woodland. The High Forest was the largest and wildest in all Faerûn, and it was far from a safe place. Gaerradh and Sheeril dealt with intruders who were few in number, and summoned help from other elf scouts and rangers when faced with foes too numerous or powerful to deal with on their own.

Gaerradh told her elf friends that she best served the People by searching out dangers before they could threaten the elven settlements of the High Forest, but in truth, Gaerradh simply loved the wide lands of the wilderness. She found solace in the wilds, and when she spent too much time among the People of Rheitheillaethor or the other settlements of the forest, she found herself growing restless and longing for the silence of the woods again. She was on her way back to Rheitheillaethor at the moment to provision herself and trade news, but she hoped to stay no more than two or three days before heading back out into the winter forest again.

Sheeril abruptly peeled away from her side, and halted to gaze intently into the woods downhill. Gaerradh needed no other signal. She halted in mid-stride, crouching knee-deep in the snow and holding herself immobile.

"What is it, girl?" she whispered to the animal.

The wolf glanced back at her and whined softly. Then

she slid into a thick stand of fir trees lower on the hillside. Gaerradh followed, an arrow on the string of her bow. She was puzzled more than anything else. They were in a region of the forest that was usually safe and quiet. The elves maintained a guard over the old ruins nearby in order to keep careless bands of adventurers from disturbing them. The watch also served to chase marauding orcs and hungry monsters out of the area as well.

She followed Sheeril down into the thicket, and she caught the scent that had attracted the wolf's attention. The smell of death lingered in the cold air beneath the evergreens. It was faint, thanks to the blanket of snow and the cold weather, but it was there nonetheless.

Then Gaerradh found the first of the bodies.

Half-buried in the drifting snow lay a wood elf warrior, frozen gore clotted around his wounds. He'd been hacked to death by sword cuts, but he still wore the simple diamond-shaped brooch of those who stood guard over Nar Kerymhoarth, the Nameless Dungeon. Gaerradh bowed her head in grief, then rose and followed Sheeril deeper into the copse.

There, in ones and twos, she found the remains of eleven more wood and moon elves. Some had died by sword, others by spells, their bodies burned or blasted by deadly magic. Eight of them she knew, and two she counted among her few close friends.

"All twelve," she murmured. "The guardians of Nar Kerymhoarth, overcome all at once. What evil is this?"

Snow had fallen since the fight, covering any tracks Gaerradh might have studied. It had last snowed two days before and scavengers—ravens, mostly—had been at the exposed flesh. They died not long before the snowfall, she decided after a quick examination of the scene. Less than a day, certainly. Possibly no more than an hour or two. The warriors on watch had been killed between two and three days before.

Sheeril padded up to her side and looked up at her face.

"I know," said Gaerradh. "We must go to Nar Kerymhoarth and see who did this."

She stood and composed herself, dropping her pack in a clump of brush nearby. Then she carefully backtracked out of the clearing, hiding her trail as best she could, and set her eyes on the nearby stony spire of the ancient citadel's barren tor, rising above the trees half a mile away.

It took Gaerradh well over an hour, since she didn't want to be seen, but she half-circled the barren hilltop and approached the deep ravine sheltering the fortress's entrance by climbing high over the shoulder of the hill and descending on it from above. Finally she got herself into position and wormed her way over the ridgeline, moving slowly to avoid the creaking of compressed snow or, worse yet, the sudden crunch of a broken ice crust. Sheeril crept along a pace behind her, trained to crawl on her belly and move only on Gaerradh's cue. Her face and throat stinging from the wet, cold snow, Gaerradh gently parted a notch to spy on the dungeon's door.

There was no door before her. In fact, there was no ravine. She blinked in astonishment. Had she somehow got her bearings wrong, and climbed over the wrong shoulder of the hill? She couldn't have made such a simple-minded mistake as that!

Gaerradh looked again, studying the scene carefully. The landscape seemed right, but there was a huge gouge in the side of the tor, laying bare chambers and tunnels in the hill. The door itself she finally spotted lying almost a hundred yards away, broken in several pieces. Someone had blasted the ancient citadel of Nar Kerymhoarth open to the sky. She could not imagine who would have done it, or why, but clearly powerful magic had been put to use there.

And they slew the watch, she reminded herself. Whoever this is, he's no friend to the People.

Rheitheillaethor, and the other havens of the People in the High Forest, had to be warned, and right away.

Gaerradh pushed herself to her knees, brushed snow

from her clothing, and whispered, "Come, Sheeril. We must travel fast and far today."

⊙ ⊙ ⊙ ⊙ ⊙

Araevin and Ilsevele stood together in the dim light of the coming dawn, listening to the sounds of the forest around them. The first notes of birdsong lilted in the distant trees, and overhead the dark sky was streaked with bright shoals of rose and pearl. The elfgate had transported them to a briar-grown hollow deep in the shadowed woods, and they'd walked through the Ardeep for half the night to reach the ruins of an ancient court, its moss-grown flagstones long broken by the growth of mighty trees hundreds of years old. Before them was an ancient palace of white stone, its walls overgrown by ivy, and large sections open to the sky.

Ilsevele shifted the bow case she wore over her left shoulder and shook her pale copper hair free of her green hood. The air was damp with dew, and beads of cold water clung to her cloak and armor.

"The House of Long Silences is aptly named," she observed. "This place has been abandoned for many years."

"In the days of Illefarn, it was a proud manor," Araevin replied. "But the realm dwindled over the centuries and finally passed away more than seven hundred years ago. Few of our folk live in the Ardeep now, other than Elorfindar."

"Elorfindar?"

"Lord Elorfindar Floshin. He is a kinsman of mine, the son of my great-great-grandmother's brother. He has taken it as his duty to guard the magical portals here."

Araevin took Ilsevele's hand and led her up a wide flight of cracked stone steps to the gaping doorway of the old palace.

The empty halls seemed a place apart from the thick stands of cedars and blueleafs beyond its facade of pale white stone. The Ardeep Forest chirped and rustled with birdsong and the soft caress of wind in the treetops, but those comforting sounds did not intrude into the ancient elven palace. Even though the empty doorway stood open to the elements behind them, Araevin and Ilsevele heard nothing in the gloomy forehall. Ilsevele turned to speak to Araevin, but the mage simply shook his head.

Measured footfalls echoed in the corridor. A dignified sun elf appeared, dressed in silver mail, with a long sword at his belt. His eyes had the dark wisdom of many years, and in the shadows of the hall he seemed almost to glow with an eldritch light.

"Greetings, Araevin," the elflord said. "I have not seen you in the House of Long Silences in some years. Come inside. And you, too, fair lady."

Araevin clasped Elorfindar's arm firmly and replied, "It's good to see you, kinsman. How goes your watch?"

"It is hard to say. Many of the old gates to Evermeet have been closed or hidden in recent years, so I have fewer to guard now. But after the invasion launched by Kymil Nimesin three years past, it has become more important than ever to ward the ways leading to the Green Isle." Elorfindar shrugged. "It is my penance, and I am not finished with it yet. I can only hope that my watch will in some small way atone for those of my fathers who betrayed the trusts they held." The dignified warrior turned to Ilsevele with a gentle expression. "Araevin, you have neglected to introduce me to your companion, for which you owe me an apology."

"Elorfindar, this is the Lady Ilsevele Miritar, a captain of the spellarchers in the queen's service. She is the daughter of Councilor Seiveril Miritar, the lord of Elion. And she is my betrothed."

Elorfindar's serious expression lifted, as a genuine smile creased his features.

"Your betrothed? Lady Ilsevele, I am delighted to meet you. And I am even more delighted to learn that you will be a cousin of mine! I was afraid that the Teshurrs would vanish all together, and leave the House of Cedars for the seabirds." He took Ilsevele's hand. "Your beauty brightens this gloomy palace, dear lady."

"As does your gallantry. Thank you, Lord Elorfindar," Ilsevele replied. She looked around at the ruined palace. "Do you live here by yourself?"

"Oh, no," the elflord said. "I live a day's ride south of here, in a much less lonely manor close to the Delimbiyr Vale. I only keep watch over this palace and its doors. My wardings warned me that someone was here, so I came to investigate."

"I apologize for forcing the journey on you," Ilsevele said.

"It was nothing. My magic shortens the trip considerably." Elorfindar gestured to the ruined palace and continued, "There are some rooms that are in better condition, where I have a store of food and drink laid by for just such an occasion as this. Before I set the table, I would like to know what brings you here, Araevin. You are always going somewhere when you pass through this house."

Araevin dropped his gaze to the floor. He did not like to carry tidings of ill news. "Evermeet has been attacked again, Elorfindar. Not an invasion like Nimesin's war of three years ago, but a raid to break into the vaults of Tower Reilloch."

Elorfindar's expression grew cold and he said, "Go on."

Araevin nodded, and launched into the story of the attack on the Tower.

"When Quastarte and I found Philaerin," he concluded, "we also discovered evidence suggesting that Philaerin held knowledge of something dangerous in Faerûn, something that he chose to conceal from the Tower's attackers. The demons and their masters escaped with the Gatekeeper's Crystal. Ilsevele's father has gone to Leuthilspar to take up that matter with Queen Amlaruil. In the meantime, I am looking into Philaerin's secret. The Tower's attackers might have been after the crystal and nothing else, but it seems dangerous to assume that was the case. Our enemies thought their prizes important enough to dare Evermeet's defenses and attack a Tower of mages."

"You said that the raiders were demons and demonic

sorcerers. I thought Evermeet's wards prevented such creatures from attacking the island directly."

"Demons and yugoloths, to be accurate," Araevin said. "I recognized creatures of both races. As for their masters, they were like winged elves with demonic blood. They had scarlet skin with fine scales, black hair and eyes, and small horns . . . and they seemed to be resistant to fire and lightning, like many demons and devils are. But they fought with sword and spell, not the supernatural powers of a demon."

"My father wondered if they might have been elves of a fallen Cormanthyran House known as Dlardrageth," Ilsevele added. "He said that they were thought to have been defeated long ago, but the description fit. Since they were elves at least in part, they might have been able to pierce Evermeet's defensive wards more easily than true demons could."

"I know of the Dlardrageths," Elorfindar said. His face was pale and his eyes dark with horror. "They were destroyed or bound long ago, along with the lesser Houses that followed them into darkness. Long ago, they poisoned the realm of Siluvanede and brought down the kingdom of Sharrven before they were halted. The shadow of their crimes stretches across many centuries and distant lands. If they have somehow returned. . . . " He looked up at Araevin and asked, "How can I help you?"

"I may need to make use of some of your portals," Araevin said. "I believe the trail I am following will lead me to some lonely places scattered far across the North. And I mean to gather some help before I set out. Using the old portals of Illefarn could save me a great deal of time."

"Of course," said Elorfindar. "The doors are at your disposal."

"What sort of help are we going to gather?" Ilsevele asked.

"During my previous travels in Faerûn, I spent a lot of time seeking out and exploring the ruins of ancient elven realms. They are dangerous places, filled with decaying wards, slumbering guardians, and sinister new occupants. The Company of the White Star assisted me in my explorations. They were courageous and trustworthy comrades."

"Where will we find these old associates of yours?"

"It's been quite some time, so I am not entirely sure," Araevin said. "But when we last parted, we agreed to honor any call from one of the company. I will dispatch a sending to each, asking them to meet us in Daggerford."

☙ ☙ ☙ ☙ ☙

Lord Seiveril Miritar sat at his customary place in the eighth seat of the council table, absently gazing up at the ceiling a hundred feet above as he waited for the queen to call the council to order. The Dome of Stars was the heart of the royal palace in Leuthilspar, a vast round chamber ringed by high galleries. By day the theurglass dome was a wondrous mosaic of stained panels, gleaming with a rainbow of color in the light. By night the magic glass was clear, showing the starry sky overhead. The floor of the chamber was finished in dark, glossy marble that seemed to hold tiny flecks of diamond in its depths, so that on clear nights those lords and ladies who met in the Dome seemed to float in a veritable sea of stars.

It was dusk, and the dome was open to the sullen colors of an overcast sunset.

"The council is assembled, Lord Seiveril," said Amlaruil, Queen of Evermeet, from her high seat at the head of an elegant table of frosted glassteel.

A moon elf of striking beauty, her hair dark and flawless as a cascade of night, her eyes thoughtful and wise, Amlaruil was one of the oldest elves in Evermeet, but unlike so many who were close to passing to Arvandor, she was untouched by the winds of the LastHome. Instead of ghosting softly away from the world as so many old elves did, Amlaruil's personal power and force of character fixed her to the firmament of the world, so that it seemed as if all Evermeet was anchored to the spot where she sat.

"Tell the council what you have told me," Amlaruil continued in her clear, musical voice, "so that we may consider the meaning of these events and decide what action to take."

Seiveril returned his attention to the table. The great galleries ringing the Dome were empty, having been cleared at his request. He quickly swept the table, eying his fellow councilors. To his right sat the High Admiral Emardin Elsydar, a sun elf of unusually serious demeanor, and at the foot of the table Zaltarish, the aged royal scribe. It was his duty to record the discussions and resolutions of the council. To Seiveril's left sat the wood elf princess Jerreda Starcloak, who represented Evermeet's forest-dwelling elves, and the highborn sun elf Selsharra Durothil, matron of the powerful Durothil clan. On the opposite curve of the table sat Grand Mage Breithel Olithir, newly appointed to his position to replace the grand mage slain during the fall of the Tower of the Sun. Beside him sat the moon elf Keryth Blackhelm, the High Marshal of Evermeet, then the wealthy moon elf merchant Lady Meraera Silden, the Speaker of Leuthilspar. Beside her was the Lady Ammisyll Veldann, governor of the city of Nimlith on Evermeet's southwestern shores.

The membership of the council was not set at nine by any law or tradition. Over time it fluctuated as new members were invited to join, or older ones passed to Arvandor. For eighty years Seiveril had sat on the council, by virtue of his governorship over the northern city of Elion, his high standing among the clerics of Corellon Larethian, and the cachet of the Miritar name.

"I must report that Evermeet has been attacked," Seiveril began. "Three days ago a raiding party of demons and demon-blooded sorcerers teleported into the great hall of Tower Reilloch. They killed more than twenty of Reilloch's People, including the high mages Philaerin and Aeramma, and wounded many more. They fled with the Gatekeeper's Crystal, an artifact stolen from Reilloch's vaults."

Seiveril heard an audible groan from the high admiral at his right hand. Other councilors winced, or drew in their breath with a soft hiss, or simply looked down at the table. Amlaruil, who had already heard the tale from him, simply waited impassively.

"As far as I can tell, the attackers came for the specific purpose of stealing the artifact," Seiveril went on. "Since they accomplished that, it is doubtful they will return, but I have dispatched warriors to reinforce the surviving mages of Reilloch Domayr just in case. I suggest that we send word to all other Towers to look to their own defenses."

"We would have done better to look to our defenses before we were attacked," Selsharra Durothil growled. Her clan was arguably the noblest and most powerful family of sun elves on the island. It was no secret that some among the Durothils, and the many sun elf Houses allied with them, resented the fact that a moon elf dynasty had been appointed to rule over Evermeet. Seiveril didn't know if Selsharra privately hungered for Amlaruil's throne or not, but for fifty years she had been the queen's most strident critic on the council. "Did no one pay attention when Nimesin invaded three years ago? For that matter, how did demons teleport through Evermeet's defenses? Haven't our mages woven wards to prevent this very sort of thing?"

"It should not have been possible—" began Grand Mage Olithir, but Selsharra Durothil simply cut him off with a cold stare.

Despite his accomplishments as a high mage, Breithel Olithir was a novice in the workings of Evermeet's council, and he knew it. He left his protest unfinished and fell silent.

Seiveril decided to help the grand mage save face.

"Those who fought the creatures at Tower Reilloch reported that the demonic sorcerers resembled winged sun elves, with scarlet skin and black, leathery wings," he offered. "Supposedly, these creatures appeared first, then created a temporary gate that permitted the passage of the demons. Some of Reilloch's mages speculated that the demon-sorcerers might have elf blood sufficient to pass unrecognized through Evermeet's wards."

The grand mage nodded slowly, a pained look on his face, and said, "Our wards can block the passage of most creatures of supernatural evil . . . but elves, or elf-kin of some kind, are not barred, regardless of their intentions. Kymil Nimesin demonstrated that three years ago."

"Then we must redouble our efforts to strengthen Evermeet's wards," Ammisyll Veldann said. A proud sun elf matron, Ammisyll was one of the younger elves on the council, but renowned for her staunchly conservative views. Like Selsharra Durothil, she was an avowed antimonarchist who had spoken out on more than one occasion against the primacy of the throne. She was also the scion of a family of Cormanthyran expatriates, sun elves who had only recently abandoned Faerûn for the safety of Evermeet. "We did not call for the Retreat in order to leave Evermeet's gates open to anyone who cared to follow us here and attack us in our haven. If we had prepared our defenses properly in the wake of Nimesin's war, this insult might not have been allowed to happen."

"We cannot defend ourselves by walling out the world and ignoring what happens beyond our shores," Seiveril said. "We gave no provocation to the sea wolves of the Nelanther or to the drow of the Underdark, but they joined Kymil Nimesin's invasion anyway."

"Why should our wards permit any gate to function without the approval of the council?" Ammisyll retorted. "Or allow the entry of any evil creature, be they demon, drow, or elf? We have failed in our vigil, Lord Seiveril. We did not take every step we might have to defend this island against a repeat of Nimesin's invasion. Or perhaps you make light of the threat Evermeet faces from the barbaric human kingdoms of Faerûn?"

"My wife died in the Tower of the Sun, Lady Ammisyll," Seiveril said. "And it does not escape my recollection that your cousin Tarthas was one of the spellsingers who helped Nimesin destroy it. I know exactly what Nimesin's war cost Evermeet."

Ammisyll Veldann flushed. She opened her mouth

to respond to Seiveril, but Amlaruil rapped her golden scepter twice on the glassteel table, sending a sharp ring through the chamber.

"You are wandering away from the matter at hand, Lady Ammisyll," the queen said clearly. "The purpose of this session is to inform the council of the theft of the Gatekeeper's Crystal, and to determine what actions are necessary in response."

Ammisyll Veldann glared at Seiveril, but held her tongue.

The council fell silent, until High Admiral Emardin shifted in his seat and said, "What is the purpose of the artifact? What does it do?"

"I am not personally familiar with the device," Seiveril admitted. "However, I am told that it is designed to negate magical fields and constructs, such as the defensive wards of a mythal."

"That is essentially correct," Grand Mage Breithel observed. "I spoke with Philaerin about the crystal when it was brought to Reilloch. It has other powers, too. It can smother certain types of magic in very large areas, for example. But its principal and most dangerous power is the ability to disjoin and collapse existing enchantments. The crystal's theft is dire news indeed, Lord Seiveril. In the wrong hands, it could work terrible harm. In fact, it may already have done so."

Seiveril looked to the grand mage and asked, "You have learned something?"

"Nothing specific. But two days ago I detected a perturbation in the Weave, as if a very powerful spell had been cast. Several other mages remarked on the incident."

"I sensed it, too," Amlaruil said quietly. The queen was an accomplished mage in her own right, the equal of any of Evermeet's high mages. "The Gatekeeper's Crystal might be responsible for the disturbance we felt, but I could not be certain of that."

"The purpose of the crystal is to destroy wards?" asked Meraera Silden. A moon elf, the elected speaker of the city of Leuthilspar, Meraera was a moderate voice on the council, though she was not a monarchist. "As we just discussed a few moments ago, Evermeet is protected by extensive magical wards. Clearly, we must assume that someone is preparing a new attack against our island. This time, they mean to destroy our protective spells entirely."

"I agree," said Keryth Blackhelm. Coarse and direct, the moon elf soldier commanded Evermeet's defenses. "We live in a castle with gates made of oil-soaked wood, and someone has just stolen a match. I propose we muster immediately and make ready to repel an attack. And if we haven't done so already, we must locate the stolen crystal and get it back."

"While I agree that we should make all possible efforts to recover the crystal," said Zaltarish, the old scribe, "we don't know for certain that we are the target of this attack. There are other wards and mythals in the world besides our own. Evereska and Silverymoon come to mind. What happened at Tower Reilloch might have been a simple theft. Perhaps our foes intend to use the device somewhere else."

"Evereska is virtually in ruins, and Silverymoon is a collection of squalid human hovels," Selsharra Durothil snapped. "Why in the world would we think this attack to be aimed at someone other than us? Where else do wards worth breaching exist? Don't waste our time with wishful thinking, Zaltarish."

"Is it wishful thinking? The invaders of Tower Reilloch have already demonstrated their ability to slip through Evermeet's magical wards," the old sage replied, unperturbed. "Why would they steal a device designed to bring down our defenses, when they seem to be able to master our wards already?"

The chamber fell silent. Selsharra Durothil composed herself gracefully, and voiced her displeasure at the scribe's logic only with a single icy glance. Seiveril kept his face impassive as well, though he allowed himself a wry smile on the inside. Zaltarish was mild and soft-spoken, and some of Evermeet's high lords and ladies were in the habit of considering him ineffectual because he rarely asserted himself. It pleased him to see the ancient scribe stand the great Lady Durothil on her head.

"Lord Blackhelm spoke of recovering the crystal," Jerreda Starcloak said to Seiveril. "Have you begun any efforts to do so?"

Seiveril nodded and replied, "As soon as I was informed of the theft, I prayed to Corellon Larethian for spells to divine the crystal's location and the identity of our foe. Unfortunately, I was unable to ascertain either. It seems our adversary anticipated that we would attempt to scry out his secrets, and made sure of his own magical defenses."

The grand mage said, "I will begin divinations of my own at once. Perhaps our foe will make a mistake and let us have a look at him."

"In the meantime," Seiveril said, "I have suggested to the queen that we should send word to our spies in Faerûn to drop all other matters and search for some sign of our foe. For that matter, we should dispatch more agents to Faerûn at once. If our divinations prove fruitless, then we will have to find our enemies with simple persistence. The sooner we begin, the better."

"Sending our wizards and knights to blunder about Faerûn chasing shadows seems pointless," said Ammisyll Veldann. She looked over at Amlaruil. "I refuse to compound negligence with folly. In fact, I find that I am not at all confident that this matter should be left in the hands of the throne's agents, seeing as the council has just learned how easily our defenses were defeated—again."

"What are you implying?" Seiveril demanded.

"I imply nothing," Lady Veldann said. "I will observe, however, that since King Zaor's ascension the throne has assumed increasing power over Evermeet's affairs and defenses, but our walls seem to be growing more and more porous. As the council has been relieved of the responsibility of overseeing our magical wards and physical defenses for some time, it is clear where the responsibility for these failures now lies. Perhaps it would be wisest if the council assumed direct oversight of the investigation of this entire affair and the organization of an appropriate response."

Corellon, grant me patience, Seiveril fumed.

For decades he had listened to Ammisyll Veldann begrudge the queen's every effort to unite Evermeet's defenders behind the throne, and she had the temerity to wonder why Evermeet was not invulnerable to attack? He started to speak, but he sensed a small wave of the queen's hand. He shut his mouth and turned to look at Amlaruil.

"I accept responsibility for the losses at Tower Reilloch," Queen Amlaruil said. Her eyes flashed, but she did not lose her composure. "The preservation of our realm's People and treasures is the single highest privilege and responsibility of the throne. When the lives of our elves are lost, then I have failed in my duty, and I deserve censure. But know this: I intend to exercise the full power and authority at my disposal to recover the crystal and oppose the purposes of our enemies, wherever they may be found.

"I swear by the Seldarine that this crime shall not go unpunished."

CHAPTER 5

29 Alturiak, the Year of Lightning Storms

The town of Daggerford was a sleepy little stopover on the Trade Way near the mouth of the Delimbiyr River. It was a human town, with only a scattering of other kindred, and though it was protected by a wall and a sturdy keep, its streets were unpaved and its buildings had a ramshackle, weather-beaten look to them. Araevin was amazed at how much the soporific little town had changed since last he walked its streets. In some ways it *felt* much as it always had. A strong wet wind blew in from the Sea of Swords. Freezing slush lined the streets. Rustic, heavy-handed craftsmanship was evident in the iron-hasped doors and thick-beamed buildings. Acrid smoke filled the air from open-air smithies, fuming smokehouses, and seemingly every home and store. But half the buildings he remembered had vanished, replaced by new ones.

"Incredible," he murmured. "I was just here only a few years ago. . . and it seems they've knocked down the whole town and rebuilt it since then."

Ilsevele stayed close to his side, warily eying the passersby in the wide, muddy street. She wrinkled her nose at the heavy smoke in the air.

"I feel no *Tel'Quessir* nearby," she said. "How strange to be in a town of this size and sense no one else."

"They are here. Humans do not experience community the way we do. Each is a lonely isle in the sea, out of sight of his fellows."

"Then why do they dwell in such close quarters?" Ilsevele muttered. Her eyes watered from the smoke of a nearby smithy. "And do they each have to have their own fire?"

"Ah, here we are," Araevin said.

The Dragonback Inn was a large, rambling building with chest-high walls of fieldstone from which rose sturdy wooden walls with thick timbers framing the structure. Dark, small-paned windows of green leaded glass looked out over the broad ford of the Deliymber below, and a creaking sign of grayed wood hung over the strong door.

Araevin noticed Ilsevele's dubious expression, and said, "It's not so bad, really. Come on, let's go in."

They pulled open the heavy door and entered the building, finding themselves in a cozy, warm common room that Araevin remembered fondly. There, at least, not much had changed. A fierce-looking dragon skull hung over the large fireplace, and battered old shields and banners draped the walls. A dozen plain wooden trestle tables were jammed into the room. It was the middle of the afternoon, so most were empty, but Araevin knew they'd be full by sundown, and likely stay that way until midnight.

"Araevin!" a deep, gravelly voice called across the room.

Araevin turned to see a tall, square-shouldered human with a deeply weathered face, a gray goatee, and a close-cropped fringe of iron-gray hair rising to hail him, dressed in a simple cassock of red. He did not recognize the fellow, and opened his mouth to request an introduction—then he realized with a shock that it was Grayth Holmfast.

The human's dark hair had gone silver-gray and retreated sharply above his brow, and his powerful, athletic build had grown lean and spare. The Lathanderite priest caught him up in a powerful embrace before Araevin recovered from his astonishment, and thumped his back with blows that might have staggered the elf mage if he hadn't been held up.

"Araevin Teshurr, as I live and breathe! It's been damned near twenty years, old friend. Where have you been keeping yourself?"

Twenty years? Araevin thought, confused. Surely it had not been that long . . . but when he thought on it, he'd last traveled in Faerûn in the Year of the Worm, 1356 by Dalereckoning, so that would make it eighteen years.

"Evermeet," he answered. "I've continued my studies at home since I left." He rallied and returned Grayth's embrace, pounding the cleric on his back. "It's good to see you, Grayth!"

The human cleric stepped back and studied Araevin from head to toe.

"Amazing," he said. "Time touches you so lightly. You have not changed a bit, my friend."

Araevin replied, "I forget how different it is with us."

Grayth barked laughter and said, "That's one way to say that the years have been hard on me!" He gestured at his receding hairline. "The hair began retreating ten years ago. Oddly enough, it's started to sprout on my back instead. So, who's your friend?"

A wave of distress crossed Ilsevele's face at the last remark, but she bravely set it aside and thrust out her hand in the human fashion. Her Common was a little awkward, and her voice lilted musically.

"I am Ilsevele Miritar, daughter of Lord Seiveril Miritar. I am Araevin's betrothed. It is a pleasure to meet you, sir."

"Grayth, please! The pleasure is mine, fair lady. And welcome to Faerûn. Unless I miss my guess, you haven't spent much time away from Evermeet."

Ilsevele shot a glance at Araevin, her surprise showing, and said, "Is it that obvious?"

"No, it's not," Araevin replied with a smile. "Grayth will never admit it, but he sees more in a glance than most people, human or elf, notice in an hour. Don't play cards with him."

"If you'll join us, I'll have some food and wine sent over, and we can trade tales of old adventures," Grayth said. "I noticed a number of mice in the stables, if your little falcon's feeling hungry."

"Whyllwyst died eight years ago," Araevin said. "I have no familiar now."

Grayth looked up and said with a grimace, "I know that's hard on a wizard, Araevin. I'm sorry. Come, we'll speak of lighter things."

The cleric motioned the two sun elves to a sturdy wooden table and bench, and sat down opposite them.

Another man was waiting for them, a strapping young fellow with sandy-blond hair and wide blue eyes. He was dressed like Grayth in the cassock of a priest of Lathander, but his robes were orange and yellow, and the emblem on his tunic was a simple half-disc of white.

"This is Brant Rethalshield," Grayth said, "an aspirant to the Order of the Aster, the knights templar of the Morninglord's faith. He is my squire. Brant, this is Araevin Teshurr and Lady Ilsevele Miritar."

Araevin took the young man's hand, noticing the well-worn calluses of a swordsman.

"A pleasure to meet you, Brant," he said.

The young fellow returned his handclasp and said, "And you, sir. The High Mornmaster has told me many stories of his adventures in your company."

"So you've simply been studying your spellbooks back on Evermeet all this time?" Grayth asked.

"I've found a few things to busy myself with, but I haven't been back to Faerûn since the Year of the Worm."

Araevin studied Grayth's accoutrements and added, "I see you have risen in Lathander's church in the last eighteen years. What of you? How are you faring? Have you heard from others of the company?"

"I am well enough, as you can see. I traveled a few more years after we parted. In fact, I rode all the way to Thesk in King Azoun's crusade against the Tuigan Horde, but my superiors in the order kept asking me to take on more and more responsibility. So for some time now I have devoted myself to serving in the Morninglord's temples, as I have been called to do." A brief shadow flickered across the human's face. "I settled down and was even married for a time, but no longer. I have two fine sons, though—ten and seven. They live with their mother. I visit them whenever I can."

"I hope I get the chance to meet them someday," Araevin said, though his heart wasn't in it.

He had always felt a little odd around human children. A long time ago, when he'd been only a hundred or so, he'd struck up quite a friendship with a little girl named Senda, the daughter of a human merchant he dealt with in his travels. She'd lived to seventy years of age . . . and she'd been dead already for longer than she'd lived. Yet still he remembered a tiny slip of a girl with long curls of golden hair and eyes that danced with mischief when she laughed at his pointed ears. He might well live to see Grayth's sons, and their sons and grandsons too, pass from the world. Araevin felt his eyes growing damp and quickly changed the topic.

"What of the others?"

"Darthen's done well for himself. He's the lord of a small hold near Scornubel, with a lovely wife and a whole tower-full of children. I spoke with him after receiving your message. He will not come, Araevin." Grayth sighed and continued, "He said that his duties did not permit him to respond, but that you could come to him for anything you needed, and he would do his best. He also told me to tell you to make sure to visit him, if you'll be staying in Faerûn for any time."

"I hope to do that," Araevin replied, concealing his

disappointment. The Company of the White Star had parted with an agreement to come together if called, but none of them were sworn to it. If he needed Darthen badly enough, he might try to change his old comrade's mind, but it sounded as if the human knight had responsibilities he could not easily lay aside. "He would have come if he could have, I suppose. What of Belmora?"

Grayth sighed again, then said, "Belmora is dead. She went back to her clan-hold in the North, and I understand that she died in battle against an orc warband."

Araevin bowed his head. He'd always liked Belmora, even though she was irascible, stubborn, and every bit as abrasive as dwarves were supposed to be. The news didn't surprise him, really. The redoubtable dwarf priestess had always spoken of returning to her mountain home to drive away the orc tribes.

"She was a stout companion," he said. "Her heart was true and strong. What about Theleda?"

"I have not heard from her for ten years now, I guess." The human shrugged and said, "She lived in Waterdeep for a time, living well off the treasure we garnered back in our day. She owned a tavern, and provisioned caravans and merchant ships on the side. I suspect that one of the guilds ran her out of town."

"It doesn't seem likely that she will show up, then."

Araevin leaned back against the wall and sighed. Out of the four companions he had parted with in that very inn eighteen years past, only one had answered his call. One dead, one missing, and one simply unable or unwilling to come.

I waited too long, he realized. *Of course I thought nothing of leaving them behind me for twenty years, but humans don't make light of such a span, do they?*

"Grayth," Araevin said, "thank you for answering."

The Lathanderite waved his hand and replied, "I live in Waterdeep. It's only a couple of days up the road, so it wasn't any trouble to make the journey. Besides, I've been looking for an excuse to get out of the temple for some time, I think."

The inn's keeper, a heavyset dwarf with a rough set of white whiskers and a beet-red nose, brought them a large earthenware jug of wine and a set of clay cups.

"Your wine, High Mornmaster," he said to Grayth. "I've just started a roast for you and your friends, so it will be a time, but I'll have Nanda bring out some cheese and bread for you. Welcome to the Dragonback, sir and miss. It's an honor to have the Fair Folk under my roof."

"It's a pleasure to find a good inn," Araevin replied.

The dwarf bowed and withdrew.

Grayth filled the clay cups with wine from the jug and asked, "So, Araevin, what is it that led you to summon us again? What in Faerûn has caught your attention after eighteen years in Evermeet?"

"Nothing good, I'm afraid," Araevin said. His eyes hardened, and his voice grew colder. "A few days ago, a band of demons attacked my Tower in Evermeet. I think they were looking for this." He fished the *telkiira* out of his pouch and showed it to Grayth and Brant. "More stones like this are buried in an ancient vault of my people. This stone has provided me with a map of sorts leading to its sisters. But I don't know why our enemies wanted this stone, or even who our enemies are, for that matter. If I find the rest of the set and unravel this riddle, I may learn more about our adversaries. We understand nothing about them now."

"And you thought that the Company of the White Star might be able to help you find more of your magic gemstones," Grayth observed.

"Well, yes," Araevin said. "But . . . but I hadn't realized how much time had gone by. Darthen has his steading to govern, and I think you have become a man with responsibilities, too."

The High Mornmaster offered a wry smile and said, "Let me be the judge of my responsibilities, Araevin. I've spent too much time lately telling others what they need to go do. Some time away from the temple might be just the renewal that Lathander intends for me."

"We would not want you to get into trouble with your superiors," Ilsevele said.

82 • Richard Baker

"You think I'm too old for such nonsense, you mean," Grayth said. He nodded at Araevin. "I seem to recall that I'm a good two hundred years younger than him. I might not be as old as you think. Now, why don't you start at the beginning and tell me what exactly has brought you back to Faerûn? I doubt you'll have any luck with the others of the company, but I am with you, Araevin."

☙ ☙ ☙ ☙ ☙

Despite the gray skies and winter chill, the gardens of the royal palace in Leuthilspar were green and lush. The gardens of Moonflower Palace were said to be blessed by the Seldarine, and Seiveril could well believe it. He had never asked Corellon Larethian the truth of the tale, but some myths did not need to be examined, did they? He chose to simply admire the perfection of the palace grounds without permitting himself to wonder how it was done, and followed the palace chamberlain through the green maze.

The chamberlain led him to an ivy-covered arbor beside a still, dark pool.

"Your majesty?" the young elf called softly. "Lord Seiveril Miritar is here."

Queen Amlaruil stood by a stone balustrade at the far end of the arbor, gazing absently into the water. Her long, dark hair was bound in a simple braid, and she wore a plain but elegant dress of green felt not much different than any elf lass might have worn to visit a friend for an afternoon. For a moment she seemed just a pensive young girl in a garden, no more than twenty or thirty, but when she glanced up, Seiveril felt the full weight of the starry wisdom in her dark eyes.

"Thank you, Dremel. You may go," the queen said.

The chamberlain bowed and withdrew. Seiveril murmured a word of thanks as well, and crossed the arbor to bow deeply a short distance from the queen.

"You sent for me, my lady?"

"Oh, stand up straight, Seiveril. You've known me far too long to genuflect like that."

"As you wish," the nobleman said. He joined Amlaruil at the rail and studied the setting. "I don't think I've ever been in this corner of the garden."

"I come here often," the queen said. "The garden has a way of guiding my thoughts, suggesting answers to questions I haven't asked yet. I feel Zaor's hand here."

Seiveril nodded. He could, as well. King Zaor Moonflower, Amlaruil's husband, had ruled Evermeet well for hundreds of years. But he had died at the hands of a sun elf assassin more than forty years before, leaving Amlaruil to govern alone. She had ruled well and wisely, too. In fact, Evermeet might have fallen to Kymil Nimesin's treachery and invasion three years past, if not for Amlaruil's firm leadership and personal courage. But the tale of Zaor and Amlaruil's centuries-spanning love and devotion to each other was known to all Evermeet.

"I have seen the Gatekeeper's Crystal, Seiveril," she said. "Not clearly, mind you. Someone is working hard to deflect our divinations. As you feared, our enemies assembled the three shards of the device and used it to undo a powerful, ancient ward."

"Where?" Seiveril asked.

"I do not know the place. It was a rocky tor surrounded by a great woodland . . . I saw that much. I think it was an old stronghold of some kind, broken open by the power of the device."

"That seems ominous, to say the least." Seiveril frowned. "We should send word to Evereska and the other realms in Faerûn, warning them. Maybe your vision will mean something to them."

"There is this: My divinations also revealed that the crystal has again been scattered."

"Thank the Seldarine for that. Evermeet is safe from that threat, at least."

"Perhaps," Amlaruil said, "but who knows where our enemy's road now leads? I will not consider Evermeet safe until we have at least one of those shards back in our hands, and I know exactly who wielded the device and where."

"I can answer that question, at least in part," said Seiveril. "I have communed with the Seldarine, and I have a name for our foes: the Dlardrageths, the daemonfey. Araevin's report of the raid on Tower Reilloch reminded me of the old stories about the Dlardrageth palace in Myth Drannor. It seems that my suspicions were well founded."

"Who are they?" Amlaruil asked.

"A House of sun elves who were influential in ancient Arcorar. They trafficked with demons for the power to seize control of that realm, but were found out. The Coronal of Arcorar destroyed their House, but some escaped to ancient Siluvanede, where they lured a number of lesser Houses into evil, as well." Seiveril spread his hands. "Supposedly they were dealt with in the Seven Citadels' War. In any event, I can find no more mention of them in any records since that time."

"Siluvanede fell five thousand years ago," the queen observed. "Do you believe anything could vanish so completely for so long?"

"Evidently they did. I cannot explain it. Perhaps even the Seldarine do not know their tale. But I am certain that we are dealing with the Dlardrageths, or their heirs."

Amlaruil nodded and said, "Very well, then. We will find out where they are hiding, we will recover what they have stolen, and we will root out this ancient evil."

Seiveril sighed and looked up from the still waters of the pool to meet Amlaruil's gaze directly. Even though he was a full four centuries in age, and a high priest of Corellon Larethian, he did not find it easy to do.

"Even that will not be sufficient to secure Evermeet's safety, Amlaruil," he said. "This time it was the Gatekeeper's Crystal. Three years ago, it was the treachery of Kymil Nimesin. In a year, or two, or ten, it will be something else. We withdrew all our strength from Cormanthor in the Retreat and virtually abandoned Faerûn to whatever fate the other speaking peoples forge for themselves, and still evil follows us here. Whatever refuge we have found here is little more than a temporary reprieve from the workings of the world beyond."

"I know that, Seiveril," Amlaruil said wearily. "I cannot walk in this garden without remembering the day Zaor died here. But what would you have me do? Even if I could undo the Retreat and open Evermeet's shores to the world outside, there are those on the council who would rise in open rebellion if I were to make the attempt."

"Durothil and Veldann. And their allies."

"You named them, not I," said Amlaruil. "Nor will I name them, unless I must. Sun elves comprise half of Evermeet's people, and almost a third of the sun elf Houses are in Durothil's camp. I must take great care when I act against the wishes of the powerful Houses on the council."

The queen sighed and turned away from the pool, moving over to take a seat on a nearby bench of marble.

"In all fairness," she said, "I must concede that the isolationists possess a persuasive argument. Less than five years ago, we boasted more than two hundred high mages in Evermeet. But Kymil Nimesin's attack on the Towers of the Sun and Moon, and our expedition to aid Evereska against the phaerimm two years ago, cost us dearly in this irreplaceable resource. We have fewer than eighty high mages today. Evermeet is weaker than it ever has been."

Seiveril studied her.

"I presume that you will soon call the council together to relay your findings about the Gatekeeper's Crystal," he said finally. "So why did you send for me, my lady?"

"Because I think you are right, Seiveril, but I may not be able to act on our common conclusions," Amlaruil replied. "Evermeet cannot exist in isolation from the rest of Toril, but powerful voices will be raised in opposition to anything we do to act on this belief. If I ignore them, I court disaster. I want you to know that even if I must remain silent in the debate to come, I do not disagree with you."

"What is it that you see coming?" Seiveril asked.

"The crystal was taken from an elven tower, by creatures who were once elves," Amlaruil replied. "I do not know what evil purpose the Dlardrageths have in mind, but I am certain that it will fall to us to oppose it."

☙ ☙ ☙ ☙ ☙

Fires danced and guttered amid the ruins of Myth Glaurach. The snow-covered buildings echoed with the sounds of ringing hammers and hissing steam. More than two thousand fey'ri soldiers, the legion imprisoned for five thousand years in the Nameless Dungeon, camped amid the ivy-grown stones of the long-fallen Eaerlanni city. Armed with powerful magic, fey'ri sorcerers worked furiously to repair the city's ancient ramparts and prepare deadly spell traps against any possible attacker. Other demonblooded elves were busily engaged in refitting the prized arms and weapons of the ancient Vyshaanti—another of Nar Kerymhoarth's buried secrets—for the fey'ri army. Hundreds of fey'ri scoured the lands nearby, foraging for food and searching diligently for signs of enemy spies.

Sarya Dlardrageth was pleased. She stood amid the broken rubble of the fallen grand mage's throne room, gazing out into the bitterly cold night. She and her followers were not much troubled by winter weather, and despite the freezing temperature she wore only a light dress embroidered with the dracophoenix emblem of her House. Before her eyes lay the strongest army for more than five hundred miles, a winged legion whose every soldier commanded magical powers, and none of her enemies even suspected its existence.

"Siluvanede lives again," she said into the night, her breath steaming. "We shall reclaim the lands and cities we once ruled, and the children of our onetime enemies will grovel at our feet. Time itself has proven to be our decisive weapon. We still exist, while the proud kingdoms of Sharrvan, Eaerlann, and Illefarn are no more."

She turned away from the firelit night. Behind her waited her son Xhalph, along with a dozen of her chosen fey'ri. Only she and Xhalph remained of House

Dlardrageth, but the proud sun elf lords and ladies in the throne room each led a House of fey'ri sworn to serve her. Cruel and arrogant as they were, they attended her every word, obedient to her will. House Dlardrageth had forged chains of fear and loyalty to ensnare the fey'ri Houses long ago, and the fey'ri nobles were zealous servants indeed. Their souls depended on it.

"Command us, my lady," said Jasrya Ilviiri. She was a tall, beautiful fey'ri whose skin glittered in diamond-shaped scales, evidence of her marilith heritage.

"Oh, I shall," Sarya answered. She moved over to a table on which lay a large parchment map taken from a merchant near Everlund a few tendays before. The fey'ri gathered close to follow her. "Since I and my sons were freed five years ago, I have studied this new world tirelessly. This is the shape of things in the North today.

"In our time, this part of the world harbored three elven realms: Eaerlann, Sharrven, and Siluvanede. All these are gone. Siluvanede, our home, was conquered by Eaerlann after our defeat and came to nothing. Sharrven perished soon after, but Eaerlann persisted until quite recently, finally falling only five hundred years ago. No strong realms have risen in the place of the kingdoms we knew, and the High Forest is almost empty. A few thousand mongrel wood elves roam the forest, living in simple bands or wretched little villages scattered here and there, but they answer to no lord or ruler." Sarya looked up from the map, baring her small pointed fangs. "They are the heirs of Eaerlann. Since time has denied us the opportunity to exact our vengeance from the Eaerlanni, the wood elves will be made to answer instead for the wrongs we have suffered."

"We will make good sport of their deaths," Xhalph promised, his four muscular arms crossed before his huge chest. "I have already tasted their blood, and I thirst for more."

Sarya smiled and continued, "Beyond the High Forest and the valley of the Delimbiyr lie more dangerous foes. South and east of us the city of Evereska still stands, home to thousands of sun elves and no small number of cursed moon elves. Evereska's sun elves will be my subjects. The moon elves shall serve us or die. No other elven realms stand within a thousand miles of us."

"Evereska was a strong city in our time, Lady Sarya," said Lord Breden Yesve. "Its walls were high, and its army strong. And it was guarded by a powerful mythal."

"It was still a strong city when I was freed five years ago," Sarya replied. "But here we have another stroke of good fortune. Two years ago Evereska was attacked by magic-wielding monsters called phaerimm. The city was virtually laid waste, its army decimated, its mythal desperately weakened. It is my belief that Evereska now lies within our grasp."

The fey'ri grinned in response, his black fangs gleaming.

"Evereska's army played no small part in our final defeat," he said. "I look forward to settling that score."

"You will," Sarya promised. "But I am not quite finished yet. To our north, in the vale of the Rauvin, lies a young, weak confederation of dwarf and human cities known as Luruar, or the Silver Marches. The chief city of the league is the city of Silverymoon. It is a city of temples and schools of magic, protected by strong wards. Many of the People live there, as well."

"With the humans?" one of her fey'ri asked. "Have they no sense of dignity?"

Sarya frowned. "Understand this: the world has changed while we slumbered. In our day the humans were crude barbarians who sometimes aped our cities and our speech. Humans are not the savages they once were. Their squalid cities and ramshackle empires cover the land like an infestation of locusts." Her face twisted into a snarl. "They have stolen our ancient lands, driven off our folk, desecrated our sacred places, destroyed the great forests. Of all the wrongs we have suffered at the hands of the Eaerlanni and their allies, this may be the greatest: In our absence they permitted the shining cities and high kingdoms of the People to fall beneath the stinking tide of humankind. Elven Faerûn has been dying for centuries, and they have done nothing to save it."

"If humans have become so numerous, and the *Tel'Quessir* so rare, are they not our most dangerous enemy?" asked Breden Yesve.

"In time they will be," Sarya replied. "But, as it turns out, no human realms now stand between the High Moor and the Graypeak Mountains. Other than the league of the Silver Marches, there are no human settlements larger than a small town for many hundreds of miles. We will have little interference from human kingdoms at first. By the time they think to intervene, we will have strengthened our position to the point where we can dictate terms to our new neighbors, or destroy them if they prove unmanageable."

Lord Yesve nodded, and returned his attention to the map.

"Good. Now attend, all of you. We are surrounded by three enemies: the wood elves of the High Forest, Evereska, and the human cities of the Silver Marches. I suspect they will object to my creation of a new Siluvanede in the lands they mistakenly regard as theirs. And rather than argue with them about the matter, I mean to retake what is rightfully ours. This is how it shall be done.

"Jasrya, you are to lead the Ilviiri against the High Forest. The Aelorothi and Dhaorothi are also under your command. Your mission is to wipe the wood elf realm from the face of the forest. Destroy their villages, slay their warriors, enslave the young and the weak. Strike quickly, and without mercy. The wood elves are scattered throughout the forest, so keep your warband together, and give them no chance to gather a force large enough to threaten you. I will send Xhalph with you to assist you in your work. These are the descendants of our ancient enemies. Visit on them the vengeance they have earned."

"Thank you, Mother," the daemonfey swordsman growled.

"Lord Mardeiym, you are to take House Reithel; with Floshin, Ulvaerren, Ursequarra, and Almyrrtel;

and march on Evereska. I will join you when I am able. It is your task to take the city by whatever means are necessary. You have nearly fifteen hundred fey'ri warriors under your command since I expect you to have the harder fight. I will also dispatch with you a strong force of our demonic allies.

"Lord Breden, you are to lead House Yesve to the eastern end of the Rauvin Vale and keep Silverymoon at bay. I will also give House Ealoeth to you. Your force is the weakest of our three armies, so I do not want you to attack unless you find the humans weaker than I thought. You are simply a screening force to make sure that Silverymoon does not interfere with our capture of Evereska or the scouring of the wood elves from the High Forest."

"As you command, my lady," Breden said with a bow.

"I have laid the groundwork for alliances with orcs, ogres, and such rabble that dwell in the nearer reaches of the Nether Mountains," Sarya continued. "Unfortunately, the phaerimm drove many of these creatures to their deaths against Evereska only a couple of years ago, so the tribes of the mountains are not as strong as I might have hoped. Do not trust these stupid creatures with anything important. Use them as skirmishers and raiders, or, if a chance presents itself, drive them into battle before your fey'ri in order to die in place of our own soldiers. We are strong, but our numbers are not inexhaustible, and we don't want a fey'ri to die when an orc will do.

"When Evereska falls, we will turn Reithel's army back to the north and repel any assault mustering in Silverymoon—or invade that city and raze it, if it lies within our power."

"Do we have sufficient strength to contemplate fighting three foes at once?" Mardeiym Reithel asked. He was a crafty old fighter, veteran of many fiercely fought campaigns in the Seven Citadels' War, and a fervent devotee of the dark powers the daemonfey worshiped.

"If we strike only at one of these enemies, the other two will come to their aid anyway," Sarya replied. "I am confident that we can triumph over the wood elves and

Forsaken House • 91

Evereska quickly. Once we have won our battles in those places, I believe that the humans of Silverymoon will see little reason to continue fighting." She studied the rest of the fey'ri, noting the glowing eyes, the feral grins. After five thousand years of magical slumber, her legions were eager to fight for her again. "Go back to your Houses and ready your warriors to fly. I mean to march at once."

CHAPTER 6

1 Ches, the Year of Lightning Storms

Araevin decided to wait at Daggerford for two days, on the chance that Theleda or even Darthen might turn up, or at least send word. In the early hours, while the humans slept, he and Ilsevele braved the bitter weather to ride or walk the countryside around the settlement. The afternoons and evenings they spent in the common room of the Dragonback, trading tales with Grayth or digesting news of distant lands from the caravan masters and traders who passed through the town.

Late in the evening of the second night, as the Dragonback's evening crowd was beginning to disperse, Araevin and his companions looked over a map of the Sword Coast over steaming goblets of mulled wine. He intended to set out on his quest soon, and he was taking the opportunity to study the roads leading south. He could feel the second *telkiira* in that direction, tugging at the back of his mind like something he had forgotten.

"Which one of you is Araevin Teshurr?"

Araevin and the others looked up, and found a young woman standing at the end of their table. She was a strikingly unusual person, her skin as pale as snow, almost a frosty blue in places. Her eyes were large and violet, and her hair was silver-white and long, streaming softly from her head as if she stood in a gentle breeze—though the smoke simply hung in the rafters of the tavern without so much as a hint of motion. Tall and graceful, she wore high leather boots, black breeches, and a soft quilted doublet over a shirt of white silk.

"Well?" she asked.

"I am Araevin Teshurr," Araevin replied. "And you are—?"

"I am Maresa Rost. Theleda Rost was my mother." Without awaiting an invitation, the pale woman dropped herself into a seat beside Ilsevele, and fixed her startling purple eyes on the others in the company. "You must be Grayth Holmfast. I don't know who you are, or you," she said, looking at Ilsevele and Brant in turn.

"Theleda's daughter?" Araevin could not keep the surprise from his voice.

Theleda had a daughter? he thought.

Theleda had been the first to leave the company, a couple of years before their last travels, so there might be as much as twenty years during which she could have had a child.

"Yes, we went over that already," Maresa said. She poured herself a large helping of their wine. "My mother told me a few stories about her old adventures. You were two of the Company of the White Star, weren't you?"

Araevin studied the young woman closely. She had Theleda's pointed chin and heart-shaped face, but her coloration was so odd . . .

"Excuse my surprise," Araevin said, "but Theleda is human, and you are—I hope you will forgive me, I am not sure what kindred you belong to. I do not think I have ever seen someone like you."

The young woman snorted softly and replied, "Well, there are not many like me. I am a genasi. Theleda was human, of course. My father was a being of the elemental planes. The plane of elemental air, or so I understand, which is why I look as I do. It was an unusual romance, I suppose, and I understand it did not last long."

Araevin shook his head. Who would have thought? Then something Maresa had said resurfaced.

"One moment. Theleda isn't—?"

"Theleda was murdered last summer," Maresa said. "One of her business rivals had her assassinated."

Araevin sat back, his heart aching. First Belmora, then Theleda too? She had always been abrasive, arrogant, armed with too sharp a wit, perhaps. But they had shared many dangers together.

"Our company is growing smaller by the day, Grayth," he said softly.

The cleric replied, "I am sorry to hear it, but the news does not surprise me. Such things happen in Theleda's line of work." He looked over to Maresa. "I am sorry for your loss. Are you well? I mean, are you in any danger from those who killed Theleda? We may be able to help."

Maresa smiled thinly and answered, "No, I am not in any danger. I found the assassin who murdered my mother and killed him. And I found out who had hired him, and killed his employer as well. I went back to Waterdeep after I saw to that."

Araevin was not sure if one should congratulate a young human—well, half-human—woman on having successfully killed the murderers of a parent.

"I see," he managed, and decided to change the subject. "How did you receive my summons?"

Maresa reached into her tunic and drew out a small pendant in a star-shaped design.

"This little keepsake of my mother's," she said. "I wear it to remember her by."

Araevin nodded. He had given the tokens to his companions when they parted in order to serve as conduits for his call, if he should ever need them again.

"So what business did you think you had with my mother?" the genasi asked.

"I have just returned to Faerûn after a long time in Evermeet," Araevin answered, "and I find that I have need of some trustworthy comrades to assist me in the recovery of some relics of my people. Theleda was an expert at traps and locks and such things, and I had hoped I might persuade her to travel with us again. But it seems we will have to do without her."

"I might be able to help you. Mother taught me everything she knew."

"It might be dangerous, and there may be little reward in it," Araevin said.

"I have reasons to leave Waterdeep anyway, and as long as I get an equal share of the profits—or am reasonably compensated for my time, if there are none—I might be interested."

"Maresa, I don't think you understand," Grayth said. "You may not have much regard for whether you yourself are in danger, but we may have to trust our companions with our lives. You are young, and we don't know you."

"I told you that I dealt with my mother's murderers myself," Maresa said flatly.

"Which we only have your word on," Grayth replied.

"Fine. Allow me to demonstrate," Maresa snapped. She stood up quickly and rested one hand conspicuously on the hilt of a rapier at her belt, a graceful weapon with a guard of gleaming silver. A slender wand of dark wood rested in a small holster next to the blade. "Who's the best swordsman among the four of you?"

Grayth folded his thick arms across his chest and said, "I don't know if that would—"

"Afraid to try your luck, priest?"

The Lathanderite stopped in mid-sentence, his face expressionless. He leaned back in his seat.

"She's her mother's daughter, all right," said the priest.

"If my eyes were closed, I would swear that was Theleda speaking. And the gods know Theleda never had a good eye for picking a fight."

Maresa bridled, but Ilsevele set a hand on her arm and said, "In all seriousness, you know something about traps, and glyphs, and such things?"

"I already said so!"

"All right, then. Open this."

Ilsevele reached into her pack for her spellbook. As a spellarcher, she studied wizardry in order to enchant her arrows. She had nothing like Araevin's skill in the Art, but she was no novice either, and as many wizards did, she had protected her spellbook with abjurations designed to prevent anyone from pilfering her spells. It was a small, slender volume bound between thin sheets of laspar wood, with clasps of silver.

"There's nothing deadly here," Ilsevele explained, "but you definitely won't like it if you open the book without passing my signs safely."

Maresa bristled.

"An audition? Fine!" she muttered under her breath.

She sat down again, peering at Ilsevele's spellbook without touching it.

Araevin sat up straight and looked to Ilsevele. He knew what sort of protections Ilsevele had on her spellbook, and they were formidable even if they weren't deadly.

He said in Elvish, "Ilsevele, do you think this is wise? If she fails, she will be shamed, and if she succeeds, she is likely to insist on going."

Ilsevele shook her copper hair, met his eyes with her sharp gaze, and answered in Elvish, "She came in her mother's place. I have a feeling about her, Araevin. I am willing to give the girl a chance, if you are."

Araevin acceded. He returned his attention to Maresa, who had finished looking over the book. The genasi whispered the words of a seeing spell, and the spellbook began to glow with a soft azure radiance. She carefully studied the book again for a few moments, examining the spells that lay over it.

"All right, then," Maresa said as she reached into a vest pocket in her doublet and retrieved a small leather folio, opening it on the table by the book. "Your glyph will be damaged."

"We will see," said Ilsevele. "Do what you need to, as long as you don't damage the book itself."

"It's your book," Maresa replied.

She found a small paper packet in the leather case and opened it, shaking out a purple-colored powder over the spellbook. Then she laid a thin piece of parchment over the powdered book. With a stick of charcoal she carefully colored the parchment, making a rubbing or etching of the spellbook's cover.

On the parchment, a string of mystic symbols appeared in her rubbing. No such symbols had been visible on the book's cover beforehand. Maresa left the parchment in place and fished a strange styluslike instrument from her case. Muttering the words of a counter charm, she picked out the symbols on her charcoal rubbing one by one and pressed each out with the stylus, changing it to a different symbol by erasing one stroke. Carefully she negated or altered each symbol in the arcane phrase, then straightened up and shook her flowing white hair. Araevin noticed that she still had not broken a sweat. With a smug smile, she removed the parchment, picked up the book and shook off her powder, and promptly opened it.

"Satisfied?" she asked.

"Damn. That was nicely done," Grayth said. "All right, so you're better than I thought."

"You can come," said Ilsevele. She took her spellbook back from Maresa with a rueful look. "I suppose I need better runes to protect my book."

Araevin set down his mug and looked up at Maresa.

"There is a little more to this than striking out spell traps," he said. "It's not wise to seek out dangerous places in the company of people you don't trust implicitly, and to put it plainly, you don't know us very well, nor do we know you."

"You knew my mother, didn't you?" Maresa riposted.

"She carried your pendant until the day she died, elf. She would have answered your call, so I am here in her place."

Neither Araevin nor Grayth replied.

"I thought so," Maresa said. "In that case, where are we going, and when do we leave?"

☙ ☙ ☙ ☙ ☙

Gaerradh knelt easily in a well-disguised tree stand overlooking the village of Rheitheillaethor. The moon was hidden behind the overcast, leaving little more than a silver patch in the darkness overhead, but an elf's eyes needed little light. She could clearly make out the simple shelters and fieldstone storehouses on the ground below, with the gleaming patches of white snow lingering around the boles of the broad weirwoods and shadowtops sheltering the village.

Rheitheillaethor was home to nearly five hundred of the wood elves, but few of them lived in the buildings and shelters on the ground. Instead their homes were hidden high in the branches above the forest floor, a cunning arrangement of disguised platforms and narrow catwalks that was nearly invisible to anyone below. Even knowing they were there, Gaerradh had a hard time picking out other stands and platforms at any distance, but here and there she caught glimpses of resolute wood elf warriors crouching in stands like hers, waiting for the enemy to appear.

She shifted her position, craning her head for a better look. Her platform was near the center of the village, away from the pickets where she would have liked to be, and she was impatient to get a look at her foes. Three days before she had brought news of the breaking of Nar Kerymhoarth to the elders of Rheitheillaethor. The next day news had followed of orc bands on the move in the forest, accompanied by winged elves, cruel and proud, armed for war. Gaerradh had no idea who the elfkin might be, but the fact that they marched in the company of orcs spoke for their intentions. Wood elf scouts had shadowed the invaders since sunrise. There could be no doubt that they were coming to Rheitheillaethor.

"The waiting is not easy, is it?" whispered a voice behind her.

The Lady Morgwais, sometimes known as the Lady of the Wood, shared the large platform with her. She was beautiful and graceful, with long auburn hair and a copper-red complexion that made her seem half a dryad. She had asked Gaerradh to stay close by her in the large tree near the village's center, along with half a dozen more sharpshooters and mages. In better times their perch served as the hall of the village elders, the largest structure in Rheitheillaethor's canopy, but the wood elves had fitted new screens and camouflaging panels to make the hall into a hidden redoubt high above the forest floor.

Gaerradh did not take her eyes from the woodlands to the northeast.

"I don't like meeting them in the village, Lady Morgwais," she replied. "I do not mean to question your judgment, but I can't help but think we would be better off in the open forest, where we could ambush and melt away from pursuit. I fear being trapped."

Morgwais frowned and said, "I think you might have found these orcs and their bat-winged allies more difficult to ambush than you think. They have held to their course and kept on toward the village, despite our illusions, enchantments, and our scouts' efforts to decoy them away. I suspect that they have some skilled wizards among them, someone who can dispel our defenses and divine a path to our village."

Gaerradh glanced around at that and said, "If they are using magic to sniff us out, then maybe we shouldn't be here at all!"

"Rheitheillaethor is no more or less significant than any other place in the forest," the noblewoman replied, "but it's as good a place as any to try our enemies' strength. And it might not hurt to teach these new foes that searching out our homes and marching on them will not be as easy as they think."

A soft owl's cry came from the night beyond the village, answered by another.

"They're here," Gaerradh whispered.

Other elves nearby repeated the warning. Gaerradh crouched back down in her chosen spot and unlimbered her bow.

She heard the orcs before she saw them. The brutish creatures were holding their tongues, but their armor clinked and jingled softly, and their sandaled feet crunched and scuffled in the thin snow and leafy debris of the forest floor. She spied the leaders, a handful of scouts and skirmishers trotting warily before their fellows, crouching and stooping as they moved from cover to cover. Behind them came a ragged line of berserkers, the champions of the tribe—powerful warriors who disdained armor, wearing little other than broad leather belts and dirty breeches, huge axes gripped in their hairy hands. After the berserkers came long, dark files of orc warriors creeping through the shadows. It was a large warband, bigger than any raiding party Gaerradh had ever seen before.

They know enough to be wary of the trees, she thought, watching the gleam of their yellow eyes as they peered into the dark branches of the weirwoods, shields held high by their heads. *But where are the others, the demons with elves' faces?*

Almost directly below their tree, a pair of the scouts halted, looking up into the darkness. The rest of the orcs continued forward, but from below Gaerradh heard a wet snuffling sound.

They smell us, she realized.

She started to signal to Morgwais, but the Lady of the Wood simply said, "Now."

Five dozen wood elf archers fired as one, sending arrow after arrow plunging down into the orc company below. Orcs screamed and bellowed, some roaring in rage, others gurgling out awful death cries as they spun or sagged into the snow. Gaerradh shifted her position and fired straight down the bole of her tree at the scouts below, taking the first one in the throat as he looked up at her, and the second high between the shoulders as he scrambled back looking for cover.

The first volleys were devastating, scything through the orc ranks with merciless efficiency. The elf archers above did not speak or shout, but bowstrings thrummed like harps and arrows hissed in the air like angry serpents. Orc after orc fell, plucking at arrows buried in chests and necks. Others quickly covered down beneath their shields, forming turtle-like knots of a dozen or more warriors crowding together to make their shields into an impenetrable wall. Even as she plied her bow with deadly skill, Gaerradh saw one of the orc shield-knots blown apart by the lightning spell of an elf mage hidden overhead. Thunder boomed in the village clearing.

"Beware the war priests!" Morgwais called to the elves in the redoubt.

Gaerradh caught the guttural sound of orc shamans chanting spells. She held her fire, searching quickly for the spellcasters. Few orcs ever studied wizardly magic, but priests devoted to the dark and savage gods of their race often accompanied the warbands. She spotted one fellow, a chanting war priest with the ceremonial eye patch worn by the servants of one-eyed Gruumsh. She aimed carefully and shot him through his remaining eye, cutting off his chant in mid-syllable.

Other chanting voices shrieked and fell off as priests fell wounded or dead. But enough of the clerics lived long enough to cast their spells together. Barking out the last words of the chant, the priests gestured and shouted.

Dense white fog filled the forest floor, rolling away from each shaman and covering the orcs below from the elves' arrows. Gaerradh peered at the ground below, but all she could make out were roiling clouds of white mist, out of which rose the black boles of Rheitheillaethor's weirwoods like pillars in a great hall. She glimpsed movement here and there, dark shapes flitting below, but nothing she could shoot at.

Morgwais joined her in leaning out carefully to study the fog below.

"Damn," she whispered. "That was a good idea. These orcs are far too clever and determined for my comfort."

"Do we have any spellcasters to dispel the mist?" Gaerradh asked.

"Yes. But they anticipated our attack from above. They'll have a counter ready. Still, we should try. We need to see them to shoot them."

Morgwais dropped back down to the main platform and started to give her commands.

Flickering orange light filled the forest as a dozen burning globes of fire appeared above the canopy and streaked down toward the elves' fighting platforms with a rumbling crackle of magic. Gaerradh glanced up to see one of the great spinning orbs heading straight at her perch.

"Fireballs!" she screamed.

She threw herself down to the main platform only a heartbeat before the globe struck where she had been kneeling and detonated. The mighty weirwood trembled in the blast as a huge gout of scathing red fire blasted through the elven house, shattering light screens and snapping the smaller limbs. Gaerradh turned her face away from the blast and cowered beneath her cloak. Pain seared her exposed limbs, and the impact picked her up and threw her back down to the wooden deck.

Elf voices shrieked in pain around her. One of the sharpshooters with whom she'd shared the post toppled out of the tree, wrapped in flame like a living torch. He plunged into the mist below like a meteor. Fires burned in many of the hidden tree blinds.

They used the orcs to learn our positions, Gaerradh realized. They got above us and watched us fire at their allies, and when they spotted our blinds, they threw their spells. How many spellcasters are up there? A dozen? Maybe more?

The orcs below whooped in delight at the burning trees and elves' screams. The weirwoods didn't burn easily—

they were guarded with protective spells, and were not naturally inclined to burn anyway—but shadowtops were a different story, and several of the towering giants were alight despite the winter weather and the damp.

"Get the spellcasters!" Morgwais cried to the elves nearby.

Her hair was singed, but she was otherwise fine, her spells sufficient to protect her against the fiery blasts. The noble wood elf recited a spell of her own and hurled a crackling sphere of blue light into the high branches overhead. The orb burst in a scintillating wave of lightning, illuminating the sinister, shadowed forms of winged warriors descending toward the village. A pair cried out and crumpled as Morgwais's spell burned them out of the sky, but others eluded the energy wave or shielded themselves with spells of their own.

Gaerradh took aim on another darting form illuminated by the blue lightning and fired, but she missed her mark. The arrow buried itself in the elf-demon's thigh instead of its breastbone. It spiraled wildly, but then regained sufficient control to drop down behind a tree and get out of her line of sight. She looked around for another target, and she heard a ragged roar of battle cries and oaths from below her.

The orc warriors scaled the trees of the village, hurling grapnels up into the branches and raising clumsy siege ladders against the trunks of the larger trees. The battle-mad berserkers swarmed up out of the mist, foaming at the mouth, red eyes rolling wildly as they roared their challenges. Quickly Gaerradh shifted her aim to pick three orcs off a ladder in a neighboring tree, though she could hear orcs scrabbling and cursing as they climbed her own.

"Sound the retreat!" Morgwais snapped. She started to cast another spell, only to break it off abruptly and duck low to avoid a bolt of green acid hurled down by one of the winged sorcerers above. "We can't fight off both assaults at once."

One of the other elves seized a hunting horn at his belt and sounded three short blasts. He was killed an instant later by a heavy iron spear hurled up from the orc ranks below.

Morgwais didn't wait on her warriors. She quickly worked a spell that covered the tree-hall with a spreading cloud of gloom, and she ran out across the well-hidden catwalks linking the tree houses together. Gaerradh followed her, groping in the darkness. She knew that other elves would be abandoning their platforms, likewise concealing their escape with clouds of mist or walls of gloom.

"What now?" she whispered to the lady as they slipped out of the village.

"We flee," Morgwais replied. Her eyes gleamed with ire and determination. "We retreat, we skirmish, and we delay until we have the measure of these demonspawn. And we call for help."

☉ ☉ ☉ ☉ ☉

"Lords and ladies of Evermeet, the queen!"

The Dome of Stars rustled softly with movement as the council and the assembled observers stood up and fell silent. Seiveril rose from his seat and turned to face the doorway as Amlaruil swept into the Dome of Stars, Keryth Blackhelm a pace behind her. A sun elf lord wearing a tabard of emerald blue emblazoned with a star and sword emblem accompanied them. Seiveril did not recognize the fellow.

Amlaruil was dressed in a simple dress of green, her only concession to formality a plain silver fillet on her brow. In all the council meetings he had attended, Seiveril could not recall being summoned so hastily, or seeing Amlaruil appear in anything less than royal splendor. It struck him as an ominous sign.

"Please, be seated," the queen said. She looked around the glasssteel table. All the council was present except for Emardin Elsydar, the high admiral, who was currently at sea and could not be recalled in time for the emergency session. "I thank you all for coming so swiftly. I am afraid there is grave news from Faerûn."

Forsaken House • 105

Seiveril frowned and studied his fellow councilors. Most wore expressions of puzzled concern that no doubt mirrored his own. Never in his memory had the council been called on only one hour's notice. Elves were deliberate folk and did not make a practice of trying to meet untoward developments with thoughtless haste. He looked across the table at Lady Selsharra Durothil, who simply studied the queen with narrowed eyes, her expression cold. It didn't matter what news Amlaruil had for the council. Lady Durothil was gathering herself for a confrontation, possibly for no other reason than the fact that Amlaruil had seen fit to summon her at short notice.

"An hour ago Lord Imesfor arrived in Leuthilspar, bearing a message from Lord Duirsar, the High Elder of Evereska," Amlaruil said. She indicated the sun elf lord who had followed her into the Dome. "I will let him present it to you."

"Thank you, my lady," Imesfor replied. He stepped forward and faced the council. "I am Gervas Imesfor of Evereska. I have the honor of serving my people as one of our Hill Elders. Forgive me if I forego courtesy in order to quickly state my message: Evereska faces a new attack. An army of orcs, ogres, giants, and other foul creatures is marching south through the Delimbiyr Vale, heading for the Shaeradim. They are accompanied by a number of demons and other fiendish beings, including a mighty legion of creatures that seem like demon-tainted elves. We have also heard from our allies in the High Forest that another army has invaded the woodland seeking out the villages and havens of the wood elves. The wood elves have fought several skirmishes against the invaders already, and have asked us for as much help as we can spare. But with an even mightier army approaching our city, we fear that we do not have the strength to aid the High Forest while defending our own people. The war against the phaerimm two years ago claimed far too many of our warriors and mages. We know that Evermeet sacrificed greatly to assist us then, but we hope that you can once again lend us your strength and help us stand against the enemies of all the People."

"You mentioned demon-tainted elves," Seiveril said. He tightened his hands into fists under the table to combat the dread in his heart. "What do you mean by that? Can you describe them?"

"I have studied them with scrying magic, my lord," Imesfor replied. "They have leathery wings, like those of a bat or dragon, and a reddish hue to their skin. I observed many wearing arms and armor of fine quality and elven workmanship. The wood elves who have engaged them described the creatures as skilled sorcerers and blademasters." The Evereskan lord absorbed the council's reaction then asked, "Do you know these creatures?"

"Yes," said Seiveril. "You have described the Dlardrageths and their minions, the daemonfey."

Lord Imesfor's eyes widened and he murmured, "So the old tales are true."

"Fifteen days ago a party of these demon-elves attacked a Tower on the northern coasts," Seiveril continued. "They killed more than twenty of our people, including two high mages, and carried away a powerful weapon. We have been searching for some sign of them, but it seems as though they have no more need of secrecy." He looked over to the queen and said, "I fear we bear some responsibility for this threat to Evereska and the High Forest, your highness. We cannot stand by and allow the crystal to be used against Evereska!"

"Did you not tell us that the crystal had been brought to Evermeet out of Faerûn only a couple of years ago?" Lady Ammisyll Veldann asked Seiveril. "The throne's servants meddled in Faerûn by bringing that cursed device into Evermeet, and now we see the price we must pay for yesterday's mistakes. I refuse to countenance any suggestion that we repair the damage caused by our unwise involvement in Faerûnian matters by involving ourselves even more!"

Lady Jerreda Starcloak, speaker for the island's wood elves, glared at Lady Veldann. "How can you propose turning our backs on kinfolk in need? What would that make us?"

"Of course we would not turn our backs on the elves still dwelling in Faerûn," Lady Veldann snapped. "Have we not always found a home for any who wish to Retreat? I would not turn away any Evereskan, or wood elf of the High Forest for that matter, who seeks safety here. That is Evermeet's purpose, after all."

"You speak lightly of asking us to abandon our homes," Gervas Imesfor observed. "Evereska is almost as old as Evermeet itself. Only two years ago we spent thousands of lives to defend it against the phaerimm. It would shame the valiant dead of that war to flee this fight."

Meraera Silden, the Speaker of Leuthilspar, stepped in.

"The point of whether or not we should aid Evereska and the High Forest may be moot," she observed. "The first question is, *can* we help them? Do we have sufficient strength? If the answer to that question is no, then our debate is without purpose."

"We ask only what you think you can spare," Imesfor said. "Five hundred archers and fifty mages would help us greatly, and would not place Evermeet itself in jeopardy. But you may need to consider more if you hope to aid the folk of the High Forest, too."

"We heard the exact same point raised two years ago, when we sent an expedition to Evereska's aid against the phaerimm," Grand Mage Breithel Olithir said. "Less than half of those we sent then came home, and none of the high mages. We cannot afford another such disaster in Faerûn."

"Talk of what we can spare and what we can afford to lose is absolutely pointless," Seiveril interjected. "If something is worth doing, then it is worth doing with all of our might! The defense of Evereska and the safeguarding of our kinfolk in the High Forest is not an act of charity on our part, but an act of *self-preservation*. The defense of Evermeet begins in the hills of Evereska and beneath the trees of old Eaerlann."

"We who Retreated to Evermeet did so because the wide seas serve as a mighty rampart against exactly the sort of threat that now menaces Evereska," Lady Veldann retorted. "If we had had the sense to leave matters in Faerûn alone, we would not have to consider this question."

"Lady Veldann, it does not matter whether we abandon Faerûn or not, because Faerûn will not abandon us," Seiveril replied. He stood and rested his hands on the cool glassteel of the table. "We learned three years ago that evil can and will follow us here, regardless of whether we 'provoke' it or not. For my part, I will take my chances with provoking those who would do us harm. They will hate and envy us no matter what we do, so it seems better to me to exert my strength against them in Faerûn than to wait until they come to Evermeet's shores."

The Dome of Stars fell quiet. Seiveril glared at Ammisyll Veldann, and she returned his anger with her own.

Lady Durothil turned to Amlaruil and said, "You have heard your council speak. Now what do you intend to do, Lady Moonflower?" Seiveril scowled at the deliberate insult the noblewoman delivered by refusing to address Amlaruil as queen, but Selsharra Durothil continued, "What is the throne's response to this latest catastrophe?"

Amlaruil didn't rise to Lady Durothil's provocation. She folded her hands in her lap.

"I will carefully weigh the question of how much assistance can be sent without placing Evermeet in undue danger," said the queen, "and I will then dispatch as much aid as I can. For today, it seems clear that we must learn all we can of the forces marching against the High Forest and Evereska." She turned to High Marshal Blackhelm. "Keryth, go with Lord Imesfor back through the elfgate to Evereska, and take a company of the Queen's Guard with you. I feel confident that we can spare that much, at least. Remain only as long as you must to survey the situation firsthand and return here to report."

"Yes, my queen," the general replied.

He rose and strode from the room, his helm tucked under one arm.

"Grand Mage Olithir," he queen continued, "redouble your efforts to scry our foes. Organize the mages of the Towers to find the daemonfey armies and spy out their strength and movements. I want to know what we are up against."

The high mage inclined his head and replied, "It will be done."

The queen stood, weariness evident in her posture, and said, "When we have learned a little more, we will meet again to consider our response."

CHAPTER 7

6 Ches, the Year of Lightning Storms

Araevin and Ilsevele set out from Waterdeep on a cold, bright day scoured by fierce westerly winds. With the two elves rode Grayth Holmfast, who wore a suit of light golden mail beneath a white surcoat emblazoned with the sunrise of Lathander, and his younger companion Brant, dressed in the orange surcoat of an aspirant to the Order of the Aster. Maresa Rost rounded out the party, wearing a jerkin of studded leather dyed deep crimson, a striking contrast with her pale skin and white hair. They had spent two days outfitting themselves, purchasing good horses, an ample supply of provisions, and equipment for their search.

"So, where exactly are we going?" Maresa asked as the keep of Daggerdale disappeared below the hills at their back. The cold waters of the Sea of Swords thundered and crashed below the cliffs a few hundred yards from the road, and the roaring wind made speech difficult.

"I am not sure," Araevin replied. "I have a sense of how far away the item we seek lies, and in what direction. I've also glimpsed the place where it lies, a ruined tower deep in a forest. Based on that intuition, I believe that we will find what we seek in the Forest of Wyrms, though it might be the Reaching Woods, or the Wood of Sharp Teeth, or possibly even some unnamed copse somewhere south of the Chionthar and north of the Small Teeth."

"You still haven't gotten around to telling me what we're looking for."

Araevin frowned. He could feel Ilsevele and Grayth endeavoring not to look at him as he answered. When it came down to it, he still didn't know Maresa well at all, and he hesitated to say too much. But he suspected that she was sharp enough to see through him if he didn't trust her with something close to the truth.

"I am looking for a set of enchanted gemstones," he said. "There are three of them. I have the first, and it permits me to sense the second."

"Enchanted? What do they do?"

"They hold spells," Araevin answered. "Like a wizard's spellbook. I'm interested in the spells that I think might be stored in the second and third stones."

"Fair enough," said Maresa. "I suppose there's no point in asking for a cut of the magic gems, but I'll require an even share of any other treasure we find."

"Agreed," said Araevin, then he fell silent, considering what else he should add.

Ilsevele spoke for him.

"There is something else, Maresa," she said. "We have reason to believe that there may be others who want these gems—sorcerers with demon servants. They will kill for them without hesitation. Be on your guard."

"There are always complications," the genasi said brightly. She patted the rapier at her hip. "Let them come."

"So we start near Soubar," Grayth said. "That's a tenday's ride, possibly more if the rains come early this spring. I guess we'll have time to get to know each other."

"I intend to cut seven days from that," Araevin said. "I know of an old portal that will shorten our journey by three hundred miles. It was built in the early days of ancient Illefarn. The gate will take us from the Ardeep Forest to an abandoned watchtower in the eastern portion of the Trollbark Forest."

"Is it safe to use?" Grayth asked, with no small anxiety.

"The portal is sound enough, though we will have to be careful when we reach the other side," Araevin answered. "The Trollbark is aptly named. But we won't cross more than ten miles or so of that forest before we meet the Trade Way again."

"Would it be better to remain on the road?" Ilsevele asked.

"I don't know. The road has its perils, too—brigands and marauding monsters from the High Moor, thieves and cutthroats in the roadside inns. On the other hand time might be important."

They rode on for the rest of the day, and by nightfall the company had reached the outskirts of the Ardeep Forest. The sea wind kept its strength all day and into the evening, though with sunset a low, scudding cloud cover set in, making for a lightless and gloomy night. The House of Long Silences was still almost ten miles farther on, so they decided to camp for the night in the shelter of a ruined hunting lodge, a moss-covered building made of rough-hewn logs and fieldstone. It was open to the sky, but with a little work they hoisted some of the fallen timbers back into place and spread evergreen boughs over the gaps. After stabling the horses in the other half of the old lodge and fixing supper over the campfire, they drew for watches and retired.

Araevin stretched himself out on his bedroll beneath a blanket, gazing up through the gaps in the makeshift roof at the gray clouds overhead. Though elves didn't sleep, they still needed a comfortable place to sit or lie down while they drifted off into the dreamlike Reverie. Anything a human could sleep in or on was more than adequate. Ilsevele lay by his side, her hand in his, her breathing slow and deep. He wondered what she thought of human-crowded Faerûn so far, and that reminded him of his first impressions when he traveled the continent. He wandered drowsily into the memories of his old journeys, and an hour or more passed as he gazed absently up at the clouds.

An electric jolt returned him to full wakefulness. Araevin sat upright with a gasp, his heart thundering. One of his alarm spells, a ward against scrying and magical spying, had been triggered. He scrambled to his feet and whirled around to see a strange, semitangible puckering in the air, the manifestation of some sort of divination magic. Within the distorted knuckle of air he glimpsed a sharply handsome face surmounted by two small black horns, one eye concealed beneath a rune-marked eye patch.

The daemonfey, he realized. *They are spying on us!*

"Araevin! What is it?" cried Ilsevele, startled by his sudden movement.

She seized her bow and groped for an arrow, rising to her knees as she searched wildly for a target.

Araevin ignored her and quickly worked a dispelling enchantment, wiping out the spell the other sorcerer was using. He sensed a growl of frustration, a snarl of pure hate, and the connection was severed. The mage closed his eyes and carefully enunciated the words of an amplifying spell, then stretched out his wizard's senses to encompass the whole camp. He could feel a distant presence, a tenuous thread linking their campsite with a far-off place many miles to the north and west.

"We have been spied on," Araevin said finally. "A scrying spell. I negated it."

Ilsevele paled and asked, "Who was it? Do they know where we are?"

"It was that daemonfey we saw at Reilloch," Araevin

replied. "The one with the eye patch. Most likely all he knows is that we are in Faerûn, camping in a forest. He did not watch us long enough to perceive more. But I wonder if he has spied on us before without our noticing him."

The rest of the company sat up in their bedrolls, looking at Araevin. Even Grayth, who had the watch, got up from the fireside and circled closer.

"Someone scried us?" the cleric asked.

"Yes," said Araevin. "I defeated this attempt, at least. I must remember to renew my defenses regularly from now on, to detect and block any such additional attempts in the future. They saw enough to recognize me, and perhaps Ilsevele too.

"Someone knows we're here."

❧ ❧ ❧ ❧ ❧

Five days had passed since Hill Elder Imesfor of Evereska had presented his city's plea to the High Council of Evermeet—five days of bitterly divisive debate, argument, and strife that left Seiveril Miritar as cold and empty as last month's ashes at the end of each day. Imesfor had returned to Evereska already, of course. Given the approach of an enemy army, the Hill Elder could not linger in Evermeet to plead his case in person. Seiveril therefore took up the Evereskan's cause as his own. He used every argument, every wile he could think of to shake the intransigence of Durothil, Veldann, and the other conservatives in the council, but to no avail. The council could not resolve to send Evermeet's army into danger again, not so soon after the costly campaign against the phaerimm and Kymil Nimesin's invasion.

As the sun fell on the eighth day of Ches, Seiveril returned to his comfortable townhouse, a small palace of white stone in the hills overlooking Leuthilspar's harbor. Even though their ancestral lands lay along Evermeet's northern coasts, like many other noble families, the Miritars had maintained a residence in the capital for some centuries. The high priest donned his clerical robes and went straight to a small grove close by his palace to perform the daily rites and invocations welcoming starrise, the time holy to Corellon Larethian. He was so exhausted and sick with frustration that he stumbled over the familiar words.

With a sigh, Seiveril halted in his devotions. He was alone in the grove. Any elves who wished the clerics of Corellon to seek some special blessing or intercede on their behalf with the other deities of the Seldarine usually sought out the Uilaevelen, the Moongrove, Leuthilspar's living temple to the elf gods. Feeling as weary as an aged human, Seiveril stared up into the sky, where a few faint and distant stars were beginning to appear in the gaps between the clouds.

"Lord of the Seldarine, give me patience and strength," he prayed. "Help me to find the way to guide your People onto the right path. I cannot do it myself."

He watched the sky darken for some time, his mind calm and empty. Then, as he turned away, he caught sight of a white owl winging silently through the treetops. Seiveril scented magic in the air. The beautiful creature hooted softly and wheeled over his head before descending to the ground. Then the owl shimmered into a fountain of silver light, growing and changing. In a moment Queen Amlaruil stood before him, dressed in a silvery gown with a cloak of soft white feathers draped over her shoulders.

"Good evening, Lord Miritar," she said. "I hope you will forgive this unusual intrusion, but I wished to have a word with you without the rest of the council at hand."

Seiveril bowed and replied, "You startled me, my lady. I sometimes forget that you were a grand mage before you were queen. What can I do for you?"

"You can listen, and perhaps understand. I have come to tell you that I have composed my reply to Evereska's request for assistance."

"You have decided not to help them," the lord said. "You wanted to tell me first."

The queen nodded and said, "I will send what help I can,

Seiveril. Without showing my hand I can send a number of mages, spellarchers, spellsingers, and bladesingers to Evereska. Some of them can journey on from there to fight in the High Forest. But I cannot send any high mages, and I cannot send more than a few dozen carefully chosen warriors. And of course, I will offer safe haven here in Evermeet to any elf who seeks it."

"It is not enough. Even if Evereska has the strength to fend off this newest assault, we cannot take the chance that the city will be weakened any further."

"And I will not be permitted to take the chance that Evermeet might be rendered vulnerable by sending more of our strength to the mainland," said Amlaruil. She folded her arms beneath the white cape. "You have seen that the council cannot reach consensus on any response that requires us to send our warriors to Faerûn. While we waste time in debate, the danger to our kinfolk grows each day. I will do what I can now."

"My queen, it is up to you to end the debate," Seiveril said. "The council serves at your pleasure. We hold no authority other than that of our collective titles and stations. If we cannot agree, then you must decide. You hold your throne to defend Evermeet, and all the People everywhere, against the threats that gather in this world. It is your paramount duty. You cannot allow Selsharra Durothil and Ammisyll Veldann to hinder you from taking whatever steps are necessary to preserve our civilization."

"Do not presume to lecture me on my duties, Lord Miritar. I may have only held the throne for sixty years, but I have stood beside it for more than five hundred."

Seiveril lowered his gaze and said, "I apologize, my lady."

Amlaruil stood in silence for a long moment. Then her face softened.

"You know as well as I that I rule by the consent of the People. I am not a tyrant who can drive my subjects in any direction I choose. The monarch of Evermeet represents the collective will of all the People and must remain subservient to their goals and desires, not her own. While I may not care for the ambitions and arrogance of Durothil or Veldann or any of the other Houses who follow them, I cannot escape this one fact: Perhaps as much as a third of Evermeet's folk believe strongly that spending our strength to defend realms in Faerûn is pure folly."

"They are mistaken," Seiveril said.

"I am inclined to believe so too, though I find that I lack your unshakable certainty on the question. But regardless of how I feel about the matter, I cannot ignore the reservations of so many of my subjects."

"Reservations or not, elves are in dire peril in Faerûn. We cannot stand by and do nothing!" Seiveril took a small step toward the queen and caught her hand in both of his. "Send something, I beg you. Whatever force you dispatch will be better than nothing. Surely, Durothil and Veldann cannot prevent you from doing that."

"Yet they can," Amlaruil said with a sigh. She extricated her hand from Seiveril's and turned away, pacing across the moonlit glade. "Soon after the council adjourned for the day, Selsharra Durothil came to speak to me privately. She informed me that if I dispatched any expedition to Faerûn, she would recall all Durothils from Evermeet's service—and with them, the Veldanns, as well as all the Houses that owe them fealty. That constitutes something like three in ten of our mages and warriors."

Seiveril's stomach ached with dread.

"Surely," he said, "not all of the Durothils and Veldanns would abandon their oaths and return to their homes?"

"Some would defy Lady Durothil, I am sure. But how many others from different families might be encouraged to express their own private reservations in the same way?" Amlaruil hugged her shoulders against the growing chill in the night air and continued, "I dare not call her bluff, Seiveril. If my actions force the strong sun elf Houses to repudiate their allegiance to the throne, I open the door for horrors such as we cannot imagine. No, I must accept that Evermeet's heart is divided on the question of whether to turn our faces toward Faerûn or away from it, and as long as Evermeet's heart is so troubled, my own must be too."

"Durothil needs to be put in her place," Seiveril snarled into the night. "The Seldarine themselves have anointed House Moonflower as the ruling House of Evermeet. If she opposes you, that is one thing, but she is trying her will against that of Corellon Larethian himself, and that I will not stand."

"That may be the case, but it is not for me to punish her, nor for you." Amlaruil looked back to Seiveril and said, "I must return before I am missed. Since you have argued so passionately for intervention, I wanted you to hear my decision first, and I wanted you to know why I made it. Needless to say, I do not want anyone else to know of the threat Lady Durothil issued me. I am entrusting you with this so that you will understand why you must yield the point."

Seiveril closed his eyes and replied, "I will not repeat this to anyone. It stands between the two of us and the Seldarine alone."

"Good." Amlaruil whispered the words of an arcane spell, and her form began to glow silver and shift its shape again. "Your passion does you credit, Seiveril. My hands may be tied, but perhaps yours are not."

An instant later, she took wing again, a white shadow flitting through the darkness beneath the trees.

Seiveril watched her fly off, his mind turning. The gods themselves had ordained the ascendancy of House Moonflower, yet still there were those who envied Amlaruil's rule and thought to govern in her place. He looked up to the stars overhead again.

"Corellon, show me the path," he whispered. "There must be something I can do."

The forest seemed chill and shadowed, empty in the growing darkness. But then a single moonbeam broke through a gap in the clouds to flood the silent grove with silver light. Seiveril turned his face up to Selûne, and an idea arose in his mind. The audacity of it staggered him, but if it worked—if it worked!—he might turn the course of events as surely as a few well-placed stones might alter a river's flow.

◈ ◈ ◈ ◈ ◈

Dank green moss clung heavily to the twisted limbs of the dark-boled trees looming overhead. Araevin and his companions had traveled three hundred miles south with a few short steps through the ancient elfgate in the House of Long Silences. The broken stump of an abandoned elven watchtower dating back to old Miyeritar stood over the southerly arch of the elfgate. Its ragged top no longer pierced the dense, close canopy of the forest, but the plaza of cracked flagstones surrounding it created a small clearing beneath the trees.

"I don't like the looks of this," Maresa said. The pale genasi led her horse away from the gate, studying the shadows under the trees. "The whole place positively reeks of trolls."

"They prefer to hunt by night," Araevin said. "With luck, we'll reach clear ground before dark. We would be wise to proceed without delay." He nodded at a thickly overgrown trail leading away from the tower, following the bed of an ancient roadway. "If we follow that path, we'll meet the Trade Way in about ten miles."

"You've come this way before?" asked Ilsevele.

"Once, about fifty years ago, when I was engaged in exploring the portals in Elorfindar's care. I was fortunate enough to avoid the trolls, but there are a couple of difficult stream crossings ahead."

"Nothing brightens a day of winter travel like the prospect of a good soaking," Grayth observed. He sighed and took his mount by the reins, leading it away from the tower. The brush and tree limbs overhanging the path were too thick for riding.

Ilsevele, as the most wood-wise of the party, took the lead, bow in hand. Araevin followed her, leading both his horse and hers so that she could watch the trail ahead without tending a mount. Maresa and Grayth followed, and the young swordsman Brant brought up the rear, leading the packhorse along with his own mount.

The trail was much as Araevin remembered it, climbing steeply up and down as it wandered eastward over a series of fingerlike ridges stretching north from the nearby Troll Hills. The forest was soggy and cold, with swift, narrow rivulets of water rushing down in hundreds of nameless little brooks that crossed their path, and when the trail reached the ravine and valley floors between the ridges, it usually met a loud, swift, and cold stream.

At the boulder-strewn bank of one such stream about an hour's walk from the tower, Araevin found Ilsevele crouched over the trail.

"Tracks?" he asked.

She glanced up as he approached and said, "How often do people come this way?"

"It's not really on the way to anywhere. Adventuring companies searching for the Warlock's Crypt might pass this way. I suppose there are a few who might seek out the watchtower, hoping to find some lost elven treasure or maybe make use of the portal, as we did. What do you see?"

"Troll sign, not more than a few hours old. At least four or five of them, I think. They're following the trail ahead of us." Ilsevele straightened and brushed off her hands. "I've seen tracks both coming and going. We may meet these fellows if they come back this way."

The company pressed on, fording the stream and climbing back up the heavily overgrown ridge on the far side. They marched for another two hours, as the overcast slowly descended and a cold rain began to fall, lightly at first but growing more steady as the afternoon wore on. The going was even more difficult than Araevin remembered. At no point did the trail open up enough for them to mount their horses, and finding ways to get the animals across the treacherous broken streambeds took far more time than he had supposed. By dusk Araevin guessed that they still had three or four more miles before reaching the forest's edge. He began to consider the question of whether they should push on, or make camp.

A shrill cry from ahead interrupted his thoughts.

"Trolls!" shouted Ilsevele. *"Trolls!"*

Araevin looked up from the trail, only to realize that Ilsevele had gotten far enough ahead of him that he could not see her through the dense underbrush. He cursed himself for allowing his attention to narrow to the trail right in front of his feet, and hurriedly threw the reins of his horse over a nearby branch.

"Trolls ahead!" he called over his shoulder, just in case the others had not heard Ilsevele's cry, and he sprinted down the trail. Ilsevele's bow thrummed twice, then twice again. From somewhere out of his sight, a wet, burbling voice howled in pain, and others joined in with cries of anger and bloodlust.

Aillesel seldarie, he thought as he dashed over the difficult trail. Let her be safe! Let me reach her before the trolls do.

He knew that Ilsevele was a highly trained warrior, as good with a bow as any he'd ever seen, but still the thought of her standing alone against blood-maddened trolls made his heart ache with terror as if a cold iron knife twisted in his chest.

He topped a sharp rise in the trail, and found the scene laid out before him. Ilsevele stood beside a gnarled oak, calmly firing arrow after arrow into a gang of half a dozen trolls who thrashed up the path toward her, loping along with their knuckles dragging on the ground at the end of their long, gangly arms. The vile creatures roared and bellowed in challenge, their mouths filled with rotten black fangs. One troll had fallen writhing on the rain-wet boulders, transfixed by five arrows, but one by one it plucked the arrows out of its body. Its spurting green blood slowed to a trickle and halted as its warty flesh puckered and healed around the injuries. Trolls were not so easily killed.

Araevin hurried down toward Ilsevele, leaping from boulder to boulder. He heard Maresa at his heels, swearing like a Calishite sailor, and behind her the heavy footfalls of the two humans as they thundered toward the fight. Ilsevele's bow sang like a harp, and her arrows hissed angrily through the air.

Head-sized rocks hurled back up the hill in response as the trolls pelted Ilsevele with anything they could get their hands on.

"Elf-meat! Elf-meat!" they cried, scrambling up the hillside.

Araevin shoved his lightning wand into his belt and fished in his bandolier for the reagents for a spell. He knew from long practice what each pocket held without even looking. As he rolled a pinch of sulfur between the fingers of his left hand he quickly barked out the words of a fire spell. From his right forefinger a single gleaming bead of orange streaked out toward the charging trolls, only to detonate in a thunderous burst of flame. Trolls shrieked and scattered, flames clinging to their malformed bodies.

"Well done, Araevin!" Grayth exclaimed.

The priest drew up abreast of Araevin and unsheathed his hand-and-a-half sword with a ringing rasp. Then he skidded down the path to meet the trolls in front, less than twenty yards from Ilsevele's perch. Brant followed half a step behind him. The hulking monsters screeched in rage, their mossy hides smoking from the flames of Araevin's fireball.

"For Lathander's glory!" the warrior-priest cried.

He leaped in close to the first troll, taking off its arm at the elbow before ducking under its snapping jaws to ram his sword deep into the creature's gizzard. Brant fought at his side, guarding Grayth's back as he fended off another troll with a flurry of shining steel.

"You need fire to kill them!" Araevin called. "They'll just keep healing until we burn them!"

"Right," Ilsevele replied.

She whispered the words to a spell of her own, and suddenly the arrow in her bow blazed with brilliant white flame. She took careful aim, and shot the troll flailing at Brant through the throat. The creature's knees buckled, and it went to all fours, pawing at the burning missile

Forsaken House • 123

lodged in its neck, at which point Brant hewed off its foul head.

Araevin felt the brilliant chill of magic rippling in the air behind him. He glanced back to see Maresa aiming a wand of her own at the trolls trying to circle around the two swordsmen holding the path. A jet of roaring flame sizzled out from the genasi's wand and she seared one of the trolls into a lump of black, burning meat.

"Hah! Take that!" she called at her foes, leaping down after them with her rapier in one hand and her wand in the other. "Who wants to play next, eh?"

Three trolls were down, and the remaining monsters wavered in confusion. Araevin chose to make their decision easy for them. He conjured up a globe of swirling green acid and hurled it at the biggest troll left. The orb arched through the air and caught the troll across the head and chest even as it tried to twist out of the way, raising one long arm to fend it off. The creature shrieked in agony and staggered back as its flesh smoked and sizzled. The other two trolls broke and ran as their leader shambled off. Grayth and Brant pursued them a few steps, slashing at their backs as they loped away.

"I'm not done with you yet!" Grayth called after them.

Ilsevele took aim at the acid-burned troll staggering blindly away, and put it down with two arrows in its misshapen skull.

"Should I take the other two?" she asked.

"No, let them go," Araevin said. "They might serve to warn off any other trolls in the area."

"Or they might go round up some friends," Maresa said. She tucked her wand into her belt and sheathed her rapier. "How many more fireballs can you cast?"

"Quite a few," Araevin answered. "I knew we intended to travel the Trollbark today, and made suitable preparations." He glanced at the genasi. "By the way, you didn't mention that you knew some magic."

"It didn't come up before. Besides, I like to keep you guessing."

Maresa grinned fiercely and turned away to pick her way back toward the horses.

The elf mage shook his head. He glanced over at Ilsevele, and took her hand.

"Are you well?" he asked.

"Of course. It will take more than a few trolls to frighten me. You should know that by now."

"I can't help it. I fear that something might happen to you."

"I can look after myself, thank you," Ilsevele replied. "You keep an eye on yourself, my betrothed. I have too many years invested in you to start over again with some other thickheaded fellow."

CHAPTER 8

10 Ches, the Year of Lightning Storms

Cold and heavy, the rain arrived in the hour before sunrise and lasted all day. Ribbons of icy water cascaded down from the green canopy far above, turning the snow mantling the forest floor into frigid slush. Gaerradh could feel the first stirrings of spring in the High Forest—after all, it was raining, not snowing—but that did not mean the day was at all pleasant. Her woolen cloak was sodden and useless, her feet were wet and cold, and she could not stop shivering.

She reached a boulder-strewn streambed and scrambled up onto a large, flat rock that had been washed clean of snow, her eyes on the band of open sky above the creek. She searched long and carefully before giving a small wave of her hand.

"It's clear," she called softly.

Behind her, a long column of marching elves threaded their way along the trail. More than a hundred of Rheitheillaethor's folk followed her. Unlike those who had fought at the village, they were not all warriors. Children and untrained youths, artisans or craftsmen who did not trust their martial skills, mothers of young children, and those rare elves hindered by age or injury, made up three-quarters of the company. A short string of pack animals—mostly elk and branta, temporarily held to their tasks with the urging of druids—carried the light shelters and furnishings the elves needed as well as a small number of wounded, but each elf also carried a pack of provisions. Two dozen archers, scouts, and mages flanked the marching line of folk who could not be expected to fight in their own defense.

Gaerradh kept her bow at hand and maintained her watch as the first of the marching elves lightly leaped from stone to stone across the stream. So far, they'd avoided additional battles with the demon-elves or their orc marauders, but only by fleeing deeper into the forest. All across the western High Forest, the wood elves were in flight, abandoning their camps and villages to seek shelter in the trackless depths of the immense woodland. Not all of the elven villages had managed to escape the invaders. In four days Gaerradh's company had found one band of refugees slaughtered in a burned glade, and a village that had been surrounded and systematically exterminated. She still saw the flayed bodies every time she closed her eyes.

"Rillifane Rallathil, Master of the Forest, hide us from our enemies," she prayed under her breath. "Spread your branches out over your People, and conceal us from our foes."

Somewhere ahead they would find sanctuary. The High Forest was simply too large a hiding place, and even the most determined pursuer couldn't hope to run all the fleeing bands to ground.

But they might catch up to a few.

A low whistle caught Gaerradh's ear. She looked back

at the column beside her. Lady Morgwais stood nearby, speaking words of encouragement to each elf passing by.

"We will halt for a short time on the other side of the stream," she called out. "Move well under the trees, so that we will be hidden from any foes flying over the riverbed. Take care to build smokeless fires, but build them anyway. We all need a hot meal and a little warmth after this dreary day."

Morgwais watched the last of the elves cross the stream. Small and sprightly, she had passed up and down the marching band constantly for days, her light laughter an instant cure for fatigue or despondency. The Lady of the Wood seemed indefatigable, and her unwavering confidence had done wonders for keeping the band moving in the face of the waning winter. She gazed after the company, and Gaerradh caught a glimpse of utter exhaustion as the lady's energetic mask crumbled.

The ranger quickly slid down the boulder to the trail. Sheeril followed, leaping down beside her.

"Lady Morgwais, are you well?" Gaerradh asked.

Morgwais rallied with a smile and replied, "As well as any of us."

"Nonsense. You've marched twice as far as anyone, and you've kept a song for us all and a laugh on your lips for days now. You must make sure to rest, too."

"I'll thank you to keep that thought to yourself. Besides, you and the rest of our scouts have covered far more ground than I have," Morgwais said. She moved a short distance under the spreading boughs of a blueleaf and found a reasonably dry log to sit on. "Come, you've earned a break as well."

Gaerradh started to decline, but then she realized that Morgwais might need some encouragement of her own. She agreed with a nod, and joined the lady on the stump, Sheeril curled up at her feet. They sat together in silence, listening to the voice of the stream and the rainwater dripping through the branches.

"Do you think they'll follow us all the way to the Lost Peak strongholds?" Gaerradh said finally. "It's nearly two hundred miles from Rheitheillaethor to the mountains."

"I don't know," Morgwais said with a sigh, "but I fear so. Look around you. What do you see?"

"The forest. A stand of blueleafs here. The Ilthaelrun, there. There's a nest of snow owls above us in this tree. The female is watching us with no small alarm."

"It's a pretty spot. We could raise a camp here and stay a season or two, and we wouldn't lack for anything," Morgwais said. "The whole of the High Forest is more or less the same to us, isn't it? Our people have no need to till a river plain, or trade at a crossroads, or build a town to house our craftsmen and merchants. We could easily settle anywhere in the forest. In fact, there is no reason we couldn't march another hundred miles farther south and hide among the Starmounts. One place in the forest is much the same as any other, so why not abandon the eastern reaches for a time? Let the orcs and the tainted ones have it."

"I don't care for the idea of giving such murderous beasts leave to poison our homeland."

"Nor do I, but that is not the mark I was shooting at. Nothing in the lands we hold in the eastern reaches of the forest is particularly valuable to us, really, which suggests to me that territory in the forest is not particularly important to the daemonfey, either, at least not for its own sake. Oh, there are plenty of old ruins they may have an interest in, but we only guard a handful of those places." Morgwais met Gaerradh's gaze and said, "They are here for *us,* Gaerradh. Not our lands, not our possessions. They intend to break our strength and scatter us, perhaps drive us out of the forest all together. And that means they will follow us wherever we flee."

Gaerradh drew in a breath. She had been looking forward to the refuges of the Lost Peaks, the secret glens and hidden vales in the heart of the forest, long since prepared as havens and strongholds in times of trouble. But if Lady Morgwais was right. . . .

"We will have to stand and fight, then," she said quietly. "Not yet, perhaps, and not here. But soon."

The lady nodded and said, "We are not prepared for an enemy like this. There are a hundred or more bands and companies of our folk scattered over this forest, but only a handful of those can muster even fifty warriors. Until we gather our strength somewhere, we will be harried and hunted. Somehow I must summon all the companies, all the clans and villages, together, and build an army to meet these foes. And I must pray that we have the strength to defeat them."

"I cannot remember any such gathering of the People in this forest."

"It hasn't happened since the days of Eaerlann, and Eaerlann fell almost five hundred years ago—long before your time, and even a little before mine."

"What of our kinfolk in Evereska or Evermeet? Have we heard from them?" Gaerradh asked. "We have no experience in raising armies, but they do."

Morgwais looked away.

"Evereska is endangered, too," she said. "I have spoken to Turlang the treant, and he tells me that armies of evil creatures, including more of the demonspawn, are marching south through the Delimbiyr Vale toward the Shaeradim. After the war against the phaerimm, Evereska has no strength to spare for us."

"Well, what of Evermeet, then?"

"I do not know. I have sent word to Amlaruil's court, but I have heard no response."

"Do you think they would refuse us help?" Gaerradh asked with alarm.

"No, I doubt that. But I do think it is entirely possible that Evermeet might take months to decide how to help, and we might not have that much time for the sun elves to think over our situation for us." Morgwais stood and dusted off her seat, shaking her head. "You know sun elves. Anything worth doing deserves ten years of second-guessing before they'll agree to it. Sometimes I wonder how they manage to pick out their clothes in the morning."

Gaerradh looked up at Morgwais and asked, "Were you not married to a sun elf?"

"Yes, long ago. It took him fifty years to propose to me," Morgwais said with a laugh. "Listen, Gaerradh, there is something I want you to do. Go north to the Silver Marches and tell Alustriel of Silverymoon what is happening here in the forest. I have no doubt that she knows much of it already, but you have followed and fought this new foe for days now. She will want to know what you have seen, and what you think."

"Do you think she will help us?"

"I don't know. The cities of the Silver Marches have enemies of their own to guard against. But she and her sisters have always been friends of the People, and she is a Chosen of Mystra." Morgwais rested a hand on Gaerradh's shoulder. "And . . . if we are driven from our refuges, then Silverymoon must know that they could face this peril next. If I cannot contain the daemonfey, it will fall to Alustriel and her confederation to do it."

☙ ☙ ☙ ☙ ☙

The galleries of the Dome of Stars were crowded with elves waiting on the high council. Seiveril studied the spectators with a smile of satisfaction. For the last two days he had spoken to dozens of friends, acquaintances, and allies, asking them to attend the open session and pass the word along to anyone they knew. Many of the onlookers were men and women of the Queen's Guard, the Spellarchers, the Eagle Knights, and other elite companies of Evermeet's armies. The clerics of Corellon Larethian and the other deities of the Seldarine were well represented too, and with them many of the temple knights and holy champions of the elven faith. Seiveril also noted no small number of nobles and merchants whose sympathies belonged to Lady Durothil and her faction. Apparently Durothil and Veldann had heard of his call to his adherents and allies, and they had made sure to summon their own supporters to the day's council meeting.

Surprisingly, he was not at all nervous. He knew what

he intended to say, and he was certain of his course. The low murmur of hundreds of voices filled the chamber. Seiveril could feel the eyes of the other council members on him, but he waited patiently for the queen.

At the appointed hour, Amlaruil swept into the Dome, clad in a formal dress that seemed to cascade from her shoulders like a shower of silver. Her diadem tiara gleamed in the soft starlight of the chamber. With the rest of the council, Seiveril rose as she entered, and bowed respectfully before resuming his seat.

Amlaruil took the golden scepter of her office and rapped it twice on the glassteel table.

"I call the council to order," she said, her voice carrying through the great chamber. "Lord Miritar has requested the opportunity to address the council before we consider our ongoing deliberations. I hereby yield the floor to Lord Seiveril Miritar."

Seiveril stood slowly and bowed to the throne. He had half-expected Selsharra Durothil to protest the breach of custom, but evidently she was not quite foolish enough to attempt to keep him from speaking out of order. Amlaruil would allow him to say what he wanted to say whether she protested or not, and the attempt would make her look petty and spiteful. He turned to face the crowded galleries ringing the chamber, and the crowd fell silent, awaiting his words.

"Ten thousand years ago," he began, "Evermeet was founded by our ancestors as a refuge from the perils and dangers of the rest of the world, a place where the People might exist apart from the savages and barbarians, the monsters and the dragons, who have always been envious of the beauty we bring into the world. Yet Evermeet has rarely been a perfect sanctuary. Early in our history we battled the evil creatures of the sea. Later we fought against enemies who came against us through extraplanar gates and hidden tunnels. And only three years ago we were faced with a terrible alliance of all our enemies, including traitors from within our own land who followed Kymil Nimesin in his war against the throne.

With courage and the favor of the Seldarine, we have triumphed over all of these foes. Evermeet has not been the place of peace our forefathers dreamed of, but it is a place of beauty and strength.

"Yet we are not the only elves who walk in this world. Across the sea lie the realms of our kinfolk, realms such as Evereska and the Yuirwood, the High Forest and the Wealdath. Just as we are one People, bound by one language, one history, one destiny, so are our realms all one. If an elf is slain in the High Forest, then Evermeet has lost a son. If a city is thrown down in ruin in the Graypeaks, than Leuthilspar has been sacked. Some among this council do not recognize this essential truth. While our kinfolk in Evereska and the High Forest face war and devastation, our leaders refuse to aid them. I cannot find it in my heart to go along with this decision.

"I have come before you today to announce my resignation from this council. It is with a heavy heart that I lay aside the duties and responsibilities King Zaor called on me to accept sixty years ago. But from time to time, we are all called to answer our own consciences. For many days now I have sought Corellon Larethian's counsel, and this is the answer that the Seldarine have shown me: I must go to Faerûn.

"I must go to Faerûn, and I call on each of you who feels as I do to join me. The council and the throne are unable to ask Evermeet's People to accept the burden of fighting in the defense of distant lands we have long abandoned. Very well; I ask none but willing volunteers to join me. Our kinfolk in Evereska and the High Forest are threatened by terrible new enemies, and I mean to help them. Our ancient lands have grown wild and dangerous, and I mean to restore them.

"If you believe that the time of our People is done in Faerûn, I do not want you. If you fear that your strength will be missed too much here, that your duties are too important to lay aside, then I do not ask you to abandon them. If you simply do not care what becomes of kinfolk who live thousands of miles away, then I despise you! But if you think, as I do, that it is an act of cowardice and complicity to name something evil, and refuse to oppose it with all your might and will and power, then I call on you to join me in this crusade.

"Make your farewells, sons and daughters of Evermeet. Lay your affairs in order, walk with your children, your lovers, and your parents in the sacred glens of this blessed isle one last time. Then gird yourself in mail, and take up your bows, swords, and lances, and come to me at Elion. There I will gather my host. In ten days' time we will pass out of Evermeet back to Faerûn, and we will show our enemies whether or not we have any strength left to do good in this world. But know this: Whether I lead a mighty host of ten thousand, a legion of a thousand, a brave company of a hundred, or none but myself, I will go."

"I will go, my friends. This is what Corellon Larethian has put in my heart." Seiveril paused, and gathered his strength for a mighty cry. *"Who is with me?"*

The Dome of Stars erupted into chaos, with hundreds of voices calling out at once. From the gallery came a chorus of "I am!" and "I will go!" and "My sword is yours!" But mixed in with the rousing cries of those willing to volunteer came catcalls and other voices shouting "Madness!" and "Treason! Treason!"

At the table, all the rest of the high councilors were on their feet, every bit as agitated as the partisans in the gallery.

"You have no right!" Selsharra Durothil screeched. "You have no right, Miritar. You cannot choose to launch a war because you, and you alone, think it is the right thing to do!"

"I cannot be expected to defend Evermeet if half my soldiers go off to Faerûn," Keryth Blackhelm snapped. "This is reckless, Lord Seiveril!"

"I will go, and I will bring two hundred of my archers and scouts with me!" the wood elf princess Jerreda Starcloak cried. "Our people are fighting for their lives in the High Forest. I will not turn my back on them."

"Lord Miritar, I cannot allow you to take high mages

away from Evermeet," Grand Mage Olithir said. His calm manner was belied by his wide eyes and pale face. "We have too few left after Nimesin's war and the fight against the phaerimm. We dare not risk the loss of any more."

Ammisyll Veldann kept her composure. She simply turned to look at Amlaruil, who remained seated in her high seat with her face impassive.

"Surely, my queen, you will not permit this act of madness to proceed," Ammisyll said in a dangerously quiet voice. "Or does Lord Miritar defy the will of this council with your blessing?"

Amlaruil betrayed no emotion, but she stood slowly and set her scepter on the table. The lords and ladies fell silent, awaiting her words, and even the chaos in the gallery diminished as the crowds there realized that the queen was about to speak.

"I do not condone this crusade," she said. "Evermeet's army will not leave this island unless I order it. Lord Miritar does not dictate policy for the throne or the council."

"You will put a stop to this nonsense, then?" Lady Veldann said sharply.

"No," Amlaruil replied. "I did not say that."

"Do you mean to say that you do not approve of Miritar's ridiculous crusade, but you refuse to stop it?" Ammisyll Veldann fought to keep the disbelief from her face, but failed. "Is it the case that you are lying when you say you intend to enforce the consensus of the council, or do you simply lack the strength of will to govern as monarch?"

"Watch your tongue!" snapped Keryth Blackhelm. "I will not tolerate such speech here."

Amlaruil drew herself up and fixed her piercing gaze on the noblewoman.

"I am not lying, Ammisyll. As monarch I do not condone Lord Miritar's call for a voluntary expedition, and any efforts he makes do not reflect the official policies of the throne. And I have no lack of strength, as you should well know. The reason I do not intend to interfere with Lord Miritar is simple: It is not my place to dictate to any citizen of this realm where he or she goes and what he or she does, provided they obey the laws of the realm and respect the authority of the throne."

"So I could gather a so-called voluntary army to go invade the Moonshaes, for instance, and you would not view it as the throne's place to stop me?" Veldann snarled. She threw up her hands in disgust. "This is anarchy!"

"That is a poorly considered example, Lady Veldann," Zaltarish the scribe observed. "In that case, you would be taking an action that would provoke war with another state. That is indeed an affair of the crown, and you would be stopped. But Lord Seiveril proposes to go, as a private citizen and on his own cognizance, to fight in the service of an elven realm that has been attacked by the same enemy who has already assaulted us once. He would not be creating any state of war that does not already exist between Evermeet and another realm."

"Bah! My point remains the same. Miritar is circumventing the decision of this council. He cannot be allowed to do this."

"And how would you stop me, Lady Veldann?" Seiveril retorted. "Would you have me imprisoned, perhaps? For what offense? Stating my intention to leave Evermeet? Are we not each of us free to come or go from this realm whenever we like?"

"I think I would begin with sedition," Lady Veldann said. "Perhaps rebellion against the throne."

"So now you call it sedition when a free citizen of Evermeet chooses to leave and asks if others will follow?" Seiveril said. "You have a broad definition of the term."

"We may not have the authority to bar any who want to follow you on your fool's errand from leaving," Selsharra Durothil said, "but it is certainly a seditious act to seduce the defenders of this island into abandoning their duties. We will not permit you to strip our defenses bare, Seiveril. If you try it, you will be stopped."

"Now you are the one who presumes to speak for the throne, Lady Durothil," Amlaruil said. "I am quite aware of what constitutes sedition, and I will decide if or when we must respond to Lord Miritar's call. Do not issue threats in my name."

The queen turned to Seiveril. She frowned, considering her words.

"Lord Miritar, I accept your resignation with sorrow. You must do what you are called to do. But I cannot allow you to leave Evermeet defenseless, and I cannot allow you to divide our citizens into two camps. Volunteers may follow you, and I will not stop them. But you are not to coerce any into coming with you, and if I ask some to remain to attend their duties here, you are not to encourage them to leave."

"I agree," Seiveril said.

He bowed, and descended from the council table to the floor of the great hall. Jerreda Starcloak followed him, sparing one daggerlike glance for Durothil and Veldann. Seiveril glanced out over the crowded gallery, and roars of approval greeted his ears along with jeers and insults.

"I hope you know what you have started here, Seiveril Miritar," the wood elf noblewoman said quietly into his ear.

Seiveril drew in a deep breath and nodded.

"I do," he said. Then he strode out of the room, beneath the great archway, as first dozens, then scores and scores of elves in the council gallery detached themselves from their comrades and companions in order to follow him out into the night.

❦ ❦ ❦ ❦ ❦

After sheltering for the night in a ruined mill near the Trade Way, Araevin and his small company arose early the next morning and left the Trollbark behind them. The weather remained cold and gray, with a light but steady rain that left them miserable and sodden as they followed the Trade Way south. They soon came to the crossroads where the Coast Way split off to head south toward the city of Baldur's Gate, while the Trade Way turned southeast toward Soubar and Scornubel. Araevin paused at the crossroads, eyes closed as he concentrated on the glimmering intuition the *telkiira* had planted in his mind, and he pointed toward the Scornubel road.

"It's almost due east of us now," he said. "We're definitely getting closer, but we're not there yet."

"I hope somebody hasn't pocketed the second stone and walked off with it," Maresa observed. "We might follow the stupid bastard all over Faerûn."

Araevin shook his head with a wry smile. The genasi had an acerbic manner that reminded him of her mother, but she was quicker to laugh than Theledra had ever been. "It's not moving, I'm pretty sure of that."

They followed the Trade Way south and east. Each day Araevin was careful to renew his defenses against scrying spells, and he kept a wary eye out for anyone or anything that seemed to take too much interest in their passing. On two occasions he felt the cold feather-touch of some enemy prying at his barriers, seeking to circumvent his defenses and spy on him again, but each time Araevin managed to parry the attempts.

Late on the second day they crossed the Boareskyr Bridge over the Winding Water, and they came to the town of Soubar early on the fourth day. The spring mud slowed them considerably. Many merchants had abandoned the roads, waiting for drier weather before trying to move their heavy wagons. They passed a dozen or so parties of fellow travelers each day—pilgrims bound for some shrine or another, caravans who packed their wares on surefooted mules instead of heavy carts, far-roving patrols of soldiers from Baldur's Gate and Scornubel, adventuring companies in search of ruins to loot, nobles and their entourages riding to visit distant kin, bands of dwarf smiths and ore cutters looking for work, troupes of acrobats and entertainers, imperious mages who often as not traveled on phantom horses or flying carpets, and more than a few gangs of ruffians, brigands, and highwaymen, some of whom thought to waylay Araevin and his friends, at least until Ilsevele shot a crossbow out of someone's hands or Araevin used a lightning bolt or similar spell to scare them off. Meanwhile, the weather warmed a bit each day, until by the time they rode into Soubar the fields were a luxurious deep green and the sun no longer rose on thick frosts each day.

In Soubar they rested for a day and a night at an inn called the Blue Griffon, drying out their clothes and re-provisioning. Then, on the morning of the twelfth of Ches, they set out again, following the cart tracks of woodcutters northeast toward the great dark verge of the Forest of Wyrms, fifteen miles from Soubar and the road. At first they passed through prosperous if well-fortified farms, homesteads with houses and barns made from thick fieldstone and guarded by small packs of wolfhounds. But the farms gradually thinned out as they drew closer to the forest, until finally there was nothing more than a wild, desolate moorland hard by the forest itself. The company crested a low rise and found themselves at the forest's doorstep.

"In there?" Maresa asked with a nod of her head.

"Yes. Not more than fifteen or twenty miles, I think," Araevin replied.

"Why is everything in a forest?" the genasi muttered to herself. "First the Ardeep, then the Trollbark, and now the Forest of Wyrms. I'm getting damned tired of trees."

"These are the places where the elven empires of long ago raised their cities and towers," Araevin replied. "The Ardeep was the heart of the ancient realm of Illefarn. The Trollbark was part of the realm of Miyeritar, which is what the High Moor used to be called before dark magic destroyed Miyeritar during the Crown Wars. In the long years since, the Trollbark has grown wild and savage, forgetful of the elves who once roamed its hills and valleys. Even the Reaching Wood and the Forest of Wyrms were part of the old realm of Shantel Othreier, which also fell during the Crown Wars."

"All this land was once forested," Ilsevele added. "A single great forest stretched from the Spine of the World to the Lake of Steam."

Maresa gave her a skeptical look. Grayth glanced at her as well.

"I knew the forests of the western lands were formerly much larger," the Lathanderite said, "But one single forest? What could have happened to it?"

"Vast reaches of the woodland were devastated in the ancient Crown Wars, or burned by dragons, or cleared during the rise of the human empires that followed the elven realms," Araevin answered.

"So the remaining forests mark the spots where the old elven realms once stood?" asked Grayth.

"Yes, but I believe that the forests remain because the elven realms were there, and not the other way around. My ancestors wove many great spells and sang powerful songs to strengthen and protect the woodlands they called home. Some small portion of that elven magic lingers still—strong in the Ardeep, almost forgotten in the Trollbark. As for the Forest of Wyrms, I am not yet sure."

Araevin closed his eyes and consulted the knowledge of the first *telkiira*. He could feel its sister close by, still east of them, but not far at all.

"This way," he said, and he led them beneath the mighty trees.

The Forest of Wyrms quickly proved to be a place of tremendous majesty. Its trees were mighty redwoods, each hundreds of feet tall and twenty feet thick or more. Along the streambeds and steeper hillsides smaller trees crowded closer, but for miles at a time it seemed that they rode through a great green-roofed cathedral, the noble silver trunks pillars holding up the sky. The air was cool and damp, with drifting mists clinging to the ground, and the rich, pungent smell of the wet wood hung in the air like incense.

Ilsevele rode close beside Araevin, her eyes wandering to the distant boughs above.

"This woodland is beautiful," she murmured to him in Elvish. "None of the People live here?"

"You forget the forest's name," he replied. "Many

green wyrms and their young live here. They make poor neighbors."

"Is it wise to come here?"

"The dragons don't often come to the western reaches of the forest. Most of them understand that they do not want to make a name for themselves in Soubar. Far too many adventurers ride up and down the Trade Way, looking for dragons to slay. But the younger and more reckless dragons might be found anywhere. I have prepared a number of spells that might be useful against a green dragon, just in case."

Ilsevele nodded and said, "I think I will keep my eyes open."

She rode ahead a short distance and uncased her bow, resting it across her saddlebow beneath her hand.

Fortunately, they ran into no dragons for the rest of the day. The ride was surprisingly easy. The forest had little underbrush, and the terrain was not very rugged. Araevin could feel the second *telkiira* drawing closer with each step, but as darkness fell, they had found nothing. Araevin reluctantly called a halt, and they passed a nervous night camping in a small thicket near a stream, doubling up on their watches and using magic to conceal their camp and horses.

The following morning greeted them with patches of weak sunshine breaking through the overcast. They broke camp and continued eastward, climbing slowly into steeper hills as they went. But they only rode for an hour before Araevin suddenly reined in, his eyes narrowed.

"We're here," he called to the others.

Ahead of him, hidden below the trees, stood the small tower he'd seen in the vision granted by the *telkiira,* hoary with age and covered in creeping vines. Looking east into the patchy early morning sunlight, the forest shadow seemed black and impenetrable around the old building. Empty windows gaped blankly at the woods, and large portions of the rooftop had fallen inward.

Grayth rode up beside him and asked, "This is the place? Strange, it isn't elven. That's a human-built tower."

Araevin dismounted, taking his horse's reins in one hand. Grayth was right. The stonework was clearly not elven, and the tower had not been abandoned for all that long. Some of the wooden shakes of its pointed rooftop, and the roof of the adjoining house, still clung to the rafters.

Fifty years? he guessed. Perhaps a hundred? Why was an elven *telkiira* in such a place?

"It's not a watchtower, and I don't think it's a temple or shrine," Grayth said. He dismounted, too. "It has the look of a wizard's tower to me. Someone wanted a strong, safe house someplace out of the way, a place where he wouldn't be troubled by unwanted visitors. I wonder if the dragons got him?"

"We'll find out soon enough," Araevin said. "Let's find a safe place for the horses, and we'll have a look inside."

CHAPTER 9

14 Ches, the Year of Lightning Storms

They found a small thicket a spearcast from the tower, and led the horses inside the bramble patch. Araevin wove an illusory shelter to conceal the horses as best he could, just in case a dragon happened by.

"All right," he said. "I suppose it's as good as we can do here."

"I don't like the idea of leaving the horses here alone," Grayth said. "If something hungry comes along, they'd be in a hard spot. Should we post a watch out here?"

"Who?" countered Maresa. "If something hungry comes along, our sentry would be in a hard spot, too."

"I think I agree with Grayth," Araevin replied as he studied the sun-dappled forest. It seemed difficult to believe that it might prove dangerous, but there was a sense of menace in the air that he didn't like. It was nothing he could put his finger on, just a single note of warning in his heart that told him to be careful, to be thorough. "I'm not worried about the horses so much as the forest. I don't like the idea of being inside that tower with no idea of what might be skulking around out here."

"I'll stand guard," Brant offered. "I can keep an eye on the horses and the tower door at the same time. If you need me inside, you can simply shout."

"Are you sure you don't mind?" Ilsevele asked.

"Well, I'd rather go in with the rest of you, but someone needs to do it." The young swordsman shrugged and looked around. "That looks like a good spot."

He trudged over to the enormous wreck of a fallen redwood, and settled himself against the moss-covered log. They left him there, and advanced on the ruin. Before they entered, Araevin cast a spell to sniff out any traces of magic in the old tower or its surroundings, while Grayth murmured a prayer to Lathander and searched for signs of evil. The others waited as the elf mage and the human cleric studied the ruins together.

"I sense no evil," Grayth said finally. "But if there are hidden chambers inside or below the ground, I wouldn't sense them from here."

"There is old magic here," Araevin said. "Old protective wards. Some have likely failed, but others may still remain functional. We will have to be careful."

"Can you dispel them?" Maresa asked.

"Possibly, but I hesitate to use such a spell until I know we need it. If I have to study my spellbooks again it would take hours." Araevin allowed his divination spell to fade. He checked his bandolier of components, and made sure his wands were holstered at his hip. Finally he loosened Moonrill in its sheath on his left hip. "All right. Let me cast some protective spells on the rest of you, in case we run into trouble."

He produced a pinch of granite dust and powdered diamond, and sprinkled it over Grayth, Maresa, and Ilsevele in turn. Murmuring the words of a potent defensive spell, he armored their flesh against physical blows. Then he cast a spell that provided all of them with the ability to see in the darkness. After that, Grayth blessed each of them with prayers sacred to Lathander, to protect them all against acid in case they encountered the horrible corrosive breath of a green dragon. With their spells in place, the small band advanced to the empty doorway in the stone house adjoining the tower, and one by one slipped inside.

The house itself was large, and likely had been quite comfortable and strong in its day. The wooden flooring was weak and rotten. Grayth, with his human weight and heavy armor, had to move with care, but the elves and the genasi were light enough to stand on it without worry. Large holes gaped in the roof overhead, and moldy heaps of fallen beams and broken shakes lay beneath each collapse. Rotten old chairs still stood around a sturdy table in the center of the first room, in front of an empty stone fireplace. The whole place was somewhat dank and musty.

"There can't be any magic that's too deadly in here," Maresa laughed. "There's a bird's nest in the rafters. Come on, let's see what's in the tower proper."

"Do you still sense the other stone?" Ilsevele asked Araevin.

"Yes," he answered, "but it is so close I cannot tell exactly where it is. All I know for certain is that it is here somewhere."

Araevin and the others followed Maresa through the empty rooms of the old house, looking in on old kitchens and disused bedchambers before they found the doorway leading into the base of the round tower at the house's far end.

Maresa studied it, and started to lean in to look around in the next chamber. A brilliant blue sigil glowed brightly above the doorway, and a sheet of coruscating azure lightning crackled across the doorway. Maresa yelped and hurled herself forward, rolling through the archway as the magical electricity snapped and popped around her. Smoke and sparks showered from the rotten wood of the lintel, and the stink of burning stone filled the air.

"Maresa!" Ilsevele cried.

She started forward, but Araevin caught her arm.

"Wait!" he warned. "The sigil is not discharged."

Araevin hurriedly worked a counterspell, striking the glowing blue symbol from its place above the door. The hissing sheet of lightning guttered once and failed, leaving bright spots dancing in their eyes and acrid smoke drifting in the air. The instant the curtain of sparks collapsed, Ilsevele darted into the tower room, an arrow nocked on her bow. Araevin and Grayth started to follow, but a massive iron fist smashed into the doorway in front of them, crushing stone and blocking the way. The hulking arm drew back, replaced by a blank-eyed visage of the same black metal. The thing turned away from them and moved ponderously in pursuit of Maresa and Ilsevele.

"Damnation! That's an iron golem!" Grayth snarled. He glanced at Araevin. "Do you have any spells that can hurt it?"

Araevin quickly reviewed the spells he had stored in his mind, trying to imagine what might damage a hulking automaton of iron.

"Not really," he answered.

"Well, that's unfortunate," said the priest. "Guess I'll have to do it the hard way."

Grayth leaped into the room and aimed a powerful two-handed cut at the towering golem's knee. Holy steel clanged against animated iron with a terrible sound, and sparks flew from Grayth's blade, but all he achieved was a thin crease in the side of the construct's leg. The hulking machine pivoted and smashed its fists down at the Lathanderite, but Grayth backed away across the uneven floor, choosing to avoid the golem's terrible punches rather than try to parry them.

Now we know why the dragons haven't bothered with this place, Araevin thought grimly.

He followed Grayth into the room more carefully. The

tower's ground floor was a large, round room with a sagging ceiling twenty feet overhead. The stairs leading to the upper stories were long gone, but rotten posts still stuck out of the sockets in the stone walls, circling the room as they led up. Once the chamber might have been some sort of workroom or laboratory. Old workbenches stood against the walls, and dusty old glassware was being smashed and broken at a furious rate by the attacking golem.

Maresa levitated in the air near the high ceiling, her white hair streaming around her as she hurled magical darts one after the other into the golem, which ignored them.

Ilsevele crouched atop a table, bow in hand. She took careful aim and fired a pair of arrows into the golem's back. One glanced off the thing's thick iron skin, but the other punctured a hole in the creature. The golem boomed and grated, its joints screeching like a rusted gate as it turned to face the latest attack.

"Maresa!" Araevin called. "Forget those spells, they can't hurt the creature."

"What do you want me to do?" the genasi snarled in frustration. "My rapier wouldn't even dent that thing!"

"Distract it from Ilsevele. She has arrows that can pierce it, but we have to keep it away from her."

"Distract it? How?" the genasi muttered, but she moved over to the wall and dislodged a large, loose stone from the wall. She grunted with effort, but managed to maintain her levitation spell and drift back over the iron golem before releasing the heavy stone. "Here, try this, you rust bucket!"

The block dropped ten feet and caught the golem square on the top of its head with a tremendous *crash!* before tumbling off its shoulder and cracking the flagstone floor. The golem staggered in its tracks, its head marred by a large dent, but the construct simply steadied itself and looked up at the genasi drifting overhead.

Araevin crouched in the doorway, thinking hard. He knew a little about golems. The living statues were common enough as defenses in wizards' towers and magical fortresses. Tower Reilloch possessed a small number of the devices, hidden in various places. Golems were built to be immune to most magic, but some spells could affect them, if in unexpected ways. Magical rust would be the best way to attack a golem of iron, but he had no such spells.

What other elements might serve? he thought furiously. Cold might make it brittle; fire was unlikely to trouble it much. Lightning? A creature made of iron couldn't possibly avoid a lightning bolt. . . .

"Grayth! Back off a bit," he called.

As the cleric backed away, Araevin leveled his lightning wand at the golem and barked out the command word. With a roar like the tearing of an enormous sheet, the brilliant bolt slammed into the golem's chest. Arcs of electricity danced over its body. The golem lurched awkwardly and toppled backward, crushing a rotten old workbench, but it immediately climbed to its feet again.

Grayth chose that moment to dart in at the creature's back, ramming the point of his sword at a joint in the device's armor. The golem whirled on him and knocked the Lathanderite flying with one backhand blow of its mighty fist, but Grayth bounced back to his feet almost instantly. Araevin's protective spell had absorbed most of the blow for him. He started circling in more carefully. Meanwhile, Ilsevele shifted a few feet back, calmly sighted on the same joint that Grayth had pried open, and sent two more arrows deep into the construct's back. Sparks showered in its innards, and the golem stumbled to one knee. Abruptly it belched out a great cloud of horrible green gas, flooding the room with fumes.

Maresa was safe above the cloud, but Ilsevele threw a hand over her face and turned to scramble up the old sockets of the vanished staircase, leaping lightly from post to post as she climbed up and out of the bilious green vapors.

Araevin retreated back through the archway calling, "Grayth! Get out of there!"

The cleric stumbled out of the mist, coughing and

gagging. He managed to get through the archway before falling to all fours, his sword clattering to the ground beside him. Blood flecked his beard, and his face and hands smoked with the awful vapor. Araevin hurried to his side, but Grayth waved him off.

"Check on the others," he gasped, "I will be fine."

He fumbled for his holy symbol and began to rasp the words of a healing prayer.

Araevin nodded and turned back to the doorway. He could hear the golem's great limbs creaking and scraping as it moved, but the thing was still hidden in the middle of its own poisonous mist.

"Ilsevele," Araevin said, "Maresa . . . are you hurt?"

"No, but we can't see the damned thing!" Maresa called back.

I may not be able to affect it directly with my spells, Araevin thought, but I can certainly do something about that.

He quickly pronounced the words of a wind spell, and blew the green vapors away from the golem. Maresa and Ilsevele huddled together at the place where the old stairs had met the floor above, the genasi holding the spellarcher steady in her precarious perch.

"That's better," Ilsevele said.

She laid an arrow across her bow and drew it back as far as she could before sending it down into the golem again. The arrow caught it in the back of the neck, sinking down deep into its iron chest. The automaton sparked and smoked, its arms jerked up and down, and it fell face-forward to the ground and didn't move again.

Araevin sighed in relief. He looked behind him, where Grayth stood unsteadily but had stopped coughing blood. The cleric plodded up to stand beside him, gazing at the wrecked golem on the floor of the tower room.

"Just like old times," he said. "Lathander grant that there aren't any more of those around."

"I'm sure it will be something worse," Araevin replied. He clapped the human on his broad shoulders. "Thanks, old friend."

"It was nothing," Grayth said, and he coughed hard, eyes watering, one mailed hand kneading his armored chest. "Your lady did all the hard work with her archery," he rasped. "I don't know if we could have beat that thing without her. Now let's find your gemstone and get out of here before we learn what else this place has in store for us."

◈ ◈ ◈ ◈ ◈

Nurthel Floshin hurried into Sarya Dlardrageth's conjury, wings trailing behind him like a great black cloak. His remaining eye glowed green with avarice and purpose, and his infernal golden mail gleamed in the lurid firelight Sarya favored in her chambers. He halted just inside the door and bowed before his queen.

"You sent for me, my lady?" he rumbled.

Restlessly, the demon-sired sorceress circled the chamber. The conjury was a vaulted stone room deep in the catacombs beneath the grand mage's palace. Five thousand years of imprisonment had left Sarya with a distaste for dungeons and deep vaults, and she therefore visited her conjury for only the most important of work.

"Lord Floshin, you would be well advised to answer with more alacrity when next I call for you," she hissed.

"I apologize, Lady Sarya. I was involved in working spells of sending to dispatch your orders to our spies in Yartar and Everlund."

Nurthel Floshin had served as Sarya's spymaster for almost five years, and continued to do so even after she had broken open Nar Kerymhoarth. He had been one of the first fey'ri she had gathered to her side on regaining her freedom, and he was far more familiar with the shape of things in the North than the ancient fey'ri warriors who made up her new armies.

"Ah. I might forgive you for that, then." Sarya's ceaseless prowling slowed a step. She glanced at her fey'ri servant, and moved over to a black silk shroud that covered some unseen furnishing in her conjury. "How go your efforts to locate the mage with the *telkiira*?"

Nurthel watched Sarya with interest. The shrouded object was something he hadn't seen before, and he was more than a little curious about it. Sarya didn't care to set foot in the conjury without good reason. On the other hand it was likely that Sarya would explain it in her own time. He quelled his curiosity and answered her question.

"Twice I have scried him briefly, but each time he has succeeded in blocking my divinations. I have dispatched two fey'ri to find him, but we are still so few in number, I did not dare send more. Just now I directed our agent in Yartar to retain the services of a certain merchant's guild, whose true trade involves dealing in information and dispensing with unwanted rivals. I have promised them a handsome sum if they locate this fellow for me."

"And what results have you achieved with all that effort?"

"I believe he is traveling on the Trade Way, heading south from Waterdeep. He is riding with four companions, including a high-ranking cleric of Lathander. I infer that he is in the process of traveling to the second stone, but I do not yet know where that is or how soon he might reach it."

Sarya trailed a hand over the black shroud and said, "That is not good enough. He might find the second and third *telkiira* before we find him! You must redouble your efforts, Nurthel. But perhaps I have failed to provide you with the proper implements for the task."

Sarya drew aside the silken shroud, and allowed it to fall to the floor, revealing a great crystal orb resting in a heavy iron stand. The device glimmered with a weird emerald light deep in its countless facets.

"What is it?" Nurthel asked softly.

"A *telthukiilir,* a High Seeing Orb—one of the many useful treasures we recovered from the depths of Nar Kerymhoarth when we freed the fey'ri legion. This is an artifact of ancient Aryvandaar itself, buried for thousands of years in that dolorous citadel."

"A crystal ball?"

"Not quite. Crystal balls are useful enough, but they are easily blocked by those who know rudimentary defenses against scrying. The *telthukiilir* is a much more powerful instrument. You will find it capable of piercing all but the most powerful of barriers your opponent may raise. But you must use it with care, since its most powerful abilities consume its magic at a prodigious rate. The orb will require a long time to restore its power after defeating the defenses of a knowledgeable enemy." Sarya invited Nurthel with a languid gesture. "Try it now, if you like. I would do so myself, but you have seen this fellow. You will find him more quickly and easily than I would."

Nurthel moved up to stand before the orb. He reached out a hand to pass above the great crystal sphere, and he felt the restless surging of its magic beneath his fingertips. He whispered a few arcane words, and called to mind the face of the sun elf mage he sought.

"Show me the elf who carries the *telkiira* of Kaeledhin," he said.

The orb glimmered, as emerald energy spiraled deep below its surface. It grew transparent in the center, and Nurthel leaned closer, peering into the orb. Sarya watched him, her arms folded. In the orb an image formed of an old vine-covered tower in a great forest. The picture reeled and blurred, as if the orb was moving closer to it, then it steadied again. Nurthel gazed on the bronzed features of his nemesis from Tower Reilloch. Distantly he heard the sounds of battle, and he realized that the mage and his friends were engaged in a fight against some unseen peril.

"I see him!" he snarled.

"Good. Study the surroundings, fix them in your mind, then gather your company and summon your demonic allies. But remember, I want him alive. He can lead us to the last of the stones."

"He may prove difficult to coerce."

Sarya laughed and said, "Do not underestimate my powers of coercion, Lord Floshin! I am certain we will be able to persuade him to help us."

❂ ❂ ❂ ❂ ❂

The forested hillsides above Elion glittered with the soft light of a thousand lanterns, looking for all the world like fireflies in a summer field. The night was cool but not cold, with a patchy silver overcast through which broad swaths of stars glittered. Seiveril stood with his hands clasped behind his back, gazing up from Seamist's green arbor at the growing army encamped about his seat. Each day more elves came, and more elves, so that the scattered camps of a hundred different bands, companies, clans, societies, and orders filled the hills above the Miritar palace.

"So many," he murmured. "So many. How can I hope to put them in some kind of order quickly enough to aid Evereska?"

"Perhaps you should have thought of that before you sent your voice ringing over all of Evermeet, calling us to your banner," said Vesilde Gaerth.

Short and wiry, even by elf standards, the sun elf knight seemed like a stern-mannered youth barely out of childhood, not the Knight-Commander of the Golden Star. He waited with Seiveril for the rest of the Council of Captains. Each captain led one of the largest contingents within the gathering crusade. Over the past few days Seiveril had drafted them into service as an impromptu staff and command structure. In the case of Vesilde Gaerth, he commanded the Golden Star, one of the militant orders associated with the temple of Corellon Larethian. Vesilde Gaerth personally led more than five hundred clerics, knights, templars, and temple guards in Seiveril's crusade.

"What did you expect from your reckless speech, Lord Seiveril?" Vesilde continued. "You have no idea the trouble you have caused within the faith."

Seiveril nodded, silently accepting the rebuke. Vesilde Gaerth was an old friend and ally within the hierarchy of Corellon's faithful. Seiveril had hoped that the clerics and temple soldiers of his own faith would hear his call, and a great number did. But an equal number, mostly from the southern and western districts where the Durothils and Veldanns were strong, had chosen not to come. In fact, he'd heard just that morning that a Highmeet of the Stargrove had been called, so that the chief elders of Corellon's temple might consider whether Seiveril's actions could be sanctioned by the faith. More than a few of Corellon's priests were sun elves of old and conservative families, and Seiveril suspected that they might seek to remove him from his position in the clergy.

"Those words were not entirely my own, Lord Gaerth," Seiveril replied. "Corellon's hand was on my shoulder."

"So you say, old friend, and I believe you. But many who stand high in Corellon's faith are not so certain. Some openly wonder whether you are indeed speaking as the Seldarine command or simply claiming so in order to realize your own private ambitions."

"Ambitions? What ambitions?" Seiveril demanded. "What could I possibly hope to gain by resigning from the council and leaving Evermeet?"

"Well, for a start, you might succeed and return a hero. Everyone knows that you are high in Amlaruil's favor. I think that the Durothils fear that you are maneuvering to present House Miritar as a successor to House Moonflower, should Amlaruil pass to Arvandor without leaving a Moonflower heir. The gods know that few indeed of the Moonflower children still live."

Seiveril shook his head in disgust and said, "When someone desires one thing above all others, she cannot believe that another person might not want it. Of course Lady Durothil thinks I'm maneuvering for the throne. She is wrong, you know."

"We are a passionate race, Seiveril. An elf's heart knows heights of glory and depths of despair that few other races can understand. You have given the People of Evermeet a great cause, a purpose suited to their longing, You should not be surprised that your words have taken root in many hearts, for good or ill."

A soft call came through the cool night air, "Lord Seiveril? The other captains are here."

"Excellent, Thilesin," Seiveril answered. "Please ask them to join us."

Seiveril waited while the younger cleric showed the other crusade leaders into the arbor. Thilesin was a priestess of middle rank in Corellon's Grove, the circle of clergy that Seiveril had led until a few days before. Like many others among the Grove, she had chosen to join Seiveril's quest. Somber and studious, Thilesin had proven to be indispensable as an aide-de-camp and adjutant. The quiet sun elf accompanied the other commanders into the arbor, and took up a position standing to one side, waiting for orders and decisions to record.

Seiveril studied his circle of captains. The first was Lord Elvath Muirreste, a tall, strong moon elf with pale skin and hair dark as shadow. He had formerly served as the leader of Elion's Silver Guard, the legion Seiveril was expected to muster and maintain on Evermeet's northerly coasts to defend the isle. Each of the high lords of the realm governing the isle's districts were required to do the same, supplementing the royal army with their own troops. Lord Muirreste served as Seiveril's marshal and captain, supervising the forces that owed loyalty to the Miritar family. Seiveril could not take the entirety of the Silver Guard with him, of course. He had promised Amlaruil that he would not compromise the safety of the realm. But the Silver Guard contingent comprised a company of knights, two of lighter cavalry, and three of infantry, totaling almost nine hundred uniformed knights and soldiers.

Jerreda Starcloak, the Green Lady of the wood elves, had been the first of the captains to arrive in Elion. Her wood elves filled the air with off-color songs and ribald jests as they trotted and gamboled along, roughhousing and boasting to each other. They did not make even the slightest attempt to form any sort of companies or march in any particular order. Each wood elf simply marched at whatever pace he and his friends enjoyed. But Jerreda Starcloak brought not two hundred, as she had promised in the Dome of Stars, but fully five hundred and fifty of the best archers, scouts, and forest-wise folk in Evermeet.

Mage Jorildyn, the fourth of Seiveril's captains, was one of the surviving mages of Tower Reilloch. A half-elf with a heavy and powerful build that seemed more suited to a swordsman than a wizard, he was in fact a very talented evoker and battle-mage who had fought alongside elven armies on many previous occasions. His beard was streaked with gray, belying his human blood, and his manner was blunt to a fault, though few dared sneer at his mixed heritage. Jorildyn represented the arcanists of the gathering army, almost a hundred mages, bladesingers, spellsingers, and spellarchers, not a few of whom had followed him from Tower Reilloch. The Circle of Reilloch Domayr needed little urging to consider a counterblow against the daemonfey and their demonic allies.

"Well, we all seem to be here," Seiveril began. "Thilesin, how stand our numbers so far?"

Thilesin consulted a small book she kept with her at all times and said, "The Moon Knights of the Temple of Sehanine Moonbow marched in an hour before sunset. They are only eighty strong, but they are all clerics and skilled swordsmen, and I understand all have some skill at healing magic. Earlier today a flight of Eagle Knights appeared."

"Yes, I saw them," Seiveril said. "I spoke with their captain."

The Eagle Knights were only thirty strong, but each was mounted on a giant eagle. They were invaluable as aerial scouts and would serve well against any flying enemies the army met. Seiveril wished dearly for a hundred more, but the Eagle Knights were indispensable to Evermeet's defenses, and he could not ask for any more to join his cause without straining his promise to Amlaruil.

"Also, Lord Celeilol Fireheart of Leuthilspar sent word that he will be here tomorrow afternoon. He is leading a company of spearmen in mail."

"I don't think I've ever heard of him," Seiveril said. He glanced at the others, who shrugged back at him. "How many in his company?"

"He reports two hundred and fifty. By my best count, that brings us to just over five thousand warriors, plus at least two thousand more in armorers, engineers, drivers, and other such folk."

"The Moon Knights are under the command of Ferryl Nimersyl?"

"Yes, Lord Seiveril."

"Please invite him to our captains' council, then. He has a sound mind and I know he fought well in Nimesin's war." Seiveril paused to organize his thoughts. He would have to be careful about asking too many captains to attend his councils, but it would be difficult to limit his invitations without offending any who weren't asked to come.

"How about the individuals?" he asked.

Thilesin grimaced and replied, "It's very hard to get a count, Lord Seiveril. They show up by ones or twos and simply set up a camp wherever they like. I have arranged for my assistants to establish a station where all who come to join can sign up, and give us a name at least. Based on our rolls, which are incomplete, I'd say we have almost three thousand volunteers who aren't a part of any company or society."

"That could be fifteen companies of infantry," Elvath Muirreste observed. "How can we equip them all?"

"More to the point, how do we organize them into companies?" Seiveril asked. "I have no idea what to do with so many."

"Best to divide them among the companies we already have, I think," said Muirreste. "It would seem to be impossible to organize and equip new companies before we march, let alone train them for battle. Any we cannot place with a real company, we should send back home."

"Do not turn away anyone whose heart is full of courage, Seiveril," Jerreda Starcloak said. "Yes, we must do something to put these fellows in order, but they are willing, and they are waiting to be led. Marching and heeding orders can be taught, but determination and courage are harder to teach. If you give them the chance, they will storm a dragon's lair for you."

Seiveril replied, "For many of them, it is simply the passion of youth. They think they are signing on for the adventure of their age, and they can't stand the thought of missing it."

"Yes, for many of our volunteers that is true," Jerreda said, "but I think you might do well to walk among the camps tonight and see who has answered your call, Lord Seiveril. They come from all over Evermeet. Many are soldiers of the Queen's Guard who resigned their positions to serve in your army. Others are huntsmen of the Silver Hills. We have dozens of noted swordsmen and archers; bladesingers, spellsingers, and spellarchers; and whole Towers full of mages. They might serve to leaven the rest."

"That many?" Seiveril asked. He thought hard. In truth, he wanted to do exactly as Jerreda suggested, and go among the newcomers, greet them, speak with them, find out who might be skilled or experienced enough to serve as a leader for the rest, but he dared not. There were much more dangerous problems demanding his attention. "All right, this is what we will do. Muirreste, Gaerth, I want you to select one third of your officers and sergeants to leave your companies and serve as leadership cadres for five new companies each, to be organized from our unattached volunteers. Make sure you pick some good and capable leaders for this duty. You will be promoting them, after all. Have the cadre commanders figure out how to build their new companies from our volunteers. In the meantime, you may go among the volunteers and see if any of them would serve to replace the captains and officers you will be losing."

"Lord Seiveril, I don't know if I can spare that many good officers," Knight-Commander Gaerth said.

"Lord Gaerth, you and Muirreste have the largest, most well organized contingents here. If anyone can spare seasoned commanders, it's the Silver Guard and the Knights of the Golden Star." Seiveril offered a stern smile and added, "I don't want to leave anyone behind who wants to go, and I can't have them organize their own companies. You will have to help them."

"We will do our best," the sun elf knight capitulated with a grimace.

"My thanks," Seiveril replied. He glanced at each of his principal officers again, and offered a rueful smile. "I know it is difficult, but time is pressing. Since we were not permitted to bring Evermeet's army to aid our kinsfolk in Faerûn, we must build the best force we can in the shortest time. I want to send at least some of our strength through the elfgates to Evereska in two days' time. Now, do we have any other pressing business?"

"I fear so," said the mage Jorildyn. "Tell me, Lord Seiveril, have you decided which elfgates you wish to use to move the army to Faerûn?"

"There's a gate to Evereska about ten miles from here," Seiveril replied. "I understand it can be held open for several hours at a time, long enough for quite a few troops to march through."

"I think we should put it under a strong guard."

Seiveril looked sharply at the mage and asked, "Why?"

"It occurs to me that your crusade could be easily defeated or delayed if it proved impossible to move to Faerûn when you would like. If you were forced to use a gate that led to some place hundreds of miles from the fight, you might conclude that you could never get there in time. There are powerful families on the council who feel that you flouted their will by arranging your voluntary crusade. They might be willing to return the favor by denying you the means to leave the isle where and when you wish."

"You think matters are that serious?" Seiveril asked with a frown.

The heavy-shouldered mage replied, "Are you confident they are not, Lord Seiveril?"

The nobleman studied his chief mage, conscious of the eyes of the other captains on him.

"Lord Gaerth,' he said, "have your troops provide a guard over the elfgates we intend to use. Mage Jorildyn,

Forsaken House • 159

assign a few of your spellcasters to assist him. We may have no cause for such measures, but perhaps it would be better to deter any trouble of this sort than to find out we were wrong."

CHAPTER 10

16 Ches, the Year of Lightning Storms

The floors above the iron golem's chamber were in dismal condition, damaged by long exposure to rain and rot. The beams supporting the wooden floors sagged noticeably, and the staircase that had once ascended the tower in a circle following the outer wall was unsafe at best, and simply missing in other places. Araevin finally resorted to casting a flying-spell on Grayth so that the heavily armored human would not have to chance a general collapse of the stairs or the floor. Grayth then helped the others ascend to the floors above, simply carrying them up through the gaping holes where the stairs had formerly climbed.

The second floor above the golem's chamber seemed to have been the personal chamber of the tower's builder. The mildewed remnants of an old canopy bed and several large chests of drawers still stood in the room.

"That's a human bed," Ilsevele observed. "Elves don't use anything like that for Reverie. Are you sure the *telkiira* is here?"

"Yes," said Araevin. He rummaged through one of the old chests, finding nothing but a couple of mildewed blankets. "Who was this fellow, I wonder? And how did an elven loregem come to be in his hands?"

"He might have stolen it," Maresa said. She was searching slowly and carefully along the walls for any sign of a hidden door or compartment. "Or maybe he bought it from someone who stole it from its true owner. For that matter, he might have just bought it from an elf or traded for it, with no duplicity or theft at all—though what's the fun of that? It's not much of a mystery, and it's one we can't solve anyway, so why bother with it?"

"She has a point," said Grayth.

Araevin shrugged. It probably didn't matter, but it might have shed some light on how Philaerin had come into possession of the first stone.

They climbed carefully to the next level, and found it divided into two rooms: a small library full of sodden, illegible books, and a conjury with an old silver circle for the summoning of extraplanar beings inlaid in the floor. Again, wind and weather had worked slow destruction on the room's contents. The ceiling above was mostly gone, showing the interior of the pointed roof, with large holes gaping in the shakes and rafters. Broad windows allowed slanting shafts of light into the room, showing green forest outside. Whatever shutters the windows might once have had were long gone. Ilsevele leaned out and looked down.

"Brant and the horses are still there," she said. "He looks bored."

"He should have fought the golem, then," Maresa grumbled.

They fell to searching the two rooms thoroughly, looking for any sign of persistent magic or treasure caches.

Araevin pored through the remains of the bookshelves, finding book after book decayed beyond any possible perusal. A few had borne the years better, and those he flipped through with greater care, hoping that a spellbook or enchanted tome of some kind might have been left behind. He found nothing of that sort, but he did find a faded mage rune printed carefully on the frontispiece of one of the more intact tomes. It was the mark of a wizard who called himself Gerardin. Araevin pulled out his journal and recorded the shape of the rune and the name, in case he ever got a chance to compare it later with some other scholar or research it himself.

"Aha! I think I found something," Maresa announced. The genasi knelt by one wall, peering closely at it. "There's a secret compartment here."

"Be careful," Araevin said. "We know this fellow placed at least one trap in his home. There may be more."

Maresa lightly ran her fingers over the stonework surrounding the suspicious spot, then rocked back on her heels and pulled her leather folio from her doublet. She rummaged through the small case, and produced another packet of paper, rolled and crimped at the ends. She unfolded the packet, revealing bright blue dust, and blew the dust over the area.

"What's that?" Ilsevele asked.

"Chalk dust, dyed blue. It sometimes helps to show details that you might otherwise miss. Such as this." Maresa pointed at the wall. "See, here is the catch for the compartment, or so it seems. You'll see that there is a faint scoring across it. That would be a spring-loaded needle scraping across the surface of the catch. If you pushed it in with your finger or thumb, you'd get jabbed, probably with some nasty sort of poison. But up here there's a small, more well hidden catch, too. To use the main catch safely, you depress and hold in that second one, which probably prevents the needle from striking. Let's see if I'm right."

She carefully pushed and held down the second catch with her left hand and used the pommel of her dagger to push the compartment catch. There was a small click, and a section of wall about a foot square popped open. Inside the hidden compartment were several small cloth sacks, some mildewed scrolls, a small wooden case, and a rusty wand of iron.

"Well, well," Maresa said softly.

Two of the sacks held coinage—gold in one, platinum in the other. Another held gemstones, not magical but valuable nonetheless. The scrolls and the wand had long since decayed into uselessness, but the wooden case was scribed with delicate arcane runes. Maresa examined it carefully, and offered it to Araevin.

"Any of those sigils look dangerous to you?" the genasi asked.

Araevin examined the box and said, "No, they're only for preservation."

He opened it, and inside lay a black-green glittering *telkiira*, identical to the one he carried in the pouch at his belt. Gingerly he picked it out of its case and held it up to his eye, studying it.

"All this trouble for a single small gemstone," Grayth muttered. "Is that it?"

"Yes. It seems to be guarded like the other one, but I don't recognize the rune it holds. I'll have to use a spell of identifying or opening to get at it. Give me an hour or two to pre—"

The terrified whinny of a horse from outside cut him off, and an instant later, Brant shouted out a warning, unintelligible through the distance and the stamping and whinnying of the animals he guarded. Grayth happened to be closest to the tower's slitlike window. He dashed over and looked out.

"Demons!" he snarled.

Without waiting, the Lathanderite dived through the open stairwell, racing down through the tower. Maresa and Ilsevele followed him. Araevin paused long enough to secure the *telkiira* and its carven box in his own belt pouch, then hurried over to look out the window for himself.

In the forest clearing surrounding the tower, Brant

battled furiously against three hulking vrocks, demons in the shape of vulturelike gargoyles, with gray shabby wings and long, filthy claws and talons. The monsters wheeled and screeched above the young swordsman, mocking him as they fluttered just out of reach before dashing in to claw or snap at him. A dozen more fiends of the stinking hells flapped or leaped toward the tower, from hulking insectile mezzoloths to blind, houndlike canoloths with long, barbed tongues and huge snapping jaws. Araevin stared in shocked amazement.

"Aillesel Seldarie," he murmured. "Where did these come from?"

A gleam of gold caught his eye, and his breath hissed in his teeth. Several of the demon-elves, including the fellow with the eye patch whom he had seen before, drove the vile warband onward. Their swords were bared, and their golden armor gleamed in the morning light.

Araevin considered attacking the daemonfey at once, but Brant needed immediate help. His sword flashed bravely against the demons tormenting him, but each of the monsters was as tall and strong as an ogre, and they were far, far quicker. They toyed with the strapping swordsman like great cats batting at their prey.

I'll give them something else to think about, Araevin swore silently.

He found a lodestone and a pinch of dust in his bandolier, and rasped the words of a powerful spell. From his fingertip a brilliant green ray shot forth, catching one of the three vrocks between its shoulder blades. The demon arched in agony, its beak gaping as it shrieked terribly. The green glow washed over its foul body and erased the creature from existence, leaving nothing but dancing dust motes in the sunlight.

"Up here, hellspawn!" Araevin cried.

"Take that one alive!" cried the daemonfey lord, pointing up at Araevin's window. "Slay the rest!"

He hurled a spell back up at Araevin—apparently an enchantment designed to bind the mage in dolorous paralysis—but Araevin muttered the words of a countercharm and fought off the creeping lethargy that momentarily settled over his limbs.

Araevin started another spell, but two of the demon-elves below were waiting on him. As he chanted out the words, they struck with simple spell missiles that streaked unerringly up through the narrow window and blasted into him. Impacts like hammer blows staggered him and caused him to lose the spell he was casting, as he stumbled over invocations that had to be spoken with care. Then one of the vrocks broke away from Brant and flapped up toward him, scouring the whole tower-top with a burning magical foulness that almost gagged the mage.

Deciding he'd done well enough in attracting the demons' attention, Araevin stumbled back from the window and followed the others down the tower steps. The sounds of fighting drifted up from below, the sharp thrumming of Ilsevele's bowstring and the harsh clatter of steel meeting steel. Araevin descended one floor and quickly dashed over to the window in the wizard's bedchamber, risking another look.

Demons, yugoloths, and the demon-elves swarmed around the tower. Several jostled and shoved toward the door, evidently waiting for their chance to get inside. Others scrambled over the rotten rooftop, searching for a gap large enough to drop into. The vrock and two of the daemonfey circled above him, watching the upper window for any additional sign of his presence. Meanwhile, Brant still battled on against the remaining vrock and a pair of canoloths closing in on him.

Araevin leveled his lightning wand at the monsters surrounding the embattled swordsman and blasted them with a powerful thunderbolt, slapping the vrock out of the air and leaving one canoloth as a smoking corpse on the ground. Brant staggered back, looking for a place to make a stand—and the other canoloth had him. It shot its arm-thick tongue at Brant and wrapped the slimy member around the young knight's sword arm. Then it clenched its powerful claws in the thick loam of the clearing and pulled

Brant off his feet, dragging him by his arm toward its clacking maw. Brant's arm vanished in its mouth up to his shoulder, and the terrible jaws closed. The knight screamed and struggled as blood sprayed and bone crunched, but the canoloth's jaws ground and dug deeper, sawing at him like some awful machine.

"Brant!" Araevin cried. He hurled a volley of his own magic missiles, digging fist-sized pocks in the canoloth's flanks, but then one of the demon-sorcerers hurled a tiny bead of glowing orange light through his window-slit, and an instant later the entire chamber erupted in a terrible blast of crimson flame. Araevin was flung to the ground and barely managed to cover his face in his enchanted cape, but still he was burned, and burned badly. Worse yet, the detonation wrecked the rotten floor, precipitating a collapse of rubble into the golem's room below. Araevin slid down the floor and toppled into the debris.

He landed awkwardly, wrenching his knee and slamming facefirst into the stone floor. Darkness filled his sight. *We can't win this,* Araevin thought hazily through the pain. *There are too many of them.* He heard the scuffle and roar of his companions fighting nearby, and with a tremendous effort of will, fought his way back to wakefulness.

"Come on, elf," said a voice nearby. A pale white hand seized his arm and dragged him to his feet. Maresa held a blooded rapier in her other hand, and her red leather armor was gouged with three deep furrows across the ribs. "This is not the time for a little rest."

In the hallway outside the chamber's door, Grayth fought furiously, his sword a whirling streak of silver in front of him as he fended off a mezzoloth and a demon-elf swordsman who were trying to get past him. Ilsevele stood just a few steps behind the human cleric, searching out clear shots at the enemies beyond. Even as Araevin glanced up at her, a demon-sorcerer that crouched over a hole in the roof hurled a smoking orb of sizzling green acid at her from above. The orb missed her head by inches as she somehow ducked under it, but it splattered against the wall beside her, spraying her with emerald drops of death. Ilsevele cried out and jumped away, stumbling to the floor.

"We've got to get out of here," Araevin said to Maresa. "We're outnumbered."

"Tell me something I don't know," the genasi snapped.

She took two quick steps and hurled a dagger up at the sorcerer overhead, striking him in the arm. The fellow cursed in some infernal language and jerked back out of the way.

"Grayth! Ilsevele! Fall back to the golem's room!" Araevin shouted. The rotten old flooring overhead—or what was left of it, anyway—smoldered and sagged, raining hot cinders and burning brands into the room. It wouldn't be a good idea to stay there for long, but Araevin judged that he'd have enough time to do what they needed.

"Brant's still out there!" Grayth replied.

He ducked down and stabbed the mezzoloth through its lower abdomen. The terrible creature snapped its beaklike maw and clawed at the Lathanderite's back, but Araevin's stoneskin still lingered, shielding the cleric from the worst of the attack.

"Brant's dead!" Araevin called.

Grayth did not reply, but he retreated a couple of steps, fighting his way back toward the golem's room. Ilsevele picked herself up, seized her bow, and dashed back as well, just as a large piece of the burning floor overhead gave way and rained fiery debris down into the corner of the chamber.

"Araevin, this is a death trap!" she said. "We can't stay here!"

"We're not going to," he answered. "Take Maresa's hand!"

Ilsevele understood him at once. She grasped the genasi by the arm, and with her other hand caught Araevin's hand in her own. Araevin quickly barked out the words of a spell, and as he finished, he reached forward and touched Grayth on his broad, armored shoulder. The whole room shimmered with white shadows, and the ruined tower vanished in a flash of light. An instant later, they were somewhere else—a cool, green forest, damp with moss and dripping water, with no sign of the demons or the tower anywhere.

Grayth wheeled at once, covering all directions with his weaving sword, still in his fighting crouch.

"Where are we?" he demanded.

"The Ardeep again, near the House of Long Silences," Araevin replied. He limped over to a mossy rock nearby and sank down, trying to ignore the throbbing in his knee and the coppery blood in his mouth. "I teleported us away from the tower."

The human doffed his helmet and let it drop with a clang, running his hand through his thinning hair.

He took a deep breath then said, "You left Brant behind."

"The demons dragged him down. He fought valiantly, and I did what I could to aid him, but there were simply too many of them." Araevin looked up at his old friend and said, "I would not have abandoned him if I had not seen him fall, Grayth."

"I know." The cleric sighed and sat down, wincing as he did so. "Ah, damn it all to the hells."

He bowed his head, elbows on his knees.

Maresa clamped one hand over the torn furrows in her side and asked, "All right, so where do we go from here?"

"Evermeet," Araevin replied. "I must examine this stone, and see if I can unlock it. And I mean to speak with some of my colleagues. I want to see if I can learn more about this enemy who pursues me."

✦ ✦ ✦ ✦ ✦

The walled city of Everlund lay astride the River Rauvin, huddling against the feet of the Nether Mountains as if to escape the icy rain. The cold, wet weather turned its streets into rivers of freezing slush and mud, and wreathed its towers with thin gray mist. Streams of people—human merchants, laborers, and teamsters; dwarf smiths; even a few elf woodworkers and mages—waded through the streets, bundled in heavy cloaks and furs, carrying on with their business despite the foul weather.

Gaerradh studied the city from the high windows of Moongleam Tower, endlessly fascinated by the sight of so many people engaged in so many different tasks, all at once. She was no stranger to Everlund. She usually found herself in the city once or twice a year for various reasons. Sometimes she came to buy weapons she could not make easily herself, such as silver arrowheads or a good dwarven axe enchanted to strike hard and true. Sometimes she carried messages for Morgwais or other folk of the High Forest. And sometimes she came when her duties as a Harper required her to consult with others of her society in the echoing halls of Moongleam Tower. She wore her harp-shaped pin openly there.

Soft footfalls whispered in the corridor outside her door, followed by a knock. She had the use of a small guestroom in the tower any time she wanted it, and for the first time in a very long time she had stripped off her well-worn leather armor, weather-stained cloak, breeches, and tunic in order to wash thoroughly and pull on a handsome dress of green with gold brocade. Gaerradh, feeling a bit ungainly in the unaccustomed clothing, pulled the door open only to stop in surprise.

In the hall outside her door stood Alustriel Silverhand, High Lady of the League of the Silver Marches. She was tall and strikingly beautiful, with hair of pure white and a perfect, flawless face. In someone else that combination of beauty and starkness might have seemed inhuman or cold, but Alustriel's eyes were warm and compassionate, and her mouth seemed more suited to a laugh than a frown. At her side stood a young half-elf man, likewise tall and silver-haired, who wore a shirt of gleaming mithral mail over his dove-gray tunic.

"L-Lady Alustriel," Gaerradh stammered. She had only arrived at Moongleam Tower two hours before, after six days of hard travel through the forest. She had planned to rest the night and continue on to Silverymoon in the morning. "I thought you were in Silverymoon!"

"Hello, Gaerradh," Alustriel said. "Eaerlraun Shadowlyn sent word that you needed to see me, so I came as quickly as I could." She took the arm of the younger man next to her. "This is my son, Methrammar Aerasumé. He is the High Marshal of the League. May we come in?"

"In? Oh, of course."

Gaerradh stepped aside, flustered. Alustriel and Methrammar entered, and found seats on the window bench Gaerradh had been sitting on a moment before. She followed them over to the window, and remembering her manners, started to curtsey.

Alustriel reached out and stopped her.

"Please, Gaerradh. No one who harps at twilight need ever kneel to me." She indicated the seat opposite her and said, "You must be exhausted. Please, sit down, and tell me what's going on in the High Forest."

Gaerradh sat, and said, "Lady Alustriel, I was sent by Lady Morgwais of Rheitheillaethor. A new enemy has appeared in the High Forest, a race of demonspawned sorcerers, creatures who have the look and manner of sun elves from the old kingdoms that once stood in the High Forest long ago. But they also have black, leathery wings, horns on their heads, and skin that is deep red. They employ demons and devils of all description as their footsoldiers, and have also allied themselves to the orc tribes of the forest."

"You said they are sorcerers?" Methrammar asked.

"Yes, though most of them wield blades as well. I've seen them hurl fire and lightning in abundance. I've also seen them use spells of invisibility and illusion. They are dangerous foes."

"How many are they?"

"We don't know for certain," Gaerradh said. "They've divided themselves into a number of warbands, each ravaging the forest. We know there are at least three different bands, and there may be as many as five or six. Each has about one hundred of these demonspawn, plus a like number of demons and devils, and two or three times that number in orcs, ogres, and other marauders."

Methrammar frowned, rubbed his jaw, and said, "So maybe five hundred sorcerers, five hundred demons, and fifteen hundred orcs and such." He looked at his mother. "If they gathered that force and marched north . . ."

"We would be hard-pressed to defend Everlund," she finished for him, nodding. "The wards of Silverymoon would prove a difficult obstacle for that army, and Sundabar is quite strong too. But I would fear for Everlund and the smaller towns of the Rauvin Vale." She looked back to Gaerradh. "How do matters stand now?"

"We've abandoned most of the villages in the eastern part of the forest, which is where they first appeared. We're withdrawing to the Lost Peaks. We have some hidden refuges there. But the demonspawn are following us, Lady Alustriel. They've caught up to and slaughtered many of our fleeing folk, and so far we've been unable to muster a force strong enough to stop them. Lady Morgwais hopes that as more of our folk reach the Lost Peaks, we will be able to assemble an army from the warriors of a number of villages, and perhaps meet our attackers on a more equal footing. In the meantime, we need help."

"I know," Alustriel said, then she fell silent, thinking.

"There is one more thing," Gaerradh said. "I don't know if this is important or not, but Morgwais said that you might understand its significance. We know where these demonspawned elves, or some of them anyway, come from. They were held somewhere in Nar Kerymhoarth, the Nameless Dungeon. I discovered the guards of the dungeon slain, and a vast portion of the hillside blasted open."

"Siluvanede," Alustriel breathed. She stood and paced away, arms folded. "I knew that many things had been buried in Nar Kerymhoarth, but I never suspected something like this. That is dire news, indeed."

"What is it, Mother?" Methrammar asked.

"I will have to ask some questions to be sure," Alustriel said. "It may take me some time, but for now, I want you to return to Rauvinwatch Keep and march the Argent Legion companies there south to the High Forest. We will aid the elves of the High Forest with all the strength we can spare."

"The council won't like sending even a couple of companies out of the Silver Marches," Methrammar said.

"I will explain to them why it is necessary." Alustriel turned to Gaerradh and asked, "Would you consent to guide Methrammar and his soldiers to the place they can best serve the High Forest folk? We don't know where the wood elves will gather or stand."

"Of course, Lady Alustriel."

"Good," Alustriel replied. She took Gaerradh's hand. "I am sorry that we have only a few hundred soldiers who can march now, but it may be that even a few hundred will make a difference. I will send more companies after Methrammar as soon as I can. If it lies within my power, I will not let the High Forest folk fall beneath these demon-spawned monsters."

✦ ✦ ✦ ✦ ✦

Snow still dusted the peaks of the Shaeradim, the rugged hills that concealed the green valley of Evereska. The elven city nestled high in the hidden vale, and drifting streamers of gray cloud wreathed the white towers and mighty trees. From his vantage on the high slopes of *Ilaerothil,* the mountain known as the Sentinel, Seiveril found that the clouds and fog revealed and covered the city, almost nine miles distant, from moment to moment.

I can see why the LastHome was built here, he thought.

The high peaks of the Shaeradim formed a mighty rampart almost six thousand feet in height, completely surrounding a maze of narrow vales, high cwms, and smaller peaks that stretched for fifteen miles between the Sentinel—the mountain at the northwest end—and the Eastpeak, the even taller mountain to the southeast. Someone traveling through the Forgotten Forest far below would see nothing more than a fence of unbroken peaks, never suspecting the green vales and forests cupped within.

Seiveril had come to Evereska with Vesilde Gaerth in order to study the approaches to the city and see with his own eyes the daemonfey army. He had passed through the elfgates early in the day, leaving the crusade to continue its muster under Elvath Muirreste in Elion. Soon he would be ready to march at least a few of the more organized and better equipped companies through the gates, but it would likely be the work of three days, perhaps four, to bring the entire army to Evereska. He'd return to Evermeet by the end of the day and begin planning the march.

"Look north," said Lord Duirsar.

Leader of the Hill Council, the moon elf elder was a short, thinly built fellow whose unassuming manner seemed at odds with his high place among the elves of Evereska. His face was marked with almost humanlike signs of age, including heavy worry lines at the corners of his mouth, and a pained expression to his eyes that spoke of too much grief and sorrow. Only two years before Evereska had fought a terrible war against invading monsters, and almost lost it. Thousands of the city's People walked in Arvandor, and those who remained knew more sadness than any elves Seiveril had ever met.

"The main body is passing the Westhorn," Duirsar observed.

Seiveril followed the Hill Elder's gaze over the wild green hills and gray mists of the lands beyond Evereska. The Sentinel offered a commanding view over the lands lying west of the LastHome. From the high pass at his left shoulder, a deep, winding valley—the Rillvale—descended from the high slopes of the Shaeradim to the shadowed eaves of the Forgotten Forest, almost four thousand feet below. The Forest lay in a broad vale between Evereska's hills and the Graypeak Mountains forty miles to the west. Toward the south the forest sank into the great Marsh of Chelimber, a gray-green flat just visible from where Seiveril stood. To the north of the forest the Lonely Vale stretched between the Graypeak Mountains and the Graycloak Hills, which were more accurately described as a more mountainous part of the Shaeradim divided from

Evereska's hills by a windswept pass. Seiveril looked to the north and spotted the distinctive Westhorn, twenty miles away in the rugged rampart of the Graycloaks.

"I cannot see them at this distance," he said.

Duirsar offered him a lens of clear crystal, held in a small gold hoop and said, "You'll need this."

Seiveril held the magic lens to his eye and looked again. The hillsides and forests blurred, and Seiveril found himself gazing on the daemonfey army as if they were only a few hundred yards away. As he expected, the vanguard was a huge, disorganized rabble of orcs, ogres, goblins, and giants, with a handful of stranger beasts mixed among them. Then came a great marching mass of horrors and abominations spawned in the darkest hells: hulking insectlike mezzoloths, prowling canoloths, hopping hezrou-demons and skeletal palrethees and babaus. Winged demons, mostly vrocks, soared over the vile horde, flapping this way and that. He also glimpsed the marching ranks of the daemonfey, slender and quick. Many of those were in the air as well, but others, too heavily burdened with arms and armor to fly easily, simply marched in orderly legions behind their rabble and their demons. More humanoids—goblin slaves, it seemed—dragged the army's train, such as it was, behind the warriors.

"At their current pace, they'll reach the mouth of the Rillvale in two days," Duirsar said. "The pass is difficult, and I think it will take them another two days to bring their main body all the way to the top."

Seiveril took the lens from his eye, turned to face Duirsar, and asked, "Do you have the strength to stop them?"

"We did before the phaerimm war," the Hill Elder said. "Now, I am not so sure. We lost almost the whole of the Tomb Guard, most of the Vale Guard, and better than half of the Swords of Evereska. We managed to preserve our mythal, but it was virtually destroyed before we restored it, and it is still weak."

"Well, if the Seldarine smile on us, I should be able to bring you a thousand swords, staves, and bows by sunset tomorrow, and as many as four thousand more within three to four days of that."

"Lord Rhaellen will be greatly cheered by that news. He despairs of defending the city." Duirsar glanced at Vesilde Gaerth, who stood a short distance away speaking with the watchpost's guards, and lowered his voice. "But will Amlaruil really allow you to march?"

"Amlaruil will not hinder us," Seiveril said. "However, I am concerned about other nobles of Evermeet, which is one reason why I want to march as soon as possible."

Duirsar said, "I am sorry that Evereska has need of help again, so soon after Evermeet gave so generously to assist us in the war against the phaerimm. Maybe it would be wiser to consider Retreat."

"Lord Duirsar, I have come to the conclusion that the Retreat was a terrible mistake. When we abandoned Cormanthor, we surrendered our first line of defense against the perils of a Faerûn dominated by other, younger races. Kymil Nimesin's attack on Evermeet convinced me of that." Seiveril studied the weary Elder. "Your desire to fight for your home is not misguided, Duirsar. Do not let anyone else try to convince you that it is."

Vesilde Gaerth joined them, shading his eyes with his hand as he studied the terrain over which the approaching army would have to march.

"Lord Duirsar," Vesilde asked, "have you contested this horde's approach?"

"No, we haven't met them yet, though we've watched their march for better than a tenday now. At first we thought they would continue south down the Delimbiyr and fall on Llorkh and Loudwater in the Gray Vale, but then they crossed from the Delimbiyr Vale to the desert verge above the Fallen Lands. Much as I would have liked to harry their march, especially through such inhospitable country, we simply don't have the strength to risk anything more than a few scouts against an enemy more than a few miles from our doorstep."

"Where do you think we should try to stop them?" Seiveril asked Duirsar.

"I would like to fight here, at the top of Sentinel Pass. The way is narrow, and we could inflict great damage with a company of archers and some mages. However, I am concerned by the number of fliers in that army. Almost half its strength, including all the daemonfey, are winged. If I send out a small force to contest the pass, the fliers will go over our soldiers to attack them from behind, and we will lose whomever we send here. If I send a large force, then I risk the possibility that the fliers will ignore Sentinel Pass all together and strike directly at Evereska."

"Where else, then?"

"The next good place of defense would be the Sunset Gate, which lies between the West Cwm and the Vine Vale. But there again we risk being bypassed by demons and daemonfey who fly."

Vesilde Gaerth thought carefully, then said, "Maybe we should invite the attempt. If we offered a strong army to hold the pass or the gate, the daemonfey might choose to split their forces, leaving their foot troops to try a very difficult defense while their fliers strike at the city. At least we might keep the non-fliers away from Evereska itself."

"A dangerous gamble," Duirsar observed. "Soldiers in the pass might face attack on both sides, including from hundreds of demons and sorcerers. You will need powerful magic to defend yourselves if the daemonfey decide to surround and eliminate your force, and you will be well outside the mythal."

"The only other alternative I see is adding our army to yours inside the walls of Evereska, and surrendering the Shaeradim and the Vine Vale to your foes," Seiveril said. He gazed at the distant army, crawling up into the mountains. "I hesitate to retreat behind Evereska's wards and invite a siege."

"What other choice do we have? We can't meet so many demons and sorcerers outside the mythal," said Duirsar. "It would be as bad as fighting the phaerimm."

"That worries me too," Gaerth said to Seiveril. He turned away from the vale. "I've fought demons before. Their physical power is bad enough, but they also possess innate magical ability that's the equal of a potent sorcerer, and many of them are virtually immune to the bite of normal steel. A whole company of archers might not be able to even scratch something like a mezzoloth or vrock before it tore them to pieces or incinerated them with its hellborn sorcery. Worse yet, many of the damned things can simply teleport from one spot to another with a simple act of will. The idea of trying to form something like a defensive line against any number of demons is laughable. And of course, there are more than a thousand of those winged daemon-fey, many of whom seem to be capable sorcerers, too." The knight-commander hesitated, then added, "We have to prepare ourselves for a fight like we've never imagined."

"Elves have fought against armies of demons before," Seiveril said.

"Yes, but the last time I know of was in the Weeping War that brought about the fall of Myth Drannor. We lost that one." Gaerth looked over at the Hill Elder and asked, "Lord Duirsar, does the mythal ward have any special powers against demons and such creatures?"

"Yes. They cannot teleport into or out of it."

"So we still have to worry about them flying past us to get at the city, but at least they won't simply transport themselves there in the blink of an eye," Seiveril said. "That's something, anyway. Come, Lord Gaerth. We have to get back to Elion and consider what we've seen today."

Elven armies had stood against demons before. Somehow he would find a way to do it again.

CHAPTER 11

20 Ches, the Year of Lightning Storms

The sea winds blustered against the stone and battlements of Tower Reilloch, chill and damp despite the brightness of the day. Fir and spruce trees surrounding the tower sighed and creaked in the wind. Araevin looked up at the tower's stark strength, surprised that he felt as if he were returning home. He'd been away so much over the years that it didn't seem that Reilloch should feel that way to him.

Ilsevele watched him. Simply setting foot back on Evermeet seemed to have filled her with a tangible radiance that almost showed through her pale skin and green eyes. She set a hand on his arm and offered a rueful smile.

"Glad homeagain," she said.

"Glad homeagain to you, too," Araevin replied. "I suppose I missed the place."

"It's been your home for a hundred years."

"As much as any place, I guess. But it won't be the same without Philaerin and the others."

Araevin turned to Maresa and Grayth, who both looked distinctly uncomfortable standing beneath the green boughs of the forest. Grayth had drawn the hood of his cloak up over his head as if that would hide his human build and heavy gait. Maresa seemed determined to hold herself absolutely still in order to appear graceful, but it simply gave her the appearance of being petrified with fear.

"Do not be afraid," Araevin said. "You are my guests, and you are welcome here. I only ask that you promise not to tell anyone of this tower, or what you see or hear while you stay here."

"Are you . . . permitted to bring non-elves here?" Grayth asked.

"It's not encouraged, but you don't need to worry about it," Araevin replied. "If you'll follow me, I'll arrange quarters for you, and a good dinner. I don't know about you, but I am exhausted, and I could use a few hours' rest before we address any serious business."

"A sound idea," Grayth said. "I'm afraid that I'm in need of something else to wear, though. Everything except my weapons and armor were with the pack horses."

A shadow passed over his face as the human cleric's thoughts turned dark, and he seemed to sag with weariness.

"We'll provide anything you need," Ilsevele answered. "Come; this is Evermeet. Walk in wonder, for you will see sights and hear songs few humans—or genasi—have ever shared."

They passed beneath the gatehouse of the keep, where Araevin found a guard of determined warriors eight strong watching the gates. The guards eyed Grayth and Maresa with no small suspicion, but agreed to allow them to pass as long as they remained with the two elves. Araevin requested the Tower's major domo to arrange rooms for his guests, and saw Grayth and Maresa to their chambers before Ilsevele and he returned to his own apartment. They bathed and changed into comfortable robes, ate heartily of the dinner sent up by the kitchens, and lay down together on Araevin's divan to drift off into Reverie.

At moonset, a few hours before dawn, Araevin rose, dressed, and carried the second *telkiira* down to his workshop. He was pleased to find that the room was much as he had left it, everything more or less in its place, but Ilsevele accompanied him despite his protests.

"I may be at this for hours," he told her. "There is no telling what spell I might need to open this stone."

Ilsevele shrugged and patted her hip, where she wore her sword and Araevin's lightning wand.

"I don't know if it would be wise for you to be alone," she said. "If demons start popping out of the air to take that loregem away from you, I intend to contest the issue. Besides, our human and half-human friends won't be up for hours yet, so I have little better to do."

Araevin shrugged and began to scrutinize the second *telkiira*. First, wary of traps, he cast a spell to study the magical aura of the stone. Philaerin's loregem might have been safe, but that didn't mean the others would be. To his surprise there was a powerful abjuration embedded in the lorestone, which might have indicated the presence of a deadly trap. He examined the defensive spell closely, and decided that it seemed to be keyed to function only against specific enemies.

"This is interesting," he murmured. "The loregem is screened by powerful defenses against divination. It would seem to be very difficult, if not impossible, to search it out by means of magic."

"But you could sense its location, once you had opened the first stone," Ilsevele said.

"Yes, but I think that might have been the only way to circumvent the defense. So, if you didn't have the first stone, you would not be able to locate the second. Even then, the loregems seem to be keyed to refuse certain users."

"Like who?"

"I am not certain. It's possible to key magical wards of all sorts to recognize or refuse particular people. You can make a magic door that only opens for an elf, or a person who does not serve evil, someone who knows the right password or performs a specific action like casting a particular spell. . . . This *telkiira* is warded against some, but open to others. Fortunately, it seems that I am not prevented from studying it closer."

"Someone went to a great deal of trouble to make sure that these *telkiira* would not be easily found or opened by the wrong people."

"Exactly. Let's see if I can open it." Araevin peered very closely into the gemstone, and glimpsed a glyph similar to the one he had seen in the first *telkiira* when he had examined it in Seiveril's sitting room. This one was subtly different. He spoke the words of his deciphering spell, hoping to identify the rune so that he might name it and thereby master it—but the glyph remained mysterious and unchanged, inscrutable.

"Well, that didn't work," he said.

"You can't open it?"

"I didn't say that. I'll just need a different approach." Araevin thought about the puzzle, and tried a spell of erasure, an enchantment designed to render glyphs and symbols powerless, but that failed as well. He followed that with an attempt to dispel the *telkiira*'s defenses and bypass them in that manner, but whomever had created the stone had been a wizard of no little accomplishment. Araevin could not begin to unravel even the least thread of the spell.

Frowning, he set down the stone and paced away, thinking hard. He had exhausted the spells most likely to be useful, though he hadn't made the effort of preparing every spell his mind could hold that morning. With a few minutes' study, he could press another spell or two into his mind. The only question was, which one would do the trick?

The only other option he could think of was a spell

invoking a vision. It was difficult and not without risk, but he had no other ideas at the moment. He went over to his shelf of spellbooks and pulled down the appropriate tome, carrying it over to a reading stand and whispering the passwords needed to open the book safely. He flipped through its heavy vellum pages to the right spot, and began studying the spell intensely. In fifteen minutes, he decided he had impressed the spell into his mind as well as he could, and he straightened up.

"That should do it," he said.

"What are you going to do?" asked Ilsevele.

"Provoke a vision."

Araevin moved back over to the table on which he had set the *telkiira,* and rested his hand atop the small dark stone. Then he carefully intoned the words of the spell. The stones of the tower seemed to reverberate with the force of his magical words, and the theurglass windows hummed and rippled in response. Ilsevele watched with growing alarm, but Araevin finished the spell, and knowledge poured into his mind.

He saw the three *telkiira,* lying together in a velvet-lined case. An old moon elf wizard in ancient robes held the case, standing in the conjury of some unknown elven tower. He handed the stones one by one to three younger elves. Faint whispers of the long-ago names crawled through the shimmering, streaming view: *Kaeledhin, Sanathar, Morthil,* and the name *Ithraides,* the name of the moon elf mage who inscribed the *telkiira* long ago. He watched as the mage Ithraides drew glyphs in each *telkiira*, and he glimpsed the names of the second and third runes: *xorthar* and *larthanos.* Then the vision spiraled away from him, and his own true surroundings returned to him in a dizzying rush. Araevin gasped and sagged to his knees.

"Araevin! Are you well?" Ilsevele asked as she hurried to his side.

"A moment," he said. He waited for the weakness to pass, then rallied. "The spell is strenuous, but I think I have what I need now."

"Maybe we don't need to see what is in this second stone," Ilsevele said as she helped him to his feet.

"I have already cast the spell. I might as well use the names I have learned." Araevin picked up the second *telkiira* again, and held it close to his eye. This time, as he studied the shimmering glyph hidden in its depths, he spoke confidently: *"Xorthar."* The inscribed symbol gave off a flash of blue light, and the *telkiira* opened its knowledge to him.

Weird symbols and arcane formulae pressed themselves into his mind, the spells contained in the second stone. Araevin shunted them to the side for later examination, and plunged deeper into the loregem. Like a distant beacon he sensed the third stone, burning clear and bright, somewhere far to the east and north—Faerûn again, somewhere farther north than the spot where he'd found the second stone. He glimpsed a deep, moss-grown gorge through which an icy white stream rushed, and a dismal cave mouth hidden beneath the overhanging rock. And he saw again the proud sun elf with the hateful green eyes that he had seen during his exploration of the first *telkiira*, a mage of great power who meticulously scribed tiny runes on a large, purple gemstone the size of a thumb.

As the old thoughts faded, he looked at the spells in the stone. There was a spell of unweaving magic, which he knew already; a spell that produced a terrible blast of supernatural cold, which he did not; a spell that drained away enemy spell shields in order to strengthen the caster; a spell for destroying undead; and a spell of binding that could imprison its victims in a number of ways. And there was another segment of the mysterious spell that had appeared only as a fragment in the first stone. Clearly, he would have to examine all three *telkiira* at once to determine what it was and how it could be mastered.

"Well?" Ilsevele asked.

Araevin leaned wearily on his worktable, steadying himself after the effort of unlocking of the *telkiira*, and briefly explained to Ilsevele what he had discovered.

"If we return to Faerûn," Ilsevele said, "the demon-elves will be waiting for us. They want those *telkiira*."

"I know. But if they reach the third stone before me, I may never unravel this little mystery Philaerin left for me." He looked out the windows, stained rose with the approaching dawn, and said, "Grayth will be rising soon; he never misses his sunrise devotions to Lathander. We should take counsel together and decide what to do next."

❧ ❧ ❧ ❧ ❧

The holy rites of Corellon Larethian, Lord of the Seldarine and ruler over the gods of the elves, were most often celebrated under the stars. But some rituals and observances seemed most fitting at different times of the day. Seiveril Miritar stood in the mist-shrouded Grove of Corellon, greatest of the elf god's temples in Evermeet, and watched the rosy streaks of dawn coloring the eastern sky. Sunrise was a time of beginnings, of renewal and rebirth, and for the magic he contemplated that day, it was the only appropriate setting.

He closed his eyes, praying that he had read the signs correctly, that he understood Corellon's will. What he prepared to do was so rarely done that he required absolute certainty in his faith and his purpose. On returning from Evereska to Elion he had spent many long hours praying for guidance in the sacred grove, consumed with the question of how to defeat an army of demons and sorcerers. And in time he'd heard an answer to his divinations and invocations. But was it the answer Corellon gave to him, or was it the answer he had fashioned in his own heart, thinking it the will of his god?

"It is time," the priestess Thilesin said. She was the highest ranking cleric of the Seldarine among the crusade besides Seiveril himself, and he had decided to bring her into his confidence, simply to voice the thought that was in his heart and hear another's opinion. "Are you certain of Corellon's will in this?"

"As certain as I can be," he replied. "I am convinced of

its necessity. We are sometimes carried by our fates like leaves swept along a swift river. Whether we desire it or not, we will go where we must go. What does your heart tell you?"

"I have sought Corellon's will as well, and I detect no disapproval." Thilesin smiled thinly and continued, "Of course, many great evils have been wrought by those who failed to see the injustice of their acts, but . . . as long as he is willing, I cannot see the wrong in this."

She stepped forward, bearing a long, flat bundle wrapped in heavy cloth. With care, she unwrapped the dark felt, revealing a gleaming silver broadsword, its enchanted steel marked by faint wavy patterns of green watermarks.

"Here is Keryvian," she said.

"Hold it while I speak the rites," Seiveril told her.

He drew a deep breath, and raised his arms to the rising sun. In a clear, strong voice, he began to declaim the sacred prayers and passages of a mighty spell. Corellon's holy power welled up from the center of his chest as a white nimbus, slowly spreading over his body until Seiveril's face shone with divine power, and argent light streamed from his outstretched fingertips. Almost at once he felt the strain of the powerful rite, but the magic seemed to stream through his soul stronger and more deeply with each word, until it felt as if he was nothing but a hollow shell, a brittle casting, through which Corellon's will and power flowed.

Between his raised arms a white door seemed to glimmer in the air, at first a lazy fountain of rising golden sparks, then growing clearer and more distinct as Seiveril continued his chant. Through the door Seiveril glimpsed a forest of silver and gold, a place of shining white skies and rushing perfect waters, and with all his heart he found himself yearning to step forward, to enter into the realm beyond and leave his empty shell behind. But he reminded himself of his duty, and held his place.

"Fflar Starbrow Melruth!" he called. "Hero of Myth Drannor! Come, come back! Your People need you again.

Fflar Starbrow Melruth, rise and walk the mortal world once more."

A shining figure began to coalesce in the doorway, an elf strong and sad and wise.

"Who calls me?" it whispered. "Who calls me?"

"I am Seiveril Miritar, the son of Elkhazel Miritar, your friend. Six hundred and sixty years have passed since you fought in Myth Drannor. Will you come back?"

"What is your need?" the spirit asked.

"An army of demonspawned elves and demons marches on Evereska. We will meet them in battle, but I do not know if we can prevail. Your deeds in the defense of Myth Drannor are legendary. You would be a mighty champion for our cause."

"I failed, Seiveril Miritar. I died, and Myth Drannor fell."

"Then this is your chance to join a new battle against the enemies of all elves, and triumph where once you fell."

The spirit remained silent as Seiveril held the door open. He could feel the hand of Corellon steadying him, supporting him, filling him with the power to attempt such an audacious resurrection. Fflar had died far too long ago for such magic to work reliably, and yet his heart had told him to make the attempt. It was what was meant to be.

"I will come."

The spirit seemed to move toward Seiveril. Like sunshine vanishing behind a cloud the liquid silver light dimmed and took on form, becoming a tall, broad-shouldered moon elf with russet hair and a broad, handsome face. He took one faltering step out of the door of light, and fell naked to the soft loam of the clearing, suddenly real and wholly in Evermeet, Arvandor a fleeting glimpse of bliss shining on his shoulders.

Seiveril swayed and reached out for Thilesin, who moved close to steady him. The coursing divine energy vanished so swiftly that he ached with the emptiness of it. For a long moment he could not speak.

Before him, the moon elf groaned and stirred, his strong fingers clenched in the soft earth, shaking with the chill of the morning air. He gasped once, sharply.

"Where am I?" he whispered.

"Corellon's Grove, near the city of Elion in Evermeet," Thilesin answered for Seiveril.

She hurried close with a warm robe, and threw it over the moon elf's shoulders.

The fellow pulled the robe close over his shoulders and pushed himself up to his knees. Then he slowly stood, looking around in silent wonder.

"How long . . . I mean, when is it?"

"The year is 1374, by Dalereckoning," Seiveril answered. He was a little more steady on his feet, and he squared his shoulders to look the elf in the face. "Myth Drannor fell more than six hundred years ago."

"Who . . . who am I?"

"You are Fflar Starbrow Melruth, and you were a great captain of Cormanthyr in the final days of Myth Drannor."

Fflar hugged his arms close to his chest and shivered.

"I am Fflar," he said. "But I was not a great captain. I failed. Why would you bring me back?"

"Because an army of fiends threatens an elven realm again, and I thought you might know more about such a foe than anyone now living. Because my father gave Keryvian into my care, and it will answer no hand other than yours. This is why I called you out of Arvandor."

"Arvandor . . . I was in Arvandor," Fflar said quietly. He took a deep breath, and looked at the sacred grove around him, and the rosy mists of dawn, and the cloud-streaked skies overhead. "I do not recall it now."

"Forgive me if I did not do as you wished, but you said you were willing to return," Seiveril said. "If you had declined, I could not have brought you back."

"I don't remember," Fflar said. His eyes fell on the sword Keryvian, lying on the altar-stone nearby, and he moved over to slide his hand onto its grip. "I remember you, though."

Seiveril watched the moon elf lift the sword and carefully feel the weight of it.

"Do you remember Elkhazel Miritar?" he asked. "Yes," Fflar replied. "He was a good friend. Did he escape the city's fall?"

"Yes. I am his son."

Fflar looked sharply back at Seiveril and said, "Yes, I think I see the resemblance. You have his hair and his frame, I think." His lips twitched in a weak smile. "Well, Seiveril son of Elkhazel, I find that I am hungrier than I ever imagined possible, and I'd like to put on something more substantial than this nightshirt you picked out for me. If you could point me toward breakfast and a change of clothes, I would be in your debt."

"Come with me," Seiveril said. "My home is not far away, and we have much to talk about."

◈ ◈ ◈ ◈ ◈

An hour after Grayth had concluded his morning prayers, Araevin and Ilsevele invited the human and genasi to breakfast with them in Araevin's apartments. Araevin had the kitchens send up the heartiest fare available, and while the four of them ate, Araevin explained what he had learned by opening the second stone.

"A cold, mossy gorge with a swift stream..." Grayth said. "That could be anywhere. I hope your sense of direction remains as sharp as it was with the second stone."

"I'm not sure I want to get anywhere near that third stone," Maresa said. "In case you've all forgotten, the competition brought a dozen demons with them to the forest tower. Clearly, they can find the stones, too, and next time they might choose to bring along *two* dozen."

"I don't believe they knew where the second stone was hidden," Araevin said. "I've had a chance to look at it closely, and I think its magic wards it against being found or used by the wrong people."

"Then how did the demon-elves and their pets know where to find the stone?" the genasi demanded.

"Simple," said Grayth, watching Araevin. "They followed us. Remember when we were spied upon in the Ardeep? Araevin defended us against that attempt, but I'd wager that our adversaries succeeded on other occasions we didn't detect."

"You have done more than your mother could have expected of you already," Ilsevele said. "You need not share this danger with us."

The genasi snorted and replied, "You won't cut me out of my share that easily. I'm not content with the few tarnished coins we grabbed in the wizard's tower."

Araevin met Ilsevele's eye, and his betrothed winked at him. He covered a smile with his hand and reached for another apple from the breakfast tray. A soft knock sounded at his door. He rose and answered it, and found that it was Loremaster Quastarte.

"Glad homeagain, Mage Araevin," the loremaster said. "Might I have a moment of your time?"

"Certainly, Loremaster. Please, come in." Araevin replied.

He showed the loremaster into his sitting room, and introduced Quastarte to Grayth and Maresa. The old elf concealed his surprise with admirable skill, and even remembered to clasp Grayth's hand in the human manner and offer Maresa a courteous bow.

Araevin motioned the loremaster toward an empty seat and asked, "What is on your mind?"

Quastarte glanced at Grayth and Maresa, and said in Elvish, "My business concerns the attack on the Tower, and what we found near Nandeyirron's Vault."

"They know of the attack. In fact, we've seen the demon-elves again and fought them. You can speak openly."

Quastarte nodded, and switched back to Common.

"We have learned a great deal about our attackers since you departed the Tower," he said. "My colleagues and I have pored through all of our most ancient texts and cast many divinations in order to gain a glimpse of our enemy, and our efforts have not been entirely in vain. Tell me, have you ever heard of House Dlardrageth?"

"My father mentioned that name," Ilsevele replied, "when we spoke to him before leaving Evermeet."

"That makes sense," Quastarte said. "Your father's family came out of Cormanthor. Naturally, he might have heard the old tales of House Dlardrageth. They were a powerful sun elf House in ancient Arcorar, one of the elven realms that later united into the great kingdom of Cormanthyr, whose capital was Myth Drannor. As the legend tells, they did indeed breed with demons, seeking the strength to reforge the long-fallen empire of Aryvandaar and reclaim the dark glory of the Vyshaanti lords."

"They are that old?" Araevin asked. "Why have we never heard of them before?"

Quastarte steepled his fingers in front of his chin and said, "The very question I asked myself once I read the old accounts of the Dlardrageths, but I will get to that soon. The dealings of House Dlardrageth were eventually uncovered in ancient Arcorar, and the powers of that realm moved against these evil elves, sealing them within their own keep behind impenetrable wards. Their House was forsaken by all other elves, their dealings renounced, their titles and lands taken from them.

"The Coronals of ancient Arcorar presumed that the Dlardrageths had been dealt with, and most of our records of the House end there. But, as it turns out, some of the Dlardrageths escaped this fate. They fled west, to the rising sun elf realm of Siluvanede in the High Forest. There they remained hidden for several hundred years, slowly corrupting and poisoning several of the influential houses of the younger kingdom; Reithel, Yesve, and others.

"Through their minions in Siluvanede, the Dlardrageths provoked the Seven Citadels' War, a conflict between the sun elf realm in the southern High Forest, the moon elf realm of Sharrven in the north, and the wood elf realm of Eaerlann in the east. However, they did not see their evil plans to fruition, because early in the war the Dlardrageths were found out and imprisoned beneath the crag known as Ascalhorn. Siluvanede, and the Dlardrageth-sworn Houses of Reithel and the rest, were eventually defeated in this war. A great number of Siluvanedan nobles and soldiers, born of unholy elf-demon heritage, were subsequently imprisoned as well, bound in the ancient citadel of Nar Kerymhoarth. Yet in the confusion of the war, and the collapse of the realms that had fought in it, these timeless prisons were forgotten. No one remembered that the daemonfey of House Dlardrageth, and the fey'ri of Reithel and the other Siluvanedan houses, had actually been imprisoned as the consequence of their defeat."

"In that case, how did you discover their existence at all?" Maresa asked.

"I found an account from Arcorar, centuries after the original confrontation with the daemonfey, that explained how several Dlardrageths were found to be missing when the wards around their keep in Cormanthor were finally lowered hundreds of years after the keep had been walled off with magic. The Coronal of Arcorar immediately commenced a search for the missing daemonfey, located them in Siluvanede, and dispatched an expedition to deal with them there." Quastarte spread his hands and added, "My sources suggest that this incident may even have sparked the Seven Citadels' War."

"So the reason that the Dlardrageths vanished from our history is that we imprisoned them, and forgot we had done so," Araevin mused. "How were they freed, then?"

"I am not sure. I believe some of the Siluvanedans who followed Dlardrageth avoided detection and imprisonment. They survived for thousands of years as a secret enemy of Eaerlann, concealing their demonic heritage and evil ambitions." Quastarte shrugged and continued, "As for those who were imprisoned . . . well, as you know, Ascalhorn eventually became the site of a mighty human city in the centuries following the fall of Netheril. In the Year of the Curse, almost five hundred years ago, Ascalhorn was overrun by a swarm of demons and devils. It became known as Hellgate Keep. If the daemonfey were imprisoned beneath it, perhaps the demons infesting the place found their prison and let them out."

"Or perhaps, when Hellgate Keep was razed five years ago, their prison was finally breached," Araevin said slowly. "The raiders who attacked Tower Reilloch might have been the descendants of these ancient, evil Siluvanedan houses, or they may have actually been the ancient prisoners, finally freed."

"You referred to some of these demon-elves as daemonfey, and others as fey'ri," Grayth asked Quastarte. "What is the difference?"

"That is a little confusing, isn't it? The scions of House Dlardrageth were the daemonfey. They seem to have possessed higher, more powerful demonic bloodlines. The Siluvanedan Houses who owed allegiance to Dlardrageth are the fey'ri, tainted and dangerous, but not the spawn of demon princes. Many of my sources use the term daemonfey to refer to both the daemonfey—the elves of House Dlardrageth—and the fey'ri, the elves of the other Houses."

Grayth nodded and sat back in his chair, silent.

Quastarte cleared his throat and said, "I hope you'll forgive me, but I must speak to Mage Araevin in confidence."

"Please excuse us," Araevin said, "My workroom, Loremaster?"

The two mages withdrew from the sitting room and left Araevin's chambers. The workroom was close by, only one floor down and a short distance through the tower's echoing halls. Araevin spoke the passwords needed to pass the magical defenses of his workroom door, and stood aside to allow Quastarte in first.

The loremaster waited for Araevin to close and seal the door before he asked, "Have you learned anything about Philaerin's *telkiira*?"

"Little other than the fact that the daemonfey are searching for it," Araevin replied. He went on to relate his success in accessing the lorestone, the story of his search for the second stone, and his encounters with the daemonfey sorcerer who seemed to be his appointed nemesis. "I have just succeeded in opening the second *telkiira*," he concluded. "It contains more spells—two I have never heard of before, the others much as you might find in any wizard's spellbook—and directions toward the third stone."

"So this moon elf wizard Ithraides created this set of *telkiira*, and gave one each to three other wizards," Quastarte said. "And you have hints of another wizard, a sun elf, and another lorestone, a *selukiira*. That would be quite a find. High loregems are not scribed on a lark."

"Do those names mean anything to you, Loremaster? Ithraides, Morthil, and the others?"

"No, but I will inquire after them at once." Quastarte frowned and said, "This puzzle grows less clear with each day. Given the fact that you found the second stone in a secret cache in a tower obviously abandoned for many years, I wonder when the story of the *telkiira* meets the story of the daemonfey. Do these lorestones date all the way back to the days of Siluvanede, or possibly even Arcorar? Or are they a more recent development?"

"I suspect I'll know when I find the third stone," Araevin replied with a shrug.

"I wonder if it is wise to seek it out? Perhaps it would be better to leave it where it lies."

"Nothing hidden can remain so forever. The third stone will be found, so I might as well be the one to find it." Araevin swept the two lorestones from the table and replaced them in his pouch. "I don't suppose you learned anything more about these?"

"Nothing in Philaerin's journals or notes so much as hints at such a *telkiira*."

"That does not surprise me. Thank you for your help, Loremaster," Araevin said.

"It was nothing. Besides, Lord Miritar may have need of what we have learned about the daemonfey."

Araevin paused, then asked, "Why is that?"

"Knowing the history of the Dlardrageths may suggest a way to defeat them, of course." Quastarte looked at Araevin, and sudden comprehension dawned in his eyes. "You don't know!" he gasped.

"Don't know what?" Araevin said.

"An army of the daemonfey has arisen in the Delimbiyr

Vale, and is marching against both Evereska and the High Forest."

"What did you say?"

"Lord Miritar is gathering a host to fight them in Faerûn. Both the wood elves and the Evereskans requested Evermeet's help. The council felt that it would be unwise to risk more of Evermeet's soldiers and mages in a campaign in Faerûn, not after the terrible losses in Nimesin's war and our expedition against the phaerimm, but Lord Miritar felt differently. He resigned from the council and called for volunteers to accompany him in a crusade against this new enemy."

"I had no idea!" Araevin said. "Where is he now?"

"Still in Elion, though I have heard they will march soon."

"In that case, Ilsevele and I must leave at once," Araevin said as he walked Quastarte to the door. "If you learn anything important, do not hesitate to perform a sending for me. I will return if I can. Sweet water and light laughter until we meet again, Quastarte!"

"And to you, my friend," the older elf replied.

He watched as Araevin hurried away.

CHAPTER 12

23 Ches, the Year of Lightning Storms

I was wondering where all the elves were," Maresa said. "Apparently, they're here."

The genasi reined in her horse on the broad track that wound past the gates of Seamist down to the city of Elion below.

Araevin, Grayth, and Ilsevele stared alongside her. Beneath the evergreens, on either side of the road, lay the encampments of elf warriors. Proud banners and standards stood by each one, identifying the contingent camped there. Hundreds of elves dressed in hauberks of chain mail or byrnies of ring-sewn leather filled the forest, all engaged in different tasks. Some mended arms and armor, some prepared food, and quite a few seemed to be engaged in striking their simple shelters and collecting their gear into manageable packs. In one meadow nearby a company of nearly two hundred archers practiced their marching and maneuvering.

"By the bow of Shevarash, will you look at that?" Ilsevele murmured.

The small company had left Tower Reilloch within an hour of Araevin's meeting with Quastarte, after Araevin and Ilsevele had gleaned most of the story of the council's debates and Seiveril's call to arms from the loremaster. Even though the evidence was right in front of Araevin's eyes, he still couldn't believe it.

"We leave for two tendays, and Evermeet decides to stand on its head," said Araevin. "What next, I wonder?"

After asking several orderlies and messengers hurrying past about Seiveril's whereabouts, they were directed to a broad hilltop glade a mile above the palace. Whole companies of elves—archers, knights, elite guards, and spearmen—waited in orderly ranks at the edge of the glade. In the center of the clearing stood a trio of weathered old stone markers. Six drummers beat an easy rhythm in the damp air as the companies formed themselves into three columns each and queued up, facing the stone markers. On the first stroke, three elves advanced to the markers, on the second, each of the three touched a stone; on the third stroke, they vanished in a golden sparkle; and on the fourth stroke the waiting columns advanced one step.

"That's astonishing," said Grayth. "They must be moving a whole company through in ten minutes or less. How long can they keep that up?"

"As long as necessary," Araevin said. "The elfgates were designed for the swift movement of armies." He looked at Grayth and Maresa. "Please, do not tell anyone else what you have seen here. This is something we would rather keep to ourselves."

The Lathanderite looked over to Araevin and simply nodded. Maresa narrowed her eyes. "I won't speak of it," she said. "It's your business, and no one else's."

"Look, there is Muirreste," Ilsevele said. "He will know where my father is." She rode over to a small party of officers who stood near the elfgates, supervising the movement of the soldiers. "Lord Muirreste! Is my father anywhere near?"

The knight turned at the sound of her voice and answered, "Lady Ilsevele! And Mage Araevin. This is a surprise. I thought you two were off in Faerûn somewhere."

"We returned yesterday," replied Ilsevele before she introduced Grayth and Maresa.

"A pleasure to meet you," Muirreste said politely, bowing, but his face betrayed his concern at finding *n'tel-quessir* at such a sensitive spot. "Lady Ilsevele, your father already passed the elfgate. He is on the other side overseeing the army's movements, while I am trying to keep some measure of order here."

"Will he return?"

"No, he does not expect to. However, you could certainly go to him, if you wish. If you'll wait until the company there clears the elfgates, you can join him. We've been leaving a few minutes between formations in order to give gating soldiers the opportunity to clear the arrival area."

Ilsevele looked at Araevin and asked, "What do you think?"

"Seiveril will want to know what we found in the Forest of Wyrms. And I promised Quastarte I would carry his tale of the daemonfey to him, too. We should find your father at once."

"I agree," said Ilsevele. She glanced back to Muirreste. "Thank you, Elvath. We will take advantage of your generous offer. Where exactly will we find ourselves on the other side of the gate?"

Muirreste looked at Grayth and Maresa, and said in Elvish, "It might be better not to say. The People of the LastHome are even more careful in guarding their secrets from *n'tel-quessir* than we are."

"Grayth and Maresa have my trust, Elvath, and through me my father's confidence as well. They have fought valiantly and endured great danger already in our cause."

"Then I will not bar their passage, though Lord Seiveril

may have to answer for them in Evereska. I hope your trust is well placed." He switched back to Common. "Fall in at the end of the company moving through now. When your turn comes, simply touch the stone marker. The magic of the gate will do the rest."

The four companions dismounted and led their horses to the back end of the archer company passing through the gate—a disorderly gang of wood elves, who laughed with delight when they saw a human and a planetouched following their column.

Ilsevele said to Grayth and Maresa, "I hope you will forgive us for leaving Evermeet so quickly. I would have liked the opportunity to show you more of the island."

"I'll carry it with me in my heart," the cleric said with a smile. "I am honored to have seen it even for a day."

Their turn came a few minutes later, as the last of the wood elves trotted through the gate. Araevin waited while Ilsevele, Grayth, and Maresa walked their horses up to the markers and touched the stones, disappearing in a sparkle of golden light, and he did the same.

The hilltop misted away from him. There was a moment of darkness and a strange, directionless sense of motion in the center of his body, and Araevin found himself standing in a dark, rainy plaza or square in an elven city. Soft lanternlight glowed around him, flickering as the wind shifted, and white stone towers rose up between towering shadowtops and cedars.

Of course, he thought. We moved several thousand miles to the east, so naturally we moved later in the day.

An elf soldier dressed in a long mail shirt took Araevin by the arm and guided him away from the arrival point. The mage noticed that a pair of Evereskan drummers kept the time of the drummers in the Evermeet glade. Already the wood elves were marching away down a broad thoroughfare, still laughing and singing with high spirits. Araevin led his horse away and joined Ilsevele and the others off to one side.

"Where will we find Seiveril Miritar?" Ilsevele asked one of the elves nearby.

"Out in the Meadow, my lady," the elf replied. "Follow the company ahead of you, they're being led there now. But leave your horses here. We'll have to take them down by another way."

They relinquished their reins, and hurried after the wood elves through the forested streets of the city. Evereska was a striking place of marvelous buildings, deep groves, and steep hilltops. Lanterns glowed above the streets, each haloed by the falling drizzle. But Araevin was startled to see signs of war amid the city's towers and trees: a shadowtop scorched badly on one side by fire, a tower with a great gouge in its side from some spell or another, windows of theurglass boarded up with simple wooden shutters.

They fought the phaerimm in the streets of the city, he reminded himself. It was only two years ago.

They reached a park overlooking the city's edge. Evereska sat atop sheer cliffs nearly a thousand feet in height, its hills and forests crowning the stark stone of its great pedestal. Below lay the Meadow, a ring of grassy open land at the foot of the cliffs, and circling that the Vine Vale, a valley of terraced fields, vineyards, and orchards surrounding the city. At one side of the park, quite near the edge, a golden circle glowed on the ground. One by one the wood elves walked into it and vanished.

"Where are we going now?" Grayth asked.

"We're descending to the valley floor outside the city," Araevin explained. They waited their turn, passed through behind the wood elves, and stepped out of a shallow niche in the cliffside, walking out into the broad, open Meadow.

Columns of elf soldiers waited here, organizing themselves before marching off. Araevin spotted Seiveril at once. He stood amid a knot of other elves, dressed in his gilded armor of mithral plate, watching as the elves who had already passed the gate and the cliff marched off into the darkness. The sight of Seiveril attired in battle-armor startled Araevin. With an abrupt and chilling clarity he realized that all the martial hurry they'd wandered through for the past hour had a purpose. The great host gathering in Evereska's green Meadow had come to fight, and perhaps die, in battle against the enemies of the People.

How could I have forgotten that for an instant? Araevin wondered.

"Father!" Ilsevele called.

She hurried over to embrace Seiveril, while Araevin and his friends followed.

Seiveril turned in surprise, but returned his daughter's embrace, saying, "Ilsevele! What are you doing here?"

"We came to find you, but it occurs to me that I might ask you the same question," Ilsevele replied. She stepped back and looked around at the marching soldiers. A long, snaking line of elves carrying their arms and armor were ascending the outer wall of the Vine Vale, following a trail that switchbacked up toward the higher hills surrounding Evereska and its valley. "What is going on?"

"It is a long story, but . . . I could not stand by and allow our people to do nothing to aid the Evereskans. If I had not done something, no one would have, and I believe with all my heart that this needs doing," Seiveril said. He looked over to the officers standing nearby. "Lord Gaerth, you know where these troops are supposed to go. Will you take over for me for a time? I need to speak with my daughter. Make sure they know to remain vigilant, our foes might attempt to pass our lead companies and strike at us here."

Vesilde Gaerth, resplendent in his golden plate armor, touched his fingertips to his visor and replied, "Of course, Lord Seiveril."

Seiveril took one last look at the mustering elves then took Ilsevele's arm, leading her to a nearby tent.

"Come, both of you, and your friends as well. I suspect we have some news to exchange. Starbrow, why don't you join us, too?"

One of the elves who had been standing with Seiveril detached himself and followed. He was a tall and strongly built moon elf, his red-brown hair pulled back into a long braid behind his back. He wore a lacquered breastplate with a large kite-shaped shield slung over his back. Araevin didn't recognize him, but then again, in the last hour he'd seen hundreds of elves he didn't know.

They filed into the pavilion Seiveril indicated, and found simple but comfortable furnishings, including light folding stools and a portable table with several maps laid out across its surface. A tray of fruit and bread filled one end of the table, along with ewers of cold water and wine.

"I wish I could claim credit for the hospitality, but I can't," said Seiveril. "Thilesin and her assistants decided to provide me with a valet so that I could devote all my attention to the challenges ahead, instead of fretting about where to rest and when to eat. Please, be seated."

"Father," said Ilsevele, "what are you doing here? Why didn't the queen send the army? Why did she refuse to help?"

"As I said, it is a long story, and it is a story that may not be for everyone to hear. I will only say that the queen has duties and responsibilities that constrain her freedom of action, and that this was the only way for those of us on Evermeet to send any real help to the People in Faerûn." Seiveril looked over at Grayth and Maresa. "You have neglected to introduce me to your guests, Ilsevele."

Ilsevele frowned, noting the change in subject, but she did not protest. Instead she introduced Grayth and Maresa, and in turn Seiveril introduced the moon elf called Starbrow. Araevin took the fellow's hand wondering who he was again, and his eyes fell to the sword hilt at the moon elf's hip.

"You are wearing Keryvian!" he gasped in surprise.

"Yes," Starbrow said. He offered a crooked smile. "Seiveril loaned it to me. I have some experience in fighting demons, and he thought I could make good use of the sword."

"I don't believe I have ever heard of you," Araevin said. "Where are you from?"

Starbrow glanced at Seiveril, then back to Araevin,

and said, "Cormanthyr. Though I have been away from my homeland for a long time."

Seiveril poured himself a cup of water from the ewer on the table.

"Well, Ilsevele," he said, "you can see what has been occupying my time since we parted. Where have you been? Araevin, did you learn anything more about the attack on Reilloch?"

"We've spent the last two tendays in Faerûn," Ilsevele said. She looked at Starbrow, and decided that the moon elf obviously enjoyed some special confidence with her father. "We learned the hard way that the daemonfey are very interested in the lorestones. We found . . . no, Araevin should tell the rest. The tale is his."

The company gathered in Seiveril's tent turned their eyes on Araevin. He gave Ilsevele a pained look, but stood and faced the others.

"We followed the first *telkiira*'s directions to a second *telkiira*, lost in an abandoned tower in the Forest of Wyrms . . ." Araevin began.

He went on to relate the course of their adventure along the Sword Coast, from their arrival in the Ardeep, to their meeting with Grayth and Maresa, their journey through the Trollbark to the Forest of Wyrms, and the fierce battle against the daemonfey at the ancient tower. Then he described what he'd discovered when he opened the second loregem, and what Quastarte and his fellow mages had divined of their secret enemy.

"So, we don't know exactly why the daemonfey want these *telkiira*. But they must be important to the Dlardrageths, if they are pursuing them at the same time they choose to launch a war against the High Forest and Evereska together."

"I've heard of the Dlardrageths before," Starbrow said to Seiveril. "Their old tower used to lie abandoned near the outskirts of Myth Drannor. I never knew the story behind it, though."

"Where is the daemonfey army now?" Grayth asked Seiveril.

"They are near the top of the Sentinel Pass, the northwestern approach to the city, about ten miles from Evereska's walls."

"What are you up against, and what do you have to stop them with?" the cleric asked.

"We face an army of perhaps fifteen hundred fey'ri, five hundred demons of various sorts, and several thousand orcs, ogres, and other such creatures," Seiveril replied. "Against that stands Evereska's army, roughly two thousand strong, plus our own expedition, which will number close to six thousand by tomorrow."

"They have that many demons?" Grayth asked in surprise. "How did they do that, I wonder?"

Araevin rubbed his jaw, thinking. His human friend had touched on something important, he was sure of it. Demons were not native to Faerûn. They could only be summoned from their foul hells for a very short time by battle-conjurations, or sometimes bound to longer service with difficult and expensive rites. If the daemonfey army had so many demons and yugoloths among their numbers, then they were clearly not using short-lived summonings or difficult binding rituals to enslave their fiendish allies.

"They must control a gate of some kind," he said. "The demons are serving of their own free will."

"Evereska's scouts have reported the presence of demons in this army for most of its approach," Seiveril said. "So, the gate must be located somewhere near the place where the daemonfey legion and their orc allies began their march. That would be somewhere in the upper Delimbiyr Vale. Hellgate Keep, perhaps?"

"Presumably, there must be some constraint on how rapidly the demons can enter the world through the gate," Grayth said. "Otherwise all the North would be overrun by hellspawn."

"Wherever they are coming from, the most pressing point is the fact that they are at Evereska's doorstep," Ilsevele pointed out. "Father, you said they were only ten miles away. Will you have time to bring the rest of the army through the elfgates before the battle is joined?"

"I don't know," Seiveril said. "We have two companies of volunteers holding the top of the pass, but we do not expect to do anything more than slow the daemonfey for a few hours. We will try to meet the invaders in the West Cwm at sunrise. We'll be marching soldiers up the track to the Cwm all night."

"Sounds like an even fight. Can you beat them?" Maresa asked directly.

Starbrow looked to Seiveril, then back to Maresa. "The numbers are about equal, but we have the advantage of defending," the moon elf swordsman replied slowly. "We could hold the Sentinel Pass or the Sunset Gate against any number of enemies—if our enemies did not possess the powers of flight and teleportation—but since they do, we can only choose our battleground against the orcs, ogres, and goblins. The fey'ri and their pet demons may choose to simply fly or teleport past the Cwm and either trap us in the Cwm or attack the city directly."

"Why haven't they done so already?" asked Ilsevele.

"I think they're being overly cautious. They know there is strength in numbers, and so they prefer to keep their army together so that we won't be offered the chance to destroy it piecemeal. And perhaps more importantly, I don't think they know we're here." Starbrow offered a fierce smile. "They brought an army sufficient to reduce Evereska by itself, but there was no army from Evermeet here yesterday. By tomorrow morning, Evereska's strength will be more than tripled."

"But they might choose to avoid fighting you at all," Grayth pointed out.

"Not without abandoning their ground forces. If they assail Evereska directly and leave their orcs and goblins to fight through on foot, we'll destroy a large portion of their army seven miles from the city walls." Starbrow shrugged. "In that case, the best move for our enemies is to concentrate all their efforts on destroying the army that meets them in the Cwm by surrounding us through the air, knowing that we dare not leave Evereska itself with

Forsaken House • 205

too little strength to defend against a direct attack."

"How can we help?" asked Ilsevele.

Seiveril looked up sharply.

"I didn't ask you to fight, Ilsevele. There is no need—"

"Nonsense," she said. "If you called for all of Evermeet to take up arms in the defense of the LastHome, then you called for me as well. I am a captain in the queen's spellarchers, and I have just as much reason to be on this battlefield as you do."

"I don't know how tomorrow will turn out, Ilsevele. If you were to be hurt, I could not stand it."

"I will be exactly as careful as you are, Father," Ilsevele retorted. "Now, I'll ask again: How can we help?"

Starbrow cut off Seiveril's protest with a motion of his hand.

"Stay close by our command group," the mysterious elf said. "We have no time to find a different place for you, and to be honest, I think we will need all the skilled fighters we can get around the standard. In my experience, demons like to use their teleporting ability to butcher the opposing commander when the fight grows heavy. There will be a point in the battle when several dozen appear at once to tear down the standard and kill any leaders they can sink their claws into."

"How can you fight an enemy that can be anywhere he wants with a mere thought?" Araevin wondered aloud.

"Simple," said Starbrow. "You set a trap and wait for him to stick his foot in it. We'll create a false standard to lure in any demon rush, and prepare an ambush around it to make sure we punish the fiends for the attempt." He looked over to Seiveril. "Lord Miritar, we need to get up to the Sunset Gate and oversee the disposition of the troops. I think our foes will wait until they get their main body over the pass, but if they have spied out the movements of our army, they may push their vanguard ahead to seize the cwm before we can get our forces there."

Seiveril said, "You go ahead. I'll be there as soon as I speak with Lord Duirsar again. I also have to send word to Muirreste to bring the rest of the expedition through in whatever order he deems best." He turned to Araevin and his companions. "None of you are bound by any oath or promise to fight here. You do not have to stay."

Ilsevele gave her father a level look and said, "I stand by what I said before."

"I suspect you have a need for capable mages," said Araevin. "I will help, too."

"Lathander opposes the forces of darkness, wherever they appear," Grayth said. "I wish I had time to summon the Order of the Aster here to join in this battle, but since I am the only one of my order here, I will stand for my fellows and do what I can."

The tent fell silent before Maresa shrugged and said, "It's not my fight. But I agreed to aid Araevin, so if he stays, I'll stay too." She jabbed a finger at the mage. "Running headlong into battles was not part of our agreement, but someone has to watch your back."

❧ ❧ ❧ ❧ ❧

Thin, freezing mists clung to the mountainsides in the dark of the night, gathering and pouring downslope like rivers of wicked moonlight. Sarya Dlardrageth stood on an ancient Vyshaanti battle-platform recovered from the depths of Nar Kerymhoarth, admiring the masterful workmanship of a war machine crafted almost ten thousand years past. Shaped like a brazen disk forty feet in diameter, the battle-platform hovered in the air, suspended by levitation magic. Its armored sides could shelter twenty skilled archers or mages, but Sarya had no intention of exposing the platform to harm. Instead, she used it as a flying dais for her throne, a mobile tower from which she could survey the progress of her army and issue whatever orders seemed needful.

"Ascend a little higher," she directed the fey'ri who operated the platform's control orb. "I desire a better view of the fight at the top of the pass."

She paced along the metal crenellations at the platform's edge, dressed in black robes enchanted to the hardness of steel. In her hand she gripped a sinister staff of zalanthar wood decorated with bright gold wire, a potent weapon indeed in her hands. She longed to join the fray herself, hungering for the heady wine of triumph over her enemies, but she restrained herself. She had a legion of fey'ri, hundreds of demons, and great tribes of orcs and ogres marching under her banner. She needed to watch how they fought together and judge how best they might be employed against a serious obstacle.

A spearcast below her brazen platform, the orcs, ogres, and goblins of her army surged up the last half-mile of the Rillvale's winding trail, pressing up against the weak line of elf archers who fought to hold the saddle of the pass. Above the archers, fey'ri and winged demons wheeled and stooped, scouring the Evereskans with gouts of hellfire and hurling iron darts down from above at the foolhardy warriors trying to bar the passage of Sarya's horde. A few of the archers found the opportunity to shoot down at the climbing ogres and orcs, but most of the Evereskans were busy with keeping their aerial enemies at bay with archery and spells.

"Not much of a fight," observed Mardeiym Reithel. The fey'ri lord, a leader of the ancient fey'ri she had freed from Nar Kerymhoarth, served as Sarya's general. His battle armor was striking, a black mithral breastplate embossed with the likeness of a snarling dragon, and his face was distinguished by an exceptionally large pair of ram's horns that curled out from under his war helm. "They are simply trying to slow us down, and perhaps exact a small price for seizing the Sentinel's pass."

"How many hold the pass against us?" Sarya asked.

Mardeiym studied the ridge top from the platform's edge.

"Two companies of archers," the fey'ri lord said, "with a handful of mages. They've certainly hurt the orcs in the vanguard. Most likely they'll disengage and fall back when the orcs crest the pass."

"I see no reason to allow them to escape," Sarya said. "Land a strong company of fey'ri and a warband of demons on the far side of the pass, behind the defenders. We will crush them between our two forces and slaughter them to the last warrior."

"As you wish, my lady," Mardeiym answered.

He barked out a set of orders to the winged imps who fluttered nearby, awaiting messages to carry. The foul little creatures streaked off to find the fey'ri captains and demons Mardeiym named.

Sarya and her general watched as two ranks of the fey'ri waiting behind the orcs and other rabble abruptly launched themselves into the air, scarlet wings beating furiously as they climbed up into the dark sky and passed over the defender's positions. From somewhere on the rocky slopes a bright bolt of lightning stabbed up into the air, bringing down a pair of the daemonfey warriors. Several of the fey'ri replied with a rapid succession of fireballs that scoured across the ridgeline in a string of lurid explosions.

"That's better," Sarya said.

Even from a distance, she could hear the screams of the wounded and the frightened calls of the elf warriors as a cloud of vrocks and other winged demons descended on the defenders.

She was so absorbed in the carnage that she did not even notice the arrival of a vrock scout until the creature alighted on the platform and spread its shabby wings, bowing before her.

"Lady S-Sarya," it hissed through its vulturelike beak. "I have flown to the edge of the mythal-l and back, as you commanded-d. There are many elves-s marching out of the city."

Sarya frowned. "Are they fleeing?"

"No, these are warriors-s. They march to meet you."

"How many?" she demanded.

"At least ten different companies-s. I s-saw their standards-s. They are w-waiting for you at the east end of the v-valley beyond this pass-s, three miles distant-t."

"Good," Sarya said. "Return and see if you can get a good count of their numbers and dispositions."

Forsaken House • 209

The vrock bowed again and flapped off, the platform bobbing as the creature's weight left it.

"Three miles," she said aloud. "It will take us hours to get the main body up and over the pass. Dawn will be close by the time we are through the pass."

"Should we send the fey'ri against them now, while they are still marching?" Mardeiym asked her. "We could strike them hard, right now."

"No," Sarya replied, "we brought our orc allies for a reason. Let's keep our forces together, so that we can crush the Evereskans in a single blow rather than send our army at them one piece at a time. That way lies defeat."

She found her seat and sat down, curling her long, snakelike tail around her feet. After twenty days of tortuous marching alongside slow, clumsy orcs and giants, Evereska was within her grasp.

☙ ☙ ☙ ☙ ☙

The first gray streaks of dawn gathering in the eastern sky did little to warm the damp chill of the cwm. The rain had finally given out in the middle of the night, but the overcast was so low that Evereska's higher peaks pierced the clouds, leaving scraps and tatters of mist to drift by only a few hundred feet overhead. The bowl-shaped West Cwm was high and bare compared to other parts of Evereska, flirting with the tree line. A large, deep lake of icy water lay close under the cliffs on the southern side of the cwm. It struck Araevin as an open and unforgiving battleground, especially against aerial foes. He would have preferred to fight under the cover of the trees, where winged sorcerers and demons would have to come well within bowshot to attack.

He peered into the night, trying to piece together what he could see of the approaching army. Elves needed less light to see by than humans did. Even in the darkness Araevin could make out the saddle of the Sentinel Pass, about three miles distant. The fight at the pass had been over for better than three hours, and very few of the elves who'd volunteered to fight there had returned. He could glimpse movement there, distant torches and large, awkward wagons threading their way over the pass and into Evereska's heart.

Marching steadily eastward toward him came a great, shapeless mass, sprinkled here and there with torches and burning brands—the army of the daemonfey. Their numbers seemed to fill the cwm, and menacing black shadows wheeled and soared above the marching orcs and ogres. A vast, many-throated rumble preceded the army, the rustle and creaking of armor, the clash of weapons on shields, the bone-shaking thunder of hundreds of war drums, hisses and screeches and roars of demons and other fiendish things from the hells beyond the world. Briefly Araevin entertained the curious impression that the whole valley was a cup being filled from the Sentinel Pass, and that in time the horde would fill it up entirely and spill out over the sides.

The leaders of the horde were less than a thousand yards from the elven ranks. Araevin could pick out individuals: bare-chested orc berserkers, hulking ogres, and demons wrapped in fire, shadow, or foulness, all prowling forward in a ragged wave.

"Not long now," murmured Starbrow, standing close by Araevin. The moon elf champion stood amid a loose knot of elves that included Seiveril, Ilsevele, Grayth and Maresa, the Blade-Major Rhaellen of Evereska, and a number of Miritar guards and Swords of Evereska. Keryvian was naked in his hand. The blade was a hand-and-a-half sword, and its cold blue steel seemed to glow in the darkness. "Not long now."

Araevin's heart hammered in his chest.

At least I know my magic can hurt their demons, he told himself.

He couldn't imagine how someone could stand in the ranks with a sword of mundane steel, watching a demon immune to such things stalk closer with every step. He looked up and down the lines, fixing in his mind for one final time the army's positions, in case he needed to know them.

Forsaken House • 211

Lord Elvath Muirreste commanded the right flank, where the terrain was more open and the mounted knights would be able to maneuver. Jerreda Starcloak and her wood elves held the left flank, overlooking the lake. A determined attacker might try to skirt the steep slopes and broken forest on the south side of the cwm, and the wood elves seemed like just the sort of light and mobile force to defend that difficult approach. Wood elf snipers and skirmishers lay hidden in other spots in the vale, as well.

Vesilde Gaerth and the Knights of the Golden Star served as perhaps the most important contingent in the crusade's army: the reserve. Since many of the knights were clerics or possessed enchanted weapons, it was thought that they could be held out of the fight until the demons engaged some portion of the army, then move to aid the endangered troops. Stationed in the rear of the army, the knights also served to guard the Sunset Gate at the crusade's back. The high, narrow cleft leading down to the Vine Vale was the only possible retreat from the West Cwm if things went poorly.

Seiveril himself commanded the center, with the moon elf Starbrow as his deputy. There most of the elven infantry were massed, in orderly ranks of spearmen, swordsmen, and archers. It was also the place where most of the crusade's mages, under the leadership of the half-elf Jorildyn, stood waiting to unleash their battle spells. The best of those companies were battle-hardened Evereskan Vale Guards, steady and unflinching in the defense of their homeland. But more than half the Evereskan army remained in the city, in case the daemonfey decided to bypass the fight in the West Cwm. Seiveril had also left almost two thousand of his own soldiers there, a full third of his army, though he had chosen the companies with the least experience and equipment for that duty.

With a loud groan and clatter, the approaching horde came to a ragged stop just out of bowshot. Orcs and other foul creatures hooted and jeered in their uncouth tongues, shaking their weapons in the air, gnashing their teeth.

On the other side of the battlefield, the elves waited with icy calm. Off to his left, Araevin distinctly heard Jerreda's wood elves jeering right back at the orcs.

"This seems like a good time for a few spells," Araevin said.

He quickly recited the words for the stoneskin spell, dusting Ilsevele, Grayth, Maresa, and himself with powdered diamond—he was almost out of the stuff, unfortunately—and reciting the words of the abjuration.

"What are they waiting for?" Ilsevele wondered aloud. "Do they intend to parley first? What in the world do they think they could offer us?"

"They're not going to parley," Starbrow replied. "They're looking for the standards. Stay on your guard."

Araevin quickly reviewed the rest of the spells he held ready in his mind, and checked the wands at his belt. Moonrill hung on his left hip, though he hoped he wouldn't need it. He was a passable swordsman, but magic was a much better weapon in his hands.

"Hey!" Maresa yelled out. "That's all they've got? You didn't bring enough orcs, you morons. Go back home and get some more! And your mothers—"

The genasi's jeering was interrupted by the tremendous blast of a heavy horn from somewhere in the enemy ranks. A dozen lesser horns caught the note and repeated it, until the West Cwm echoed with the sound. With a ground-shaking roar, the dark ranks surged forward, crooked swords and notched axes held high, while behind them a whole legion of the fey'ri leaped into the air, mighty wings thundering as they climbed above the rabble.

It begins, Araevin thought.

He raised his hands and hurled his first spell of the battle.

Forsaken House • 213

CHAPTER 13

27 Ches, the Year of Lightning Storms

Five hundred yards stood between the two armies when the daemonfey horns sounded their charge. The orc berserkers, unburdened by heavy armor, raced out ahead of the surging horde, running full out for the elven lines, roaring like dumb beasts as they came. Ogres and trolls loped along just behind the berserkers, covering two yards with each stride, frighteningly fast for their bulk and power.

"Archers, at the leading ranks!" Seiveril called. "Casters, watch the airborne troops!"

Dozens of captains and sergeants echoed the orders up and down the elven line, and at their command more than a thousand archers bent their bows and fired. Arrows flashed down at the onrushing warriors like a rain of silver death. Orcs died by the hundreds, stumbling to the ground with arrows feathering chests, throats, and eyes. Ogres reeled and roared in agony, clutching at deadly shafts stuck in faces and necks. From the corner of his eye, Araevin saw Ilsevele draw and fire, draw and fire, so quickly that her hands were a pale blur.

The charge faltered, but still the orcs came on. Foaming at the mouth and bellowing like boars, orc berserkers shrugged off wounds that would have downed any warrior not consumed in the blind blood-frenzy of the berserker. And while some ogres fell, they were hard to kill with arrows. Many of the hulking brutes came on with arrows sprouting from arms, shoulders, and chests like white pins, sticking in muscle and sinew but failing to find the life of the monster.

"Casters, at the ready! Casters, summon, cast!" cried Jorildyn, the Reilloch battle-mage. Araevin was not under his command and had no obligation to follow his orders, but he chose to lend his strength to the other mages. He'd spoken with Jorildyn earlier, and knew what the battle-mage planned to do. Scattered through the ranks of the archers and swordsmen, disguised under soldiers' tunics and cloaks, more than one hundred elf mages and clerics began to cast their spells. Araevin barked out the words of his summoning, shunting the sights and sounds of the battle off to a corner of his mind where he would not be distracted in his effort to remember the complex symbols and tedious chants of the spell.

From the flying daemonfey a hundred and fifty feet over the battle line, dozens of bright orange streaks appeared, hurling down at the ranks of archers. Fiery blasts rippled and thundered through the elf ranks, hurling bowmen through the air or simply hammering them to the ground. Screams rang in Araevin's ears, and blasts of heat singed his face and hands, but he endured and finished his spell, as did many other mages hidden in the ranks. In the air above the elven line a hundred or more swirling knuckles of air appeared, slowly condensing into crudely humanoid forms of mist, smoke, and cloud—a host of air elementals, beings called to life from the very substance of the sky.

"Elementals, destroy the flying ones!" Seiveril called.

With a great and terrible rush of wind, elementals both huge and small streaked up and away from the battle line, seeking out the winged fey'ri sorcerers and warriors who waited above. The fey'ri were quick and strong fliers, but they could not outfly creatures composed of the elemental power of air itself. Like a seething wave of tornadoes the elementals slammed into the daemonfey, battering and blasting their victims with blows that could uproot trees or scour flesh from bone.

Araevin shouted in delight, as did many others. Though the winged daemonfey outnumbered their elemental attackers ten to one, for the moment the fey'ri legions were fully engaged in defending themselves against the ferocious onslaught, and that left the elf spellcasters on the ground free to turn their power against the surging sea of orcs, ogres, goblins, and trolls thundering into their ranks.

"A good plan," Grayth said. The Lathanderite stood close by Araevin and Ilsevele, busy with spells of his own, weaving holy wards and protections over all the elves he could reach. Elf clerics were doing much the same across the battle line. "But those elementals won't keep the winged demons busy for long."

Araevin looked down at the melee in the front ranks. Screaming with battle-rage, orcs threw themselves headlong into the elf ranks, hewing furiously with axe and sword. Ogres hammered down at their smaller foes with huge clubs and maces. And here and there, like storms of destruction, demons, yugoloths, and other terrible fiends strode among the orc ranks, smiting down elf swordsmen and spearmen with gouts of demon-fire or tearing their foes to pieces with fangs, claws, stings, and barbs. The furious dark tide threatened to overwhelm the elven line entirely.

What now? Araevin thought.

His spells could be decisive in any number of tactical engagements, and he had to make sure each one counted. He spotted a mezzoloth stalking forward, wreaking terrible carnage with its huge, powerful claws. The yugoloth struck down an elf swordsman only twenty yards from Araevin, shredding the breastplate of the warrior as if it were nothing more than soggy paper. Then it leaped forward to rush at a knot of archers, who fired desperately at the monster, only to watch their arrows shiver on its thick, chitinous armor.

Araevin hurried through the words of a spell designed to banish the creature back to whatever hell it had crawled from, but just as he finished the spell, a rampaging ogre appeared, seemingly out of nowhere, and caught Araevin full in the ribs with its huge, stone-headed hammer. Araevin flew through the air, crumpling to the ground a dozen feet away.

"Araevin!" screamed Ilsevele. She leaped down beside him, pausing only to send a burning arrow straight through the ogre's forehead as the creature lumbered forward to strike again. The ogre groaned and fell. "Grayth, come quickly. Araevin has been hurt!"

Araevin rolled to his side and pushed himself up.

"Not as bad . . . as it looked," he gasped. "Stoneskin spell absorbed . . . much of the blow."

His side ached abominably, and he couldn't draw a breath, but instead of crushing his ribcage the ogre's hammer had simply knocked the wind out of him and spoiled his spell. He staggered to his feet, and realized that the mezzoloth he had meant to dismiss was no longer there, though two of the archers lay dead or dying, clawed by the ferocious monster.

He looked around for the next foe to deal with, Ilsevele close by his side. Grayth dueled a pair of orc berserkers, sword flashing as he parried strike after strike of their heavy axes. Since Araevin couldn't trust himself to speak a spell, he snatched a wand from his belt and riddled the first berserker with four bright darts of magical power that blew fist-sized holes in the orc's torso. The creature crumpled to the ground, and Maresa sidled up behind the second and ran him through with her rapier, transfixing him until Grayth stepped up and knocked off his head with a fierce slash of his broadsword.

"Are you well?" he called to Araevin.

Araevin still couldn't answer, but he gave the cleric a sharp nod and turned to search out another foe. This is pure madness, he thought desperately. He looked wildly about himself, trying to decide what to do next. The cwm was filled with the ring of steel on steel, the roars and screams of the wounded, and the thunder and detonation of powerful spells.

"Which way?" Ilsevele asked him.

For the moment they seemed to have cleared the area immediately around themselves, so Araevin picked a fierce skirmish off to his left and hurried toward it, drawing a second wand. Ilsevele followed him, picking off lone enemies as she saw them. Together they fell on the flank of a band of bugbears who were pressing an Evereskan company. Araevin blasted terrible swaths of destruction through the heavily armored goblinkin with his wand, singling out sergeants and leaders, while Ilsevele rained arrows at any of the savage warriors who turned to face Araevin's attack.

A rain of flaming orbs pelted down from overhead, each exploding in a gout of evil green flames. Emerald fire scorched Araevin, hurling him to the ground again, and more of the vitriolic spheres blasted nearby, incinerating elves unfortunate enough to be struck directly. Araevin rolled to his feet and looked up. A band of daemonfey thirty strong wheeled over the Evereskan company, hurling spells down at the elves below.

"Fey'ri above!" he cried.

The Evereskans scattered and sought cover, some of them unlimbering bows to shoot back up at their airborne attackers. The daemonfey climbed away from the archers, though a few of them crumpled in midair and plummeted to the ground, brought down by good or lucky shots. He looked for Ilsevele, and found her picking herself up out of a thicket, her cloak and surcoat smoldering.

"Damn them," she growled. "We've got to draw those winged warriors closer to the ground!"

Araevin watched them, and a fierce joy kindled in his breast.

"Or go up after them," he snarled.

He quickly barked out the words of his flying spell, and leaped up into the air after the winged warriors circling overhead. The smoke and fog rushed by his face as he streaked upward, and he glimpsed the great expanse of the battle filling the cwm from side to side. He paid it no mind, keeping his attention honed on the fey'ri ahead, even though he saw hundreds more winging over the battlefield.

These at least will know they've been in a fight, he told himself.

The fey'ri noticed his ascent, and a dozen of them wheeled to meet him. Two sorcerers blasted at him with stabbing tongues of brilliant blue lightning, but Araevin swerved aside from one, and his protective wards served to blunt the worst of the second. He tumbled awkwardly, flailing in midair as he tried to shake off the bolt, and when he looked up again fey'ri warriors were closing in on him, blades bared, fierce grins on their faces.

"Fool," hissed one. "We own the sky!"

Araevin bared his teeth, and incanted the words of a spell of his own, stretching out his hand toward his foes. A scintillating blast of brilliant colors flayed the dozen nearest fey'ri. Yellow rays wreathed one in crackling electricity. Red beams scorched the wings from another. A sinister purple ray blasted one into some distant plane, banishing her from the world entirely. In the space of an instant seven fey'ri tumbled down out of the sky, some fluttering vainly to stay aloft, others already dead. Distantly Araevin noted a ragged cheer from below, as the embattled elves saw his brilliant spell and its results.

He started another spell, but a fey'ri sorcerer a short distance away from him struck Araevin with a spell that abruptly dispelled his ability to fly. Araevin plummeted toward the ground, already starting a spell to arrest his fall. But he didn't complete it quickly enough. Even as his descent slowed, he plunged through the branches of a hemlock, breaking through the boughs as they snapped under him. He landed badly on the uneven ground below the tree, stunned by the impact.

He tried to rise again, but his arms and legs didn't want to work, and his head swam. He was just about to drift off into comfortable darkness when Ilsevele and Grayth appeared at his side, scrambling down to where he lay.

"Araevin, that was the stupidest thing I've ever seen!" Ilsevele snapped. "You were outnumbered a hundred to one up there."

"It might not have been wise, but it was a valiant gesture nonetheless," said Grayth. The cleric looked up at the fight still going on around them. "No time to rest, Araevin. This battle isn't done yet, not by a long measure."

He laid his hands on Araevin and began to speak a healing prayer.

※ ※ ※ ※ ※

Sarya watched the battle from the vantage of her Vyshaanti platform. Off to the right of the enemy center, a brilliant prismatic blast streaked the sky. Fey'ri crumpled and fell from the air, but then the enemy mage plummeted after the daemonfey he'd defeated. She scowled, stung by the cost of the exchange. Her fey'ri were irreplaceable, and the longer the battle went on, the more of them would fall.

"This is taking too long," she growled.

Mardeiym Reithel stood next to her, arms crossed before his chest.

"The Evereskans have found help," he said. "This army is too large for them to field while maintaining the garrison our scouts have reported in the city."

"Evermeet," Sarya spat. "Who else could it be? We should have abandoned the orcs and other rabble instead of staying with them for twenty days of marching. We gave them too much time to prepare."

"Without the savage tribes, we'd have less than half the strength we do," Mardeiym answered. "They may have slowed us down, but today they're killing paleblood elves, and they're dying in place of our fey'ri. Evermeet's army would have met us sooner or later anyway."

Sarya gripped the rail of the platform, watching the battle. She longed to plunge into the fray herself, to slay with spell and talon, but she dared not. Once she immersed herself in the fight, she would be unable to exercise any form of control over her army. She could count on the fey'ri to follow orders and fight with cunning and resourcefulness, but the demons and yugoloths would take orders from no one other than her. The orc warbands and ogre marauders might break off and retreat from the unexpected Evereskan resistance without the threat of demons behind them to drive them forward.

The sinister crackle of magic rippled through the air at her shoulder. Sarya turned as a vrock suddenly appeared in a puff of sulfurous smoke. The vulture-demon carried two elven arrows snapped off in its right wing, but it seemed untroubled by the wounds.

"Lady S-Sarya," it hissed. "I have f-found the enemy commander-r. He stands th-there, a hundred yards from the s-standard."

The creature extended one filthy talon to point at a spot in the enemy center.

Sarya leaned closer to peer in the direction the demon indicated. The day was growing brighter, and while her orcs would not like that much, it was becoming easier to descry detail at a distance. She could see a small number of paleblood elves behind a strong line of Evereskan guards. Spell shields sparkled and glimmered over them. At the very least, there were some accomplished clerics and mages among that group.

"That will do," she decided. "I want those elves torn to pieces. Let's see if that disheartens the defenders a bit."

The vrock bobbed its vulturelike head. It flapped down to the high hillside below, where a great and terrible company of demons and yugoloths—vrocks and hulking, toadlike hezrous, skeletal babaus, and huge, gargoyle-like nycaloths—waited for Sarya's command. Each one of the

Forsaken House • 221

infernal creatures on the hillside could teleport itself, appearing out of nowhere to maim and rend. At the head of the company towered the glabrezu Grushakk, a terrible monster the size of a storm giant, with four arms and a canine face whose eyes glowed red with malice. Grushakk looked up to Sarya, who flung out her arm to indicate the direction of the prey.

"There!" she cried. "If you cannot find the commander, slay any mages you see."

Grushakk howled in glee, and clacked his pincers together.

"Rise!" the demon hissed. "Now we slay!"

The other demons stirred and spat. The glabrezu barked out his commands, and the demon company vanished in a ragged volley of teleportation.

Sarya wheeled on Mardeiym and said, "Pass the word to left, to right, and to center: Press now! We want to keep any help far from those the demons attack. This is our chance."

☙ ☙ ☙ ☙ ☙

Seiveril studied the battle from the small prominence he'd chosen for its view over the Cwm. Since the elven army had formed ranks near the eastern end of the vale, directly before the Sunset Gate, they held land that was generally higher than that their attackers had to cross to reach them. Not only did that provide the elf archers and mages with good fields of fire, it also slowed the rush of orcs and ogres, and it gave the elf commanders a good view of the entire battlefield.

A strong company of fey'ri swooped down over the Vale Guards directly in front of him, hurling their darts and blasting with deadly spells. Seiveril groaned as new gaps appeared in the ranks, elves falling to their knees with heavy javelins piercing shoulders and chests, others hurled limply through the air by jabbing forks of lightning or turned into living torches by gouts of evil fire. But the archers standing behind the infantry raised their bows and sent a storm of arrows skyward, even as the daemonfey climbed again to avoid the missiles. Fey'ri staggered in midair as arrows tore through them, spinning from the sky or simply crumpling and dropping.

"Jerreda doesn't seem too busy over on the left," he said to Starbrow. "Let's get some more of her archers over here to help cover our infantry against those damned fey'ri."

"I concur," Starbrow said. He called a runner over. "Find Jerreda on the left flank and ask her to send one hundred archers back to the center."

The messenger repeated the message back to ensure that he had it right, and dashed off toward the steep forests surrounding the tarn on the south side of the Cwm.

Seiveril looked toward the right. Lord Muirreste's mounted elves were hard-pressed, as well. The knights and lighter cavalry were much less numerous than the horde of orcs and ogres attacking them, but the open ground of the Cwm favored them. As long as they stayed in motion, the fey'ri had a hard time hitting them with any kind of massed magical assault. He wanted to send Muirreste some help, but he didn't know if—

"Demons!"

In the space of three heartbeats dozens upon dozens of demons and yugoloths, crackling with sinister magic or stinking of brimstone, appeared all over the hillside surrounding Seiveril. Even though he had been expecting it, Seiveril was paralyzed with horror for an endless moment.

So many of them! he thought. So many!

"Vesilde!" he called. "Vesilde!"

He wheeled to look for Vesilde Gaerth's knights, just as the demons struck out with their vile sorcery. Demon fire and destruction blasted the hilltop. Dozens of elves died at once, consumed by foul flames, scoured by unholy power, or hurled like broken dolls by the invisible might of demonic magic. Seiveril endured two searing waves of fire that scorched him even inside his enchanted elven plate. A mighty telekinetic buffet sent him hurling through the air. He picked himself up slowly, and looked up to find a hulking nycaloth rushing at him, its great claws as long and sharp as daggers. Seiveril just had time to raise his shield before the creature was on him, roaring with rage.

The nycaloth's claws scored his armor and almost wrenched his shield away, but Seiveril crouched low and held on while he found the haft of his silver mace with his right hand. He surged up and counterattacked, smashing the holy weapon at the nycaloth. He caught it with a glancing blow across the shoulder, but the mace detonated with a pure, white light that charred a great black scar in the nycaloth's flesh. The fiend screeched and reeled back, and Seiveril used the space he'd bought to quickly shout out a spell, dispatching the creature back to its infernal home.

He turned, searching for another foe, and found himself looking up at three massive hezrous, demons the size of ogres, with wide, toadlike mouths full of needle fangs and huge, powerful talons. The monsters croaked and scrambled toward him.

"Kill the cleric," they snarled. "Break his bones, and suck the marrow. Rip his heart out!"

The fearsome stench of the things gagged Seiveril. He went to one knee, trying to keep from losing his stomach as the monsters closed in. The hezrous hissed in glee and moved closer, their jaws gaping wide.

Then from one side Fflar Starbrow Melruth leaped in among the monsters, his sword Keryvian glowing like a shining white brand too bright to look at. He hewed off the arm of the hezrou closest to him, the sword slicing through demon flesh with a pure ringing sound. The monster roared in pain and tried to recoil, but Starbrow followed closely and rammed the point of the long sword deep into the hezrou's side, taking the monster under the ribs and stabbing it through its foul heart. The ancient magic of the weapon burned everything inside the hezrou's ribs to a foul gray ash, and smoke poured out of the demon's wide mouth as it collapsed.

The second hezrou raked at Starbrow with its huge

claws, but the moon elf ducked beneath the blow and rolled up under the demon's guard. He took off its left leg at the knee as he passed by. The demon toppled, black blood pouring from the wound, but snapped and clawed at Starbrow even as it fell. The elf champion danced back out of reach, and darted in to bury Keryvian's point between the hezrou's eyes. Again the sword flashed with its terrible white light, and another demon lay dead.

The third demon wheeled to face the threat of Keryvian, turning its back on Seiveril.

"I will take that sword from your dead hand!" the creature snarled.

It hammered Starbrow with a blast of unholy power, staggering him, but Seiveril hurled himself at the demon's back and smashed the base of its spine with a mighty blow of his holy mace. The hezrou shrieked and threw its arms up in the air, toppling forward—and Starbrow took its head with his white sword.

Seiveril looked over the bodies of the hezrous to Fflar and said, "My thanks, friend. You saved my life."

Fflar offered a smile and replied, "It only seems fair. Here, stay close by me. You watch my back, and I'll watch yours."

Seiveril glanced around at the furious battle. Elf bodies lay everywhere he looked, but many demons had fallen with them. Straight ahead, the Seldarine Knights of the Golden Star advanced with the sunrise behind them, gleaming like titans of gold as they battled against the foul tide. And to his right Ilsevele, Araevin, and their friends fought a terrible glabrezu. Ilsevele sent arrow after arrow into the creature's torso, while Araevin hammered at the monster with powerful spell blasts, and the cleric Grayth warded them all with his divine spell shields.

"There!" Seiveril called to Fflar. "The glabrezu!"

Fflar nodded and dashed off down the hillside, leaping down at the monster. Seiveril followed, only a step behind. The towering, dog-faced demon seized Grayth in one of its pincer hands and began to squeeze the armored human in its grasp, but then the genasi Maresa darted in and skewered its hamstring with her rapier. The monster roared and batted her away with a backhand slap of another arm—and Fflar and Seiveril were upon the monster. Fflar laid open its thigh with two great cuts of his sword, while Seiveril smashed its kneecap with his holy mace.

"I will destroy you all!" the demon rumbled.

It hurled Grayth aside and reached for Fflar. Then a silver arrow lodged in the side of its neck, and black blood foamed through its mouth. The demon groped closer, catching Seiveril with a weak blow that the cleric easily parried with his shield, and it collapsed facedown in the heather of the hillside.

"Well met, Father," said Ilsevele. She hurried forward, her bow still in her hand. Seiveril winced when he saw that she limped badly, blood streaming from a long cut on her hip. Araevin's cloak was tattered and singed, and the human Grayth was slow in picking himself up from the ground. "How are we doing?"

"We're still holding," Seiveril managed.

He looked around to see what had happened while he had been busy fighting for his own life, and he was surprised to see the daemonfey army falling back. Those demons who had survived the fray on the hilltop vanished one by one, teleporting away from the charge of the Knights of the Golden Star. The surging tide of orc warriors and marauding ogres retreated as well, their charge finally arrested by the terrible losses to bow, spell, and sword. Even the fey'ri overhead were falling back, unwilling to engage the elven army without the savage tribes of orcs to divide the elves' attention.

Maresa followed his glance.

"Actually, I'd say you've held," she observed. "Damn, but was that a fight!"

Fflar turned to Seiveril, clapped him on the shoulder, and said, "Congratulations, Seiveril. You've won your first battle."

Seiveril looked out over the carnage of the elven lines. He felt weary beyond words, weary enough that a breath of wind would be sufficient to carry him to Arvandor. With the sounds of battle fading into a few isolated clashes of steel and occasional spells instead of the deafening crescendo of a few minutes before, he could hear the piteous cries of the wounded and dying—elf, orc, and ogre alike—over all the battlefield. He looked down and noticed that his armor was spattered with blood.

"Have I, Starbrow?" he said quietly. "Because if I have, I don't know how many more battles we can afford to win."

⊛ ⊛ ⊛ ⊛ ⊛

At the end of the day Seiveril summoned Araevin, Ilsevele, and their companions to the post he had picked out for his standard, a simple guardhouse close by the Sunset Gate. In peaceful times it had served as a watchpost and a place for a dozen or so of Evereska's soldiers to stand guard over the path leading from the West Cwm to the Vine Vale. It had come to serve as the center of a sprawling field hospital. Hundreds of wounded elves lay beneath light shelters quickly raised to protect them from the elements. Several strong companies of knights and mages stood guard in case the daemonfey decided to mount a raid against the wounded.

None of Araevin's companions had been seriously hurt, so they had spent their day combing the battlefield for elves whose lives might still be saved by a cleric's spells or a potion of healing, while standing guard against a resumption of the fight. But the daemonfey had retired all the way to the Sentinel Pass, hard pressed by Muirreste's cavalry and Vesilde Gaerth's Golden Star knights. They did not mount another attack, though Araevin suspected that they might try the gate again under cover of darkness, when the orcs were not exposed to the daylight they so detested.

They found Seiveril working among the wounded, Starbrow standing guard over him. As a powerful cleric of Corellon Larethian, Lord Miritar knew much of the healing arts. Even though he had long since exhausted any healing magic he could muster, he still used his knowledge and lore to do what he could for the wounded. Seiveril looked up from the injured wood elf he'd been tending and offered Araevin and Ilsevele a weary smile.

"Ah, there you are," he said. "I am glad to see that you're all in one piece. Too many of our folk have fallen today."

"How bad is it?" Araevin asked.

"More than we can bear," Seiveril said. He stood and showed them out of the shelter, leading the way as they walked back toward the stone watchpost. "So far we've counted over five hundred dead, and at least that many wounded seriously enough that they'll need a cleric's spells before they can fight again. And we lost some irreplaceable leaders, as well."

"Who fell?" Ilsevele asked, visibly steeling herself.

"Celeilol Fireheart died in the first rush, standing at the head of the Leuthilspar spearmen. He was hacked down by a band of orc berserkers. The bladesinger Haraeth Echorn was slain by demon fire. Geren Festryth was torn apart by trolls." Seiveril sighed. "Jorildyn tells me that we lost almost twenty of our mages and spellsingers, and you well know that they are worth their weight in gold. And I just learned that Elvath Muirreste died an hour ago, pursuing the daemonfey horde on the shoulders of the Sentinel. I never imagined such a disaster."

They reached the small stone building, and Seiveril threw himself down on a plain wooden bench in the guard post, his head in his hands. The others followed. Araevin sank down with his back to the wall, too tired to stand any longer. He watched Seiveril, head bowed in grief, and glanced at Ilsevele and Grayth.

Grayth watched the elf commander, and took a breath.

"Each death is terrible," the human cleric said, "but you have not fought in vain, Lord Miritar. You repelled the daemonfey horde, and you inflicted grievous losses against them. Thousands of orcs and ogres and such lie dead in the Cwm, and we destroyed dozens and dozens of the demons and fiends who came against us. And you brought down many of the fey'ri, too. Your enemy is far less pleased with the day than you are."

"I've tried to explain that to him," Starbrow observed, standing with his shoulders to the doorframe. "Seiveril doesn't want to see it that way."

"All who died here, died because they answered my call!" Seiveril snapped, ire in his face. "I bear the responsibility for each of them. If I—"

"Did you summon the Evereskans to fight in their own defense?" Ilsevele interrupted. "Did you bring the daemonfey here? If you had not launched your crusade, Father, Evereska would even now lie under siege, surrounded by the whole of the daemonfey army. Warriors from Evermeet have laid down their lives to protect the innocents of Evereska. It is a terrible price, but our dead do not begrudge this victory. You should not either."

Starbrow looked at Seiveril, and stepped up to grip the elflord's shoulder with one hand.

"Seiveril," Starbrow said, "trust me when I say this: You did nothing wrong today. This is the cost of defending our homes and our lives from those who would take them from us. It's a hard cost, but the only thing more awful than a battle won is a battle lost. Give thanks for that much."

Sensing it was time for the subject to change, Araevin asked, "What did you want to speak to us about, Lord Seiveril?"

"I want to know more about this enemy," Seiveril said. "This is a war that is just beginning. I want to know where they came from, and why they're here. I suppose we've fought them to a stalemate today, and perhaps we may have the strength to drive them out of the Sentinel's pass and repel the daemonfey from Evereska. But even if we do that, I still don't know how to finish this war. What blow can I strike to mortally wound this foe? I am not content to chase the daemonfey into the wilds of the North and scatter their orc allies."

"How can I help you?" Araevin asked. "Whatever it is, I will do it."

"You know more about the daemonfey and their designs than anyone," said Seiveril. "I think that your *telkiira* are at the bottom of this mystery. Unravel the story of the lorestones, and you will learn something about the daemonfey that they are desperate to keep hidden from us. I want you to continue your quest for the next loregem, and find out what it is that they are hiding from us."

"Are you certain you do not need me here?" Araevin asked. "We've lost many wizards, and I can stand spell-for-spell against any sorcerer the fey'ri have revealed so far."

"Of course your spells would be useful, but no one else has studied these loregems, and I cannot stand the thought of abandoning them to the daemonfey. The *telkiira* are important, I know they are."

Araevin glanced at his companions. He met Ilsevele's eyes, and she offered a slight nod. He looked to Grayth, who shrugged in his heavy armor.

"If this is the deadliest blow we can strike against the daemonfey, I am all for it," the cleric said.

"What about you, Maresa?" Ilsevele asked. "You are under no obligation to stay with us."

The genasi crossed her arms, tossed her head, and replied, "I'm not likely to leave now, am I? I want to see how this turns out, or I'll spend the rest of my life wondering what in the Nine Hells was in that third gemstone."

"Rest for tonight in Evereska," said Seiveril, "and leave in the morning."

"But what if the daemonfey attack again?" Araevin asked.

"We'll hold them," Starbrow promised. "We will have to."

CHAPTER 14

1 Tarsakh, the Year of Lightning Storms

At the dawning of the day after the Battle of the Cwm, Araevin and his companions rode out of Evereska, heading north into the rugged heart of the Shaeradim. The third *telkiira* glimmered in Araevin's consciousness like a lingering daydream or a few notes of a familiar song that refused to be forgotten. When he closed his eyes, he could sense the gemstone, feeling its direction and closeness just as he might feel the sun on his face with his eyes closed and know whether it was a bright or cloudy day. From Evereska it lay north and somewhat west, and based on his experience in following the second *telkiira*'s pull from Waterdeep to the Forest of Wyrms, he knew it was far off.

Had he more time, Araevin would have been content to follow his trail on foot, closing in on the lorestone slowly and methodically. But the presence of the fey'ri army—encamped high in the Rillvale, driven back but not defeated—urged him to move faster. If the *telkiira* in fact harbored some secret lore that might be turned against the daemonfey, if it truly contained some useful knowledge or weapon, then it was needed in Evereska as soon as he could retrieve it. And if the *telkiira* quest proved to be a vain hope, then the sooner he followed the trail to its end and returned, the sooner he could lend his arcane strength to the crusade's next battle. So, instead of creeping out of the Shaeradim through one of the secret trails to the north, they spent the morning following the track deeper into the mountains, traversing higher and higher vales that not even the Evereskans visited often, until at last they reached the barren stone plinth of a high, thready waterfall that coursed down from a cliff above them. A moss-grown stone marker stood beside the pool, leaning crookedly to one side.

"Not another one of these," Maresa observed. She dismounted and set her hands on her hips. "It can't be good to tempt Tymora's luck too often. Sooner or later we're not going to go where we think we're going."

"Where does this one lead, Araevin?" Grayth asked.

"If I understand the Evereskan records, it will take us to the Moonwood, somewhat north of Silverymoon."

"Is that where the third loregem lies?"

"Possible, but unlikely." Araevin swung himself down from his own mount, and checked to make sure his saddlebags and gear were secure. "I can feel the *telkiira* quite a long ways north and west of here, and this is the nearest *portal* I know of that leads a fair distance to the north. It's my hope that transporting ourselves to the Moonwood will bring us closer to our goal, and save us some travel."

"We might overshoot the mark," Ilsevele said. "The Moonwood might be farther from the goal than we are right here."

"I know, but this seems worth a try. If I feel that the *telkiira* is farther away once we pass to the other side of the portal, we will simply step back through and proceed from here. It costs us no more time than it took to climb up here if I'm wrong, but if I'm right, we may save days of hard riding."

"So what sort of horrible monsters infest the Moonwood?" Maresa muttered. "Trolls and dragons again? Or something else this time?"

Araevin replied, "The Moonwood doesn't have quite the same reputation as the Trollbark or the Forest of Wyrms. But it's been almost eighty years since I was last in Silverymoon and the lands about, so my information may be out-of-date."

He moved over to the stone marker and studied it, softly tracing the weathered Espruar runes carved into its lichen-covered surface. Evereska's high vales concealed a handful of ancient elfgates leading to elven realms that no longer existed. Araevin cast a spell that let him study the ancient device and perceive its condition, its destination, and the method of its awakening.

"This gate linked Evereska to a northerly outpost of the fallen realm of Sharrven," Araevin said, "on the far side of the River Rauvin. This is the right one. Be ready to move swiftly when the gate opens, for it will not remain open for long."

Dutifully, his traveling companions ringed themselves around the elfgate, and waited for his signal. Araevin straightened, caught the reins of his horse, and led the animal closer. He spoke the ancient words needed to wake the portal, and quickly touched the device. A golden shimmer arose around him, warm and electric, and he was standing somewhere else, an overgrown clearing in a deep forest. He led his horse away from the weathered stone post marking the northern end of the portal, and watched as his companions came through one by one.

Maresa made a show of patting her arms and legs, as if part of her might have been left behind.

"Well, what do you know? I'm all here," she remarked.

Ilsevele looked to Araevin and asked, "Are we closer, or not?"

Araevin hesitated only a moment, pausing to make

sure of the magical intuition dancing in his mind, then answered, "Yes. The loregem now lies east of us, not close, but not terribly far."

Grayth glanced at the brooding sky.

"More riding, then," the cleric said. "Unless you know of another portal leading in the right direction."

"No elven realms ever stood between the Moonwood and Anauroch. I could try a teleport spell, but we'd have to leave the horses behind. And I would be guessing at where I'm going, which is not wise with such magic." Araevin shook his head and concluded, "We'll have to ride from here."

They mounted their horses again and headed east, riding beneath a cold but thankfully sparse drizzle. Winter might have been fading in the lands of the North, but spring's grip was still frail. Large patches of snow lingered under the tall trees of the forest, and the air was damp and chilly. After an hour's ride, they broke out of the eastern eaves of the Moonwood and rode across more open land, rolling hills crowned with bare, windswept heather, interspersed with thicket-filled vales and swift, cold streams. South of them rose the white peaks of a low but rugged mountain range marching off toward the east.

Early in the afternoon they struck upon a clear track running north and south across their path. Araevin couldn't recall the exact lay of the land, but Grayth prayed for Lathander's guidance and directed the company to follow the track to the north. Toward the end of the day the track crossed a broad, swift river, icy cold but fortunately less than knee-deep at the ford.

"We're lucky," Grayth called to Araevin over the rushing of the water. "If we come back this way in ten or fifteen days, the snowmelt will make this ford impassable!"

"Does any of this look familiar?" Ilsevele asked Araevin.

"I think this might be the Redrun. If we followed it south for quite a ways, we would eventually reach Sundabar."

"This track leads in the wrong direction, then."

"I'm not so sure." Araevin pointed at a stout marker that stood overlooking the ford. "Those are Dethek runes—Dwarvish. I think this track might skirt north of the Rauvin Mountains and head east through the Cold Vale toward Citadel Adbar."

"I think you may be right, Araevin," Maresa said, studying the Dwarvish writing. "I can make out some of this, I think . . . ah, that's not good."

"What?"

"The trail glyphs warn of orc lands ahead. And someone called Grimlight," said Maresa. "It's going to be a cold and lonely ride. I don't think there's anything between here and Adbar, and that's more than two hundred miles off according to the dwarves' glyphs. No civilization anywhere."

"The dwarves must pass this way," observed Grayth. "They raised a stone here, anyway."

"Yes, but look at the track," Ilsevele said. "Not much traffic at all."

They made another five miles before camping for the night in a small, sheltered hollow. The night was bitterly cold, cold enough that they decided to build a fire in spite of the risk of attracting orc marauders, but the night passed by without event. They pressed on in the morning, and rode as hard as they could reasonably push the horses for the next several days. The track skirted just to the north of the stark, forbidding foothills of the Rauvin Mountains, passing through a desolate land of tumbled boulder-fields covered in moss, boggy green fells, and sudden deep gorges across their path where icy streams plummeted down out of the mountains and carved paths through the hills. It was cold and wet, wreathed in dense fogs at night, empty except for the sound of countless white rills and falls amid the stony hills. Crumbling old dwarven bridges crossed stream after stream, some in such bad repair that Araevin or Grayth were forced to resort to magic to get the company across safely.

At noon of the fifth day since leaving Evereska, they reached another old bridge spanning a narrow gorge less than fifty feet wide, but twice that in depth. A nameless mountain stream rushed by below, plunging from rock to rock as it descended. The bridge was sound enough to cross, but in the middle of the span Araevin halted and looked downstream.

"Here," he said. "This is the gorge, I'm sure of it. We need to follow it downstream from here."

Ilsevele studied the landscape and said, "It will be impossible for the horses."

"We'll leave them, along with all the gear we don't need in a fight. I'll hide the animals and our cache with a spell."

They led their mounts back a few hundred yards to the empty shell of an old, long-abandoned wayhouse along the road, and left the horses in the moss-grown ruin, concealed by an illusion Araevin wove to make the whole place seem like one more tumbled boulder den to anyone passing by.

The company returned to the bridge and with great care picked their way down the slippery walls of the gorge to the stream at the bottom. The stream snaked back and forth between huge boulders and steep shoulders of rock and filled the gully with cold spray and roaring water. But by leaping from stone to stone or scrambling over tumbled rock falls they were able to pick their way downward. Fortunately, it seemed that spring was just slow enough in coming that the bottom of the gorge was still passable. Araevin could easily see that a few days of heavy rain or snowmelt would have filled the channel from side to side.

The gorge turned to the east in a sharp bend that took quite a scramble to negotiate—and they saw the cave mouth. Beneath an overhanging shelf of rock, about fifteen feet above the stream below, a great dark tunnel gaped in the moss-covered wall of the gorge. Araevin halted, riveted by the sight of the place that had hovered in his mind since finding the second stone. It was not quite exactly as he had seen it. The stream was higher, some of the boulders seemed to have shifted or moved, and the vagaries of light and weather were not the same. But he could feel the closeness of the third stone. And as he looked closer, he realized that some of the smaller boulders and water-soaked branches clustered below the cave mouth were not rock and wood, but crushed and splintered bones.

"That's it," he replied in answer to the question he had not yet been asked. "It's in there."

Grayth doffed his helm and mopped his brow with the sleeve of the loose surcoat he wore over his plate armor. "Good, I was getting tired. Can't say I like the looks of it, though. That's a monster's lair if I've ever seen one."

"What do you think it might be?" Maresa asked.

"Maybe it's the lair of Grimlight, whoever or whatever that is," Ilsevele offered.

Grayth replaced his helm, looked up to Araevin, and asked, "So what's the plan?"

"Rest a few minutes, then ready ourselves with spells and go in," Araevin said.

He looked around at the gorge. He could feel the menace of the place, and wished he had Whyllwyst with him to keep an eye on their line of retreat once they entered the cave. He didn't like the idea of not knowing if anyone else might be coming up behind them.

"I suppose we'll have to find out the hard way who lives here," Araevin said, "and whether or not they're willing to part with the lorestone."

❂ ❂ ❂ ❂ ❂

It took Methrammar Aerasumé almost ten days to gather a force from the cities of the League. Most of the confederation's soldiers were scattered all over the Silver Marches in small detachments and companies, doing their best to check the depredations of raiding giants and marauding orcs. The High Marshal stripped whole companies from other tasks and sent them up the Rauvin by barge, gathering them in Everlund's Great Armory, the walled barracks compound overlooking the busy riverfront of the city. His agents scoured the city's markets and caravan yards, buying up every pack animal in sight as they amassed a tremendous store of food and supplies for the march.

Gaerradh was impressed by the martial array Methrammar assembled, even though she was more anxious with each day that passed. Two hundred of Silverymoon's famous Knights in Silver rode at the head of the column—human, elf, and half-elf soldiers strengthened by a dozen mages of the city's famous Spellguard. Four hundred sturdy dwarf warriors—Iron Guards from Citadel Adbar, and a small company from Citadel Felbarr—tromped along behind the riders, openly discontented with the notion of marching off into the trackless woodlands to fight in the service of wood elves who weren't even members of Alustriel's league. Several small companies from smaller towns such as Auvandell and Jalanthar followed, including a handful of human huntsmen and trackers almost as comfortable in the forest as Gaerradh herself. And finally, Methrammar had prevailed upon the First Elder of Everlund to lend him three seasoned companies of the Army of the Vale. All told, Methrammar's expedition numbered well over a thousand soldiers.

After assembling his force, Methrammar did not lead his army straight south into the wood, as Gaerradh would have expected.

"If your folk are retreating to the Lost Peaks, then that is where we should march to," he explained. "The forest is a road to elves, but this army we have gathered will not make good speed on elven trails."

Instead, they marched southwest along the trade road known as the Evermoor Way, skirting the western edge of the forest for fifty miles before turning south into the forest on the fifth day of their march. From there, Gaerradh led them along the remnants of the elven highways that had once crisscrossed the High Forest in the days of Sharrven and Siluvanede.

On the sixth day out of Everlund, soon after Methrammar's army entered the forest, the daemonfey struck.

Gaerradh was with Methrammar, riding with the Knights in Silver at the head of the column. Behind them the other companies were scattered over close to a mile of trail, threading their way among the rugged, dense forest of the hills that climbed ever southward to the hidden slopes of the Lost Peaks. Suddenly, from the dark hillside above the trail, a barrage of magical fireballs whistled down into the marching column.

"Ambush!" Methrammar cried. "To arms! To arms!"

The fireballs exploded a bowshot behind the lead company, huge orange gouts of flame blossoming in the gloomy, dripping forest. The heat of the magical fire was so fierce that Gaerradh could feel the flames from where she stood. Before the flames fully vanished, brilliant bolts of lightning stabbed down from the hillside above the track, splintering trees with tremendous *cracks!* and *booms!* that left Gaerradh's ears ringing. Everlundan soldiers staggered and screamed, burned or maimed by the deadly magic.

Methrammar wheeled his horse about, his handsome face hard and flat with anger.

"Damn! Where did they come from?" he hissed. Then he shouted at the Silvaeren knight who commanded the vanguard, "Take defensive positions and spread out! They're going to try to swarm the vanguard while the rest of the column is cut off by the spellcasters!"

I should have been scouting the trail instead of riding with Methrammar, Gaerradh thought angrily. *No fey'ri sorcerers would have ambushed Sheeril and I!*

Few others came close to matching her woodcraft, but Methrammar had asked her to stay close by him, pointing out that her knowledge of the trails and landmarks of the forest was irreplaceable. In truth, she had not minded the opportunity to keep the company of the handsome commander. She cursed her own foolishness and swept the woods nearby with her keen eyes, looking for the next step of the ambush.

Dark, swift forms dropped down from wooded hillside above the trail with bared steel in their filthy talons.

"Here they come!" she cried. "Watch upslope!"

Gaerradh slipped off her own mount and unslung her bow. She had no skill in fighting on horseback, and she suspected that anyone on a horse would be singled out by enemy archers and wizards.

Forsaken House • 239

Sheeril growled at her heel, baring her fangs at the forest. Gaerradh quickly knelt down beside the wolf and tapped her shoulder, pointing downslope.

"Scout!" she commanded.

She didn't think the ambushers would try to struggle up the hillside to get at the Silvaeren soldiers, but having just been fooled once, she didn't mean to be fooled again. Sheeril was trained to seek out hidden foes and stay out of sight. The wolf yipped once and bounded off down the hillside. Then Gaerradh darted over to take cover by a huge dead spruce, already seeking out marks for her arrows.

Orcish war cries filled the air, and a ragged line of berserkers leaped down the hillside through the trees, shrieking like blood-maddened beasts as they hurled themselves on the humans and elves of Silverymoon's company. A barrage of fireballs preceded the orc charge, but the Silvaeren mages among the vanguard were ready and countered many of the attacker's spells. Gaerradh searched the treetops and high branches for the daemonfey spellcasters, ignoring the orcs. She glimpsed a bat-winged fey'ri in dark mithral armor gliding overhead, its hands gesturing as it shaped another spell. Gaerradh drew and fired in one smooth motion, sending two arrows at the enemy wizard. One glanced away from a spell ward of some kind, but the other struck true, taking the fey'ri just under its breastbone. The demonspawned sun elf crumpled in midair and began to fall.

Gaerradh looked for another target, but with a terrible crash the orcs reached the waiting soldiers. Axes rose and fell, swords flashed, and the dead and wounded began to fall. Steel clattered and rang, and angry human battle cries rose to match the bellowing of the orc raiders. A hulking orc with a great hooked axe ran straight for Gaerradh, hurling past the human and elf swordsmen around her. She didn't have enough time to shoot, and had to parry quickly with the strong shaft of her bow until she managed to draw one of her gracefully curved axes from her belt.

"Die, elf!" the big orc shouted. His mouth was flecked

with foam, and his eyes rolled wildly in his porcine face. "Kill! Kill!"

One blow of his huge axe tore Gaerradh's bow from her left hand, and he reversed his swing and brought the sharp hook on the back of his weapon whistling at her neck. Gaerradh ducked under the blow and yanked her off-hand axe from her belt. Then she straightened up and launched herself at the orc, weaving her two axes before her in a deadly double arc of whirling elven steel. She slashed him once across the forearm, a second time across the ribs, and the savage warrior simply shoved her away with the thick haft of his war axe. Gaerradh stumbled back three steps and almost fell.

The berserker roared in glee and stepped forward, whirling the axe with the full length of his long, powerful arms, but then he grunted and staggered as a barrage of streaking globes of blue magic pummeled him from the side. Gaerradh risked a quick glance that way, and saw Methrammar Aerasumé standing, sword in one hand, wand in the other. He offered one quick, fierce smile, and whirled away to aid another soldier.

The orc recovered from Methrammar's spell and snarled, blood streaming from his mouth. He fixed his eyes on Gaerradh and shambled closer, kept on his feet by nothing more than hate and bloodlust. Roaring in rage, the bestial warrior swung wildly, but the wood elf used her right-hand axe to pass the orc's swing over her head. She stepped inside his reach and split his forehead with her left-hand axe.

More spells blasted into the melee, silver forks of lightning and furious jets of azure fire dropping orcs on all sides, while simmering spheres of acid and lances of black ice streaked down from the fey'ri sorcerers skulking on the hillside above, wreaking carnage among the Silvaeren soldiers. Gaerradh stooped to retrieve her bow and crouched beside a tree, searching for another fey'ri spellcaster, but in the space of a few moments the battle suddenly ended. The orcs broke and ran, the surviving warriors fleeing into the trees or snarling defiance at the Silvaeren company. Overhead, the fey'ri spellcasters vanished as well.

"Gaerradh!" Methrammar Aerasumé called. He stood among the soldiers of Silverymoon, his long sword spattered with red. "Gaerradh!"

"I'm here," she replied.

She looked around. Despite the furious assault, the Silvaeren company had not fared too badly. More than a few of Silverymoon's soldiers would not return to their city, but even more orc warriors lay dead at their feet. Farther back in the column, where the fey'ri had concentrated their first barrage of deadly spells, she expected the carnage would be worse. She slung her bow, then stooped and wiped her axe on the ragged wolf skin worn by her orc adversary.

"We walked right into that," she said.

Methrammar grimaced and replied, "I know. You warned us about these fey'ri, but after so many days of seeing nothing of them . . ." The high marshal sighed and sheathed his sword. "At least we slew many of them, too."

"Only their orc allies. The daemonfey spellcasters are the real threat. I shot one, but I didn't see any more fall." Gaerradh looked up at him, and smiled thinly. "Thank you for the help with this big one, by the way. You gave me just the opening I needed."

"We'd never find our way to the Lost Peaks without you. And I find that I've grown too fond of your company to let an orc deprive me of it," replied Methrammar. He sighed and looked over the soldiers who stood nearby, searching to see who among their fallen comrades still lived. "We will have to post a strong watch at night. If they're willing to attack us by day, they will certainly look for a chance to harry us while we're trying to rest."

❖ ❖ ❖ ❖ ❖

Amlaruil, Queen of Evermeet, entered the Dome of Stars at a sedate pace. She was dressed in a regal dress of gold brocade, her scepter of office transmuted into a willowy golden wand to match the gown. The Dome's galleries were dark and silent, empty of courtiers and spectators. By chance the tidings from Faerûn had come an hour before the beginning of a royal ball, so she had arranged for the council members to be diverted to the Dome as they arrived at the party.

Faint strains of music echoed from the distant ballroom. Some of her guests would undoubtedly note that the queen and her councilors were late for the revelry, but Amlaruil hoped that they would be able to sweep in together as a gala entourage, and appear fashionably late.

As one, her councilors rose to meet her. If Ammisyll Veldann and Selsharra Durothil stood a little slower than the others and did not bow as deeply or as long, they at least observed the forms of courtesy. Like Amlaruil, each was dressed for the formal dance to follow, bedecked in the finest robes or flowing dresses as appropriate. It lent a strangely humorous atmosphere to the scene.

Amlaruil suppressed a smile and said, "Thank you for answering my summons. I have received news from Evereska. There has been a fierce battle in the passes approaching the LastHome."

"Lord Miritar's expedition?" High Admiral Elsydar asked.

"Yes. It seems that his host transited the elfgates to Evereska just in time to meet the daemonfey onslaught. They fought the invaders on the shoulders of *Ilaerothil* and halted their advance."

"A victory, or a defeat?" Keryth Blackhelm asked, steeling himself for the answer.

"The fighting was fierce. I understand that Lord Miritar lost hundreds of warriors, but he won the day. The daemonfey army suffered far greater losses, and they were stopped short of the Vine Vale."

"Recklessness," muttered Selsharra Durothil. "He led his mob of volunteers away from the safety of Evereska's walls to fight in the open field? Here we see the cost of Miritar's folly—yet more of Evermeet's sons and daughters dead

Forsaken House • 243

on meaningless fields in Faerûn's pointless battles. When do you intend to put an end to this, Lady Moonflower?"

"None of us was there to judge whether Seiveril Miritar's generalship was foolish or sound," Keryth Blackhelm growled. Lady Durothil's discourtesy had not escaped him. "I for one will withhold my censure until I know more."

"For what possible purpose did he lead an untrained army into such a terrible battle?" Selsharra asked. "I am no war leader, but even I know that a wise general does not abandon impregnable fortifications to hazard his soldiers in an even fight on open terrain. Was it simply a matter of Seiveril's crusading zeal overriding his common sense? Or was he determined to demonstrate to all of us that his courage brooks no question?"

"Among other things, it occurs to me that Lord Miritar could do little to succor the wood elves of the High Forest if he sat on top of Evereska's cliffs and did nothing else," the High Marshal retorted. "If you take up arms against an enemy, you must be willing to hazard losses in order to defend positions you must defend, or attack positions you must take. That is the nature of war."

"That is the problem, isn't it?" Ammisyll Veldann observed. "Evermeet is not at war, yet here we learn that hundreds of our soldiers are dying in distant battles."

Amlaruil refused to let Veldann and Durothil bait her any further.

"I will provide a full account of the fighting as soon as I am able to," she said firmly. "Hill Elder Duirsar of Evereska informs me that Seiveril's warriors won a hard-fought battle and halted the enemy advance. For that I give thanks, since the daemonfey are enemies of all elves. I regret that warriors have died, but I do not regret that they died to spare the folk of Evereska a deadly siege or bloody assault."

The table fell silent, until Zaltarish the scribe cleared his throat and said, "Have you heard anything of Lord Seiveril's intentions, Your Majesty? What has happened since the battle? Where is he now, where are his foes? Wars are rarely won in a single day."

Amlaruil shook her head and answered, "I know nothing more than what I have already said. I will send a representative to Evereska tomorrow to confer with the Hill Elder and obtain a better account of the fighting in the Shaeradim."

"I will go, if you permit me," Keryth Blackhelm said.

"Of course, Lord Blackhelm." Amlaruil looked around the table. "That is all I had to say. If there is nothing else—"

"There is one thing," Selsharra Durothil said.

Amlaruil smoothed her face and refused to show any irritation when she asked, "Yes, Lady Durothil?"

"Your council now stands at seven members, Lady Moonflower. While there is no law that dictates the size or composition of the Council of Evermeet, tradition would indicate that we should replace Miritar and Jerreda Starcloak. I have given the matter some thought, and it occurs to me that we could fill Miritar's seat immediately."

Zaltarish folded his hands before him and said, "Lady Durothil, it has been less than a month. Council seats have sometimes gone unfilled for years. There is no need to hurry such an important decision."

"I disagree. First of all, it is not clear to me that Evermeet's peril allows us to delay this decision as we might in more peaceful times. Secondly, if an ideal candidate is available, I see no point in delaying his or her accession."

"I presume you have some ideal candidate in mind?" Meraera Silden said dryly.

"Lord Miritar was, of course, the High Cleric of Corellon's Grove, a very senior representative of the Seldarine's clergy. I find myself concerned that we have no high-ranking cleric on the council now who might advise us of the will of Corellon Larethian when we engage in our deliberations. Therefore, I propose that Elder Star Mellyth Echorn should be elevated to Miritar's seat. He is the highest-ranking cleric of Corellon in Evermeet, and a member of a high and noble family as well. Who could be a better choice?"

Amlaruil leaned back in her seat, her expression neutral. Clearly, Selsharra Durothil thought that a conservative cleric of Corellon Larethian might be a powerful new voice on the council, a voice sympathetic to the traditionalist sun elf Houses. By suggesting Mellyth Echorn, Selsharra put Amlaruil in the position of accepting her nomination—not something Amlaruil was particularly inclined to do, though in truth she didn't know if Echorn was unsuitable—or declining the Elder Star, which would appear to be a deliberate slight to those of Corellon's faith. She had no doubt that Selsharra would see to it that word got out that the Durothils had pushed for the Elder Star's nomination. Lady Durothil gained in either case.

I wonder how badly it would go if I told Selsharra Durothil that her seat was vacant, too, Amlaruil thought.

The queen offered the sun elf noblewoman a warm smile.

"The councilors serve at my pleasure, as I am sure you know," she said. "I will consider the matter carefully, and I thank you for your suggestion. However, I would rather examine our needs thoroughly and make sure that I select the right candidate than act hastily and perhaps choose the wrong one. I will let you know when I have decided." She rose, and indicated the chamber's doors. "Now, let us join the festivities, before our absence creates undue alarm."

◈ ◈ ◈ ◈ ◈

The cave mouth led into a warren of dank, twisting tunnels, filled with swift, icy rivulets of water that poured down through the wet rock. Araevin summoned a magical light in order to illuminate their path. More bones, splintered and crushed, glimmered in the yellow magelight, and a damp, musky scent hung in the chill air.

"Damn," whispered Grayth. "That's a hill giant's skull, or I'm a goblin. Are you sure this is the right cave, Araevin?"

"I won't be upset if you say no," Maresa added.

Araevin replied, "Sorry to say so, but yes."

He paused to examine the chamber. As had happened in the Forest of Wyrms, he was too close to sense the exact location of the next stone. They would have to find it the hard way. Several passageways burrowed off into the blackness, but they seemed somewhat small and contorted for anything large enough to make a meal of a giant. To his right, though, a V-shaped cleft seemed to go back into the rock for quite a distance, and a good-sized stream poured out of its bottom to run across the cavern floor and out into the gorge.

"This way, I think."

One by one, they clambered up into the cleft, icy water running swiftly over their feet, and followed the subterranean streambed deeper into the caves. The way was difficult and wet. Though the stream was rarely deeper than mid-calf, the path was obstructed by numerous boulders and awkward shelves and columns of stone, and the stream descended sharply from above. They scaled several small cascades and chutes, until Araevin's teeth chattered from the cold and his hands were numb.

Forty or fifty yards from the entrance, they climbed up into a large, open cave. The air stank of old meat, and the smell was overpowering. Grayth drew his sword and carefully moved up out of the streambed, peering into the twisting galleries of stone that framed the chamber. Araevin followed the Lathanderite, glad to have a strong friend in heavy plate armor a few steps ahead of him. Ilsevele and Maresa brought up the rear, Ilsevele's bow at the ready, Maresa carrying her rapier and crossbow. Clearly, something lived in the chamber at the top of the stream. More discarded bones lay scattered about, and more tellingly, rotten old wooden chests bursting with silver and gold coins stood haphazardly at the far end of the room. But there was no sign of the cavern's denizen, though more of the small, halfling-sized tunnels led away from the room.

"Is your gemstone here, Araevin?" asked Grayth.

"It's close," the mage said. He kept his wand of disruption in hand, watching the shadows carefully, and moved over to investigate the hoard gathered in the dry end of the room. That at least spoke of intelligence. A dumb beast would not gather the gold of its victims.

Ilsevele followed Araevin over to the treasure, lowering her bow, and said, "Let's find the *telkiira* and get out of here before this thing comes home."

"Too late, heh!" croaked a horrible, rasping voice from the shadows. "Grimlight is home, heh!"

Araevin and the others whirled at the sound, looking for whomever or whatever had spoken, but then, from one of the small tunnels, a brilliant stroke of lightning blasted out, spearing Ilsevele and Grayth. Ilsevele threw herself aside, somehow avoiding the terrible blast, but the bolt caught the Lathanderite dead center in his steel armor. Azure fingers of electricity crawled over the cleric, snapping and popping, as he jerked and thrashed, pinned in place by the lightning. Then it ended, and Grayth collapsed to the cavern floor, his limbs twitching and smoke rising from the joints in his armor.

"Who is in Grimlight's den? Must be Grimlight's dinner, heh!"

Something seemed to chuckle with a sly, throaty sound, and a huge, blunt snout appeared in the tunnel mouth. The creature slithered forth, revealing first a gaping, crocodilian maw, then a draconian face with two curling horns, and a long, powerful body covered in thick scales with pairs of small, clawed legs that it held folded close to its body as it crawled out of its tunnels.

"What in all the screaming hells is *that*?" Maresa snarled.

The genasi didn't wait for an answer, but instead leveled her crossbow and loosed a bolt at the monster. Grimlight jerked its head aside with a surprisingly quick motion, and the quarrel glanced away from the thick scales above the creature's eyes. Maresa swore and yanked back on her crossbow's string, loading another quarrel.

Araevin retreated three quick steps away from the huge creature, narrowly avoiding a great snap of its fang-filled jaws, and pointed the disruption wand at its head, barking out the command word. A tremendous shriek of sonic power burst from the wand, blasting a yard-wide ram of distorted air at Grimlight that hammered the monster like the club of a giant. But Grimlight recovered with startling speed and barreled straight at Araevin, hurling the mage headlong with a quick toss of its horned head. Araevin crashed into the hard rock of the cavern wall. Ribs cracked and his breath exploded from his mouth in a deep grunt.

Ilsevele picked herself up from the floor and found her bow. Whispering the words of a fire spell, she ensorcelled her arrow and shot it at the scaled worm. The arrow kindled in flight and plunged deep into Grimlight's side, a flaming bolt that set the monster to thrashing with such violence that its long, thick tail smashed foot-thick stalagmites to flinders.

"Grimlight will eat you all!" the monster hissed in rage. "Room for many in Grimlight's belly, yes, yes!"

Ilsevele shot again, a pair of arrows that stuck in the thick scales of the monster's face but did not penetrate deeply enough to inflict any serious injury. The arrows did succeed in attracting Grimlight's undivided attention, though. The wyrm hissed so loudly that Araevin's ears rang, and launched itself at the archer like a living battering ram, lunging across the cavern floor.

Araevin managed to draw a breath deeply enough to speak a spell. He pointed his finger and fired a deadly green ray of disintegration at the huge creature. The terrible emerald beam chewed deeply into Grimlight's flank, gouging out an awful wound for ten feet or more along the worm's side. Black blood spewed from the injury, and Grimlight's charge at Ilsevele faltered. The creature bucked and thrashed—incidentally knocking Grayth twenty feet across the cavern, as the cleric began to grope his way to his feet. It opened its jaws wide and blasted Araevin at point-blank range with a blue-white spear of lightning. The monster's lightning breath hurled Araevin head-over-heels through the air, and he landed in the icy streambed and struck his head on stone. Bright white lights flared in his vision, and a great roaring sound filled his ears.

I have to get up, he told himself.

He seized on that simple thought with all the desperation of a drowning man and slowly rolled over onto his belly, pushing himself upright with arms that felt as weak and empty as burned-out cinders. He wiped away the blood streaming down his face and looked up, even though the cavern tilted crazily from side to side.

Grayth, sword in hand, fended off Grimlight's snapping jaws, slashing its snout and face with quick thrusts and cuts. Ilsevele danced back away from the monster, sinking arrow after arrow into its thrashing body while Maresa riddled its other flank with her own magic. Araevin groped about in the icy water for his holster of wands, and finally found it. He fumbled with a simple wand for conjuring magic bolts, and took aim at the long, deep wound his disintegration spell had carved from the monster's side.

"Take that," he gasped, and fired four glowing darts into the gaping hole already scored in Grimlight's body.

Grimlight shuddered and groaned, coiling up its great serpentine body into a squirming ball. It threw up its head to the ceiling, hissing and bubbling deep in its throat, and Grayth staggered forward. One hand cupped on the pommel, the human drove his sword up through the soft white underside of the neck, the jaw, and into the monster's brain. The creature shuddered once and lay still.

Grayth collapsed across the monster he'd just killed, leaning on his sword.

"Thank Lathander that's done," he groaned. "I think I'm getting too old for this."

Ilsevele straightened, lowering her bow. She looked around and caught sight of Araevin.

"Araevin! You're hurt!" she cried, and ran over to take his arm.

Araevin tried to shrug off her help, but his legs felt rubbery and weak.

"I'll survive," he managed. "Let's find the *telkiira* before we do anything else. And keep an eye open for the daemonfey. The last time we were near a *telkiira*, they appeared."

Ilsevele looked closely into his face and frowned.

"Are you trying to break my heart?" she asked. "First that insane flight of yours against the whole fey'ri army, and now this. Are you trying to make a widow of me before we even marry?"

"You're taking every chance I am," he replied. "I'll stop when you do."

He moved over to Grimlight's hoard. Several of the rotten old chests had been smashed into splinters by the creature's thrashings, and coins and jewels lay scattered all over the cavern floor.

"So what was that, anyway?" Maresa asked. "Some kind of legless dragon?"

"A behir," Grayth replied. "A little like a dragon." He straightened up and sheathed his sword, turning to join the search. "So, will this stone look like—"

From the shadows by the steep cleft of the cavern stream, a bright blue ray shot out and struck Araevin in the middle of his torso. Araevin staggered back in surprise, but he was no more wounded than he had been a moment before. Instead, a shimmering blue field of dancing light clung to his body, sparkling in the darkness of the cave.

A dimension lock! he realized.

"Watch out! The daemonfey!" he cried.

Six demons appeared in the behir's cavern, wreathed in foul-smelling smoke. From the cleft more of the fey'ri poured into the room, their eyes glowing red with hate. Behind the demonic warriors came Araevin's enemy, the fierce sorcerer with the armor of golden scales and the jeweled eye patch.

He gestured at Araevin and his comrades and shouted, "Take them alive! The mage is anchored to this plane and cannot escape us this time!"

Araevin heard Ilsevele's bow thrum, while Maresa swore a vile oath and Grayth drew his sword with a shrill

Forsaken House • 251

ring of steel. Araevin snapped out the words of terrible ice blast he'd learned from the second *telkiira*, directing a great white fountain of unendurable frigidity at the fey'ri clambering up into the chamber. The first fey'ri paled into translucent scarlet ice and shattered, and two more staggered under the weight of the magical rime that covered them, stumbling to the cavern floor with the creaking of frost and cracking of ice.

The fey'ri countered with spells of their own. Araevin tried to leap aside from a shimmering hoop of magic that formed in the air and settled down over him, pinning his arms to his side. He managed to gasp out a counter and dismiss the binding spell, only to be knocked senseless by a word of power spoken by the fey'ri captain. He reeled drunkenly across the floor, and a pair of vrocks seized his arms and bore him to the ground.

Distantly, he saw Ilsevele immobilized by a pair of webs that glued her in place with thick, ropy strands of white. Another fey'ri sorcerer captured Maresa with a will-sapping enchantment that bereft her of the volition to move and fight. Her chin sank down to her chest, the point of her rapier drooped to the ground, and the fey'ri warriors hurled her to the ground and began binding her with strong cords.

Stinking of blood and filth, the vulture-demons pinning him wrenched Araevin around and jerked up his head by his hair, laying their talons at his throat. Grayth, fighting with his back to the cave wall, reluctantly stopped and threw down his sword. He, too, was seized and bound with cords.

The spell that had struck Araevin senseless began to fade, and he could hear and comprehend again. The vrocks gripping his arms croaked and chuckled with evil glee, clacking their beaks.

"Let us kill just-t one," they begged. "We'll make it slow and delicious-s. Elf tastes so good-d."

"They are not to be killed until I tell you to kill them," said the fey'ri captain.

He approached Araevin, his one eye gleaming with

malice. He held up his hand the third *telkiira* pinched between his thumb and forefinger.

"I suppose I should thank you, paleblood," the demon-elf sneered. "Not only did you lead us to this stone, you dispatched quite a formidable guardian for us. After all the trouble you've caused me, it is only fitting."

Araevin rallied enough to raise his head and meet the sinister demonspawn's gaze.

"You've . . . got your prize," he gasped. "What do you need us for, hellspawn?"

"I need you to find me one more gemstone, paleblood," the fey'ri said, grinning. "As for your companions, well, I have no use for them at all—unless you prove uncooperative, in which case you'll get to watch them beg for death before we're done. I suppose it's up to you."

CHAPTER 15

7 Tarsakh, the Year of Lightning Storms

The ruined city of Myth Glaurach seemed empty indeed, without the fey'ri legion encamped among its broken walls and shattered domes. Sarya Dlardrageth prowled the palace she had claimed as her own, restlessly stalking the halls where less than a month before she had held her council of war with the leaders of the fey'ri Houses.

For the past five days her army had retreated north through the desolate vales leading away from Evereska. The vengeance she intended for Evereska would have to wait until she replaced her losses from the failed assault on the Sunset Gate. Of course, she had no shortage of demons and yugoloths. Given a tenday or two to summon more, she might even be able to field an army stronger than that with which she had initially attacked, whereas the Evereskans had no such source of replacements available.

Time, she thought. After five thousand years of imprisonment, now I have so little of it.

She looked up at her son Xhalph, who stood watching her, and said, "I don't like the idea of leaving my army without supervision, and I must return soon. So, quickly, how are you faring in the High Forest? Be honest."

Xhalph bared his fangs and folded his four arms in a double row.

"I have driven the wood elves to the foot of the Lost Peaks," he said. "I destroyed a dozen of their villages and slaughtered hundreds in each place, but they have finally assembled in strength in the mountains. Now that they have been driven together, I am gathering my wolves into one pack. We will fall on them soon."

"Have you seen any soldiers from Evermeet?"

"No, but there is an expedition from Silverymoon on its way to reinforce the wood elves: humans, dwarves, and paleblooded race traitors, a little more than a thousand strong."

"Breden Yesve's warband was supposed to keep Silverymoon out of the High Forest," Sarya said. "Did he just allow the palebloods to march right by him?"

"The Silvaeren marched south from Everlund and passed west of Yesve," Xhalph replied. "He had to march far and fast to meet the humans when they left the Yartar road, and all he has been able to do is harry their advance. Since he could not stop them, I recalled his warband to add it to my own forces."

"That is sound. I approve," Sarya said. She thought over the suggestion, her slender tail slithering anxiously from side to side. "Evereska has proven harder than I had thought. A strong expedition from Evermeet has reinforced the LastHome. We were checked in our first attempt to enter the Vine Vale."

"Abandon the orcs and giants," Xhalph rumbled. "Evereska can be taken with an aerial assault while the palebloods' army sits in the mountains. You can sack the city without even engaging them."

Sarya looked over her shoulder at her towering son, and cocked an eyebrow. Xhalph had little use for stratagems of maneuver, but from time to time he surprised her—which did not mean that he was right.

"We lack the numbers to take the city with fey'ri alone," she said.

"Each of our fey'ri is a formidable opponent, Mother. Elf for elf, our warriors are better fighters than the palebloods."

"I have studied Evereska's defenses exhaustively through the *telthukiilir,* Xhalph. The forces that guard the city outnumber our fey'ri legion, and include many mages and clerics. And you discount the mythal," Sarya said as she paced back and forth. "It may be that we could take the city, but we would suffer dreadful losses. More demons can be summoned, more orcs and giants bribed or threatened to march in our forces, but my fey'ri are irreplaceable, and they would be the ones who die in an aerial attack. Your suggestion would also leave our enemy's true strength, the army at the Sentinel pass, untouched. We would not keep the city for long."

"Do we need to?" Xhalph growled.

Sarya glared at him.

"*Yes*," she hissed. "It means nothing to win a battle if ultimately it will cost us the war. When I take Evereska, I mean to keep it. Our enemies destroyed our homeland, leaving us an army without a realm. We will not long survive in this new age if we remain such."

"Should I abandon my attack on the wood elves and bring my warriors to join you at Evereska?"

"No. I need to draw out their army and expose it. You must press your attack on the wood elves with all your strength and ferocity. Meanwhile, I will retreat from Evereska's gates, and feign a disordered withdrawal while I rebuild our numbers. The palebloods will be tempted to pursue. After all, they will want to make sure that my army is truly defeated, and does not make its way to the High Forest to finish the destruction of the wood elves. But I will lay a trap for them."

Xhalph grinned and said, "Turning an enemy's hopes to disaster is the essence of strategy. But what if the Evereskans do not give chase?"

"Then I will in fact bring the entire fey'ri legion to the High Forest, and we will make a smoking hell of the mongrel elves' homeland. After which, we will add your soldiers to mine, and return to Evereska to finish what we started. Now go, and redouble your efforts against the wood elves. I have some special preparations to make."

Xhalph bowed and said, "I will make you a throne of Eaerlanni skulls, Mother."

He stepped back and teleported away, vanishing in an orange cloud of brimstone.

"You'll have to catch them first," Sarya said after him.

She took one more look from the portico and stepped inside the hall. The city was not completely empty. A hundred or so fey'ri remained behind to garrison the place and guard the treasures Sarya had brought to the city, and bands of orcs and trolls encircled the hilltop with their squalid camps, making ready to march on the High Forest and join the fighting there.

She abandoned the ruined splendor of the grand mage's hall, and descended into the secret delvings beneath the hill, passing through the steep tunnels and great caverns, taking wing when it suited her. She disliked so much stone over her head—how could she not, after so many centuries of living entombment?—but she was not so weak-willed that she allowed herself to avoid going where she must.

Powerful magic wards defended the hidden depths of her buried citadel, defenses that not even the fey'ri were permitted to pass. With long familiarity she made the signs and spoke the passwords, finally spiraling down through a great vertical shaft to a mighty chamber far below.

A great boulder of pale pink stone lay at the bottom of the shaft, hundreds of feet below the Grand Mage's Hall above. A beard of green moss clung to the rock, staining its glossy surface. To anyone with arcane sight the stone virtually pulsed with power. It was an artifact of pure magic, the keystone of the great mythal of magic that had once shielded Myth Glaurach, and while the city above had long since fallen into ruin, the mighty enchantments laid into the stone over decades of work still endured. Once the stone had rested in the grand mage's garden, near the center of the city above, but Sarya guessed that during Myth Glaurach's final days it had been moved to the buried pit in order to protect it from the attackers, in hopes that someday the folk of Eaerlann might return and wake its slumbering power to rebuild their realm. That had never happened; she had found it instead.

"Welcome, Sarya." A deep, melodious voice filled the chamber, speaking from the air itself. "How goes your war against Evereska?"

"Our first attack has been repulsed," Sarya said. She suspected that the unseen speaker knew perfectly well how matters stood. "Evermeet reinforced the city with much greater strength than I expected. I need more demons and yugoloths to destroy this foe. Many more."

"You have summoned a great number in the last few days."

"I have no other choice. I need soldiers—powerful soldiers."

"You will have to sustain them in your world with the mythal's power, as before."

"That takes time," Sarya growled. "I need a great army of mighty fiends, enough to scour all this land of my ancient enemies. Is there nothing more you can do to help me?"

"You could empty the nether planes to fill your ranks, Sarya, if you could reweave this mythal in the proper way. Without the proper high magic rites you cannot alter the basic purposes for which the mythal was raised over Myth Glaurach."

"I know," Sarya snapped. "You have told me many times, Malkizid. Unfortunately, only one of my line ever mastered high magic, and his knowledge is not available to me—though I may soon be able to remedy that shortcoming."

"You have found Saelethil's arcana?" the voice said, surprised.

"Not yet, though I am closer than I have ever been. Nurthel is seeking the third of Ithraides's *telkiira* even as we speak." Sarya caressed the mythal stone, feeling its magic stir beneath her fingertips, and continued, "Deciphering the *telkiira* may be the work of tendays or months, and my army requires reinforcement now."

"I eagerly anticipate your success."

"So do I."

Sarya bared her teeth in a fierce smile. Then she drew a deep breath, gathering her strength for the ordeal ahead. She had prepared her spells for the day with that task in mind, and so dozens of powerful conjurations filled her mind, a jumble of arcane symbols and words of binding that she could scarcely hold. By herself, she could call up another dozen or fifteen demons with her spells, and that would be useful, of course, but by drawing on the power of the mythal she would be able to re-use her spells over and over, and fix the demons she summoned to her plane by the power of the ancient device. All it took was time and her own personal attention.

She raised her hands and called the first of the demons.

☉ ☉ ☉ ☉ ☉

The fey'ri stripped Araevin and his companions of their weapons and armor, binding them securely with shackles of enchanted steel. Then the captain of the fey'ri, the one-eyed sorcerer in the armor of golden scales, drew a scroll from a case at his belt and read out a spell quickly and surely, the arcane words falling from his tongue with a sibilant hiss. In the cold damp of Grimlight's lair, a shining gold hoop appeared on the wet stone floor.

Exactly like the one we saw them use in Tower Reilloch, Araevin realized.

He was not given much time to wonder about the destination. The fey'ri soldiers dragged him to his feet and marched him to the circle, their taloned hands firmly gripping his arms.

A faint golden aura rose around Araevin and his escorts, and his stomach dropped away from him in the disconcerting way it often did during teleportation. Then he was somewhere else, a great, dark hall with a floor of smooth black marble and walls of glittering rock. Globes of crimson mage-light drifted aimlessly high overhead, illuminating a sheer rift at one end of the room, from which a breath of stale, cold air sighed.

"Where are we?" Araevin asked. "Who are you, and what do you want with us?"

The sorcerer-captain studied him with his single green eye, and deliberately stepped forward and slapped Araevin with all his might. The blow snapped Araevin's head back and set bright white stars reeling in his vision. His knees buckled and he would have fallen, but the fey'ri swordsmen beside him held him upright.

"You will address me with respect," the sorcerer stated. "I am Lord Nurthel Floshin. You need know nothing else for now."

Araevin sensed magic at work as the teleportation hoop functioned again, and Ilsevele was dragged through by more of the fey'ri. He managed to catch her eye and he shook his head subtly, encouraging her to remain silent. In a few moments the rest of their captors had joined them, the last demons dragging the coin-filled chests the behir had hoarded. Araevin took the opportunity to study the room as best he could. It was deep underground, that much was clear. The very air seemed to glimmer with a strange quality—a powerful, pervasive magic, harnessed to the place.

We're inside a mythal of some kind, he realized. *Where do mythals still stand?*

Araevin's guards stirred, and he was jerked around to face a hallway behind him. Light footfalls sounded beyond the archway, and a daemonfey woman appeared.

Short and girlish in appearance, she was strikingly beautiful in spite of her clearly demonic heritage—her scarlet skin, slender tail, and long, leathery wings gave that much away. She wore black robes with a scalloped, stiff cut, finished with elaborate gold embroidery. Her eyes glowed with green malice as she circled Araevin and his comrades, studying them.

"I am weary, Nurthel," she said. "Is this who I think it is?"

"Yes, my queen. I brought them directly to you," the fey'ri captain said.

"Kneel, paleblood dog!" growled one of Araevin's guards. The elf mage was shoved to his knees, as were his companions. "Grovel before your queen!"

"Go to hell," Maresa snapped, but she was quickly hammered to the ground by three or four cruel kicks and blows.

"Well done, Nurthel," the woman said. She gazed at each of them before fixing her emerald eyes on Araevin. "I am Sarya Dlardrageth, and you will be my guests for a short time. The comforts of your visit are largely up to you. Now, who are you?"

Araevin briefly considered a sullen silence, but given the way Maresa had been mishandled, it seemed likely that the daemonfey would eventually compel him to speak. He decided to save his resistance for something that mattered.

"Araevin Teshurr," he said, his jaw still aching from Nurthel's open-handed slap.

"And your companions?"

"So you *are* the Dlardrageths," Araevin said. "You have survived all the long centuries since Siluvanede's fall . . . and no one knew. Where are we?"

Sarya snorted softly and said, "You forget who is asking the questions." She glanced at Nurthel. "Has he opened the third stone?"

Nurthel shook his head, then he produced the *telkiira* from a hidden pocket and carried it to Sarya's divan.

"Good," said Sarya.

Forsaken House • 261

Sarya examined the gemstone closely, turning away from her captives.

Over her shoulder, she said, "Since you have not told me who your companions are, Araevin, choose one of them to die—the human dog or the planar mongrel, I don't care. If you don't pick, I'll kill them both."

"Wait!" cried Araevin. He indicated them with a nod of his head. "He is Grayth Holmfast, a cleric of Lathander. She is Maresa Rost. And this is Ilsevele Miritar." He drew a deep breath, and fixed his eyes on Sarya's back. "You've won. You have your damned *telkiira*. The others had no part in this affair. I asked them to join me in recovering the stones. Let them go, and you can do as you will with me."

Sarya laughed aloud—a husky, predatory sound—and said, "Why, Araevin, I believe I will do with you as I please, regardless. You have little to bargain with."

"They'll most likely kill us anyway, Araevin," Grayth growled. "There isn't much point in trying to spare us any trouble."

"I thought I heard a dog barking," Sarya remarked.

Nurthel turned at once and snapped a vicious circle kick to Grayth's chin, smashing the cleric to the floor. Grayth groaned once and lay still, knocked senseless by the blow.

In spite of his determination to endure whatever petty malice the daemonfey chose to inflict, Araevin surged to his feet before the demons behind him caught his shackled arms and hurled him back down to the cold, marble floor.

"Get on with it, then!" he snarled, spitting blood from his mouth. "Whatever you're going to do, do it."

"Ready to die already?" Sarya laughed.

Araevin simply glared at her. The daemonfey queen arose and paced near. She leaned down close to him, and held the green-black gemstone before his face.

"Don't you want to find out what is in this third stone," Sarya teased, "and puzzle out the little mystery Philaerin left for you, the old fool?"

Araevin glanced up, despite himself. Sarya smiled and drew away, her sharp nails gliding across his cheek.

Araevin forced himself to say, "If Philaerin had lived, you never would have found any of the *telkiira*."

"That is not entirely true, paleblood. The second and third stones we never would have found without your help. But the first stone . . . that one belongs to me. I took it from Kaeledhin more than five thousand year ago, and I gave it to Nurthel to conceal on Philaerin's body once he'd killed the high mage. I knew that some enterprising young fool just like you would find it and seek out its sisters."

Araevin looked at her blankly. He couldn't make sense of it. The daemonfey had the stone, and hid it in the stronghold of their enemies? Were the *telkiira* some form of insidious trap? Had the daemonfey manufactured them to destroy Philaerin? It explained how the daemonfey found him so quickly with their scrying spells and anticipated his efforts to find the stones. In fact, they had likely prepared the *telkiira* with enchantments that would make its bearer easier to find. He felt sick.

"You spied on me, waiting for me to find each stone. They are sealed against you."

Sarya paced away again, pausing to study Ilsevele before nodding in approval.

"A fine-looking girl," said Sarya, looking at Ilsevele. "I should give you to my son. We need more Dlardrageths." Ilsevele's face paled, but she refused to look away from Sarya until the daemonfey turned back to Araevin. "Yes, they are sealed against us. You can open the *telkiira*, but we cannot. Before my imprisonment, I spent years trying to open Kaeledhin's key with no success."

Araevin shook his head, horrified. All his efforts since the raid on Tower Reilloch had played directly into the hands of the daemonfey queen.

Ilsevele drew herself up and looked Sarya in the eye.

"What are the stones for?" she demanded. "Why are they important?"

"We were *betrayed*," Sarya hissed. "The *telkiira* are the key to redressing many wrongs. My family was destroyed by the Coronal of Arcorar and his High Spellstar, Ithraides. Only a few of us escaped from Arcorar.

"Of all the heirlooms we abandoned in Arcorar, the greatest was the *selukiira* known as the Nightstar. High mages of my House preserved many of the old secrets of glorious Aryvandaar in its depths. After the Coronal of Arcorar destroyed my family, Ithraides discovered our *selukiira* in the ruins of our palace. He hid it away very carefully to make sure it would never fall into our hands again, but he recorded the hiding spot in these three *telkiira* you have helped us find.

"During the days of my exile in Siluvanede, I searched assiduously for the Nightstar. With the secrets of the *selukiira*, I could remake Siluvanede in the image of glorious Aryvandaar, and take the throne denied my House for generations. I found Kaeledhin, and from him I extracted the tale of what Ithraides had done with my family's heirloom. But I could not defeat Ithraides' wards guarding the *telkiira*, and so I could not follow it to its fellows or discern the hiding place of the Nightstar."

"Siluvanede fell almost five thousand years ago," Ilsevele said. She tossed her head and studied Sarya with determination. "Why wait for so long?"

"Because my enemies buried my son and I in a forgotten tomb, and claimed that they were showing us *mercy*!" Sarya whirled away from Ilsevele and stalked over to Araevin again. She stooped and cupped his face in her hand. Her iron-hard nails dug into his flesh. "And that is where you come in, my paleblooded friend. We cannot use these *telkiira*, since they were made to deny us access. You, on the other hand, can read these stones and tell us where our heirloom lies."

"I will not help you," he rasped.

"I have waited five thousand years to come into my inheritance," Sarya said. "I am not about to be balked by any inconvenient stubbornness on your part, paleblood." She gripped his face until blood ran from the points of her fingernails. She leaned close to whisper in his ear, "You understand what I am capable of, I think. I will not harm you, not at first. But the things that will happen to your companions, they will be hard to watch. When shall we begin?"

"Once I do as you ask, all our lives are forfeit. Now or later, what is the difference?" Araevin quivered with terror, but he kept his voice even and level. "If you let the others go, I will do as you ask. But I must know that they are safe before I cooperate."

"As you wish," Sarya said. "I would love to explore the question of how much pain you could stand to inflict on your comrades. But it might take a little time to persuade you to cooperate, and I am out of patience."

She wove her hands in arcane passes, and began to speak the words of a spell. Araevin recognized it at once and steeled his will to resist. Sarya's spell settled over his mind, seeking to shackle his will to hers. Shadowy fingers seemed to creep into his soul, insidious as serpents, their merest touch enough to render him cold and numb. He bared his teeth in a fierce snarl and battled against the enchantment, refusing to buckle beneath the daemonfey queen's sorcery.

"Your will is strong. I should have expected that," Sarya observed. She glanced at Nurthel. "Kill the human dog."

The fey'ri lord drew a dagger of black iron at his belt and strode over to Grayth. He knelt behind the Lathanderite and seized the semiconscious cleric by his hair. Araevin watched in horror, still battling against Sarya's spell, as the fey'ri fixed his remaining eye on Araevin's face and buried the knife in Grayth's throat. Bright blood poured from the wound. Grayth's eyes opened wide, and an awful gagging sound came from his mouth as blood drowned him.

"*Grayth!*" cried Ilsevele.

She wrenched herself free of the fey'ri gripping her shoulders and surged to her feet, only to be knocked down again. Maresa swore a vile oath and struggled as well, her hair streaming with her fury.

Grayth's feet clattered against the stone, and he shook,

as if trying to free his bound hands. Then his eyes drooped, and he sank down to the cold marble, face down in the spreading pool of crimson. Nurthel jerked out the dagger, and held its bloody edge in front of him.

"I've soiled my blade with a dog's blood," he complained. "I'll never get the stink off it now."

Twenty years and more he has been my friend, Araevin thought. This is the end he comes to for leaving his temple and helping me.

He thought of the sons Grayth had mentioned, and wondered how he could ever apologize to them for their father's death. And that moment of black despair was all that Sarya's spell required. As swiftly and surely as the fey'ri had clapped him in irons, the deadly shackles of the sorceress's will enchained his mind.

"That's better," Sarya said pleasantly. She looked to the demons behind Araevin. "Unbind him, let him stand. He is under my dominion."

The vrocks clacked and hissed behind Araevin, but they undid his fetters. He found himself on his feet, without knowing exactly how he had stood.

"We could play some very entertaining games," Sarya said. "I could command you to do terrible things to your companions . . . or to yourself. However, I must indulge myself another day."

Araevin stood motionless, unable to move his limbs. His thoughts were unimpaired—he reviewed spell after spell that he could hurl to blast Sarya and her minions or free Ilsevele and Maresa—but he could not join them to any action. Sarya took the third *telkiira* and placed it in his hand.

"Decipher this stone, as you did the others," she commanded.

He held the *telkiira* up to his eye, helpless to do otherwise, and sent his mind into its dark depths, seeking out its secrets. As before, he spied a fearsome glyph in the gemstone's facets, barring any deeper approach as surely as a rampart defended a castle. But he still remembered the name of the sigil from the vision he invoked in his workroom in Tower Reilloch, when he'd investigated the second stone.

"*Larthanos,*" he whispered, and the *telkiira* opened to him.

Information poured into his mind: glimpses of distant memories, arcane formulae, dazzling vistas of elven cities long fallen and swallowed by forest. Again he saw the scene of the moon elf Ithraides giving his three *telkiira* to his younger colleagues, and the image of the sun elf with the bright green eyes and the cruel smile, who contemplated a thumb-sized crystal of purple, its surface covered with intricate runes. Saelethil Dlardrageth, the Dlardrageth high mage, and the Nightstar, the *telkiira*'s frozen memories told him. Then Araevin's vision whirled and shifted, as arcane formulae and complex patterns flashed before his eyes, the record of spell after spell contained in the *telkiira*.

He recognized several of the spells, as he had before—a spell for seeking out hidden things, a spell to reflect an enemy's spell back at him or her, a spell that would transfer one to a different plane of existence. And he viewed the mysterious spell, the one left incomplete in the first two gemstones. In his mind's eye he saw the three parts of it merge, the missing symbols arranging themselves, organizing into a pattern he could decipher and recognize. It was unique, he could see that at once. It could only be cast in one place, for one result.

It was the spell that would pass Ithraides' wards.

Araevin blinked, starting to lower the gemstone, but then his vision blurred again and a quick, final vision imposed itself on his sight. He glimpsed a spherical chamber of perfect white stone, in which the Nightstar hovered. Then he saw a mist-filled hall of silver pillars, and an old elven tower half buried by the forest. He sensed the tower, as if he followed the path of a lighthouse's searching beam across dark and unseen waters to a distant goal.

It still exists, he knew. *And I know where it is.*

"Well?" demanded Sarya, calling him back to awareness.

"Tell me what you have seen! Do you know where the Nightstar lies? Can you find it?"

"Yes," Araevin said. "It is buried in a stronghold in Cormanthor. I can show you where it lies, but you will be unable to approach it. Powerful wards will bar your entry."

Sarya's face grew dark, and she whirled away, frowning. Araevin watched her fuming, wondering if she would slay him out of hand or perhaps indulge herself by murdering Maresa or Ilsevele first. But then Sarya halted, her eyes thoughtful. She turned back to him slowly.

"What about you?" she asked. "Could you reach it?"

"Saelethil's High Loregem will destroy anyone not of your House who touches it. It would burn out my mind and take possession of my body in order to have itself carried to a suitable wielder, one of House Dlardrageth."

"But you could reach it and bring it out to us?" Sarya asked, her eyes avid and hungry.

Araevin felt himself nodding, and was appalled.

❖ ❖ ❖ ❖ ❖

The Lost Peaks were aptly named. So dense was the forest cover on their lower slopes that the soldiers marching under Silverymoon's banner could not see the mountaintops towering over them as they ascended the steep river valleys climbing up into the peaks. Every now and then a break in the trees permitted a glimpse of green, mist-wreathed mountains high overhead. The trail from time to time skirted a great mossy wall of stone or traversed a jumble of boulders and rubble that had slid down through the trees from the unseen slopes above. Even elves could not march swiftly over such rugged terrain.

Methrammar led his horse a few steps from the trail to let his soldiers continue past. Dressed in his armor of mithral mail and forest-green cloak, he resembled an elf warlord of old. He waited for Gaerradh and Sheeril to follow him off the trail.

"How much farther is Daelyth's Dagger?" he asked her.

"Seven miles. If we push hard, we can reach it tonight."

"Will your folk be there?"

"I can't be certain, but I think it's likely," Gaerradh replied. "It's a deep dell, with old fortifications overlooking the valley floor. There's a narrow trail alongside a swift stream winding between two huge shoulders of rock, so that any foe pursuing you must come single file along a treacherous path. It won't discourage the fey'ri, of course, but they'll have to leave their orc allies outside."

"Is there any exit?"

"There is a hard trail at the top of the dell that climbs steeply up the valley head, leading to the higher slopes of the mountains. And there is a secret way through the caverns in the valley walls, leading to the neighboring valleys."

Gaerradh watched the soldiers march past, while Sheeril pranced anxiously about. The wolf was uncomfortable with so many humans and dwarves in her forest.

"If there is any place to stand against an attack," Gaerradh finished, "that is it."

Methrammar studied the sheer cliffs rising above them on their right, and the rugged slope falling away from the trail.

"This will be hard ground to fight on," he said. "Mounted troops will be useless, but the dwarves will like it well enough."

"Lord Methrammar!" A half-elf officer approached, walking back against the direction of the march, calling, "There is a party of wood elves here to speak with you, my lord."

"Bring them," Methrammar called back.

He and Gaerradh waited a few minutes and the officer returned, leading a small band of wood elf archers who trotted along the trail, mixing with their moon elf cousins from Silverymoon or slapping human soldiers on the back, grinning and laughing.

Gaerradh recognized several and raised her hand, calling out a greeting of her own: "Well met, Silverbow! Fomoyn! It is good to see you!"

Forsaken House • 269

Among the archers, she saw Morgwais, the Lady of the Wood, who wore the green leather of a wood elf ranger. Sheeril bounded up to Morgwais with a happy yip, tail wagging like a pup.

"Well met, Gaerradh—and Sheeril," Morgwais said. She ruffled the thick white fur of the wolf's neck, one of the very few people who could try that without losing a hand. "I see you have brought us help from Silverymoon."

"Lady Morgwais," said Gaerradh. She gestured to the Marshal at her side. "This is Methrammar Aerasumé, the commander of Silverymoon's army."

"Thank you for your help, Lord Methrammar," Morgwais said. "There are no words to express our gratitude. We need all the swords and bows we can muster."

"I only wish we could have brought more soldiers to aid you," the high marshal replied. He bowed deeply to Morgwais. "Unfortunately, these daemonfey and their orc minions threaten Everlund and the towns of the Rauvin Vale as well as the High Forest. We had to leave a strong force behind to guard our homeland in case they turned north."

"Where are the fey'ri now?" Gaerradh asked.

"Mustering at the Rivenrock, about twenty miles south of here. We've gathered the warriors of a dozen villages at Daelyth's Dagger. We've already fought off one assault, which is why they're drawing together now. They hope to overwhelm us at a place where we have decided to stand."

The Lady of the Wood looked over the Silvaeren company and said, "Lord Methrammar, I know your troops must be weary after such a long march and a bitter fight, but you must join us at Daelyth's Dagger as soon as you can. The daemonfey will certainly try to cut you off and keep you from reinforcing us, and if their whole army came upon you here, it would go poorly for you."

Methrammar nodded and said, "We will do as you ask, my lady. The swords of Silverymoon are at your service."

CHAPTER 16

8 Tarsakh, the Year of Lightning Storms

An early spring had come to the great woodland of Cormanthor. The endless dreary rains from the Sea of Swords that kept the western forests cold and wet vanished as they passed over the great desert Anauroch. Warmer winds from the Dragonmere carried gentle showers that draped the eastern forest in a green so deep and vivid that even by the pale light of the crescent moon its color leaped to the eye. Araevin tasted the warm rain on his face and breathed in the fragrance of the new blossoms, and for an instant he could almost forget the misery of his situation.

"Come along, paleblood," sneered Nurthel. "You have work to do."

Araevin complied, turning to follow the fey'ri sorcerer without any effort of his conscious mind. He fell in behind Nurthel, arms still shackled behind his back, ribs aching from the blow Grimlight had dealt him. Behind him half a dozen fey'ri warriors and a pair of foul vrock-demons marched, watching him carefully for any sign that Sarya's compulsion might be fading. The daemonfey queen was not present, having left to return to her army, but she had ordered Araevin to obey any command given him by Nurthel, instantly and without resistance, and the malignant compulsion she had used to crush his will was sufficiently strong to force Araevin to do exactly as she commanded.

Sooner or later he knew that he would be able to shake off the insidious spell—especially if Nurthel ordered him to do something he could not help but revolt against, like injure himself—but for the time being Araevin was merely a spectator in his own body, unable to conceive of refusing Nurthel's orders, even though he knew exactly how Sarya's spell had affected him. He had never cared for enchantment spells and rarely used them himself, because he'd always found it distasteful to enslave another's will, even if the subject was an enemy and the enslavement nothing more than a temporary assault to halt an attack or sow confusion among his foes. Having personally experienced the effects, he had no intention of ever using such a spell again. It was simply abominable to have one's volition stolen away.

"Which way?" Nurthel asked.

The ruined remnant of an old elven highway intersected their path, a ribbon of pale white stone buried beneath leaf mould and moss. Araevin and his captors had been walking for several hours, after teleporting from the Dlardrageth stronghold to Cormanthor's forests. The *telkiira* had warned Araevin that magic was unpredictable in the area surrounding the Nightstar's crypt, and he had duly warned the fey'ri of the danger of teleporting too close to the *selukiira*'s hiding place.

Araevin examined the path, and consulted the inner beacon guiding him onward.

"To the left," he replied. "It's less than a mile from here."

He wondered whether Ilsevele and Maresa still lived. The daemonfey had separated them as an additional guarantor of Araevin's cooperation, promising a fate worse than death for the women if he should lead Nurthel astray.

The demonic company hurried along the ancient white stones of the elfroad. Alternating showers and moon shadows made the scene eldritch and unreal. That portion of Cormanthor was the fabled Elven Court, a woodland of cathedral-like shadowtops that had once been home to countless elven palaces, temples, and towers. From time to time they passed old ruins, jumbled heaps of pale stone that seemed to glow beneath the soft touch of Selûne's light. Then he spied the tower, a slender finger of white rising up beneath the mighty trees like a silver ghost.

"Wait," he said. "We're here."

"In there?" Nurthel demanded. The fey'ri sorcerer studied the place, and nodded. "Fine. You will lead. Inform me when we are at risk."

Araevin led the way to the tower's door, a blank archway of stone. No door or gate stood there. The portal was filled with a smooth, unbroken wall of stone. But Ithraides had recorded the secret of the door in his *telkiira*. Araevin spoke a simple password, and the stone sealing the arch became ethereal and vanished from sight.

"On the other side of the doorway there is a powerful sigil that will destroy any who enter without speaking this password: *sillevi astraedh*," Araevin said. "Then we will find stairs leading down to a misty hall, guarded by a powerful watch ghost. You must fight it if you wish to proceed."

He did not point out that the daemonfey could simply remain outside the tower, since the watch ghost would not attack him. Nurthel had instructed Araevin to lead and to warn him of the dangers they encountered, but he had not asked Araevin to be explain how each peril could be avoided. It was not much of a victory, but Araevin was determined to exploit every misstep in the instructions the fey'ri gave him.

Forsaken House • 273

They passed the sigil on the far side of the doorway, and found themselves in the tower's ground floor.

It seems to be my destiny to look for crystals in old ruins, Araevin thought bleakly.

He indicated a stone staircase leading to unseen levels beneath the tower, and led Nurthel's party down the smooth steps. At the bottom the fey'ri sorcerer stopped him.

"Remain here, and make sure you do not get hurt," Nurthel said. "We will need you once we deal with this guardian." He gestured to the fey'ri warriors and the demons who accompanied them. "Destroy the guardian."

Nurthel stayed on the steps beside Araevin, watching his soldiers prowl into the room below, curved swords in their taloned fists. The vrocks followed, their vulture heads swinging from side to side on their long, wattled necks as they looked for their foe. The chamber was exactly as Araevin remembered it from the *telkiira*'s vision, a large misty hall with shining silver pillars.

A sheet of purple lightning crackled out of the swirling fog, blasting through a vrock and two of the fey'ri. Crawling arcs of violet energy coruscated around the demonspawn, charring great black burns across their flesh. The fey'ri shrieked and fell writhing to the floor. The vrock attempted to teleport itself away from the deadly spell, only to reappear in a terrible burst of black gore, materializing in the exact same spot as one of the bright argent pillars.

"I see that you did not lie when you warned us of teleporting here," Nurthel hissed. "Is there anything you have kept from me, Araevin?"

Araevin opened his mouth to reply, but the mists parted, revealing a bright and terrible figure of silver light. Ghostly and yet powerful, the guardian seemed to be a beautiful moon elf maiden, her dark hair streaming around her head, her white robes fading into translucent starshine.

"Depart!" she demanded in Elvish, her clear voice strangely high and distant, as if she were speaking from far away. "Depart, fiends! I will not suffer you to pass this chamber."

In answer two of the fey'ri drew out wands of bronze and blasted the ghostly sorceress with crimson darts of magical power. The sorceress's features twisted with a cry of dismay, and her substance seemed to boil away from the holes punched by the fey'ri spells. She countered by seizing one of the wand-wielders in a viselike grip of unseen force and hurling him against the wall, leaving him crumpled across the chamber. At the same time she chanted out a piercing melody of her own, her arms weaving in the gestures of a spell, and she threw a charging mezzoloth screaming back into its native hells.

A second mezzoloth stalked close and rammed its brazen trident through the center of the ghost's torso, but the infernal weapon passed through her ethereal substance without so much as a ripple. She turned on the creature and wove a spiraling spell chain around it that sliced deep into its evil flesh, slowly cutting it to pieces. But the fey'ri with the wand struck again, riddling her with more of the crimson darts, while another fey'ri warrior—one with a sword glowing with enchantment—darted close to slash at her, tearing great rents in her misty form.

Araevin took half a step forward, intending to help her in some way, but Nurthel set a hand on his shoulder.

"Oh, no," the fey'ri captain said. "You are not to interfere."

He wove a spell of his own and hurled a crackling azure lance of magical force at the ghost, driving a bolt of arcane power through the center of her form.

The ghost wailed in deathless agony, transfixed by Nurthel's spell, her substance fraying away from the wound. She fixed her dissipating gaze on Araevin.

"Do not lead them any farther," she whispered. "Do not let them do this!"

"We do not intend to give him much choice in the matter," Nurthel laughed.

He drew back his spell lance, and rammed it through the center of the ghost's forehead. There was a great, silent burst of spectral energy, blindingly bright, and the ghost discorporated into streamers of mist and vapor that faded to nothing. The fey'ri laughed as he allowed his spell to end, subsuming the crackling lance back into his hand.

"How long has she waited here to turn us away, only to fail in her duty at the end?" Nurthel said. "It seems almost tragic, doesn't it?"

Araevin refused to answer. He was under no compulsion to reply to rhetorical questions. Nurthel folded his arms and looked him in the face.

"Well? What now?"

"There is a portal in the far wall. Touching it will transport one directly to the chamber of the *selukiira,* which is a sealed sphere of stone some distance beneath our feet. I must first wake it by casting a special spell." Araevin hesitated, but Sarya's spell forced him to continue. "If you, or any creature with evil intent, touches the portal, you will be destroyed."

"Could that be dispelled?"

"It would be difficult, and you would deactivate the portal, so that you could no longer reach the *selukiira* chamber safely," Araevin admitted. "As your demon ally demonstrated, teleporting here is dangerous."

"That does present a problem," Nurthel said. "Fortunately, we have you, so I need not test my intentions against the standards set by the ancient paleblood wizard who built this place, or settle for excavating my way to the Nightstar. You will go get the Nightstar for me. Can you do that?"

"Yes," Araevin admitted, though it turned his stomach to say it.

"And what if the *selukiira*'s touch destroys you?"

"The device would take possession of my body. It would likely seek to return itself to your hands."

"I like the sound of that," Nurthel said. "You have caused me no end of trouble over the last few months, even when you were unwittingly doing our work. I can think of no fitter end for you." The fey'ri studied him closely, and asked, "Do you know of any reason why I would not want to send you to retrieve the Nightstar?"

"No."

"Very well, then. Show me this portal."

Araevin led Nurthel across the mist-filled hall, flanked by the surviving demons and fey'ri. With all the power of his will and heart he tried again to throw off Sarya's spell and regain his freedom, but for all his effort his feet still carried him forward without hesitation, and his hands remained shackled behind him. Evidently the potential hazard of the *selukiira* was simply not immediate enough to give him the chance to overthrow the spell of dominion. On the wall opposite the stairway, a large design of silver inlaid in the stone depicted Selûne and the diamondlike Tears trailing behind it.

"I must have my hands free to use the portal and retrieve the Nightstar," Araevin said.

Nurthel undid his bonds, watching carefully for any sign that Sarya's compulsion was weakening.

"You will use the portal to reach the *selukiira* chamber," the fey'ri said. "You will then take the Nightstar and bring it back here to me. Do not do anything except what I have instructed you to do. If something prevents you from accomplishing this task, you will return immediately for further instructions. Now go."

Araevin longed to rub his wrists and shake the stiffness from his arms, but the fey'ri's orders left him no latitude even for so simple an act. He chanted the words of the secret spell taught him by the three *telkiira,* the only spell that could awaken the portal. The silver diagram inlaid in the stone woke to life, glowing with white fire. Then he reached out and touched three of the Tears, avoiding the silver stars that would have triggered all manner of deadly spells. He felt the ancient magic awake beneath his fingers and snatch him away from the silver hall.

◉ ◉ ◉ ◉ ◉

Seiveril stood in the silent grove, eyes closed, his face tilted up to the sky, and listened for Corellon Larethian's whispers in his heart. The wooded hillside was a remote place indeed, old and wild, a small outpost of the strange and ancient Forgotten Forest that lay two days' march behind him. The trees were gnarled and stooped like senescent men, tangled with beards and hoary coats of moss, and somewhere deep in their old black hearts they dreamed of days when their fathers stood wakeful and alert across all of northern Faerûn, a single unbroken forest. Not even the elves were welcome beneath their branches.

Seiveril felt the warm glow of other elf minds nearby, the Seldarine knights and clerics of Vesilde Gaerth's Golden Star order. As the soldiers best equipped with the magic needed to fight off demonic assaults, the knights of the Golden Star never strayed far from Seiveril's banner, guarding him within a ring of holy steel and powerful protective prayers. He didn't like the idea that he required an elite guard, not when Gaerth's troops could have been gainfully employed in the close pursuit of the daemonfey, but he recognized the necessity. In the six days that the crusade had been following the retreating daemonfey army his foes had made no attempt to launch any more decapitating attacks against his standard like the one in the Western Cwm, but just because they hadn't done it so far didn't mean the daemonfey might not try it at any time.

The sun elf lord stilled his mind and looked past the nearby auras of his friends and allies, seeking the great golden presence of Corellon's will. When he felt himself calm and still again, Seiveril began to pray in earnest, reciting the spell prayers he had readied for the day. Every day since the battle in the cwm, as his host had descended the Rillvale on the heels of the horde of orcs and demons and harried them into the wild and empty lands north and west of Evereska, Seiveril had set aside an hour to wrestle with his foes, seeking to divine their secrets and their plans. Sometimes he succeeded, gaining glimpses of the daemonfey array or the ruined old city that served as their citadel. More often the spellcasters of the daemonfey horde succeeded in deflecting his divinations, blinding his magical sight. And so, while company after company of archers, swordsmen, and cavalry hurried northward on the grass-grown roadway along which the daemonfey fled, Seiveril struggled to see what would happen next and understand what he had to do.

The day's spells brought little to comfort him. He saw a terrible battle gathering in the High Forest, a fight he desperately wished to influence but was simply too far away to affect. He saw that his own army would likely be fighting again very soon, a rematch with the daemonfey horde, and he was not certain of the outcome. He could not see any hint of Ilsevele or Araevin, or the progress of their quest. It was as if they had been removed from the face of the world. He sensed that they were in danger, and that his own fortunes were tied up with theirs, but little more.

With a sigh, he allowed his arms to fall, and brought himself back to awareness. The brooding woodland returned to his eyes, its silence broken only by the soft whisper of cool, rain-speckled wind in the small green leaves of spring. He watched the woodland for a time, curiously drawn by its ancient, slumbering resentment, then he turned and picked his way down the slope.

Fflar was waiting for him, sitting cross-legged on a flat stone, Keryvian leaning within easy reach. He glanced up as Seiveril returned.

"Well? What did you see today?" Fflar asked.

"There will be a fierce battle on the slopes of the Lost Peaks, and soon. The wood elves have retreated as far as they can go, and still the daemonfey pursue them."

"How soon?"

"Within a day, perhaps two."

Fflar said, "Even if we left our footsoldiers behind and took nothing but our fastest cavalry, it would take a tenday to reach that corner of the High Forest. The wood elves will have to make do without our aid."

"Perhaps I can ask Jorildyn's mages to assist," Seiveril thought aloud. "At least thirty of our wizards and sorcerers know teleportation spells. We could spare half that number to bring fifty or more spellcasters and chosen troops to assist the wood elves."

"Jerreda Starcloak will insist that you must do something. I don't like reducing our own magical strength, not with that daemonfey army ahead of us, but I don't see any other way to help out the wood elves," Fflar said. He stood easily, unfolding his long legs, and buckled Keryvian to his hip again. "What about us? When will we fight again?"

"The daemonfey will turn and stand on the Lonely Moor," Seiveril said as he swung himself up into the saddle of his war-horse, and thanked the young warrior who held the reins.

The elven vanguard was less than ten miles from the round, scrub-covered hills that climbed up to the moor's boggy plateau. Difficult terrain lay ahead of them. The cavalry would not do well on the moorland, but on the other hand archers would exact a terrible toll from adversaries seeking to close over the uneven ground. Almost no one—elf, human, orc, or otherwise—traveled those lands often, though Seiveril's Evereskan scouts told him that bands of gnolls and bugbears hunted the moor.

"We should meet them tomorrow in the middle of the day," Seiveril went on, "if we continue our pursuit."

Fflar nodded and said, "I suppose that explains why the daemonfey haven't abandoned any poor bastard who can't fly. They could have escaped by taking to the air, and there would've been damned little we could do about it."

"They still have that option," Seiveril pointed out.

☙ ☙ ☙ ☙ ☙

The crusade marched the rest of the day, beneath gray skies and a cold, damp wind that slowly numbed the fingers and toes until they ached as if they were on fire. That night, they bivouacked on two large knolls on the long, rumpled slope climbing up to the moor proper. The overcast hid the stars, and the cold wind simply grew stronger, until the pennants and banners fluttered and snapped like brightly colored sails. Seiveril ordered his captains to rest the soldiers as much as possible and prepare a good, hearty meal from their stores, knowing that they would need their strength the next day.

Seiveril ate little and rested not at all, finding himself too troubled to slip into Reverie. He settled for circling the camp, watching the warriors of Evermeet making ready for battle. Beneath the songs sung by the windblown cookfires lay a note of determination and confidence that he could not have imagined when he recklessly invited any willing fighter to follow him to Faerûn. How many of them would not greet the next moonrise, lying dead on a distant and useless battlefield far from home? How long might they have lived if they had remained on Evermeet?

He sat down heavily on a boulder, bowing his head in the dark night, weary with all the weight of his four and a half centuries. His mind turned to his wife, Ilyyela, dead for three short years after centuries at his side.

Am I doing the right thing, Ilyyela? he asked the night. Is this what I am supposed to do?

A soft footfall drew his attention. Seiveril looked up, and saw Fflar approaching. He waited as the moon elf hero joined him on his boulder. They sat a while in silence, each wrapped in his own thoughts against the night.

Finally Fflar said, "Where are your thoughts, Seiveril?"

"My wife, Ilyyela. She died in the war three years ago. The Tower of the Sun was destroyed by a spell cast by a circle of traitorous spellsingers, and she was in it."

"I am sorry for that, my friend," Fflar said, staring off into the blackness of the night. "I had the good fortune of preceding my wife to Arvandor. She and my son were among the last to escape Myth Drannor, in the days before the city's fall. Yet here I am now, walking the world once again, and now it is she who is gone, and my son as well. It has been six hundred years, after all. I wonder if he had children? It would be something to meet them, would it not?" The moon elf paused, and laughed softly at himself. "I miss them, Seiveril. I should not have come back."

"What do you remember of Arvandor?"

Fflar shook his head and replied, "It is only a dim dream, as you might remember a house you lived in when you were a very small child. I remember contentment, joy . . . I think that the gods must veil our memories when we return from death to life. Otherwise it would be an abomination to call us out of bliss, would it not? How could I stand to be parted from my wife and son a single hour otherwise?"

"Yet you agreed to return," Seiveril said. "You made that decision while Arvandor was still unveiled."

"The difficulty with attaining everything you want is that it's not enough. I recall contentment, yes, but I also recall regret. I died as a failure, Seiveril. Despite all my efforts, my city fell, my people were slaughtered, our light was extinguished. I do not know for certain why I returned, since my mind is clouded now, but I think I came back to finish what I had left undone in my mortal days." Fflar looked at Seiveril, folded his arms, and said, "You are high in the faith of Corellon Larethian. You must understand all this. Why did you call me back?"

"Because Ilyyela told me to," Seiveril said. He did not meet Fflar's gaze, but instead studied his hands, folded in his lap. "Soon after Amlaruil rallied us to repel Nimesin's attack, I attempted to resurrect my wife. Perhaps I should not have tried it, but the grief . . . the thought was in my heart that we were both young still, young enough to walk the world for centuries yet before departing for Arvandor together.

"Corellon did not deny me the spell. I think he knew that I had to make the attempt. At sunset of a warm summer evening I chanted the prayers and cast the spell of resurrection, and Ilyyela's spirit answered my call. But she would not cross back into life. 'Ilyyela, my love, come back to me,' I begged. Yet she refused. 'My time is done,' she said. 'Do not mourn for the years we might have shared in Evermeet, for we will be together in Arvandor's summer forever.'

"I pleaded with her. 'I cannot stand to be apart from you, not for the long years I might remain. I will join you in Arvandor, if you will not return.'

"Then Ilyyela regarded me with sadness. 'That is not for you to decide,' she told me. 'It is not for any to decide. There is a great labor before you, my love, which you must begin before you come home. And you will not have long to wait. You will come to Arvandor very soon, Seiveril. Until that day you must live the life allotted to you.'"

Fflar smiled in the darkness and said, "I suppose you must wonder what she meant by 'very soon.' But what does this have to do with me?"

"I said my farewells to Ilyyela's spirit then," Seiveril said. "Before she departed entirely, she told me this: 'I cannot answer your call, love. But there is one here who will. Heal him, Seiveril. His wait has been long.'"

The moon elf was silent for a long time.

"And you thought she meant me?" he said finally. "Why me, Seiveril? I never knew you in life."

"No, you did not. But you did know my father, Elkhazel. He told me many stories of your valor in the Weeping War. When he finally passed to Arvandor himself, he told me where to find Keryvian. I suppose I have regarded you as something of a hero, since I was a small lad."

"I'm only one hundred and fifty years old, Seiveril. I can't abide the notion that a fellow three times my age regards me as his boyhood hero. Nor can I believe that I was unhappy in Arvandor," Fflar said. He stood up, shaking his head. "You'd better get some rest, old man. You'll need clear wits and all your strength for tomorrow."

At daybreak the elves broke camp and began to climb the flanks of the moor, marching in battle order—tight, disciplined companies instead of the loose columns of the past few days. They marched not more than two hours before an Evereskan scout galloped up to Seiveril and Fflar at the false standard.

"Lord Seiveril! The daemonfey army has turned!"

Fflar looked at Seiveril and said, "You were right. It seems they've stopped running."

The sun elf flicked the reins of his mount and followed the messenger as they rode ahead, climbing up a sparsely wooded hillside flanking the valley through which wound the weathered old track they followed. To the north the gray, flat emptiness of the Lonely Moor stretched unbroken for mile after mile. In the distance to the east Seiveril glimpsed the brown-gold desolation of Anauroch. On the rugged downlands of the moor the daemonfey army had halted, spreading out from the ragged, misshapen column the elves had chased for days into long lines facing south.

"Can we take them, do you think?" Seiveril asked.

Fflar replied, "That is your decision, not mine."

"I am asking you for your assessment of the situation."

The big moon elf studied the enemy ranks for a while then said, "You can't win this war by seizing some piece of territory these demonspawn control. They have no cities for you to raze, no castles to pull down. If you want to end this threat, you have to beat their army, and that means you have to wait for them come to you, or you have to run them down. I faced this same dilemma in the Weeping War, except that time I faced an army that outnumbered mine by ten to one. This foe you can defeat, if you are certain that the fight is necessary."

Seiveril studied the distant ranks of the enemy army, searching for certainty. He frowned, recalling his misgivings, and wondering what had changed for the daemonfey that had encouraged them to halt their retreat and turn back. Did they like the battleground? Had they garnered reinforcements? Or had they simply reached the right time to execute some greater plan of which he was not aware?

"Well?" asked Fflar.

Corellon, grant me wisdom, Seiveril prayed silently.

He wheeled his horse around to face the officers and messengers who followed him and snapped, "Send word to all the captains. We will attack!"

◉ ◉ ◉ ◉ ◉

Araevin found himself standing in a strange, spherical chamber of pale white stone. The room was perhaps three times his height, and the center of the floor had been leveled, so that it was not a true sphere. The walls shone with a pale radiance that illuminated the entire chamber with a strange and threatening light. He could feel the powerful spell wards that pervaded the place, spells to foil scrying, spells to make the walls impervious.... The room was without exit, as he knew it would be—the chamber had been carved out of the bedrock hundreds of feet below the ghost's hall, and it was only accessible by magic.

The Nightstar hovered in the center of the room, held aloft by the spells of the ancient wizard who had built the place. It was exactly as Araevin had seen, a dagger-shaped crystal about three inches long. In color it was a deep, iridescent purple reminiscent of the last gloaming of a storm-clouded sunset, and pale lavender glyphs were etched into its surface. Unseen emanations of magical power ringed the device like heat shimmering in the air, an aura of arcane potency that halted Araevin even in the face of his compulsion to seize the gem.

For all his years of study alongside high mages and loremasters, he had never seen a *selukiira* before. Like their lesser kindred the *telkiira,* they served to store knowledge—memories, spells, secrets, whatever their creators chose to infuse them with. But the high loregems were also reputed to be teaching devices, a means by which the arcane study of a hundred years might be conferred to the wearer in the blink of an eye. A *selukiira* might make a novice into a powerful mage in a single searing instant. If what Sarya had said was true, then locked inside its violet depths lay the secrets to high magic, knowledge of ancient rites and mighty spells that otherwise might take decades of study to encompass.

This was made by a Dlardrageth, he reminded himself. A Dlardrageth who studied firsthand the forgotten magic of old Aryvandaar, the most powerful realm of elves that ever existed. From their mighty towers in the North the High Mages of Aryvandaar launched spells that destroyed entire nations and enslaved half a continent. What would Sarya do with such knowledge?

It did not matter. He didn't have the ability to refuse.

Since the gemstone hovered ten feet above the marble floor, Araevin cast a simple spell to catch hold of it and draw it down to him—but the spell failed. The Nightstar was not to be moved by such a minor magic. He stood silent, thinking, then he muttered the words of his spell of flying, and willed himself into the air. Moving slowly, as if he watched himself in a dream, he reached out to touch the crystal. Dread welled up in his mind as his fingertips neared the gem, yet he was helpless to turn away his face or even wince in anticipation of what might happen when his flesh touched the crystal.

Selukiira burn out the minds of those who are not meant to handle them, he reminded himself. They recognize those who are false, and destroy them utterly.

"I refuse," Araevin whispered.

For an awful moment he fought to keep his hand from moving an inch nearer, his muscles straining to obey Sarya's command while his mind and will woke to full power, shaking off the daemonfey enchantment. He closed his eyes and bared his teeth, throwing the entirety of his consciousness into the simple effort to hold his hand still.

"I refuse!" he snarled, and he drew his hand back half an inch. Sarya's spell enticed him toward his doom with the seductiveness of a high, rocky clifftop and the lure of the leap, but Araevin proved the stronger.

He snatched his hand away, and howled, "I *refuse!*"

The Nightstar hung before his face, less than an arm's length from his eyes. It stood quiescent, showing not a hint of the fearsome doom it held for him. Araevin drifted back in midair, thinking hard. He took a deep breath.

"Now what?" he asked aloud.

Though his free will had been restored, the fact remained that he could not escape the chamber except by means of the portal, and that would return him to the hall where the daemonfey waited. Any teleportation he attempted there would destroy him, as surely as the vrock had been destroyed in the rooms above. He could try to surprise Nurthel with his sudden return, and attack—but Araevin had not had the opportunity to replenish his magic since before they entered Grimlight's lair, and few of his spells remained. It did not seem realistic to hope that he could defeat Nurthel, the other daemonfey, and the surviving demons with a single swift assault.

Would I have time enough to flee? he wondered. If I could escape the misty hall . . . but there again the barrier against teleportation would foil me. At best I could try to outrun the daemonfey, but they have wings, don't they?

He could try to feign compliance, returning to offer Nurthel a fake Nightstar. It was possible that the fey'ri sorcerer didn't know what the device would look like. That might give him an opportunity to flee later, but if Nurthel discovered the deception he would know that Sarya's compulsion had failed. Perhaps the best thing would be to simply wait in the buried chamber without ever returning, and make sure that the daemonfey were denied the Nightstar forever. Would it be worth his life to keep the *selukiira* out of their hands?

"Not just *your* life, Araevin," he reminded himself.

Sarya still held Ilsevele and Maresa in her stronghold. If he did not return there quickly, and with his will untrammeled by the daemonfey enchantments, Ilsevele and Maresa would suffer for it, and he could imagine only too well what form their tortures might take.

There is no way out, he realized.

Even if he regarded his own life as forfeit, he could not do the same for Ilsevele and Maresa. He had to find the path that offered him some chance to return and free them.

If he simply seized the gemstone and let it have him, there was a chance that Ilsevele and Maresa might be rescued by some other agency. Seiveril might divine her location and send help. At the very least, Araevin's resistance would not be an excuse for Sarya to kill his companions. There was at least some small possibility that the *selukiira* was not programmed to destroy its defiler. How much of a risk it would be, he had no way of knowing.

And when it came down to it, he was curious. Even if it destroyed him, he wanted to know what secrets the Nightstar concealed.

"Damn," he breathed.

He reached out and grasped the Nightstar.

His vision whirled, and in a flash of lambent light he felt himself drawn into the dormant consciousness of the gemstone. It engulfed him like a violet sea, smothering him in its power. He felt its might rising around him, ramparts and battlements of dangerous lore looming around him on all sides, penning him in, trapping him. Then the edifices vanished, leaving him to plummet screaming into a terrible and dark abyss, falling for what seemed to be hours through a cosmos of purple facets and white-glowing runes of fire. Darkness came, and a flash of brilliant light.

Araevin opened his eyes, and found himself standing in a wondrous and terrible garden. Walls of perfect white stone, graced by elegant arches, seemed to wall out some place of infernal terror. Brutal red firelight shone through the gaps, and the sky overhead was a sickly yellow-brown, streaked with columns of toxic smoke. The garden was home to scores of exotic plants and stunningly colorful blossoms, but they were alive and predatory, slow-moving things that writhed like serpents and dripped venom from their delicate structures. The golden fountain showed a marvelous sculpted scene of elf maidens and dancing satyrs, yet on a closer look the maidens' faces gaped with terror and the satyrs were scaly devils.

A flicker of light caught his eye, and he turned to look. From a soft sparkle of lavender a handsome sun elf stepped into the garden, appearing from the air itself. He was a regal fellow, tall and broad-shouldered, and he wore long crimson robes with a shorter vestment of gold-embroidered black over his torso. His face was sharp-featured, and his eyes were a startling, powerful green in color.

"Well," he said, his voice lilting with sinister beauty. "You are not what I expected. Who are you?"

Araevin steeled himself, determined not to show his dread, and replied, "I am Araevin Teshurr. Who are you?"

"I am Saelethil Dlardrageth. Or at least, a facsimile of him—me. I am the Nightstar."

"What is this place?"

"I am holding your mind within mine, as I assay you. Of course, your body still holds me in its hand." Saelethil paced nearer, his hands clasped before him, a sinister smile on his face. "I have taken the liberty of examining your predicament, at least as you perceive it. I am rather astonished to find that five millennia have passed, while I waited in Ithraides' prison. Saelethil did not—that is, *I* did not—anticipate this turn of events. If he had, I would know better what to do with you."

"If you mean to destroy me, then get on with it. I have had enough of bantering with daemonfey."

"Destroy you? Why, it's a lovely offer, but I am afraid I cannot oblige."

Araevin narrowed his eyes and studied the strange apparition more closely.

"I thought *selukiira* destroyed those unfit for their use," Araevin said.

"Of course I would do that. However, you are not unfit," Saelethil replied. His smirk faded a bit, and his eyes darkened with ire. "My purpose, as Saelethil himself inscribed it within me, is to teach sun elves of House Dlardrageth the secrets of Aryvandaar's high magic, provided they are sufficiently skilled in the study of magic to comprehend such things. You are a mage whose skill, while modest, still falls within acceptable limits. Therefore, I am not to destroy you."

"But I am not a Dlardrageth," Araevin replied, even as he wondered how hard he ought to argue that point with the Nightstar.

Saelethil laughed darkly and said, "Well, you may think you are not, but evidently you are. I have an infallible sense for this, and cannot be mistaken."

Could it be true? Araevin wondered. He thought back to what he knew of his ancestors . . . and he recalled his kinship to Elorfindar Floshin. Elorfindar and he shared an ancestor, a Floshin. And House Floshin had been one of the Houses of ancient Siluvanede, a House whose name was claimed by some among the fey'ri.

"I am a Floshin," he mumbled.

"That does not make you a Dlardrageth," Saelethil observed. "However, I would guess that one of my family chose to favor one of the Floshins with a child. The Floshins served us long and well, after all. Your heritage likely derives from such a dalliance." The cruel sun elf shook his head. "I was not nearly specific enough when I created the descriptions of who could use this device. Of course, I had no idea that five thousand years and dozens of generations would pass, allowing Dlardrageth blood to surface in some unexpected places."

"If I am a Dlardrageth, then how did I manage to unlock Ithraides' *telkiira* or gain access to this chamber?" Araevin asked. "These things were locked against the daemonfey."

Saelethil pursed his lips in displeasure and said, "Take up that question with Ithraides' shade, not mine. If I were to guess, I would suppose that his defenses were designed to hinder those with the stain of evil marking their souls. Your high and useless morals likely met the stodgy old bastard's approval."

Araevin closed his eyes and laughed bitterly.

"So I represent the one contradiction that neither you nor Ithraides foresaw," he said, "a Dlardrageth free of the supernatural evil of the rest of the House. Had I been evil, I never could have found this place. Had I not been a Dlardrageth, I never could have survived it."

"The irony overwhelms me," Saelethil said, grimacing.

"So, what now?"

"What now?" Saelethil repeated. He fixed his emerald eyes on Araevin, and a cruel smile grew slowly on his features. "What now? Now, my weak-minded bastard whelp who happens to be blessed with a genealogy you do not appreciate or deserve, I am going to do what I was made to do and instruct you in the things that Saelethil wished to see preserved. And we'll see if you are Dlardrageth enough to survive the scars I'm going to sear into your soul."

Saelethil stood before Araevin, who started to protest, but Saelethil seized his head with both hands and pressed his fingertips into Araevin's skull.

The world exploded with crimson pain.

CHAPTER 17

11 Tarsakh, the Year of Lightning Storms

Silver moonlight streamed down the shoulders of Daelyth's Dagger until the stark cliffs of the forest mountain shone like white beacons in the night. Nervous, Gaerradh studied the sky and the high slopes overhead, searching for any sign of daemonfey sorcerers above the vale. The deeply cleft valley was so narrow and high that the winged fey'ri would have to choose between staying so far above the gorge that they could not reach the elves below with their spells and quarrels, or descending into the straits of stone where it would be difficult to maneuver between the cliffs. On the other hand any fey'ri who remained above the Dagger could simply hurl stones into the deeps below and create no small danger for anyone sheltering on the valley floor below, even if their boulders were dropped at random.

"It's a clear night," Methrammar remarked. "That favors us greatly. As long as there's any light at all, we'll see as well as the orcs, and the moon shadows will help to hide us from unfriendly eyes."

The commander of Silverymoon's legion stood dressed in his great crimson cloak, his mithral mail gleaming like starshine beneath his mantle. All around him, hundreds of Silverymoon's Knights in Silver and their dwarf comrades from Citadel Adbar's Iron Guard filled the Dagger's mouth, standing in easy ranks to guard the narrow trail winding along the swift white stream.

Faint lanterns had been positioned high up on the rocky walls of the trail and the lower vale, throwing soft verdant light over the way the enemy must come if he came on foot. But Gaerradh thought that the dense ranks of waiting soldiers would make an excellent target from the air.

"The orcs do not concern me," Gaerradh murmured. "It's the daemonfey I fear. If they do not enter the vale . . ."

"If they do not enter the vale, they'll never get us out of here," Methrammar finished for her. "We can stand a siege of a month or more if we have to, and the mages of Evermeet tell us their army is marching here next. No, the daemonfey want to take the Dagger by assault. They don't have the time to starve us out."

"Your soldiers are too exposed. I don't like this."

"They're where they need to be." The half-elf turned to look Gaerradh in her eyes and said, "Our warriors are best suited for this task, Gaerradh. We've got heavier armor than your wood elves, and we're trained to fight in ranks. Holding this trail is our kind of fight. The rest of it is up to you."

"I know," she said.

She studied Methrammar's clean visage and fine features, finding no trace of fear in his eyes, only a shadow of anticipation—not that she should have expected less from a son of Alustriel. Still, the Argent Legion bore the greatest hazard, and that meant Methrammar did as well, since the high marshal was not in the habit of leading from the rear. He would be in the forefront of the fighting, his banner flying behind him, and Gaerradh knew what a prize he would be for the daemonfey and their allies. She did not want to see him wounded, or worse.

"Be careful," she managed.

Methrammar rolled his eyes and started to answer, but then a harsh, brazen horn blast sounded in the darkness beyond the vale. Red torchlight bobbed up and down in the darkness beneath the trees, and the rumble and clatter of iron-shod feet filled the echoing gorge.

"I told you they wouldn't wait," Methrammar said. He stepped out and called to his soldiers, "Get ready, lads. We'll hold them here until the mountain itself cries for mercy. Iron Guards, take your position!"

The dwarves of Citadel Adbar raised a hoarse cheer and jogged forward, forming a wall of dwarven steel across the trail, with their right flank bending back along the streambed in case any foes came at them by climbing up the cold, rushing stream. Fitted head to toe in heavy dwarven plate, with big steel shields and deadly war axes, they were an unshakable obstacle in such a small space. The humans and half-elves of Silverymoon's Knights in Silver stood back a short distance, fighting afoot since there was no room for mounted troops. Dozens of seasoned Spellguards stood within their ranks, alongside a handful of the crusade mages sent to aid the beleaguered wood elves. It was their job to protect the dwarves under the brunt of the first assault.

The orc horns sounded again, along with a rising chorus of war cries and screams, and the ground shook with the thunder of the orc approach. The savage warriors appeared at the far bend of the Dagger's trail, rushing up the old road in a reckless, screaming mass. Gaerradh recoiled a step despite herself, and started searching for targets worthy of arrows.

An instant before the orc berserkers crashed into the dwarven line, the air itself seemed to lurch and thunder as dozens of demons teleported to the mouth of the Dagger, behind the Iron Guard dwarves.

The sheer violence of the collision staggered Gaerradh. The dwarves had expected demons to show up behind them, and with uncanny swiftness the powerful company turned turtle, sealing the road like a cork in a bottle. Demons shrieked and clawed, trying to tear into the dwarven ranks from behind or scour the sturdy fighters with their terrible spells of hellfire and destruction. But Silverymoon's Spellguards countered many of the spells or threw hasty defensive wards over the Iron Guards, while the rest of the knights—led by Methrammar, who brandished his sword and bellowed commands—charged against the vrocks, hezrous, and babaus who sought to surround and overwhelm the dwarves. The whole time, the orcs roared and hacked at the front line of the dwarf fighters, while the dwarves roared their own challenges back and hewed down orc berserkers like farmers threshing grain.

Gaerradh calmly nocked an arrow with a point of blessed cold iron, a weapon no demon could shrug off, and sighted carefully to make sure that she would not strike an ally. She spotted a hulking hezrou laying about itself with its long, powerful claws, froglike mouth gaping with needle-sharp teeth. She buried two arrows in its thick neck, her hands blurring with the speed of her shot. The creature coughed black blood and disappeared at once, teleporting away from the battle—wounded or dying, Gaerradh did not care. She sighted another demon and fired again, slipping her arrows through lightning-quick openings and shifting, battling figures as a master duelist might wield a rapier.

Silverymoon's knights counterattacked the demons who'd thought to surround the dwarven company with such ferocity that the foul creatures were forced to turn away from the Iron Guards. In turn, the demons hurled themselves against Methrammar's soldiers with blind fury, claws rending and jaws tearing, all the while blasting and scouring any warrior who stood against them with sickening blasts of evil power, great gouts of clinging hellfire, and billowing yellow clouds of poison vapor.

Human soldiers died screaming under the claws and fangs of the hellspawned monsters or staggered down into death, bodies charred, poisoned, or ruptured by demonic spells. Methrammar stood in the center like a shining silver tower, cutting down any fiendish creature who came against him and hurling blasts of his own magic at demons who avoided him. Around their high marshal the knights of Silverymoon rallied, and held.

Gaerradh shot and shot until her quiver was empty, then she slung her bow across her shoulder and drew out her paired fighting axes, looking for a way to help. The furious melee around the Iron Guard dwarves and the demon-battle among the Knights in Silver were fights she wanted no part of. She was at her best with her bow, and did not wear anywhere near enough steel for that sort of brawling. She held back and waited, axes in hand. Sheeril growled anxiously at her side.

"Patience, girl," Gaerradh told her.

A streaking ball of fire arced down from overhead to detonate amid the Iron Guard dwarves and their orc adversaries. The vale thundered with the sound of the blast, and dwarves and orcs flew through the air like ninepins. The dwarves in their heavy armor and defensive enchantments fared better than their adversaries. More fireballs streaked down into the battle, filling the mouth of the valley with orange and red blasts of flame that charred the very rocks black. Gaerradh threw herself behind a big boulder and ducked under her cloak, trying to stay out of the worst of the flames.

"Methrammar!" she cried. "The fey'ri are in the valley!"

"Up and at them, lads!" called Silverymoon's champion.

Shielded by his defensive magic, the fey'ri spells washed over Methrammar with no more effect than a gentle shower. Other Knights in Silver stood by as well, likewise protected by their spells and enchantments. Some of their comrades did not rise, but more stood than fell. Gaerradh quickly looked over to the open trail where the Iron Guards had been fighting. The dwarves lay in a great crumpled mound, scorched and still. She stood on the edge of black, dizzying despair, but then she saw the tangled mass of dwarves shift and move. Awkwardly, the heavily armored warriors of the Iron Guard contingent picked themselves up, disentangling themselves from their comrades, and set their shields and weapons right, reforming their turtle-like formation.

"Is that your best?" cried one dwarf sergeant, shaking his axe at the sky. "Is that all you can do?"

Gaerradh looked up, waiting for the fey'ri reply. A great company of the bat-winged demonspawn descended into the gorge, hurling spells and iron javelins at the Argent Legion troops below. There were hundreds of them, and the air between the walls of Daelyth's Dagger seemed to broil with magical energy and supernatural power. Dressed in armor of scarlet and gold, the daemonfey wheeled overhead like sinister angels.

Exactly where they were supposed to be.

"Let's see how you like the marksmanship of the wood elves," Gaerradh murmured.

A clear horn call echoed high up in the rocky walls of the vale, and the air between the gorge's sides was filled with a black storm of arrows. From a hundred perches high up on the cliffs overlooking the narrow valley, wood elf archers—including a score of Evermeet's best spellarchers, brought to the Lost Peaks only hours before—threw aside their concealment and loosed a terrible fusillade of arrows against the flying fey'ri warriors. Many of the archers were actually shooting *down* on the airborne fey'ri, as the daemonfey company had descended past the uppermost shelves of hidden archers in their rush to eradicate the dwarves and humans who held the valley mouth.

Fey'ri wheeled and fluttered in desperation, pierced again and again by the merciless onslaught. More than a few arrows blazed with holy spells or crackled with whispered enchantments as they sped on their way, finding fey'ri chests and throats. In a single deadly volley scores of the fey'ri died in midair, wings folding as they plummeted to the boulder-strewn floor of the valley.

Those who survived the first volley searched wildly for escape from the killing zone, but even fey'ri flying over the center of the valley were not more than one hundred yards from one wall or the other, and that was well within the wood elves' range. To descend was to brave even more arrows, to climb would be murderously slow, and to seek cover on either wall was to simply come closer to one nest of archers or another. So the fey'ri struggled and flew east along the vale, fleeing for the mouth of Daelyth's Dagger as they ran the terrible gauntlet. A few quickly worked spells to turn themselves invisible, or cover themselves in obscuring darkness, or simply teleport to safety. But with every beat of their wings, more daemonfey warriors crumpled and fell to the hard boulders below.

"It worked!" Gaerradh cried, elated.

She had thought Methrammar was insane to offer his soldiers as bait to draw the fey'ri spellcasters, but the high marshal's plan was proving to be nothing less than pure genius. Broken and pierced, the demonspawned warriors littered the valley floor.

Avoiding the arrows and debris clattering down from the ambush overhead, Gaerradh sprinted over to where Methrammar stood. Sheeril flashed at her heels, growling. The Knights in Silver had beaten off the worst of the demon assault, though a few savage skirmishes still continued around the edges of the company. Methrammar watched the fighting in the air, blood streaming from a nasty bite on his left arm and a sword-slash on his thigh.

"Great work, friends!" he cried. "That will teach them some wisdom!" He looked down as Gaerradh reached his side, and he offered her a fierce grin. "I knew that all we had to do was to get the fey'ri in front of wood elf bows!"

"What now?" Gaerradh called.

"We finish this," Methrammar said. "We can drive these orc marauders all the way to Hellgate Keep if we strike now." The son of Alustriel laughed with delight, and whirled away to dash up the road, brandishing his blade.

"To me! To me!" he cried. "We're taking this fight out of the valley and into their teeth, lads!"

The Knights in Silver rallied to Methrammar's cry, and the dwarves of the Iron Guard as well. With a deafening clamor of battle cries and roars of challenge, the warriors of Silverymoon and Adbar clattered forward, battering their way back down the Dagger's trail to meet the oncoming orcs head-on. Gaerradh shouted in martial fury and followed, axes in hand, Sheeril snapping and slashing to guard her back.

At dawn the orcs broke and fled.

❧ ❧ ❧ ❧ ❧

Araevin plumbed the lambent depths of the Nightstar for what seemed like hours, examining the spells Saelethil had stored within, cataloging the deep reaches of hidden lore for later study, confronting the fiery secrets of high magic and mythalcraft preserved by the Dlardrageth high mage. He could sense Saelethil's cruel persona graven in the very substance of the high loregem, observing his fumbling explorations with a sneer of disdain, though he decided he did not care what the sinister apparition happened to think of his efforts. It would take some study yet before he could master many of the secrets waiting within the *selukiira,* but he knew enough to comprehend mythals and other such wards of high magic in a way he had never dreamed possible. Araevin suspected that some at least of the things Saelethil taught him had been forgotten—or shunned—by other high mages for many centuries.

More importantly, the Nightstar offered him the chance to turn the tables on his captors. Nurthel had likely thought that he posed no threat so long as his spellbooks remained out of his hands, but like the *telkiira,* the Nightstar itself also served as a spellbook. The three *telkiira* stored twenty spells between them, and the Nightstar by itself recorded more than seventy. Of course, many of the spells were difficult or impossible for him to cast until he acquired the correct materials—pinches of reagents, herbs, tiny charms carefully readied under the right conditions—but Araevin had found a number that he could manage. An hour's study sufficed to fill his mind with spells, ranging from insignificant cantrips to mighty dweomers he never could have managed before Saelethil's lore had burned itself into his brain. He was as well-armed as he could possibly hope, and then some.

When he was finally ready, Araevin touched the portal design in the Nightstar's chamber and instantly transported himself back to the silver hall of the ghost. The *selukiira* lay over his heart, the purple crystal embedded in his flesh and fused to his breastbone. He had considered leaving it exactly where he'd found it, but there was too much in the gemstone that he needed to know, and so he risked bringing it with him.

A moment of dizziness and darkness, and he stood by the wall in the mist-wreathed hall of the silver pillars. He felt strong and certain in a way that frightened him, doubting as he did the source of his strength. It was not simply a physical vitality, his mind was sharper, clearer, more focused, and the spells the high loregem had taught him girded his very thoughts like eldritch armor. He turned and faced the hall.

The daemonfey waited for him. Apparently the sudden operation of the portal had caught them off guard. Two of the fey'ri warriors cursed as they drew their blades, and the hissing mezzoloths rose up from crouches, seizing their iron tridents. Nurthel Floshin spun to face him, his single remaining eye alight with ire.

"Where have you been?" he demanded. "Where is the Nightstar?"

Araevin stepped away from the wall, carefully noting the positions of Nurthel and his band: A fey'ri spellblade and two more fey'ri swordsmen, standing close by Nurthel; the two surviving vrocks, skulking in the shadows to his right; and the two mezzoloths, standing up on his left.

Eight of them, he thought. And only one of me.

"Where have I been? The vault of Ithraides," he answered. "And as for the Nightstar, I have it."

Nurthel bared his pointed teeth and held out his taloned hand.

"Come here and give it to me," he hissed.

"No, I don't think I will," Araevin replied.

He looked over at the vrocks, gestured, and calmly spoke the words of a spell, banishing them back to the foul Abyss from which they had been summoned. The creatures clacked and hissed in rage, starting toward him, but before they had even taken wing azure fire flickered over their hideous forms and hurled them into their native dimension.

"He has broken the dominion spell. Subdue him at once!" Nurthel screamed.

He began a spell of his own, barking out the magical words, while the mezzoloths charged at Araevin from his left side and the fey'ri swordsmen approached more carefully from his right, sword points weaving in lazy circles before them.

Araevin darted to his right, avoiding the mezzoloths. One of the insectile creatures hurled its trident at him. The heavy weapon struck him on his left shoulder blade, spinning him around with the impact and throwing him to the floor. But the trident rebounded from his flesh, which was hardened to the denseness of granite by the spell he had cast on himself before activating the portal to return to the silver hall. He rolled to his hands and knees, looking up at the two fey'ri warriors closing in on him, and he spoke a word of power that blasted both swordsmen off their feet. Streaming blood at ears and nose, the armored daemonfey skidded across the floor and groaned, both struck senseless by the spell.

Nurthel finished his own casting and conjured a great golden hand of magical force that lunged for Araevin, seeking to seize hold of him. The second of Araevin's hastily prepared defenses came into play. As the mighty hand closed on him, Araevin's turning spell triggered, deflecting the glowing apparition back at Nurthel. The fey'ri sorcerer cried out, startled, as his own spell grappled him, fingers like a giant's arms curling around his golden armor and pinning him in place.

"Kill the paleblood!" he screamed in frustration.

Araevin gained his feet just in time for the other fey'ri spellcaster to hurl his own spell, an enchantment intended to mire his body and mind in a dolorous lethargy, dulling his reactions and slowing his efforts. He fought off the spell with a gesture and a thought, turning his attention to the two mezzoloths who stalked him. The creatures clawed at him, their foul talons scraping across his hardened skin and tearing gashes in his clothes without causing him serious injury. Still, Araevin knew that he could not ignore them for long. Sooner or later his spell would wear out, or the mezzoloths would give up on trying to tear him to pieces and instead just tackle him, and he could not allow the powerful creatures to pin him. He dodged back and immobilized one with a spell of holding, rooting it to the spot. The other stayed after him.

The fey'ri spellblade hurled a bolt of fire at Araevin that burned away the last of his turning spell. The creature was clever enough to anticipate the return of his own spell, ducking out of the way as his fire-bolt struck Araevin's spell shield and rebounded. In return, Araevin charred the fellow to a black husk with a terrible bolt of purple lightning. The smell of burning flesh and smoke filled the room. Nurthel continued to struggle against his own spell, snarling vile curses the whole time.

"I will dismember you myself!" he hissed. "Your woman shall pay for your treachery, paleblood!"

With a tremendous effort, Nurthel managed to slip one arm free of the magical hand holding him. He brought it to his face to raise his eye patch, and Araevin glimpsed a bright green stone in the socket. Nurthel looked down at the golden force around his body and snarled a word. From his eye-gem leaped out a green ray that instantly disintegrated the hand holding him. He stumbled awkwardly to the ground, then looked up and grinned at Araevin, already beginning another spell.

The remaining mezzoloth finally managed to catch Araevin by the arm, its horrid pincers seizing him in an inescapable grip. Araevin cried out in dismay, not really hurt yet since his spell still protected him. The creature's mandibles clacked and dripped before his face, and it wrenched him half around as it sought to catch hold of his other arm. But Araevin steadied his mind with a conscious effort, and set his free hand on the monster's chitinous torso.

"Let go of me!" he snarled, and cast a disintegrating spell of his own at the yugoloth.

A brilliant flare of green energy gleamed from within the mezzoloth's thick carapace, shining forth at joints and eyes, and the creature abruptly vanished into a gray, stinking haze of dust.

Araevin shook himself free of the mezzoloth's drifting ash and spun to face Nurthel. The fey'ri lord hissed out the last sibilant whispers of his own spell and raised a globe of shimmering colors around himself. Araevin recognized the spell at once as a potent ward against many magical attacks. Nurthel advanced a couple of steps, and the crawling globe of color moved with him.

"You have done well to eliminate my warriors and demons," the fey'ri said. "You surprised me. I admit it. I don't know how you found the opportunity to conceal so many spells, but you will find that I am not so easily overcome as my fellows."

"Your confidence is misplaced," Araevin replied.

"Is it?" Nurthel smiled. "Not many spells can pierce this defense, as I am sure a mage of your accomplishment must know. And I observe that, while you may still have spells at your command, you are unarmed." He drew a short sword of dark, rune-scribed iron from a sheath at his side, and advanced another two steps toward Araevin. "Now, before I kill you, where is the Nightstar?"

Araevin did not bother to reply. Instead he began another spell, one he had learned from the *telkiira* stones. Speaking the words loudly and swiftly as he moved, he turned his hands in the proper manner.

Whatever Nurthel's confidence in his spell shield, the fey'ri sensed danger. He scowled and leaped forward, charging close to reach Araevin before the elf mage finished his spell.

Nurthel fell three steps short. Araevin completed his casting and seized the fey'ri's spell shield, inverting the magical protection on its caster. The magical power swirling around Nurthel froze, motionless, and contracted in upon him. Brilliant flashes of green and blue wrapped around him as the spell shield turned on its master, flaying his flesh with crawling arcs of power. Nurthel screamed and staggered one more step before collapsing at Araevin's feet, charred and smoking.

Araevin knelt slowly and took the fey'ri's sword from his crumbling fingers. He tugged open his shirt, and showed the dying sorcerer the Nightstar embedded in his chest.

"As I told you before," he grated, "I have the *selukiira*." Then he took Nurthel's own sword, shoved it through the fey'ri's throat, and watched as the daemonfey lord died. "That was for Grayth, you black-hearted hellspawn."

He took his wands back from the corpse, then strode out of the mist-filled hall. Ilsevele and Maresa were still in Sarya's hands, and more importantly, Sarya had control of a mythal stone. Saelethil had known many things about what could be done with unattended mythals. Thanks to the *selukiira*, Araevin did too.

☙ ☙ ☙ ☙ ☙

The battle on the Lonely Moor began an hour before sunset.

It had taken the army of Evermeet most of the afternoon to climb up to the plateau and form themselves in their battle-order. As he had feared, the ground was too difficult for his cavalry to make much use of their mobility. They could fight mounted, but they could not use their speed to much effect, not without crippling their horses in unseen soft spots and deep, narrow gulches.

"I don't understand why the daemonfey did not defend the hillsides climbing up to the moor," Seiveril said to Fflar as the army advanced.

The enemy had chosen to make his stand several miles inside the boggy highland. The daemonfey army, only a thousand yards distant, waited before them, divided into a large center and two sweeping wings. Most of the soldiers in the ranks were orcs and ogres, a serried line of dark figures who hooted and jeered and shook their weapons at the approaching elves. Seiveril spotted numerous demons waiting amid the savage warriors, flexing terrible claws and snarling with needle-fanged jaws. The fey'ri waited behind their orc allies, a glint of gold and scarlet shining through the surging mass of tribal warriors.

"Maybe they just wanted us to have to walk a few more miles to get to them," Fflar suggested. "Better to fight a tired soldier than a fresh one. Or maybe they were afraid that we would encircle them by climbing up a different route while they were engaged in the defense of the old road." The big moon elf shrugged. "It hardly matters now. This is where the battle will be."

Seiveril wasn't entirely satisfied with that answer, but unless he was willing to halt and see what the daemonfey did in response, he would not find out for sure. He guessed that the enemy commander would expect him to draw near and take a defensive posture to invite attack. He hoped that a swift hammer blow at the very beginning of the fight might rout the orcs and ogres, leaving the daemonfey and their infernal allies to fight alone.

He took one last look at the ragged enemy formation, and raised his voice to call, "Companies, oblique to the left, march! Sound the signal!"

Marching in swift ranks, the elven companies veered toward the left flank of the daemonfey army. At Fflar's suggestion, instead of marching dead into the center of the enemy horde, Seiveril wanted to hurl all his strength against a portion of the army. He believed that his forces were swifter and more easily maneuvered than the daemonfeys' unruly horde, and the enemy center and right would have difficulty moving to defend the left. Of course, that meant that his own right flank was exposed to the bulk of the enemy army, but he had prepared for that by building his right flank from the heaviest and most dependable of his footsoldiers, his own Silver Guards from the northlands of Evermeet and two stout companies of Evereska's veteran Vale Guards.

"That threw 'em," Fflar said with a smile. "They can't match that move."

The ragged ranks of orcs and ogres seethed, as if they were not sure what to do. Then the harsh voice of a brazen trumpet sounded from somewhere in the enemy center, and the orcs and ogres on Seiveril's right started to move forward and in, trying to wrap around behind the elf's right flank. But the difficult terrain the daemonfey had chosen for themselves worked against them. The savage warriors trying to move swiftly to get behind the crusade's right flank found that they had hundreds of yards of wet, boggy ground in front of them. The orc spearmen farthest out on the enemy right had no hope of keeping up with the intended wheeling movement, and fell behind at once, even though they were running at their best speed to try to keep their place.

"It's only bought us a few minutes," Seiveril replied.

The shining silver ranks of the elf infantry flowed over the uneven ground, rippling like a stream of steel pouring across the moorland. The gap between the armies narrowed moment by moment, closing by two hundred yards a minute at their swift pace. Seiveril glanced to the west. The sun had descended from the day's overcast and gleamed, orange and cold, in the gap between mountains and clouds. It was a spectacular sunset, really, the skies streaked with shadow and gold.

Corellon, let our work be done swiftly and well tonight, he prayed. *Speed our arrows to our enemies, confuse and foil them so that no more of your sons may go to Arvandor before their time.*

"Archers!" he cried. "Fire at your pace as we advance. Look for fey'ri and enemy banners."

Strong bands of wood elf archers marched alongside the spearmen and swordsmen of Evermeet. The battle of the cwm had taught Seiveril that his archers were the best answer to the fey'ri spellcasters. By salting his ranks with small companies of Evermeet's wood elves and the elite spellarchers, he would make it difficult for the fey'ri legion to attack from the air without enduring at least some danger of their own. With easy skill, the archers kept the pace of the advancing swordsmen and spearmen, pausing a half step every twelve heartbeats to loose an arrow at the army waiting ahead.

More than a thousand bows began to speak as the elven force drew close to its adversary, sending ragged flights of white arrows whistling through the space between the armies. The fire was nothing like what they might have achieved if they had halted, but elf archers trained long and hard at firing on the move, and from the first volley their deadly shafts began to work destruction among the ranks ahead.

The orcs and ogres of the daemonfey army screamed and bellowed in anger. Banners fell, their standard-bearers slain. Captains and sergeants choked on slender arrows fired by keen-eyed elf marksmen. Seiveril considered ordering a halt to allow his archers even more time to rake the enemy ranks, but then the daemonfey decided matters for him. Again the heavy trumpet blatted out its deep note, and the uneasy ranks of savage warriors shouted in delight, breaking into a clumsy, ragged charge.

"Halt and hold!" Seiveril cried. "Archers, break the charge! Mages, stand by for the fey'ri and demons. Don't waste your spells on orcs unless you have to."

The elven army slowed to a stop, heavy infantry in the front grounding their shields and setting their spears and swords, the archers redoubling their fire. The ragged volleys of the advance became a withering storm of white shafts. For one endless minute, the archers scythed down hundreds of orc berserkers and rampaging ogres as the feral warriors struggled to reach the elves across the rough moorland.

The first of the orcs and ogres reached the elf ranks, while the fey'ri legion took to the air, their wing beats as great and terrible as thunderclaps.

"Beware the daemonfey!" Seiveril called.

He readied his own counterspells and defenses, prepared to withstand a magical assault. But the fey'ri stayed out of reach and flew over his army, in one swift and precise movement sealing off his retreat.

The sun sank below the dark, cold mountains, and shadow fell over Seiveril and the army of Evermeet.

❖ ❖ ❖ ❖ ❖

Sarya Dlardrageth watched her orcs and ogres hurl themselves upon the elves' army, breaking on the rampart of the elven line like a stormy sea unable to overcome a stone breakwater. In truth, she was impressed by the speed and handiness of Evermeet's army, as well as their sheer determination. She hadn't been sure that they had the stomach to press their pursuit to the point of another pitched battle, but so much the better.

"It's going poorly for the left flank," Mardeiym Reithel said. "Without our fey'ri behind it, I think they will break and run."

"No matter," Sarya replied. "The palebloods will have to turn to meet the attack of our center and right. And we are about to give them something else to worry about, anyway."

She paced across her Vyshaanti battle-platform, watching the fray closely. She was dressed in golden mail of exceptional quality and exquisite workmanship, a highly enchanted artifact she had found among the spoils of Nar Kerymhoarth. Sarya intended to lend her own mastery of the Art to the attack, and she was well prepared to do so.

The fey'ri, hovering well above arrow-reach, passed over the entirety of the elven army and alighted behind her foes. The sorcerers and warriors of her daemonfey legion began to attack the rearmost companies of the elven army, guarding themselves with potent spell shields as they scoured and blasted the elf ranks with their terrible spells and fire wands. She had deliberately ordered her captains to allow Evermeet's host to reach the moorland unchallenged in order to draw them well and truly into the open. The elven army was engaged on three sides by her left flank, her center, and the fey'ri.

The moment was as right as it would get.

Sarya laughed with malice and hissed, "Now we shall test the mettle of our enemies. Mardeiym, you will take command of the center. Send word to the right that I want them in the fight in five minutes, or I will personally slay every captain in that host."

The fey'ri general struck his fist to his chest and replied, "As you wish, Lady Dlardrageth."

Sarya made a gesture with her hand activating one of the useful enchantments in her battle-platform. Switching to the Abyssal tongue, she barked out her orders.

"Time to spring our trap," she grated. "All of you, follow me and slay to your hearts' content!"

Lurking in the shadows sheltering her from sight, hundreds of demons waited—virtually all who could transport themselves from place to place with a simple act of will. Many were survivors of the Battle of the Cwm, but better than threescore were newly summoned and bound to her service. Sarya spoke a command word, and her platform teleported from its place of concealment to a barren, sandy stretch on the unengaged left flank of the elven army. An instant later, the first of her demon marauders followed her, appearing from midair like a rain of horror.

Her army surrounded Evermeet's host on all four sides.

"Destroy them!" she cried, sweeping her arm at her foes.

Demons howled, barked, and laughed in response, and threw themselves against their prey.

CHAPTER 18

12 Tarsakh, the Year of Lightning Storms

Araevin trotted swiftly through the damp, rain-soaked trees of Cormanthor, distancing himself from the vault behind him. He deliberately avoided the old elfroad, just on the chance that the daemonfey might discover his freedom and their dead comrades and come looking for him. The side of his chest still burned with the broken ribs the behir had given him, and various other injuries announced themselves as he traveled, but he refused to give the pain a place in his thoughts, and instead considered what to do next as he jogged on.

Ilsevele first, he thought. And Maresa too. I have to get them out of Sarya's hands before the daemonfey discover my escape. All I have to do is walk into the demons' den.

Armed as he was with a mind full of spells

and abjurations as potent as anything he could ever have prepared in his own workroom, Araevin didn't shy from returning to the daemonfey halls. He even thought he might have an unpleasant surprise or two for them.

This should do, Araevin decided.

He looked around at the wet woodland and shivered. The vault of Ithraides, with its teleport-distorting spell wards, lay two miles behind him. He was well outside its magical mantle.

"Now, for the difficult part," he breathed.

Gesturing absently, he prepared a couple of defensive spells to protect himself—one that covered him in an intangible shield of magical force, and another to turn himself invisible. He gazed around at the forest, breathing in the scent of spring rising from hidden roots and deep places.

Hold it in your mind, Araevin, he told himself. It might be the last good thing you look on in this life.

Then he incanted the teleport spell, fixing in his mind the image of the marble-floored cavern in the daemonfey stronghold.

The forest reeled away into darkness, and he felt himself falling through icy void for the space of an instant—then he appeared in the dim, lamplit halls of the daemonfey.

Araevin did his best to avoid making any sound as he arrived, but he couldn't stop a soft gasp as the suddenness of the change staggered him. Fortunately, no one was in the hall. It was cold and forbidding even in the absence of its infernal masters, a stark and comfortless place where the air carried a subtle taint of blood and hot metal. Several passageways led away from the room, he presumed to other halls and chambers. At his back the hall ended in a crevasse or natural chimney that climbed up into the dark and fell away into measureless shadow below.

"What is this place?" he muttered.

He turned, studying the room again and trying to guess which way his friends might have been taken. His eye fell on the dark pool of blood where Grayth had died.

Any fear or uncertainty he might have entertained vanished like yesterday's winds.

Information is the first order of business, he decided.

He held himself still and closed his eyes, listening and feeling for the magical ward he had noted when Nurthel brought him before Sarya. If he was right about it. . . .

"I thought so," he murmured.

As before, he felt the peculiar magical vibration or resonance of a mythal ward embracing him. It was not a sound, a smell, or any sort of physical sensation he could accurately describe, but something in the very air and rock of the place announced itself to his wizard's senses. There was no doubt the daemonfey stronghold was protected by a mythal stone, and a strong one at that.

How did Sarya raise a mythal in secret? he wondered.

More likely she'd found one and repaired it, he answered himself. It would require patience and lore, but there's no reason to think that the daemonfey lack either.

Araevin paused, considering his next move. He glanced around to make sure that he was still alone, and moved to a somewhat more sheltered corner of the room just in case. He had intended to immediately set about searching for Ilsevele and Maresa with his divinations, but it occurred to him that the mythal's properties might include alarms or spell traps against intruders. Each one of the old mythals was unique, and there was really no way of knowing what spells might or might not have been woven to shield the place before the daemonfey found it, or for that matter, whether or not the original spells still worked as intended. Old mythals tended to fray with time, and their powers sometimes faded away or decayed into new and dangerous properties unplanned by their makers.

It would help him judge the dangers of the mythal if he knew how long ago and by whom it had been raised. He was pretty sure Sarya's stronghold was somewhere in the North. After all, the daemonfey army had marched on Evereska from somewhere in the vicinity of old Hellgate Keep—but Hellgate Keep itself had been completely destroyed. Most likely he was in some forgotten hold or vault of ancient Siluvanede or Sharrven, but he could not be certain.

"Enough speculation," he told himself.

He spoke one of the spells Saelethil had taught him, coaxing the mythal's woven web of ancient spells to become visible to him. All around him a bright golden network of drifting strands of magic slowly appeared.

Araevin carefully observed the tangible dweomers pervading the hall, analyzing them. First he looked for signs of alarms or spell traps that would catch the unwary. He spotted an alarm first, a spell designed to warn anyone within the mythal if a non-daemonfey spellcaster entered the ruins—a reasonable precaution, given the nearness of Silverymoon and Alustriel. He grimaced, realizing that again the faint blemish in his bloodline turned to his advantage. Then he examined the drifting thread more closely, and saw that it was a dark and potent red-gold in color. It was clearly something new, something added to the existing mythal.

Sarya has modified the mythal! he realized.

"I didn't think that was possible," he breathed.

Of course it's possible, Saelethil's memory told him. If none of the mythal-raisers contest your efforts, you can modify a standing mythal. It is strenuous and requires a little lore, but it can be done.

Araevin examined the mythal-weave again. There he saw a corrupted thread that would cause spells of magical force to fail if cast within the mythal's field. Another fraying weave allowed a knowledgeable caster to control the temperature within the mythal's bounds. A more intact strand would permit him to use the mythal's powers to enhance his own spells, making them swifter and more powerful.

"That's a useful trick," he noted.

More wards blocked scrying by those who did not know the proper key.

Araevin turned his attention to the founding ward, the strongest and most pervasive of all the magic streams, and there he found the lethargic golden trunk of the original ward warped by a strong new stream of burnished red-gold, like a strangling vine parasitizing an old tree. Sarya had twisted the first and primary warding the mythal offered. Araevin frowned and studied it more closely. In ancient times, he could see that the ward had been designed to absolutely bar the entrance of creatures who had knowingly consumed elf- or man-flesh. In the days when orcs, trolls, and demons besieged the North, it would have been a formidable bulwark against their armies. But Sarya had perverted that ward, and instead was using it to anchor something else in place. Hundreds of fine red filaments frayed out from the great ward, disappearing into the ether.

"Demons," he whispered. "That is how the Dlardrageths are summoning so many demons. They're using the mythal to do it."

Despite the fearsomeness of Araevin's newfound lore, he still felt sick. To see an ancient and noble work such as the mythal enslaved to a purpose its builders would have reviled simply turned his stomach.

He might be able to do something about that. But first he had to locate Ilsevele and Maresa.

Araevin closed his eyes and murmured the words of a powerful and unusual divination. In the air above his head, a dozen faint, ghostly orbs appeared. Each was a semitangible spell construct the size of a small apple, with a single black pupil in its center. They were not invisible, but they were small and translucent, hard to see unless someone happened to look right at one.

"Spread out and search this place," he whispered to them. "Return and report if you find Ilsevele or Maresa, or in ten minutes if you don't."

At once the orbs wheeled and arrowed off in all directions, speeding through the shadowed stronghold and quickly vanishing from Araevin's sight. While the mythal prevented scrying divinations, if he was right in his assessment of the mythal's capabilities, it would not interfere with that particular spell. He folded his arms and waited, straining to detect the least sound that might indicate that his spying orbs had been seen or his own presence detected.

The moments crawled by as he waited motionless in the dimly lit hall. Then the first of his orbs returned, speeding to him. He caught the tiny thing in his hand and focused his attention on it.

"Report," he said.

Araevin's mind filled with the image of a rapid flight through one of the passages exiting the room, up a set of stairs, down one corridor to a dead end, then to the other end of the corridor where a pair of fey'ri swordsmen stood guard over a short hall filled with cell doors. He seemed to peer into the cells one by one, spotting Ilsevele and Maresa almost at once. They had been stripped of their weapons and armor, and seemed a little worse for the wear, but both were alive and awake. The view spun away again as the orb returned. Fortunately, it seemed that the jailors hadn't noticed its passage.

The orb dissipated in his hand, its task complete. Araevin looked up at the hallway it had followed. His companions were not far off, but he decided to wait a few minutes and see what else he might learn from his spying spell.

One by one his orbs returned, and he examined the findings of each. By the time he was finished, Araevin had a good sense of the layout of the place. The rift led up to a ruined city above, and from it, like the spokes of a buried wheel, radiated passages and halls. Forges, armories, storerooms, barracks . . . the place was a small fortress, hidden beneath the forgotten ruins above. He glimpsed a dozen or so fey'ri in various places, plus a handful of demons and yugoloths, most of whom seemed to be assigned to guard duties. Otherwise, the stronghold was almost vacant, and the majority of its halls and corridors were empty and silent. Sarya's army was not at home.

The final orb to report held a surprise he had not expected: Below him, near the bottom of the shaft, he glimpsed a large boulder of pale pinkish stone, half-covered with green moss.

The mythal stone! he realized.

Araevin filed away the glimpses shown by his orbs, and set out down the hallway leading to the daemonfey dungeon.

☙ ☙ ☙ ☙ ☙

"For Evermeet!" Seiveril cried.

With Fflar at his side and the Knights of the Golden Star at his back, he hurled himself headlong into the foul tide of demons who sought to encircle the crusade. There was nothing to gain by avoiding the fighting anymore. No orders he might give could possibly affect the outcome, as the battle of maneuver was clearly done with. All that remained was to slay or be slain.

The Golden Star raised a high, clear war cry that echoed across the twilit moorlands. Chancing falls and broken legs, they spurred their elven coursers toward the wave of demons, who gladly leaped forward to meet them. Hellborn fangs, claws, and sorcery met elven steel magic in a tremendous collision that shook the battlefield.

Seiveril's war-horse reared and plunged, beset on both flanks by the hulking, chitinous forms of mezzoloths. One jabbed its iron trident at Seiveril while the other lunged low, seeking to gut his horse. But the elflord managed to wrench his mount's reins aside and dance the horse away from the second fiend while parrying the strike of the first with his holy mace. He turned toward the first mezzoloth and rode close up on it, standing in his stirrups to smash down at its head and shoulders with all his strength. Chitin split and ichor flew, and the monster went down beneath the stamping silver-shod hooves of his mount.

Seiveril wheeled to parry the attack he expected from the second mezzoloth, but that one was gone, swept away by the tide of battle. In its place a grossly obese hezrou battled with its back to him, battering at one of Gaerth's knights with its long, clawed arms. He rode three steps closer and slammed the spiked mace head between the toadlike demon's shoulder blades. The thing howled abominably, but it did not die—demons were difficult to kill, at best. Instead it spun around and struck him a backhand blow with its ogrelike fist that knocked the elflord clean out of his saddle.

Seiveril grunted as he hit the ground, but there at least the moorland was a blessing—he landed on a tuft of stiff grass that helped to break his fall. The elflord glanced up just in time to find demons scrabbling toward him from all sides, fangs dripping with venom, eyes aglow with the power of the hells.

From his knees he spoke a single word of power, a holy word of Corellon Larethian so mighty that no evil creature could endure its utterance. Several of the demons nearby disappeared with wails of agony, instantly banished back to their infernal domain by the power of the word. Others reeled away stunned, black blood trickling from their ears, smoke rising from their foul bodies.

"That's better," Seiveril managed, and found his feet again.

All around him the battle between the Golden Star knights and the demonic allies of the daemonfey raged without respite. The collision of armies had devolved into hundreds of individual encounters. Fortified by their magic, the elf knights were giving as good as they got. Blasts of argent light and bursts of holy wrath tore through the demonic ranks, while hastily raised spell shields parried or deflected many of the demon's own unholy blights and scourges of hellfire. But elves were falling on all sides, dragged down into blood and death by their infernal foes, and powerful sorcerers in the daemonfey ranks strove to pull down or pierce the elven spell shields. Horses screaming in mortal agony, the awful din of metal on metal, angry war cries, and roars of bestial wrath threatened to drive all thought from him.

"By the Seldarine, what a disaster," he breathed.

"Seiveril! Are you hurt?" Fflar called as he rode into the small circle Seiveril's holy word had cleared.

Keryvian agleam like a bolt of pure sunlight in his hand, Fflar struck left and right as he approached, cleaving demon flesh and searing yugoloths with the sword's terrible power.

"I'm well enough," Seiveril answered, even though he was surprised to find that something had torn deep furrows in the mailed skirt guarding his hips. He limped over to his war-horse and awkwardly swung himself back up into the saddle, while Fflar stood guard. "We have to reform, regroup! This is not the battle we meant to fight!"

Fflar shook his head and replied, "There's no place to go. We're hemmed in on all sides. We have to stand our ground, or press forward and cut our way out. There is no retreating now!"

"But we are being slaughtered!"

"Yes, but so are the daemonfey. We will simply have to slaughter a little better than they do tonight, my friend," Fflar said. He wheeled his horse, and pointed with his sword. "Look there!"

Seiveril followed his captain's sword point. Amid a foul phalanx of demons hovered a great brazen disk or platform, its sides armored and scribed with ancient Elvish writings. From its deck he glimpsed fey'ri hurling spell after spell into the melee.

"I see it," he answered.

"Our scouts reported seeing it at the Battle of the Cwm. The daemonfey general is there!"

"Guard me," Seiveril replied.

He began to cast a powerful summoning. His voice rose and fell in the ancient holy words of the invocation. He noticed that Fflar turned to drive off another trio of demons prowling closer, but he paid it no mind, focusing on completing his spell. He called out the last words and held Corellon Larethian's symbol high—and the ground shook again, fountaining water and mud. Before Seiveril rose up a titanic mound of animated earth and rock, an elemental the size of a small tower.

"Destroy the battle-platform!" he cried to his summoned elemental.

The colossal creature turned ponderously and marched

toward the enemy spellcasters, simply burying lesser demons and fiends who could not get out of its way. A whole barrage of magic abruptly shifted to the elemental. Seiveril watched its progress, but then Fflar grabbed him by the shoulder and pushed his head down, just as a thrown spear sailed over him. The battle was returning, and quickly.

"We need a plan!" Seiveril growled, turning to face the newest threat.

"I advise, fight hard and don't get killed," Fflar answered.

The moon elf warrior raised a war cry and charged at the enemy ranks. Seiveril hesitated, then followed the champion of Myth Drannor into the fray again.

◉ ◉ ◉ ◉ ◉

Padding quietly through the chill stone corridors of the daemonfey stronghold, Araevin followed the path traced by his orb, still cloaked in his invisibility spell. It seemed that he need not have bothered, since he met no enemies as he passed through the empty hallways. Sarya's war against Evereska and the High Forest had emptied the place, or close to it.

Araevin climbed the long, winding steps leading up to the level of the prison, and turned to the right as he had previously seen. Ahead he saw a dim glimmer of lamplight, and heard the low sound of voices in conversation. He slowed his steps even further and crept close to the guardroom's entrance, staying near to the right-hand wall even though he was mantled in invisibility. There were spells that negated invisibility, after all, and the fey'ri were skillful enough as sorcerers to know such invocations. He reached the doorway and risked a quick glance inside.

Three fey'ri stood watch over the hallway with its cells.

There were two of them a few minutes ago, he thought. *Is there a change of the watch coming?*

He decided that it didn't matter. He was too close to Ilsevele and Maresa to wait on events, not when he couldn't be certain of avoiding discovery for long. Stepping around the corner, he quickly evoked a devastating blast of multicolored rays at the three fey'ri. Potent beams of brilliant yellow, sullen red, and vivid blue lashed out at the daemonfey even as they scrambled to their feet, warned by the arcane words Araevin used to unleash the spell. Magical power filled the air with a deafening crackle, and the bright rays destroyed the dark shadows of the room with a sudden burst of light as bright as the sun.

When Araevin's sight cleared, one fey'ri stood petrified, transformed to stone by one of the prismatic rays. The second slowly picked himself up from the floor, his scaly flesh puckered and sizzling from the terrible acid of the orange ray. The third fey'ri was simply gone—disintegrated by multiple rays or blasted into some far plane, Araevin neither knew nor cared. His invisibility spell spoiled by his attack, he drew Nurthel's iron short sword with one smooth motion and charged the remaining fey'ri.

The fellow bared his fangs in a sinister snarl and started a spell of his own, but Araevin closed on him before he could finish casting. He took three fingers off the fey'ri's hand and spoiled the enemy's spell.

"You will die for that, paleblood!" the demonspawn hissed.

He drew his own sword with his good hand—a short blade of sinister reddish iron—and parried two more of Araevin's attacks before going on the offensive, snarling and spitting as he tried to bat the elf's sword aside and get inside his guard. Their blades met two times, then three, and Araevin circled his point under the fey'ri's blade and sank Nurthel's sword just under the fellow's ribs, where his breastplate met the mail of his shirt. The fey'ri staggered back two steps, then sank to the floor.

Araevin seized a set of keys hanging from a peg on one wall, and hurried into the dungeon. He found Ilsevele's door first, and after fumbling with the keys, he threw open the cell.

"Ilsevele!"

Ilsevele stared up at him in amazement and said, "Araevin? But how—?"

"Explanations can wait," he promised her. He knelt beside her and took her in his arms. "Are you well? Did they hurt you?"

She shook her head and replied, "I was not handled at all gently, but it could have been much worse. They said they were saving me for one of their lords, who was away fighting in the High Forest." She shuddered. "What they told me about him . . . I think I would have taken my own life first."

"That won't be necessary," Araevin said.

Beneath her bruised visage he could glimpse the marks despair and fear had left on her, but she rapidly rallied, her courage and hope rekindling like a blaze springing up from a tiny ember.

"Maresa is nearby," she said, struggling to her feet. "We must free her, too."

"I know. Here, take this in case we get into a fight."

Araevin handed Ilsevele Nurthel's short sword, then he moved to the cell where he had seen the genasi and quickly unlocked that one as well.

"Maresa?" he called.

The genasi looked up at him, her snow-white skin pale as moonlight in the shadows of the cell.

"Could you have made any more noise in the guardroom?" she snapped. "It sounded like a damned thunderstorm out there."

Araevin asked, "Do you want me to go back and try to do it more quietly?"

"Too late for that now," Maresa said. She climbed to her feet and brushed off her scarlet tunic. She met Araevin's eyes, and the determination in her face softened just a bit. "Not that I'm ungrateful, of course. How in the world did you manage this? The last I saw you, you were enslaved by Sarya's enchantments."

"I will tell you both the whole story later. Suffice it to say that I am no longer under her control." Araevin looked up and down the hall. "Here, Maresa, you take this wand. The command word is *nemehl*. It fires a bolt of disrupting power, so make sure you do not point it at anyone you are fond of."

"Don't worry about that," said Maresa.

She took the wand, baring her teeth in a predatory smile.

"Araevin, there's another prisoner here, down at the end of the hall," Ilsevele said. "I heard her sobbing yesterday. We must take her with us, if we can."

Araevin and his companions quickly checked the other cells, finding them all empty except for one. A small sun elf woman, hardly more than a girl really, lay curled on the floor, so weary and heartbroken that she had actually passed from Reverie into actual sleep, something that elves did only when gravely ill or wounded. They unlocked the door and moved in to rouse the girl.

"Hello? Are you well enough to walk?" Ilsevele asked, kneeling by the elf lass.

The girl roused herself, and looked up at the three of them with astonishment. She was dressed in the sturdy pants and tunic of a traveler, and Araevin noticed that she wore the padded arming coat of a suit of heavy armor that had obviously been taken from her. She seemed a little on the slight side to be a warrior.

A cleric? he wondered.

"Who are you?" she managed.

"I am Ilsevele Miritar. Until a few moments ago, I was a captive like you. This is Maresa Rost, and this is Araevin Teshurr, our rescuer."

"I am Filsaelene Merwyst. Can you really get me out of here?"

"We will try," Ilsevele promised. "How long have you been here, Filsaelene? How did the daemonfey capture you?"

The girl sat up, her arms wrapped around her torso, and said, "About two months, I think. I was traveling with a company of adventurers, heading for the old ruins of Elvenport. The fey'ri ambushed us near the ruins of

Hellgate Keep. They . . . they killed my companions, but they told me that they spare sun elves." She shivered, and added dully, "They said I would make good breeding stock."

"*Aillesel Seldarie*," Ilsevele breathed. "Did they—?"

"No, not yet," Filsaelene said. "They seem to have almost forgotten me. I think they are engaged in some dark enterprise or another, something that has absorbed their attention for several tendays now. I heard many more fey'ri here for a time before most of them left."

"How did the fey'ri bring you here?" said Araevin.

"I was marched here. It's only thirty miles or so from Hellgate Keep."

"Do you know where this place is?" Araevin asked.

Despite his success in teleporting to the daemonfey hall, he had no idea where it stood.

"Beneath the ruins of Myth Glaurach. We're in the northern end of the Delimbiyr Vale, in the foothills of the Nether Mountains. You teleported here, then?"

"Yes," Araevin answered. "And that is how I intend to leave."

Araevin looked at Ilsevele and Maresa. All he wanted was to take them out of danger at once, but if he did so, Sarya would soon discover their escape. For that matter, she would not be long in discovering Nurthel's failure. When she did, she would likely reexamine the defenses she had woven over Myth Glaurach's mythal, and she might have skill enough to ensure that Araevin would not be able to easily return. He had an opportunity that he might not have later, an opportunity important enough to hazard his life, as well as the lives of his companions.

"We should get moving," he said. "There is something I want to do before we leave."

"What is that?" Ilsevele asked.

"This place is guarded by a mythal stone that the daemonfey have turned to their own purposes. I think I can do something about it. Without the mythal's defenses, there will be nothing to obscure our scrying spells or deflect our attacks against this place. I suspect that the daemonfey would find its loss hard to bear, though it means delaying our departure for a short time."

"You can damage mythals?" Ilsevele asked in surprise. "I didn't realize you knew such lore."

"I didn't, but I do now," Araevin answered. "I will explain that later, as well."

"I can't say I like the idea of staying here one minute longer than I have to," Maresa said. "But if we can set something on fire before we leave, I'm all for that."

"I trust your judgment, Araevin," said Ilsevele.

"This way, then."

He led them to the guardroom, where the two dead fey'ri lay crumpled on the floor. There they found a sturdy vault in which the prisoner's belongings—or most of them, anyway—had been stored. In a few moments, Maresa had her rapier on her hip and her crossbow in her hands, while Ilsevele shrugged her mithral shirt over her shoulders and restrung her bow. Filsaelene put on a breastplate emblazoned with the symbol of Corellon Larethian, and armed herself with a slender long sword.

"Everybody ready?" Araevin asked.

His comrades nodded, determination plain on their faces.

Araevin began another spell, and drew a glowing portal of blue energy in the air.

"Follow me quickly, before the door closes," he said, then he ducked through, reappearing an instant later in the well of the mythal stone.

The chamber was much as he had envisioned it from the glimpse his spell eyes had afforded. It was a bell-shaped space, high and wide, at the bottom of a shaft that rose up into illimitable darkness. The floor was natural rock, rough and uneven, and in the center stood the mythal stone, a boulder about eight feet in diameter and somewhat flattened. The only remarkable thing about the stone was its color, a rosy pinkish hue that seemed almost translucent. Striated bands of green moss clung to its lower surface. He could feel the magical power in the air, as intense as a slap in the face. The only illumination in the room was a thin golden phosphorescence that seemed to dance on the walls, as faint as an aurora.

Ilsevele, Maresa, and Filsaelene followed him through the blue doorway, which faded an instant later. They stared at the mythal, silent with awe.

"Keep watch for me," Araevin told them. "I will be busy for a short time. Be on guard against enemies teleporting into the room. My efforts may be detected."

"That's a cheerful thought," Maresa muttered, but she moved to comply. The women spread out, surrounding Araevin and the mythal. Araevin glanced at his companions to make sure he knew where they were in case he had to flee quickly. Then he turned to address the mythal.

First he cast his spell of magesight again. As before, the mythal's weave of interlocking enchantments and wards became visible to him, brighter and even more clear than before. The mythal itself was a great, blazing sphere of gold, its depths complex and ever-shifting like the dancing of a great flame. The red-gold strands of the daemonfey modifications crisscrossed the surface of the sphere, but did not enter its depths. Much as a red glass held before a lantern would change the color of the light produced, so Sarya's spells altered the effects produced by the mythal without changing its essential nature.

She knows something about what she is doing, he decided. But her understanding is incomplete. She could have anchored those strands in the very fundament of the mythal, but she lacked the mythalcraft to do so.

Of course, he himself could not have perceived even that much without the knowledge the Nightstar had grafted to his mind.

"It's a good thing Sarya did not get her hands on the Nightstar," he murmured. "If she had had access to Saelethil's lore, she could have done terrible things indeed."

"What do you see, Araevin? Can you do what you thought you might be able to do?" Ilsevele asked.

Even with the magical training she had, it was clear that she did not perceive the mythal stone as he did.

"I believe so," he said.

Forsaken House • 325

He took a deep breath, and began to speak the words of a high and complex spell he was attempting for the first time. One of the spells recorded in the Nightstar, it was not a spell of high magic, but it was close. It stood near the pinnacle of what was possible without high magic, and few mages could have mastered its difficult symbology and intricate weavings. When he had prepared spells from the *selukiira* in Ithraides' vault, he'd readied the powerful evocation on the chance that his suspicions about Sarya's mythal might prove true.

The spell allowed a knowledgeable mage to modify mythals. It would never work against a mythal whose creators could oppose it, or even against a mythal secured in the proper way by a new master, but Myth Glaurach's mythal had no living defenders—or none who chose to present themselves, anyway—and its powers were open to all spellcasters who stood within its bounds. In the days of Eaerlann, that might have been a sign of trust: trust in the power of the mythal's wards to keep evil influences outside, trust in the wisdom of Myth Glaurach's leading wizards to intervene against any abuse of the mythal's power, even a sign of trust in the good intentions of those who entered the City of Scrolls. Araevin doubted that Sarya shared such trust. She simply lacked the mythal-craft to seal the device, or possibly even understand that it could be sealed. On the other hand Saelethil had no such lack.

Araevin felt his perception sinking into the great golden orb at the mythal's heart. Carefully he sifted through the strands of magic until he found the shining white filaments that represented the laws binding and governing the device. With the care of a master musician seeking to elicit a single perfect note from his instrument, Araevin focused his willpower into a pure blade of thought, and reached in to adjust the mythal's governing.

Stop.

Araevin looked up, startled. He sensed that he was in two places at once. On the physical level, he stood a few feet from the pale pink stone, his eyes closed in concentration, one hand extended toward the device. His companions watched him anxiously. But the voice had not come from there. The voice had emerged from the metaphysical, the level of thought and magical consciousness in which his mind was engaged.

You are not Sarya, the voice continued. It was a melodious and powerful voice, a voice that hinted at great beauty and wisdom, but there was a dark timbre to it that Araevin did not care for. He studied the mythal closely, but he saw no sign of another mind. *Who are you?*

Who wants to know? he replied, standing on his guard, summoning his willpower to repel a mental assault if such a thing should come.

I am not to be bantered with. Identify yourself at once.

Araevin sensed the menace and towering willpower behind the words, but he relaxed his guard. The speaker was not present in the mythal. He was speaking *through* the device in some way, using the mythal as a medium.

I am Araevin Teshurr. To whom am I speaking?

Sarya will destroy you for playing with her toy, the voice observed. *You would be well advised to desist in your use of the mythal, and flee before she returns.*

I intend to take Sarya's toy away from her. And I note that you have still not answered my question.

Is this a coup of sorts? Do you think to overthrow your mistress and replace her? The voice laughed, a curiously childlike sound for the menace and power behind it. *All right, then. If you succeed, I will consent to extend to you the same arrangements I offered Sarya.*

What arrangements? Araevin asked. *Who are you?*

I am Malkizid. You may contact me through the mythal stone. But do not trouble me until you have deposed Sarya. I have no interest in dealing with underlings.

Then the voice was gone, and with it the sense of menace.

He returned his attention to the governing concordance of the mythal, and with one decisive stroke he imposed a new set of rules to restrict access to the mythal's powers. Only spellcasters without the stain of evil in their souls would gain the benefit of the mythal's abilities. Then he added a secure lock to prevent the governance from being rewritten again, creating a magical password to protect the mythal from further changes. An original creator of the device, if any still lived, would be able to contest Araevin's restrictions. But Sarya would find them difficult to overcome indeed.

With that attended to, Araevin looked for the brazen strands of Sarya's weaving. With one quick cut he unbound them all. Spells and wards of a dozen varieties abruptly discorporated, fading into nothingness. The myriad strands anchoring Sarya's summoned demons to Faerûn vanished as well. Araevin was not certain if the monsters would be destroyed, banished, or simply fade back into their own native dimensions, but he was sure that they would not long remain in Faerûn, whatever happened. He ended his spell and brought himself back to wakefulness in the real, physical world.

"It is done," he announced.

Ilsevele glanced around, surprised and asked, "Are you sure? It doesn't seem like anything has changed."

"I've severed the daemonfey from this mythal. They will miss its power very shortly, I think. We should get out of here before they do. Everybody, join hands."

"I'm all for that," Maresa replied. "Where are we going?"

Araevin hesitated.

"I hadn't thought that far ahead," he admitted. "Evereska?"

The others nodded agreement. He stepped over to his companions, rested one hand over Ilsevele's and the other over Maresa's, and cast the final teleporting spell he had readied for the day. The four of them disappeared from the daemonfey vaults beneath Myth Glaurach.

ϴ ϴ ϴ ϴ ϴ

"What in the world?" Seiveril whispered.

He paused in his fighting, staring at the scene around

him. He was not alone. Elf, fey'ri, orc, and ogre alike looked up in amazement.

Every demon on the battlefield stood transfixed, screeching in immortal rage and agony as brilliant white spears of light struck down from above, pinning each in place. Tendrils of colorless power arced and snapped from demon to yugoloth, covering the battlefield in an electric web of magical fire.

The white spears of light grew brighter still, broadening into shining columns that engulfed the monsters of the lower planes.

The pillars of light vanished all at once, and with them each of the demons, devils, yugoloths, and fiends who had marched with the daemonfey army. Seiveril sensed the abrupt banishment of the monsters from Faerûn as a wave of icy severance that rippled across the battlefield and back again. He blinked the afterimage of the brilliant spears from his eyes, astonished.

"Seiveril! What just happened?" Fflar demanded.

The moon elf shielded his eyes with his left forearm, holding Keryvian in his right. Despite all the blood the ancient baneblade had spilled that evening, its steel was still pure and unsullied. The holy fire of the sword burned it clean of demon blood.

"The demons were unsummoned," Seiveril answered. "They're banished. Whatever was holding them here has failed."

"Will they return?" Fflar turned, sweeping his eyes over the battlefield on all sides. "Are they truly banished, Seiveril?"

"I believe they are," Seiveril replied.

He had sufficient skill in summoning spells to recognize the end of one when he saw it. He surveyed the battlefield, looking for any sign of the fiends. Everywhere he looked, the remaining warriors of both sides still stood amazed.

The left flank, where the Knights of the Golden Star and Seiveril's bladesingers and spellsingers had battled against hundreds of the daemonfeys' demon allies, was virtually denuded of enemies. In a single stroke Seiveril's best warriors had been left in complete command of their corner of the moorland with no more enemies surrounding them or keeping them from going to the aid of the hard-pressed center and right.

The battered battle-platform began drifting back toward the fey'ri legion that stood behind Seiveril's force, awkwardly climbing over the jumbled remnants of the huge elemental Seiveril had sent to attack it. From somewhere far away came the single, solitary ring of steel meeting steel, and the battle began to resume, as more and more warriors turned back to their foes and redoubled their efforts to overcome each other.

"The sorcerers in that damned floating fortress are retreating," Seiveril observed.

"That is a good sign," Fflar grinned. "I think I like these odds a little better. So what now?"

"Reform the knights. We'll swing back toward the south and turn east to take the damned fey'ri in the flank. If we can defeat them, the orcs and ogres will break."

Seiveril glanced up into the dark skies overhead. Stars were beginning to appear through the violet wisps of the day's overcast, illuminated by the last faint rays of the sunset far to the west. The clouds were breaking up. It would be a clear and starry night.

"I don't know what became of the demons," Seiveril said, "but the Seldarine are smiling on us tonight."

☙ ☙ ☙ ☙ ☙

The western skies still glowed with the fading gold of sunset over Evermeet. Amlaruil strolled along a balcony of the palace, looking down over the dark streets of Leuthilspar as one by one the warm lanterns of the elven city began to wake beneath the stars. The night was cool and the sea-breezes growing stronger. She listened to the voice of the waves and the wind, even as her handmaidens laughed and chattered behind her.

Zaltarish walked at her side, a thin staff in his hand.

"You must give Lady Durothil an answer of some kind soon," he said. "If nothing else, she will insist on a date by which you will reach your decision concerning the council."

"I meant what I said," Amlaruil began. "Filling the council is my prerogative, not hers, and I will do so in the time and manner that—"

Her eyes opened wider, and she drew in a small gasp. There was something in the Weave, subtle, a distant vibration as if a great, deep harp string had been touched a great distance away. Her step faltered and she gripped the balustrade, turning to peer east over the dark sea.

"What is it, my queen?" Zaltarish asked softly.

"High magic in Faerûn," the queen said. "Not a true spell of high magic, only the . . . touching of one. It resonates in the Weave."

The scribe followed her eyes toward distant Faerûn and asked, "What does it signify?"

Amlaruil gazed into the night for a long time, then lifted up her face, smiling at the stars.

"I am not certain, old friend, but I think a mighty blow has been struck against our enemies. Sunrise will find new things in Faerûn."

☙ ☙ ☙ ☙ ☙

The damaged Vyshaanti battle-platform hovered high over the battlefield of the Lonely Moor, its deck canted slightly to one side. Sarya didn't know if the device could be repaired or not, but she was unwilling to abandon it, even with its crumpled and scorched armor plates. But sooner or later the platform would certainly draw another attack from the elf spellcasters below, and it was only a tool, after all. Broken tools were to be discarded, and that was that.

The savage warriors who had fought and died as the fodder for her army were rapidly reaching the status of broken tools as well. Untold numbers of orcs, ogres, and such had fallen in the futile attempt to overwhelm the deadly steel core of Evermeet's army. They'd done well enough while the elves were beset by hundreds of demons and flanked by her fey'ri, but the demons she'd seeded among their ragged ranks had served to drive the tribal warriors onward with suitable zeal. With the demons gone, the orcs and their kin didn't seem so eager to try their chances against elven arrows and battle magic.

"The battle is lost, my lady," Mardeiym Reithel said. He bowed and continued, "We must withdraw the fey'ri before our losses grow any worse."

"I know," Sarya snarled.

She was tempted to punish the fey'ri for his temerity, but she held her hand. Mardeiym was competent and respectful, and it was certainly not his fault that he'd lost a quarter of the army—the fiercest and most powerful quarter, really—in one terrible moment. She had to get back to Myth Glaurach right away to see what had happened to the mythal stone. Had it finally decayed past the point of usefulness? Or had one of her underlings attempted something rash? Was Nurthel capable of such a brazen act of defiance?

"Signal the legion to disengage at once," she commanded. "Leave the orcs and the rest to the mercy of the elves. They shall serve to cover our retreat."

Mardeiym called to the messenger fey'ri who waited on his orders. "Sound the retreat!" he said. "We'll retire by air."

The messengers sounded their brazen trumpets, and from the melee of flashing swords and crackling spells below, the fey'ri began to rise, taking to the air. Better than a thousand of Sarya's demonblooded warriors had started the battle at sunset, but she guessed that a third of her fey'ri would not return to the halls of Myth Glaurach. Demons could be summoned again. Orc tribes could be enticed with promises of loot and easy victory. But her fey'ri were indispensable.

"What will we do now, my lady?" Mardeiym asked quietly.

Sarya clenched her fists on the iron rail of the platform

until the strength in her fingers left marks in the armor plate.

"Preserve the fey'ri," she answered. "Fall back and regroup to fight another day. You will gather the fey'ri and lead them back to our city at your best speed, but do not abandon the wounded if you can help it."

"Where will you be, my lady?"

"I must return to Myth Glaurach immediately to see what has happened there. Now go."

"Yes, Lady Sarya," the fey'ri warmaster replied.

He struck his fist to his breastplate in salute, and took to the air to join the fey'ri flying away from the battle.

Sarya spared the elf soldiers beneath her one hateful hiss, then she teleported herself away from the battle-platform. It was rash of her, but she chose to send herself directly to the mythal stone in its deep well of living rock. She needed to know what had happened to the spells with which she had anchored her demons to the physical world.

She appeared in a gout of sudden flame, her spell shields crackling into life, her staff held in guard as she readied herself to strike. But no enemies awaited her.

"What is this?" she snarled into the cold air.

There was no reply.

Angrily, she stalked over to the great rosy stone and set her hand on it, commanding it to reveal what had been done to it. But the mythal refused to answer. It did not recognize her presence at all.

"Who did this?" she screamed aloud. *"Who did this?"*

Ah, Sarya, I see that you have returned. You may be pleased to learn that I can answer that question, Malkizid's beautiful voice spoke from the mythal stone, melodious and perfect.

"Malkizid! What has happened to the mythal?"

I regret to inform you that a sun elf wizard with some skill in these matters appeared in this chamber a short time ago, and performed some alterations to your mythal stone. I presume from the outrage in your voice that he has sealed the mythal from any further contact on your part.

"Why did you not *stop* him?" Sarya raged.

I had no power to do so. I can communicate through this device, but I can exercise none of my powers at your end. Malkizid allowed himself a small laugh then added, *I warned the fellow that you would be terribly angry.*

"This is no laughing matter," the daemonfey queen snarled. "The loss of this mythal just now wrecked my army on the Lonely Moor. I had the palebloods trapped between my demons and my fey'ri, and my demons vanished all at once. My victory was *stolen* from me, damn you!" She whirled away in anger, stalking the floor of the mythal chamber, eyes aflame with emerald fire. "This is intolerable. I must resummon those demons and yugoloths at once."

Alas, this mythal will no longer serve you for that purpose. The sun elf who came here made certain of that. Malkizid's golden voice paused then added, *But . . . there are other mythals you might turn to your purposes.*

The daemonfey queen stopped in mid-step and snapped her gaze to the rose-hued boulder, even though she knew that Malkizid was not really there.

"Myth Drannor," she said

I have no ability to manipulate the mythal of Cormanthor, for I am not an elf. However, with your elf's blood and my knowledge of mythalcraft, we could accomplish far more in Myth Drannor than you could in Myth Glaurach. Is it really necessary to begin your reign by reclaiming Siluvanede? Or are you willing to found your dynasty here instead?

Sarya folded her wings close behind her back, and narrowed her eyes.

"Before my family came to Siluvanede, we sought the throne of Arcorar. I am not without a claim to Cormanthyr's throne." She considered the offer, examining the possibilities, and said, "Your suggestion interests me. I gain the kingdom denied my House for six thousand years, but what do you gain, Malkizid?"

The light tones of the golden voice vanished for an instant.

Freedom, Malkizid answered. *And the dream of a new Aryvandaar ordering the world as it should have long ago. Our paths run together for quite a long time, Sarya Dlardrageth.*

The daemonfey queen weighed Malkizid's words, and assented with a predatory smile.

"Very well. I will bring my fey'ri to Myth Drannor, and we will make ready an army even greater and more terrible than the one I just raised."

I await your arrival, then.

Sarya nodded. She did not entirely trust Malkizid, but she couldn't see what he might gain from leading her astray, and what he said made sense to her. Already she was considering the questions of how to carry away the treasures and armaments she had stored beneath Myth Glaurach. There was much to do, and not much time. She started to turn away, but then one more thought struck her.

"One last thing, Malkizid," she rasped. "Tell me—who ruined this mythal for me, and where can I find him?"

EPILOGUE

Seven days after the Battle of the Lonely Moor, Fflar watched Seiveril Miritar raise his banner in the forest-grown ruins of Myth Glaurach. The daemonfey were gone. The crusade's Eagle Knights had cautiously followed the retreating fey'ri legion to their hidden stronghold in the Talons of the Delimbiyr, but a day before the rest of Seiveril's army reached the outskirts of the ancient Eaerlanni city, the fey'ri had vanished without a trace. Having lost their demon allies and abandoned their orc and ogre warriors, the fey'ri seemed disinclined to meet Evermeet's army again.

"It was a handsome city in its day," Seiveril observed.

Along with Araevin, Ilsevele, and Maresa, he had wandered through the ruins with Fflar for a time, studying the stinking forges and warrenlike barracks where Sarya's soldiers had formerly worked and lived, exploring the deep vaults and passages that Araevin had dared in order to rescue Ilsevele, Maresa, and the young cleric Filsaelene.

Fflar followed Seiveril, one hand on Keryvian's hilt in case the daemonfey had left any unpleasant surprises behind.

Myth Drannor must look much like this now, he thought.

As he understood things, Myth Glaurach had fallen only fifty years or so after his own city.

"The ruins remind me of Myth Drannor," he said. "What became of this city, Seiveril? How did it fall?"

"I do not know. A horde of orcs, I believe." Seiveril gazed at the wreckage of the former grand mage's palace, open to the sky. "I wonder what we should do with the place. Now that the daemonfey have abandoned it and Araevin has done so much to secure the mythal, it seems a pity to leave it empty again."

"It won't be empty," Ilsevele replied. "I have spoken to the wood elf emissary, Gaerradh. She told me that the folk of the High Forest and the Silver Marches will keep watch over the place when we leave. They don't intend to allow the daemonfey to come creeping back."

"Where do you think the daemonfey have gone?" asked Thilesin.

"It hardly matters, does it?" Maresa asked. "They're not here, and that's enough for me."

Seiveril glanced at the young genasi and said, "No, I am afraid that is not enough. Once before we allowed the Dlardrageths to vanish from our knowledge. I will not permit that to happen again. Checking the threat to Evereska was important, but I intend to root out the daemonfey wherever they are hiding. And I also intend to make sure that the People in Faerûn will have the strength to defend themselves against the next such peril to arise."

"That is not the work of a day," Araevin murmured.

Seiveril offered a small, hard smile, his eyes fierce with determination.

"I did not call for a crusade in the Dome of Stars, my

friends," he said. "I called for a Return. Our work is not yet done."

The others fell silent, sensing the sternness in the elflord's voice. Seiveril studied each in turn, and his smile softened.

"For now," he said, "the fey'ri are nowhere to be found. Come, friends; join me for supper in my tent."

Ilsevele took her father's arm, and Araevin fell in close beside her on the other side. But Fflar found himself hanging back. The dead ruins of Myth Glaurach still had more to say to him, and in the melancholy mood stealing over him, he felt more kinship to the ghosts of that place—so like his own lost city—than he did to the elves with whom he lived a second time.

Ilsevele glanced over her shoulder, noticing his absence, and asked, "Lord Starbrow? Aren't you coming?"

"Go on ahead. I'll follow shortly."

Fflar watched the sun elf lord and his entourage descend back to the crusade's camp. The sun was setting, and the lanterns of the elven army surrounded the foot of the hill like a garland of candles amid the trees. The evening was fine and clear, with little of the cold wind that often raked the Delimbiyr Vale in the early spring, but Fflar could tell that it would be quite cold later on. It suited his mood.

The open square before the ruined palace was not unlike the broad plaza that had stood before Castle Cormanthyr. He remembered a hot, humid day with a brassy sky and the smoke of burning homes thick in the air, and he shuddered.

What is this place? he wondered. What am I doing here? A lifetime ago I fought for the People, and now I live and fight again.

"Did I know peace in Arvandor?" he asked the emptiness, but he found no answer.

He sighed and sank down on the low, jumbled stones of an old stone wall, listening to the silence of the ruins.

Dramatis Personae

Aillesel seldarie
(ale-LEH-sell sell-DAHR-ee)
An ancient prayer translated as "may the Seldarine save us."

Tower Reilloch Folk

Araevin Teshurr
(ah-RAY-vin teh-SHUR), a sun elf mage of Tower Reilloch

Whyllwyst
Araevin's familiar (deceased)

Philaerin
(fi-LAY-rin), moon elf, Eldest of the Circle of Reilloch Domayr

Aeramma
(ay-RAHM-mah), a sun elf high mage of Reilloch Domayr

Kileontheal
(kil-ee-AWN-thee-all), a sun elf high mage of Reilloch Domayr

Quastarte
(kwah-STAR-teh), a sun elf loremaster of Reilloch Domayr

Eaglewind
a wood elf sorcerer and mage of Tower Reilloch

Yesvelde Shaerim
(yez-VELL-deh shay-RIM), an illusionist and mage of Tower Reilloch

Jorildyn
(joe-RIL-dihn), a half-elf mage of Tower Reilloch

Faelindel
(fay-LIN-dell), an abjurer and mage of Tower Reilloch

Olleile
(ohl-LAY-leh), a mage of Tower Reilloch

Starsong
a mage of Tower Reilloch

The Council of Evermeet

Seiveril Miritar
(say-VERR-ill Mih-rih-TAR), sun elf lord of Elion and a high priest of Corellon Larethian

Zaltarish
ancient sun elf scribe and advisor to Queen Amlaruil

Keryth Blackhelm
moon elf warrior, commander of Evermeet's defenses

Selsharra Durothil
sun elf matron of House Durothil

Breithel Olithir
(bray-THELL oh-lih-THIR), Grand Mage of Evermeet, sun elf

Jerreda Starcloak
(jeh-REH-dah), a high noble of the wood elves

Meraera Silden
    (meh-RAY-rah sill-DEN), a moon elf merchant of Leuthilspar

Ammisyll Veldann
    (AHM-miss-ill vell-DAN), sun elf, Lady of Nimlith

Emardin Elsydar
    (eh-MARR-din el-SID-ar) sun elf, admiral of Evermeet's fleet

The Company of the White Star

Grayth Holmfast
    human swordsman and High Mornmaster of Lathander

Baron Darthen Ironwright

Theleda Rost

Belmora
    dwarf cleric of Moradin (deceased)

Daemonfey and Fey'ri

Sarya Dlardrageth
    (sahr-YAH dlar-DRAY-geth), matron of House Dlardrageth

Xhalph Dlardrageth
    (zahlf dlar-DRAY-geth), Sarya's son

Nurthel Floshin
    (nur-THEL FLO-shin), a fey'ri lord and Sarya's spymaster

Mardeiym Reithel
(mar-DAME rye-THEL), warmaster of the ancient fey'ri

Jasrya Ilviiri
(jaz-REE-ah ill-VEER-ee), a leader of the ancient fey'ri

Breden Yesve
(BREH-den YEZ-veh), a leader of the ancient fey'ri

Saelethil Dlardrageth
(say-LETH-ill dlar-DRAY-geth), an ancient high mage of House Dlardrageth

Evereskans and High Forest Folk

Gervas Imesfor
sun elf high mage of Evereska

Lord Duirsar
moon elf Hill Elder of Evereska

Morgwais—the Lady of the Wood
a noble wood elf (mother of Galaeron Nihmedu)

Gaerradh
(GAYR-rathe), a wood elf ranger

Sheeril
Gaerradh's wolf

Rhaellen Darthammel
(RAYL-len dar-THAM-mell), Blade-Major (current war leader) of Evereska

Seiveril's Crusade

Elvath Muirreste
(el-VATH murr-RES-teh), a moon elf knight in Seiveril's service

Thilesil
(thih-LEH-sill), a sun elf cleric of Corellon Larethian

Celeilol Fireheart
(kell-LAY-loll), a sun elf lord of Leuthilspar

Vesilde Gaerth
(veh-SILL-deh GAYRTH), Knight-Commander of the Order of the Golden Star

Ferryl Nimersyl
(FAIR-rill nih-MER-sill), leader of the Moon Knights of the Temple of Sehanine Moonbow

Other Folk

Elorfindar Floshin
(ell-ORF-ihn-dahr FLO-shin), master of the House of Long Silences

Maresa Rost
(mah-RAY-sah ROST), a genasi of Waterdeep

Brant
a squire in the Order of the Aster

Gerardin
mage of the tower in the Forest of Wyrms

Eaerlraun Shadowlyn
master of Moongleam Tower in Everlund

Alustriel
(ah-LOO-stree-ell), High Lady of the Silver Marches, Chosen of Mystra

Methrammar Aerasumé
(meh-THRAMM-ar AY-rah-soo-MEH), Alustriel's son and High Marshal of the Silver Marches

Ithraides
a grand mage of ancient Arcorar

Kaeledhin
an apprentice or ally of Ithraides

Sanathar
an ally of Ithraides

Morthil
an ally of Ithraides

Mellyth Echorn
a sun elf high cleric of Corellon Larethian

The Seldarine
the pantheon of elf gods

Corellon Larethian
ruler of the elf gods

FORGOTTEN REALMS®

LISA SMEDMAN

The New York Times best-selling author of *Extinction* follows up on the War of the Spider Queen with a new trilogy that brings the Chosen of Lolth out of the Demonweb Pits and on a bloody rampage across Faerûn.

THE LADY PENITENT

BOOK I
SACRIFICE OF THE WIDOW
Halisstra Melarn has been a priestess of Lolth, a repentant follower of Eilistraee, and a would-be killer of gods, but now she's been transformed into the monstrous Lady Penitent, and those she once called friends will feel the sting of her venom.

BOOK II
STORM OF THE DEAD
As the followers of Eilistraee fall one by one to Halisstra's wrath, Lolth turns her attention to the other gods.

September 2007

BOOK III
ASCENDANCY OF THE LAST
The dark elves of Faerûn must finally choose between a goddess that offers redemption and peace, or a goddess that demands sacrifice and blood. We know what a human would choose, but what about a drow?

June 2008

FORGOTTEN REALMS, WIZARDS OF THE COAST, and their respective logos are trademarks of Wizards of the Coast, Inc. in the U.S.A. and other countries. ©2007 Wizards.

FORGOTTEN REALMS®

RICHARD LEE BYERS

The author of *Dissolution* and The Year of Rogue Dragons sets his sights on the realm of Thay in a new trilogy that no FORGOTTEN REALMS® fan can afford to miss.

THE HAUNTED LAND

BOOK I
UNCLEAN

Many powerful wizards hold Thay in their control, but when one of them grows weary of being one of many, and goes to war, it will be at the head of an army of undead.

BOOK II
UNDEAD

The dead walk in Thay, and as the rest of Faerûn looks on in stunned horror, the very nature of this mysterious, dangerous realm begins to change.

March 2008

BOOK III
UNHOLY

Forces undreamed of even by Szass Tam have brought havoc and death to Thay, but the lich's true intentions remain a mystery—a mystery that could spell doom for the entire world.

Early 2009

ANTHOLOGY
REALMS OF THE DEAD

A collection of new short stories by some of the Realms' most popular authors sheds new light on the horrible nature of the undead of Faerûn. Prepare yourself for the terror of the *Realms of the Dead*.

Early 2010

FORGOTTEN REALMS, WIZARDS OF THE COAST, and their respective logos are trademarks of Wizards of the Coast, Inc. in the U.S.A. and other countries.
©2007 Wizards.